To Beverly

ACKNOWLEDGMENTS

THE AMERICAN REVOLUTIONARY WAR was far more widespread and complex than my wife and I realized when we set out to write this novel. Our research trips have taken us to England, St. Eustatius, Barbados, and all up and down the eastern seaboard of the United States. We have read scores of books and talked to dozens of people knowledgeable about the American Revolution.

Five of those persons deserve special mention for their sympathetic and critical reading of the manuscript. They are:

● Dr. Gerald S. Brinton, former assistant superintendent and history teacher in the West Shore School System, Camp Hill, Pennsylvania.

● Dr. Robert G. Crist, lecturer in American history, Pennsylvania State University.

● Mr. and Mrs. Anthony Bitonti of New Cumberland, Pennsylvania. He is a member of the Ninth Pennsylvania Regiment of the Brigade of the American Revolution. She is a clinical psychologist. Both are knowledgeable about uniforms and artifacts of the period.

● Col. John B. B. Trussell, chief of the history division of the Pennsylvania Historical and Museum Commission and a leading authority on the Revolutionary War in Pennsylvania.

Each of these five readers found different errors that, had they not been caught, would have caused me much embarrassment. I am grateful to them. Any mistakes that remain are my fault and not theirs.

My wife and I made a pact that neither of us would ever write a soppy tribute to the other in a book introduction. It is enough to say that she is the Beverly to whom this book is dedicated.

—Robert H. Fowler
Camp Hill, Pennsylvania

JEREMIAH MARTIN

PART ONE

1

No matter what lies they may tell about me in Philadelphia, I am a true American patriot. I have been one from the start of this war, and remain so even in my present unusual circumstances. I have contributed far more to the cause of freedom from British tyranny than anyone who blackguards me back home as a turncoat, and I have done so since Lexington itself.

Although I care naught for what my enemies on either side of the Atlantic may think, time hangs so heavy upon my hands as I await my trial that I propose to set down a candid account of the past six years, without thought for my reputation or safety. And what better place to begin my story than at Lexington?

Yes, I was there all right, but confess that it was neither patriotic zeal nor historical foresight that led me to spend the fateful night of April 18, 1775, in that backwater village. No, I had meant to pass those hours rapturously in the arms of one Widow Ledbetter, who lived six miles west, beyond Concord.

In that unhappy period of my life I had been reduced to peddling household items. On my last tour of those parts the widow had hinted that on my next visit she might permit something more intimate than the single prim kiss she granted me on my compliments of her rosy cheeks.

Alas, I was to be disappointed. The problem, as often in that low time of my life, was Demon Rum. On the way down from Marble-head with a rented cart full of smuggled combs, mirrors, and small pots and pans, I stopped at Wright's Tavern in Concord for a bit of grog to buck up my courage. The first cup called for another and still another, the result being that I arrived at the widow's cottage in a boisterous mood.

I had assumed that the late Master Ledbetter was a prosperous, industrious wheelwright. But it turned out that he had been so notorious a tosspot that his young wife had come to hate strong drink. Mistress Ledbetter had assumed that I was the scion of a rich Virginia family, a graduate of the College of William and Mary no less, temporarily down on my fortunes, having lost my schooner to British confiscation. That was partly true, of which more anon; I have never claimed to be sober and reliable.

At any rate, she readily accepted the comb and mirror I pressed upon her but turned her pretty head and made a face when I tried to kiss her. When I attempted an embrace, she pushed me away so forcibly, I nearly fell into her kitchen fire.

It was out of the question for me to spend the night, not in my disgusting condition, she indignantly informed me. She had thought me a southern gentleman. Why, I was no better than Homer, her late husband. Were all men alike?

I protested, first mildly and then with some rough words, which gave her such offense that she seized her broom and drove me from her house. But the bitch kept my gifts.

So, angry at my own gullibility and at the widow's rebuff, I climbed back into the cart and unsteadily drove my good horse Ned off into the dark along the Boston road, past Meriam's Corner, through the township of Lincoln, and at last to Lexington.

On previous selling tours through this region, I had spent several nights at Buckman's Tavern just across the road from the meeting-house that dominates the village common. There, at the Sign of the White Bull, for only ten cents one could rent a straw tick in a commodious third-floor room reserved for New Hampshire cattle drovers and other rough men of the road. Buckman also maintained a large stable, where I consigned Ned and the cart to a groom before making my way into the taproom.

I had never seen the place so packed with locals, and all were armed. One bald old fellow even displayed an oversize sword. And a boy of about sixteen stood about with a drum. Even in my drunken state I recognized them as minutemen, the so-called pick of the local militia, but I was little impressed by them. After all, when I was barely older than that drummer boy, I had been in a real war, against Pontiac.

But keeping my feelings of contempt to myself, I pushed my way through the crowd and rapped on the bar.

"Cup of grog, there my good fellow."

The proprietor, a dark, broad-faced man, looked at me with an amused expression and said with sarcastic edge, "Ah, it's Master Martin, himself."

"Aye, and Master Martin is waiting for his grog."

"And so he shall have it, soon as he shows his money."

Until recently, I could have bought Buckman's entire establishment—indeed, the whole village of Lexington—without blinking an eye. But back in 1775 all I could do was assume the dignified air of one whose late father had been a member of the Virginia House of Burgesses and had owned five hundred acres of good Appomattox River land, not to mention several dozen slaves. Indeed, had not misfortune befallen me at seventeen, I would have completed my education at William and Mary and become a lawyer, as my family had wished.

I glared at this impudent publican and growled, "You think I can't pay?"

The fellow raised his voice and cut his eyes around the crowded room to make sure he had an audience before replying in imitation of my Tidewater drawl, "It's not that, Mastah Mahtin. Ah thought you might be aftah bahterin' for drinks, as you did last time. Or were you too deep in yo cups to recall?"

I looked over my shoulder at the other patrons to see if they had heard this affront. A few laughed, but most were too engrossed in their endless talk against the British to have taken notice. In other circumstances I might have clouted the barman. But I merely stared him in the eye and said, "It's money you want to see? There, I'll just have two cups."

Even as I uttered the words, I realized that I had only enough cash to pay for my lodging and breakfast. For an instant I considered refusing to accept service from this impudent tradesman. That way I could have departed with an air of wounded pride and still retained enough money for my lodging. But the cups had been placed on the bar, and the fellow was waiting for his money.

A warm place to sleep or more grog? It was too late to back down. I slapped my coins onto the counter and took up a cup. What the hell? I could sleep in the stable. Might be better to keep an eye on my wares anyway, what with all these armed bumpkins knocking about the place.

I turned my back to the bar to survey the crowd in the taproom. An old man with long gray hair and a corded neck was jabbing his finger at the drummer lad.

"Tell you this. If they come this way, I don't intend to take a backward step. You'll never see me run from the British."

"They may not come, you know, Uncle Jonas. Captain Parker says it might be only a rumor."

I closed my eyes and drank deeply, trying to forget about the Widow Ledbetter and older, darker sorrows. Then I felt a hand on my shoulder.

"What say?"

It was the militia captain, a sallow-faced man in his mid-thirties. He coughed and repeated his question.

"John Buckman tells me you are a peddler."

"Only temporarily."

"From Boston, mayhap?"

Other militiamen had stopped talking to listen.

"Boston?" I laughed. "Hell, no. Want no parts of Boston. I'm a Virginian. What's it to you, anyway?"

"Take no offense, friend. Was just wondering if you might have been on the road twixt here and Boston this afternoon or evening."

"I am based at present in Marblehead. Came by way of Medford this morning. Been in Concord since afternoon—on business."

"Ah well, thought you might have seen British soldiers."

"No, and if I never lay eyes on another lobsterback, it'll be too soon for me."

The militia captain laughed. He must have suspected me of being a British spy. "You sound like a true Son of Liberty."

"I am an American like everyone else in this room. All I want is to be left alone to make an honest living. Now you answer me: What are you all doing out at night and under arms?"

"Never mind that. Better drink your other cup before someone drains it off for you."

Even after my second grog, I remained too full of resentment toward the Widow Ledbetter to enjoy myself. I felt out of place in that assembly of farmers and artisans gabbing about what they'd do to the British should they venture from their base in Boston. All that talk about their precious rights. Which of them had suffered the loss I had—a quarter interest in a small ketch (not a schooner, as I had led the Widow Ledbetter to think)—and been reduced to peddling knickknacks to rude New England yokels—I, a member of the Virginia gentry?

"You want another grog, Master Martin?" the barkeep asked.

"Nay, I've had enough. I'll just see to my horse before turning in."

The cool of the spring night cleared my head. At the stable, as I had feared, the groom had gone off and left the tack room unlocked and my wares unguarded. I helped myself to a horse blanket and climbed into the hayloft. I had slept in many a worse place in the past dozen years since I had run away from my Tidewater home at seventeen. What the hell? I settled down in the straw and was soon asleep.

4

2

How DID I, of good Virginia family and passably good education, come to be far from home amongst rude New Englanders, working in partnership with a rough Yankee seaman—Lovejoy Brown— first in smuggling and then in door-to-door peddling? Except for some bad turns of fate, I might well have ended up like my father, a burgess. Indeed, had I completed my course of study and passed the bar, I might have been preparing to take my place in Philadelphia as a Virginia delegate to the Second Continental Congress, which was set to convene in just three weeks.

My early years were pampered ones. I am the son of a well-off planter who could trace his ancestry in Virginia back for a hundred years—indeed, much longer when you consider that my great-great-grandmother is reported to have been a princess of the Powhatan tribe. I have only happy memories of my father. He taught me to ride and hunt and fish and encouraged me to read his Plutarch and Shakespeare. At thirteen my young life was shaken by his sudden death from a fever; it was shattered a year later, when my lovely mother foolishly remarried, to a widower from a nearby plantation, a man not fit to clean the boots of my father.

Horace Gouge was a coarse, hypocritical bully who persuaded my overly trustful mother that little Jeremiah wanted more discipline and that he was just the man to provide it. He tried without success to break my spirit, which he said was tainted by my Indian blood. I was glad to escape his domination at William and Mary. But during the spring of my first year there—well, I have resolved to be candid—I became involved with the daughter of a tavern owner in Williamsburg. So were two of my college friends, but when her father discovered that she was with child, it was me he sought with fowling piece and minister. Whether his daughter preferred me to the other candidates for the honor or the tavernkeeper realized my comrades were from poorer families I cannot say.

Lacking the luxury of time to debate the question, I fled to what I assumed would be the haven of my ancestral home. But my mother was humiliated, my stepfather outraged. She wept. He took down his razor strap and attempted to thrash me.

Master Gouge failed to consider that in the past year I had shot up to nearly six feet in height and had added many pounds of hard muscle. Before I knew what I was doing, the strap was in my own right hand, while my left grasped the greasy locks of my stepfather, forcing him down upon his knees in our front hall. While my mother screamed and the house servants—who hated my stepfather as much as I—danced with glee in the background, I repaid

Horace Gouge many times over for his unjustified punishments of my younger self. I beat him until he begged for mercy. And after my right arm ached so that I could no longer wield the strap, I let him fall to the floor senseless. Losing all self-control, I kicked him in the ribs. Blood suddenly gushed from his mouth.

"He is dead!" my mother cried. "Oh, Jerry, you have slain my husband!"

She fell into a faint. The female slaves screamed.

We had an elderly house servant, Virgil, who had loved my father and me as well. It was he who swept together a bag of clothes, saddled the plantation's finest steed—good old Ned, then only half grown—and set me on my way north.

"I'd go with you, young master, but I'm too old," Virgil said. And then he promised that he would tell the authorities that I had slain my stepfather in self-defense.

I shall eschew details of my flight and simply explain that I headed for the Pennsylvania frontier to avoid more settled sections, where word could have spread of my crime. Ned and I reached Carlisle in July of '63, as Colonel Bouquet was organizing an expedition to march west to relieve Fort Pitt and put down Pontiac's uprising. To make a long story short, I enlisted as a ranger to accompany Bouquet. That is how I fell in with a Pennsylvania frontiersman named Jason McGee, a red-headed crack marksman who was then about thirty and truly one of the most admirable men I have ever known. Without asking embarrassing questions, he took me under his wing. Thanks to him, I survived the battle of Bushy Run and returned east with my scalp intact.

Jason McGee lived north of the Kittatinny Mountains and west of the Susquehanna River in Sherman's Valley. He was married to an estimable German woman, Kate. They had three children at the time—Ephraim, Gerta, and Christopher. (Twins—a boy and a girl—were born to them later.) For a year they took me in and treated me like an older son. Despite the differences in our origins and stations in life, they became the closest thing I have ever had to a real family, at least since my father's untimely death. They had no inkling that I feared a hangman's noose awaited me back in Virginia. Their rude log cabin was a good place in which to hide out. My chief difficulty was that the McGees—and Kate in particular— held to the view that he who did not share in the labor should not share in the eating of the fruits thereof. And I had not been reared to work with my hands. So, I learned, both to do (but not like) manual labor and to love (but not emulate) the McGees.

When I first met Gerta McGee, she was a little girl of only eleven with a mass of dark curls and a row of freckles over a saucy pug nose. At the time I thought her a bright and winsome child and no more.

Ephraim, her older brother, was frail and blond. Chris, two years younger than Gerta, reminded me very much of myself at that age. I undertook to teach him good horsemanship and the finer points of fishing. In the evenings, after helping Jason clear timber and work in the fields, I instructed all three of the McGee children in reading, writing, and doing sums. I thought that that might win me some respite from physical labor, but no, not only was I expected to help farm, I had to break my back hewing logs for an addition to the McGee cabin.

I will ever be grateful to the McGees, but after a year I was ready to risk quick death on a Virginia gallows to escape a slower demise from overwork on a frontier farm.

The sea had always intrigued me. In my childhood I had often accompanied my father down to the mouth of the Appomattox to watch ships unloading goods from the West Indies and taking on tobacco to be hauled to England. Surely at sea I could escape the law and enjoy the adventure of travel. So I left Ned in the care of Jason McGee, said my farewells to Kate and the children, and set out on foot for Philadelphia. There I persuaded the British captain of an East India merchantman to take me on as a supercargo. I spent the next five years plying the seas aboard that tub. The captain was as big a tyrant as my stepfather, and in the bargain he despised Americans. But I got on well enough with the crew, especially with the bosun, Lovejoy Brown of Marblehead, Massachusetts. The work—mostly keeping records and reading and writing letters for the nearly illiterate captain—was not onerous. And Lovejoy and I had some glorious flings in Bristol and Le Havre and one memorable voyage around the Cape of Good Hope to Bombay.

At last our worn-out vessel returned to North America, to New York, to be sold for salvage. Nearly twenty-five and weary of the sea, I collected my accumulated wages, said good-bye to Lovejoy, and set out for Pennsylvania to look in on the McGees and reclaim old Ned. I considered it out of the question to return to Virginia, but I thought I might find refuge and a fortune by taking up land out on the Ohio.

The McGees were delighted to see me again. Ephraim was away at school in Philadelphia, while Chris had continued his studies with the local Presbyterian minister. The twins, now four years old, were lovely children. Jason and Kate had changed little during my five-year absence, but Gerta, now sixteen, had become a new person. Her beauty took my breath away. Her hair had grown even more luxuriant, her eyes were a clearer blue, her freckles had faded, her figure had filled out, and in general she shone with good health.

By that time I had possessed many women of all colors and temperaments, but I had never fallen in love. In Gerta's presence I felt like a tongue-tied child. It made me sweat just to look at her. But

7

with her beauty had also come a baffling sort of standoffishness. No longer was she the eager little girl who had sat worshipfully at my knee to learn her letters and ciphers. Now it was I who worshipped her.

It pains me to relate that I, usually so glib and self-assured, struggled to find the courage to ask for her hand. Jason listened to me quietly, but Kate came right out and said no. We should wait a year and "allow for a little more growing up."

"Many girls marry even younger than sixteen," I pointed out.

"How do you know I ain't talking about you?" she replied.

Embarrassed by his wife's bluntness, Jason explained that they were wondering just how I might support their daughter. They knew I had saved a bit of money at sea, but they weren't sure I had the steady qualities needed to survive in the edge of the wilderness.

"Take no offense, Jerry. I know you for a brave fellow and we all like you, but you have always been so close-mouthed about your family and early circumstances that sometimes we wonder about you."

I could have wept from frustration. How could I tell them that I was wanted in Virginia for murdering my stepfather?

To avoid further questioning, I suggested that they give Gerta the opportunity to speak for herself.

I spent several anxious minutes watching that girl's fresh, beautiful face as first her father explained that I wanted to make her my wife and take her west and then her mother ventured that it wouldn't hurt to wait a year and see "how things go."

When they had finished, Gerta cast those magnificent eyes on me and said as calmly as if she were talking about the weather:

"I like Jerry well enough, I reckon, but it appears to me that Mama is right."

My heart fell. But her next words buoyed me up again.

"Besides, I don't want to move west and live on a farm. I would rather wait until we could afford a fine house in Philadelphia or someplace like that."

It struck me that I did not really know the young woman Gerta McGee had become. What further mysteries lay behind that lovely young countenance? At last I found my tongue.

"You mean, if I build up a business or something in the next year, you'd marry me?"

She smiled and nodded.

My mind worked furiously. Philadelphia was too damned close to Virginia for comfort.

"I hear Boston is a grand city," I blurted out. "There might be better opportunity there."

Gerta looked at her parents. Jason frowned. Kate said in her usual forthright way, "You have always been a great talker, Jerry.

But talking and doing are two different things. Show us that you can provide for our daughter. There'll be time enough to decide where you will live after you do that."

For the next few days, Kate kept such close watch over Gerta and me, it nearly drove me mad. I would have given my soul for a single kiss. All I got were teasing smiles. But they could not deny me an embrace upon my leavetaking. I held that marvelous girl in my arms and tasted the sweetness of her lips as long as I dared, then mounted Ned and rode once more to the north.

That was how I came to settle in Massachusetts. I found Lovejoy Brown back in Marblehead, reduced to working on a fishing boat. He was glad to see me. Lovejoy loved three things: rum, his hard-bitten old mother, and the sea. My knowledge of seamanship was limited, but I recognized that great profits were to be made transporting goods from one part of the world to the other. Lovejoy, a bachelor in his midforties, had forgotten more about navigation and general seamanship than I would ever know. During the war with the French he had shipped out on a privateer and earned enough to provide his widowed mother with a sturdy saltbox cottage in Marblehead "and a bit for me old age." And like me, he had his accumulated earnings from our long cruise.

Eager to make my fortune and return to claim my Gerta as quickly as possible, I pooled my money with Lovejoy's, and we each purchased a quarter share in a ketch from a sly Marblehead merchant, who retained a secret half interest.

Those next few months were the happiest of my life. Lovejoy drank only between voyages of our craft back and forth to New York and Halifax. I kept the books and arranged for cargoes, legal and otherwise. And all the while my heart sang with hope for the future. I made two visits to Boston looking for just the right house in which to settle with Gerta. Meanwhile, I wrote her letter after letter describing my work and sharing my dreams of our future life together.

It was many months before I received a reply. But that one letter dashed my hopes, broke my heart, and very nearly ruined my life. Written in Jason's stilted hand, it informed me that only a month after my departure a sheriff's constable from Virginia had visited Sherman's Valley inquiring as to my whereabouts. I was wanted back in Virginia not only for attempted murder and horse theft but also on bastardy charges.

That was when I learned that my stepfather had not been killed, only crippled. For a moment, my spirits revived. No hangman's noose awaited me after all. But when I read on I learned of a worse sentence.

"We did not disclose your whereabouts, Jerry, but under these and other circumstances, you'll have to forget about marrying our

Gerta. I wish you had told me of your troubles when first we met. Maybe you could have cleared yourself. I have delayed informing you, but fresh circumstances force me to divulge that Kate would not have heard of allowing our Gerta to marry you . . ." To hell with Kate, I thought to myself. I would sneak back to Pennsylvania and steal her away at night. But then I read on: ". . . even if she were still free."

All my happiness drained away as I read that Gerta had just been married to "a schoolmaster from New York, Chester Peebles, who stopped here on his way to Carolina to open a school there."

I took scant comfort from Jason's assurance that "he would not have been my choice as a son-in-law, but Kate finds him acceptable and, more important, so does Gerta."

The letter concluded with a report that their eldest, Ephraim, now was studying medicine in Philadelphia.

I despise self-pity. I do not engage in it now, and I did not then. I also scorned those who let rum rule their lives. But that was before I received that letter. Thereafter I began drinking so that Lovejoy Brown often had to go thirsty to keep me sober. I gave up shaving and grew a thick, reddish beard.

A second blow befell us both one night a few weeks later, when a British cutter intercepted Lovejoy as he was unloading smuggled goods off the Marblehead coast. Lovejoy and our crew jumped overboard and waded ashore. The British confiscated our ketch. Our secret partner was outraged but had to swallow his loss in silence. All I had left was my good old Ned and my southern charm. Lovejoy took me in to live with him and his sour old mother, and we continued as partners, now in the grubby business of peddling—when we were sober, that is.

So that was how one of the Virginia aristocracy came to be at Lexington, Massachusetts, at the start of the war. That was how I nearly became a hopeless drunkard. But I have strayed from my tale.

3

GETTING BACK to Lexington and Buckman's barn: sometime about midnight, I awakened to the sound of hoofbeats and someone shouting something about the British. I quickly drifted back to sleep, only to be awakened a little later by the clanging of a bell in the odd little one-story belfry that stood across the village green between the meetinghouse and the school. This hellish racket was followed by a hubbub of voices that grew in volume as more and more minutemen gathered behind the meetinghouse.

Burrowing deeper into my bed of straw and drawing the horse

blanket over my head to drown out the voice of the company clerk calling the roll, I drifted off again. I did not hear Captain John Parker dismiss his 130 men at one-thirty with orders to reassemble quickly at the sound of the company drum, as I now know he did. About three hours later, the rat-a-tat-tat of that drum penetrated my consciousness.

Why didn't that lot on the green pipe down and let a man get his sleep? Damn it, the sun was nearly up! That was when I heard a new sound, from the east, faint at first, but growing steadily louder and more ominous. It was the sound of hundreds of booted feet, marching in military cadence to the shrill of a fife and the beat of drums.

Suddenly I was wide awake, the hair on the back of my neck tingling. I put my eye to a crack and looked east down the long, level stretch of road from Boston. In that dim dawn light I saw what appeared to be a giant machine of red-coated men, led by two mounted officers.

I scrambled to the other side of the loft and peered out upon the common. About three dozen militiamen were forming themselves into two strung-out lines, and a like number scuttled about the tavern and meetinghouse fetching muskets and powder.

With the rim of the sun just appearing, events moved so swiftly that neither I nor any of those seventy Lexington minutemen nor the seven hundred British soldiers could possibly say for certain just what happened in the next few minutes.

The Lexington Common occupied a two-and-a-half-acre triangle at the point where the road divided, one branch leading on to Concord and the other to Bedford. The three-story meetinghouse stood at the apex. The two British officers, coming upon this activity on the Common, shouted to their soldiers and rode to the left around the meetinghouse. Then here came these little fellows, the men of their light infantry companies, with muskets at the ready and bayonets fixed, trotting up into skirmish ranks, shouting as they passed Buckman's Tavern and stable.

One of their officers yelled from the other side of the meetinghouse, "Don't fire! Surround them. Disarm them." And then the same officer ordered the militiamen, "Lay down your arms, you damned rebels!"

The militia captain shouted something I could not hear above the cries from the onrushing British, and the minutemen began to drift out of formation toward the edge of the Common. That old man who had sworn never to take a backward step kept his place, however, emptying his musket balls into his hat, which he set at his feet, and then standing with weapon raised to face the red-coated horde.

I have talked to many a person who claimed to know exactly who fired the first shot. It was a British officer—no, it was a soldier in

11

their ranks—one of the militia—even a spectator. Whoever it was fired the first shot of a war that swept around the world, changing my life as it did that of thousands upon thousands of others. A few other shots followed. Then came a pause, and suddenly the air was filled with sound and clouds of smoke as British muskets began their deadly work.

The defiant old man went down but still managed to fire his piece from the ground. It sickened me to see a soldier plunge his bayonet into the old fellow and kick his hat aside.

The militiamen ran in all directions as the British soldiers fired at their backs. The British officers screamed vainly for them to cease fire. One officer's horse panicked and carried his rider through the scattering minutemen, far down the Bedford Road. Then the minutemen started shooting back from behind trees and stone walls. Puffs of smoke appeared from Buckman's Tavern and the meetinghouse.

Meanwhile, the rest of the British column—the taller, heavier men of their grenadier companies, led by a great, fat officer on horseback—crowded into the scene. Just as the light infantrymen were starting to break down doors of houses facing the common, the officer roared to a drummer to beat cease fire and soon managed to get the soldiers back into marching ranks.

I slid down from the loft, and as I approached the barn door, seven hundred muskets fired all at once. Imagine my relief when I looked out and realized it was a victory salute.

After that, the bloodthirsty fiends gave themselves three cheers. Then with drums beating and fifes sounding, they headed off toward Concord.

So there it was. Although not by design, still I was present at the beginning of the war. And I must confess that I came close to harnessing up Ned and carrying my trade goods back to Marblehead as fast as I could. But I was deterred in part by the sight of a young fellow piteously dragging himself toward a handsome house that faced the common from the north. I saw that poor man collapse on his stoop just as his wife and small son opened the door.

I was deterred, also, when I spotted the bleeding owner of the great sword leaning on his ancient weapon and shaking his fist at the backs of the British.

And my resolve to get myself away from Lexington melted completely when the militia captain, hurrying back to the now-bloody common, saw me in the doorway of the stable and implored, "Come help! We need assistance."

What could I do but pitch in and help carry the bodies of the eight slaughtered militiamen into the meetinghouse until their families could claim them? I assisted the local doctor and his son in binding the wounds of another nine men. It was heartwarming to hear the physician praise my medical skills and receive the thanks of the injured and their families.

As I told them, I had seen worse during my service with Bouquet in Western Pennsylvania. At least the British did not scalp their victims or burn them at the stake.

Meanwhile, shocked (as was I) by the unprovoked brutality of the British and fearing their return, many of the women and children who lived near the common and along the Boston road fled for refuge with friends and relatives. Word of the dawn massacre spread with amazing speed. Throughout the morning, other minutemen drifted in. So did several British stragglers, some drunk from plundered rum.

Never one to miss an opportunity, I took custody of the short-barreled fusil and other accoutrements of a befuddled member of the Welsh Fusiliers and hung about as Captain Parker questioned the little Redcoat.

The British column was not the efficient machine it appeared. They had gone without sleep for twenty-four hours. During the previous night many had spent hours jammed aboard longboats on the Charles River waiting for the commander of the expedition—fat, slow old Lieutenant Colonel Francis Smith—to arrive with his contingent from his Tenth Regiment. Once ferried across to marshy Lechmere Point near Cambridge, the light infantry had to wade ashore and stand about stamping their wet feet while the boats brought over the rest of the men and then make a third trip with provisions and extra ammunition. By the time their boots had dried and Colonel Smith gave the order to march, the tide had lapped in around their debarkation point, and they had to wade over to the road that would lead them past Cambridge and onto the route to Concord.

" 'Tweren't so bad for the grenadiers," our prisoner said. "Water only came up to the knees of those great louts. Me, I got wet clear up to me arse. At last, Colonel Smith came to his senses and let us leave our packs behind."

As all know today, General Gage, commander-in-chief of the British forces and the nominal Royal Governor of Massachusetts, had planned for his expedition to be carried out in secrecy and with speed by the flank companies of ten regiments—that is, one light infantry and one grenadier company from each regiment—plus a contingent of marines under Major Pitcairn. They were supposed to descend on Concord well before daylight and seize the stores of military rations, ammunition, and artillery pieces that the rebellious citizens reportedly had accumulated.

According to our prisoner, it was already 3 A.M. before the column reached Menotomy. As for secrecy, "Bells was ringing in the night as if 'twere Sunday morning. And then two of our scouts rode up saying there might be as many as five hundred rebels under arms here in Lexington."

I snorted at this Jonah of a tale.

"How was we to know? Anyhow, that was when Colonel Smith sent a rider back to Boston to ask for reinforcements. Then he turned us light infantrymen over to Major Pitcairn and ordered him to hurry on to Concord and secure the bridges over the river there, leaving the grenadiers to follow and search the town. As we got close here, Major Pitcairn halted us so we could load and prime our muskets. I slipped behind a tavern down the way to relieve my bladder. Off my mates marched to fife and drum. I seen the back door of the tavern was open and went in to refresh meself. . . ."

Captain Parker turned him over to be marched with his fellow stragglers to the jail at Woburn. Then around noon, he came round to shake my hand and thank me before striding off to remuster what was left of his company.

I packed my sacks of wares into the cart and hesitated outside the stable before backing Ned between the shafts. On the common, the militia clerk was once again calling the roll.

"A true Son of Liberty," Captain Parker had called me the night before. And the doctor had dubbed me "a fine patriot." It had been many months since I had received, or deserved, such respect. And the British were a vicious lot.

I watched the Lexington minutemen form into marching ranks and move across the common toward the Concord road, on the trail of the British. The fifer and drummer struck up one of my favorite tunes, "The White Cockade." To my amazement, the wounded old gentleman with the great sword marched along with the rest.

I debated the question for only a moment. Then I rolled the cart back into the stable and hid my sacks of goods under some hay. I paused to load and prime my captured fusil, then mounted Ned bareback and rode off after the column.

4

CAPTAIN PARKER led us two miles west, just to the edge of the Lincoln township line, where the road to Concord curved eastward around a wooded hill and down to a small creek. He stopped his men at the woods and ordered them to hack down bushes to provide a clear field of fire.

Ned wasn't the horse he used to be, but I would not have taken a hundred pounds for him that nineteenth of April 1775. Captain Parker, recalling my tale of serving in the Indian wars, assigned me to scout the road to Concord and report on what I observed.

The countryside swarmed with militiamen. Some wore broad-brimmed hats, others tricorns; some bore military-type smoothbore muskets, and others carried fowling pieces. Among the scores who milled about on the next hill, I saw not a single man wearing a uniform or armed with a bayonet.

That lot let me pass without a challenge, but an ever larger group blocked the road at the next hill, Hardy's. They demanded to know my business.

I explained that I was on a mission from Captain Parker of the Lexington militia.

At that they crowded closer, clamoring for news of the shooting that morning. Was it true that scores had been slaughtered, women raped, and the entire village burned by the evil British?

They seemed disappointed at my only slightly exaggerated report, which I ended with, "Now, what's going on over at Concord?"

To hear that lot tell it, the British had burned the town and been defeated in a "terrible battle" at the North Bridge over the Concord River. That was not true, of course. The British had found and spiked three cannon, burned their carriages, dumped militia supplies of flour and musket balls into the millpond, and helped themselves to the goods of a few of the households they searched. As for the battle, it is well known that after a bit of name-calling and glaring, the militia and a few companies of British light infantry exchanged volleys across the Concord River, causing the lobsterbacks to flee back to the town, leaving behind two dead and taking with them several wounded.

I interrupted the flow of misinformation to ask, "Well, where are the bloodthirsty scum now?"

A militiaman pointed to the west, where the long ridge bordering the road from Concord ends at a crossroads.

"Look for yourself—there, at Meriam's Corner."

A long column of British soldiers, their ranks still in good order, moved wearily—fifes and drums now silent—across a narrow bridge in our direction, while several hundred militiamen watched from a barnyard north of the crossing. Apparently unaware of the throngs of colonists waiting down the road, the last company—grenadiers—halted just beyond the bridge and leveled their muskets at the lurking militia.

Looking back, I think maybe that is when the war really began in earnest. Stupidly and deliberately, that company of grenadiers fired what I suppose they thought would be a parting volley.

Within seconds the landscape on the other side of the creek fairly erupted with billows of smoke. Several grenadiers fell. The others ran to catch up with the column.

The head of the column remained in good order, marching along as if the disturbance to their rear had naught to do with them. Like bears swatting at a swarm of bees, the strapping grenadiers, in their tall, peaked helmets, would fire a volley and then re-load on the run. One giant stumbled and then pitched onto his face—dead, I assumed—and another dropped his musket and clutched his shoulder.

Meanwhile, the militiamen were crossing the creek and racing ahead to the cover of stone walls and trees from which to blast away at their massed red-coated targets.

Captain Parker and his fellow Lexington militiamen left their hiding place in the woods to listen to my report.

"Good, we'll have our chance for revenge," he said. "Remember, men, hold your fire until I tell you. Aim low, at their knees. And keep your heads down."

Having carried out my assignment, I could have ridden back to Lexington, recovered my wares, and returned to Marblehead with honor—doing a little trading along the way. But I was too caught up in this adventure to leave. So I led Ned well off the road and tied him to a tree. I found myself a place behind a rock outcrop-ping and waited with my new-found comrades, these brave veterans of Lexington, to ambush the British column.

Here they came at last, splashing across a small stream and then laboring up a long slope toward our woods. The same fat officer who had halted the firing at Lexington—Colonel Smith—rode at the head of his beleaguered command. The rattle of muskets still sounded far down the road as minutemen continued to harass the rear guard.

Except for an occasional groan from a wounded soldier, they marched in silence. In the woods, as I checked the priming of my fusil for the hundredth time, I was conscious of a pair of birds sing-ing nearby and of the distant cawing of crows. Onward crunched the British boots, up the hill and onto the curve of the road past our woods.

Captain Parker got to his feet and raised his sword. I cocked my weapon and fitted the butt to my shoulder. Beside me a young man with chattering teeth gripped his fowling piece hard to stop his hands from shaking. An old man, blood oozing through the ban-dage I had tied around his arm that morning, ground his teeth and mumbled curses.

The fat officer's overburdened horse drew even with us. Captain Parker brought the point of his sword down and shouted, "Fire!"

I was surprised at how hard the light fusil kicked. I stood up and reloaded as fast as I could. As the smoke cleared and I brought the butt up to my shoulder again, I saw that the fat officer had fallen from his horse.

"Fire! Keep firing!" Parker cried.

Now the British officers were screaming at their men, some of whom were running down the road to escape our fusillade, while

16

others had halted in their tracks to return our fire. Bullets sang around my head. The road seemed littered with fallen redcoats. Another volley crashed into the woods, and the frightened young chap beside me spun around and fell across his fowling piece.

"Flankers out!" I heard a British officer shout.

Here came their light infantry, bayonets at the ready. My Lexington friends were not cowards, but neither were they fools. They took to their heels. Thinking as much of the safety of old Ned as of myself, I rode off as fast as he would go across the fields.

By the time I reached Lexington, the houses around the common were deserted. John Buckman had boarded up his buildings, but I managed to pry open a stable window. My sacks of knickknacks were untouched. Within a few minutes I reloaded them in my cart, harnessed Ned, and started along the road toward Boston, the incessant sound of musketry to my rear.

What more could be expected of a man who was not from those parts to begin with? I had my horse to think of and the cart to be returned to its owner. And there was the interest of my old friend Lovejoy to consider.

I thought I would just stop off at Munroe's Tavern, about a half-mile down the road to refresh myself with a bit of grog and a bite to eat and then press on for Marblehead, richer with a store of tales to tell Lovejoy and his ancient mother and with a British fusil to sell.

I had just crossed Vine Brook and was nearing the junction of the Woburn Road when I saw a sight that caused me to halt Ned with a jerk of the reins. I stood up in the cart for a better view. No doubt about it—there came a fresh column of British soldiers, more by far than had marched down that same stretch of road that morning, and they had two cannon with them. I recalled that our prisoner had said something about Colonel Smith sending a request back to Boston for reinforcements.

For a second I considered dashing ahead to take the road to Woburn. But then I saw a glint of bayonets spreading across the hills on either side of the road as the British deployed into battle position. I turned Ned around and whipped him into a trot back into Lexington and past the common, and damn it to hell, we nearly ran into the head of Smith's bedraggled column.

Several musket balls whistled around me. I turned Ned back across the common to the safety of the burying ground and was amazed to find concealed behind the stone wall a fresh lot of militiamen under the command of a portly, balding chap wearing a blue uniform. This worthy ordered me off the road and proceeded to interrogate me about the reinforcements.

I answered him civilly enough at first but finally demanded to know who in the hell he was to be detaining me.

"I am William Heath, brigadier general, by authority of the Massachusetts Provincial Congress. I have just arrived from Roxbury to assume command of this situation. I see you are armed. I invite you to leave your horse with the others behind those trees over there and join me and my men."

Damn that fusil! I was trapped. Resignedly, I tied Ned out of range and took up a position behind the stone wall.

Those twenty companies of light infantry and grenadiers, the flower of the British army, presented a sorry sight. They stumbled past the scene of their early-morning massacre of the Lexington militia and into the rain of fire that we poured upon them from the burying ground. In their haste to get through the village, they acted like a uniformed mob, not bothering even to shoot back. Indeed many of them, as it turned out, had exhausted their ammunition.

Colonel Smith limped alongside his horse, which now carried two more seriously wounded soldiers. Others hung on to the poor animal's saddle and reins. Pitcairn, also on foot, restored some order by blocking the road and forcing his men to get back in ranks before pressing on.

It is safe to say that if the relief force had not been waiting just beyond Lexington, Smith and the survivors of this expedition would have been wiped out. They were whipped dogs. We left the safety of our cemetery wall and swarmed out into the common, ready to chase after the tail of the column.

Then we heard two things. First, we heard a cheer from Smith's column as they saw the fresh force waiting to succor them. And then we heard the boom of a cannon from a knoll about a thousand yards away and the crash of a cannonball. It went in through the front wall of the meetinghouse and out through the back wall.

We scattered for cover. Peppering away at a demoralized column from a safe distance was one thing, but standing up to artillery fire was quite another.

That relief column—1,100 strong under General Percy—was more than we could handle. It would have been foolhardy to go up against trained, fresh British soldiers in battle ranks with cannon in position. Back in the haven of the cemetery, General Heath was striving to impose order on the hundreds of excited militiamen swarming about him. He called together their captains and suggested that some of them bypass the British position with a group of the fresher, younger fellows and lie in wait down the road.

"They will have to march eleven long miles back to Boston. We must harass them every step of the way. Encourage others to do so. The rest of us will follow close upon their heels and keep them occupied. This day is far from over."

General Heath was dead right, of course. The heaviest and most costly fighting for both the British and the Americans lay ahead, on the long march back from Lexington to Boston. But I had had enough. It was time to return to business.

Imagine my outrage when I discovered that someone—it could only have been a militiaman—had made off with my stock and left me with only an empty cart and a weary horse. Someone had dared do this to me, Jeremiah Martin, while I was valiantly risking my life at the express request of General Heath. Oh yes, I still had the fusil, the cartridge box, and other accoutrements I had taken from the Welshman. But they would not bring in enough to cover the loss of my trade goods.

Surely General Heath would right this monstrous wrong. But my efforts to gain his attention were in vain. I looked again at my fusil. I thought of the red-coated figures lying along the road. It stood to reason there would be even more before the day had ended. And that was when my fortunes—indeed, my entire life—took a fresh turn.

By the time nightfall overtook me at Menotomy, my cart was overflowing with the boots and muskets of dead and wounded British soldiers. One outraged housewife came out of hiding to call me a ghoul. An aged militiaman, too tired to pursue the British anymore, chastised me for "robbing the dead" rather than taking up the chase. I informed them and others that General Heath had requested that I do what I could to help and that I was gathering materials of war. I did not lift so much as one item from any American lying along the road; indeed, I lost much time dispensing water to our wounded.

The British were another matter. Their watches, money, and rings went into my pockets; their weapons, boots, and knapsacks into my cart. If I had had a full-sized wagon and a few more hours of daylight, I could have retired for life on the plunder I picked up in the wake of the running battle with the British.

Today it amuses me to recall how incensed I was by the theft of my trade goods. Whoever stole those pots and pans did me a service. I shall always be grateful to the fellow.

5

IN MY ABSENCE from America for so many years, I had taken little notice of colonial politics. I realize now that all of America—especially New England—had become a powder magazine, partly through the pigheadedness of the British and partly through the activities of our own strifemongers. When those British soldiers fired upon the Lexington militia, it was like tossing a firebrand into the powder magazine.

Over the next few days, relays of horsemen spread the news of the battle south to New York, Philadelphia, Virginia, and the Carolinas. Massachusetts militiamen trooped into Cambridge by the thousands to help first General Heath and then his successor, General Artemas Ward, keep the British holed up in Boston. Many of these overnight warriors lacked weapons or equipment. I got a grand price for my British muskets and other loot.

Lovejoy Brown could not believe the size of the purse with which I returned to Marblehead. With his long narrow face and faded blue eyes, he had never been an impressive man—physically, that is. He wiped his nose on his sleeve, cut his eyes toward his inquisitive old mother, who pretended to doze by the kitchen fire, and said in a low voice, "What shall we do with all this money, Jerry?"

I had been preparing for that question all the way back from Cambridge. He listened to me without changing his hound-dog expression, thought for a few minutes, and then shook his head.

"I'd rather buy us another ketch."

"There isn't nearly enough for that, you old bonehead," I replied. "But there is more than enough to buy a team of horses and a good stout wagon, yes, and a keg of rum, and—"

"I have had a bellyful of peddling!"

"So have I. But don't you see, there are thousands of militiamen down there eager for drink and blankets and tents. This won't be peddling. We'll be in the military supply business."

Lovejoy's mother dropped her game of 'possum to join the debate. As usual, she referred to me in the third person, saying, "He has just got carried away, as usual. It's like that smuggling business he talked you into. He has had a bit of luck, and he thinks it will go on like that forever. I say stash the money away and wait until better times."

"Ah, Mother Brown," I said, "that might be a long time, if by *better* you mean 'peaceful.' Nearly three hundred British soldiers were shot down between Concord and Boston last week, and nearly a hundred Massachusetts men. There will be other battles, believe me. And there is money to be made."

Lovejoy turned down the corners of his mouth. "I am a seafaring man."

His mother joined in with, "And you are my only child. Who will look after me in my old age if you get yourself kilt?"

"Lovejoy, I am talking only about starting out. This is a way to get enough money to return to shipping. And as for you, Mother Brown, a woman who has sacrificed as you have should be living in a two-story house on a hill with a widow's walk and servant girls to look after you."

She tossed her head and turned her back.

Lovejoy drew me outside, out of her hearing.

"You promise me we'll get another ketch?"

"Maybe even a schooner or a brig, in time."

The only way to get around his New England pessimism was to appeal to his greed or, on occasion, his pride. If all else failed, you could work on his devotion to his mother.

That very afternoon we purchased a pair of matched bay mares and a good wagon. The next morning we bought up all the spare blankets in Marblehead, contracted with a sailmaker for the manufacture of a gross of stout tents, and talked an old smuggler friend out of two kegs of rum.

By afternoon, I was headed south on Ned for Cambridge, leaving Lovejoy to drive the team and our goods down the next day. It occurred to me as I rode through that aroused countryside that for the first time since I had received Jason McGee's letter, I was no longer sunk in misery. And I had not had a drink since those two cups of rum at Buckman's Tavern. War is a powerful antidote to personal despair and boredom. But like rum, it exacts a heavy price in the end.

The pandemonium in and around Cambridge had grown worse during my brief absence. The yards around Harvard College were crowded with ill-matched tents. Some had been made out of drapes stolen from the homes of rich Tories who had left to take refuge with the British army in Boston. Their houses had been turned into barracks, as had the main building of the college itself.

Thousands of militiamen came and went as they pleased. Grouped into companies commanded by elected officers, they displayed a most unmilitary assortment of smoothbore muskets and fowling pieces. Luckily for them, the British, across the Charles River in Boston, did not realize the true condition of the New England militia that was supposedly besieging them.

Having been born and reared in class-conscious Virginia and sheltered for a time by steady Pennsylvania frontier folk, I was appalled by the behavior of these independent-minded New Englanders. Everyone regarded himself as the equal of the next fellow, even if that next fellow happened to be his captain or colonel. If they thought an order made no sense, they ignored it.

There was much speculation in the camps that the British might come charging out of Boston to avenge their humiliation on the road from Concord—yes, and much bold talk about what they, the militia, would do in such a case. Actually, to get at us by land the redcoats would have had to advance over "the Boston neck," the narrow strip that connected the city with the mainland near Roxbury, and a contingent under General John Thomas was digging earthworks to block that approach. The Charlestown Peninsula, where General Percy had taken refuge after Lexington and Concord, now lay unoccupied by either army. Like Boston, it too was connected to the mainland by a slender so-called neck.

The undisciplined New England militiamen may have been poorly led by lethargic old General Ward, but another group was also at work for the American cause, and it was directed by men who knew what they were about. These architects of the rebellion—for that is what I now regard them—were headed by one of the most impressive gentlemen I have ever encountered, namely one Dr. Joseph Warren of Boston.

I met him by accident—in retrospect, a most fortuitous accident—when I presented myself at the Hastings House near the Harvard common. I had a view to offer to supply tents to the still growing numbers of militiamen coming now from New Hampshire, Rhode Island, and Connecticut as well as Massachusetts.

It was impossible to see General Ward; he was much too busy, I was informed by a pimply-faced aide, one of the few Harvard students who had remained after the influx of militia.

As a William and Mary man, I was not about to be so easily put off by a mere Harvardite. When I persisted in demanding to see General Ward, this officious underling demanded to know my business.

"Tents," I replied. "This army needs shelter. Any fool can see that. I propose to supply General Ward with tents."

"We are dealing with that difficulty. The companies are supplying their own tents—" he began, but I cut him off with, "I must have been mistaken when I said any fool can see they need shelter. You apparently cannot."

The chap's face turned as scarlet as a lobsterback's jacket.

I heard someone behind me laugh and turned to see a tall, elegantly dressed gentleman several years my senior. He introduced himself as Joseph Warren, the newly elected president of the Provincial Congress of Massachusetts. Unbeknownst to me at the time, Dr. Warren was the man who had dispatched couriers to arouse the countryside the night the British marched out to Lexington. He had also helped to concoct the official reports of the Lexington Massacre that so incited the other colonies.

He invited me into his office on the second floor of the Hastings House and listened with great interest to my story of my part in the Lexington affair.

"I wish I had met you sooner, Martin. We could have used the deposition of a Virginian to go with those we just sent off to England."

As he explained it, he and some friends had taken the sworn statements of dozens of eyewitnesses (including British prisoners) and hired a fast Salem-based schooner to carry the reports to England.

"Certain friends have informed us that General Gage has sent off his official report to the government, but we think our vessel will overcome their head start and reach London first."

He went on to express his hope of inflaming public opinion in England against the government's American policy.

I listened to all this politely enough, but I could hardly wait to switch the conversation back to tents. He must have noted my wandering attention, for he brought up the subject.

"So you have tents. What kind and how many?"

He seemed surprised at my ready answer and my promise to deliver 144 shelters within thirty days.

After that it was an easy matter to agree on a price. Without further ado, he wrote out a purchase order in the name of the Provincial Congress. That done, he leaned back and asked in an offhand way whether I had any military experience and if I owned a good horse.

It was a lucky accident, my meeting Dr. Warren. And I do not refer to that order for 144 tents, welcome as it was.

The trick to getting ahead in this world, I am convinced, is to find a need (or desire). Then see that that need is filled by someone else who can do the job better than you, thereby freeing yourself to undertake yet another enterprise.

There is more to it than that, however. Timely information can be a more important commodity than physical goods. And so can influence with the right people.

All of which is by way of explaining that I set out for Philadelphia on a confidential mission for Dr. Warren as soon as Lovejoy Brown reached Cambridge with our wagonload of blankets and rum. Lovejoy was delighted at the good news about the order for tents, but he objected to my leaving him to handle our new business all on his own. I could not tell him how important it was to put ourselves in good with the Provincial Congress of Massachusetts. Nor could I divulge the fact that I would also be establishing a relationship with the Second Continental Congress that was about to convene in Philadelphia. That was what Dr. Warren wished me to do— deliver certain reports and messages to various delegates at that Second Congress and return with their replies.

At last the old seadog got it through his head that he was to carry on the work I had begun for us in Cambridge while I undertook my mysterious mission. Lovejoy was not blessed with the gift of vision. Perhaps I, on the other hand, enjoyed a surplus.

6

I DEPARTED CAMBRIDGE thinking that I had been involved—voluntarily or not—in a rebellion of New England farmers rather than the outbreak of a long war between America and Great Britain. That illusion faded when I passed through New York and saw mobs with weapons stolen from the public armory marching up and down Wall Street. It evaporated completely when I reached Philadelphia. Every vacant space in the City of Brotherly Love had been turned into a parade ground for newly reformed "Associator" or militia companies.

I had been in Philadelphia only once before, on my furtive visit in 1765, when I had slipped aboard ship as a supercargo thinking I was wanted for murder. Now, with the entire country in a turmoil and letters of introduction from Dr. Warren in my pocket, I felt safe from apprehension by Virginia authorities. Besides that, my appearance had changed over the past decade. No longer was I a downy-cheeked, fearful stripling. And I had recovered my self-respect and will—not just to live, but to prevail.

So the Jeremiah Martin who swaggered into The White Swan on South Street near the Delaware waterfront was quite a different article from the rum-soaked peddler who had been treated with such disdain two weeks earlier at John Buckman's Tavern.

This tavern was owned by one Phineas Oliver, a slow-moving chap in his midthirties who was very bland in manner and almost too solicitous of his guests. His wife, Elizabeth, really ran the establishment. A short brunette of about thirty, she displayed a ripe figure that might have been considered plump by some. She had a vivacious manner and a teasing way of talking to men. It didn't take long before it was "Liz" and "Jerry" between us.

The delegates who were to receive my messages from Dr. Warren had not yet arrived, so I set out to see what I had missed on my previous visit to Philadelphia. With forty thousand residents, it was the largest city in North America and second in size only to London in the British Empire.

During the next two days, while Ned recovered from our long journey from Cambridge and I waited for the congressional delegates to arrive, I walked from one end of Philadelphia to the other, from the busy waterfront to its western suburbs and beyond to the undeveloped shore of the Schuylkill. I was impressed by the city's orderly grid plan fronting on the Delaware and by the sheer busyness of its shops and workplaces. Its main streets paved with cobblestones, some even lighted; its grand buildings, such as the State House and Christ Church; its richly dressed, self-assured people—all these elements made Philadelphia a magic city to me.

On my second night in Philadelphia, after a long day of stretching my legs about the streets, I stopped off for a goodly supper at the new City Tavern, visited the stable behind the White Swan to make sure that Ned had no complaints, and then entered the rear door of the Olivers' establishment.

I halted in the back hall to listen to a high-pitched voice emanating from the taproom.

"Of course our people beyond the Susquehanna will fight if it comes to that. Didn't we bear the brunt of the Indian war, whilst you Philadelphians sat on your asses?"

"But our sister city to the north is in distress," a lower, more cultivated man said in a Philadelphia accent.

The first voice continued with a slight stutter, "There is no reason as yet to go rushing up to Boston, not until we hear what King or Parliament have to say about the conduct of the British soldiers. Gage may have exceeded his authority. He may be recalled for bringing all this on."

I put my head around the corner. My guess had been right. I was listening to the voice and looking at the back of my old friend and once prospective father-in-law, Jason McGee. My affection for a man who had saved my life and treated me like a younger brother contended in my breast with my bitter resentment toward him and his family for their ultimate rejection of me as a husband for their Gerta.

I was at the point of bolting from the tavern in my confusion when Liz Oliver bustled out from the kitchen bearing mugs. Was she acquainted with the tall fellow holding forth before the fire? I asked her.

"Sure, and that is Captain McGee. He came in this afternoon with his son Christopher. He stayed here last January for the Pennsylvania Provincial Convention. A fine figure of a man he is. Not a one in that room can hold a candle to him, in my opinion. Would you like to meet him?"

"Not just yet. I'll sit in the corner and listen."

In the candlelight, Jason looked younger than forty-one. Except for touches of gray, his hair still gleamed as red as it had when we rode together on Bouquet's expedition and labored side by side on his farm. Unlike the other men with whom he talked, he appeared lean and hard, as in the old days.

The Philadelphia accent was owned by a pompous little man in a velvet coat. "But it was the King who decreed Massachusetts to be in a state of rebellion. If we don't back New England, what's to stop the British from treating Philadelphia as they do Boston?"

"Ah, Ph-Philadelphia," Jason stuttered. "Th-the shoe pinches here at last. We must tie the British down in Boston to keep them away from your p-precious Philadelphia."

A man with a southern drawl like my own protested. "It's not Boston or just Philadelphia that we should consider. It is all thirteen colonies that are involved now, whether we like it or not. Let King and Parliament learn they can't trample on our rights any longer."

The southerner ticked off the litany of American complaints: the Townshend Acts of '67, which had imposed import duties to pay the salaries of unwanted royal officials and had authorized smugglers to be tried without juries; the Boston massacre of 1770; the Tea Act, which had given the East India Company a monopoly on the commodity; and the more recent Boston Port Act, which had closed that harbor in retaliation for the Boston Tea Party.

"Don't forget the Quartering Act," the man in the velvet jacket added. "I'd like to see them try to lodge their soldiers in my house without my permission."

At that point the front door of the tavern opened, and in walked Ephraim and Christopher McGee. My two former students walked right past me and up to their father, who paused to introduce them.

They joined the circle around the fire, and Jason resumed. "I know of all those complaints. The business that most concerns me is the King's prohibition against settling lands beyond the mountains. I lived out there among the Indians in my youth. My wife had to flee with Ephraim here as a babe in arms back to her parents in Lancaster County in '55. I went with Colonel Armstrong in '56 out to the Allegheny to destroy Kittanning and back again in '63 with Bouquet. What is Boston to me? I haven't heard any mention of the Quebec Act. Reserve the lands I fought for to the Canadians and the Indians? Horseshit. The British just want to block our expansion to the West, hem us in on this side of the mountains. But does any one in Boston or Philadelphia care?"

At that point I could sit still no longer. I set down the mug Liz had served me, drew my sailor's cap over my eyebrows, turned up the labels of my jacket around my beard, and walked across the room with a false limp.

In a husky voice, copied after Lovejoy Brown's accent, I broke into the conversational circle.

"Gentlemen, you will forgive me I hope, for interrupting you, but I have been much interested in your discourse."

They paused and before they could speak, I turned to Jason.

"Much as I dislike disagreeing with a stranger and speaking as a seafaring man, I can't think why folk along the coast should care about the West. The Indians deserve a place of refuge. Seems to me that our settlers—and I speak in particular of Ulstermen—have brought most of their Indian problems upon themselves."

I stopped just long enough for Jason to start sputtering, and then added quickly, "Now, as I see it, and I pray you will not take of-

26

fense, the folk out on the frontier should have defended themselves, not come whining to the Pennsylvania Assembly for militia. I recollect, and I hope you will correct me if I am wrong, that Bouquet's expedition in '63 was made up almost entirely of British troops. He was unable to persuade more than a handful of settlers to accompany him."

By now Jason's face had become almost as red as his hair. "W-W-Who the hell—" he began, but I pressed ahead. "If you will persist in agitating the poor Indians beyond the mountains and will not defend yourselves, why not at least be willing to pay the cost of British soldiers?"

Both Ephraim and Chris wore puzzled expressions as they stared at me. Their father struggled to find both words and an opening. He looked as if he were on the verge of a stroke.

"Now, you take the Battle of Bushy Run," I began.

"Y-You take the Battle of Bushy Run!" Jason fairly roared. "I was th-there, by God! Don't you t-try to t-tell me about Bushy Run, damn it to hell!"

I stepped back with a conciliatory gesture.

"Were you indeed, sir?"

"Indeed I was. And I was not the only American there—n-not by a long shot."

"Then I fear I have offended you—without meaning to, I assure you. Would you be so kind as to tell me your name, sir?"

"M-My name is Jason McGee, and by G-God you have offended me. You don't k-know what you are talking about."

I think my old friend might have struck me if Ephraim had not taken his arm. "Father, you mustn't agitate yourself so. The gentleman has apologized."

"W-Well, he goddamned well ought to. The Indians killed my mother in '44 and tried to kill your mother and you in '55."

"I apologize to you, sir, and to all your friends for intruding myself into your conversation. By the way, sir, I was given my information about Bushy Run from a source that may not be reliable."

Far from mollified, Jason demanded, "Who?"

Judging by the wide grin on his face, Chris had recognized me at last. I winked to signal him to remain silent.

"Why, it was a low fellow from Virginia. He had some Indian ancestry himself, and that might explain his prejudice."

"I should know him. If he really was at Bushy Run—"

I put my hand over my face as if searching my memory and then said in my normal drawl, "Seems to me he called himself *Jedidiah* Martin."

Jason frowned.

"You must mean Jeremiah Martin. But I would not call him a low fellow. Where did you know Jerry?"

I whipped off my cap and raised my hands. "Why, I have known him ever since I can remember."

Chris nearly bowled me over as he threw his arms around me. Ephraim seized my hand and wouldn't let go. Jason never did think my deception was half as humorous as his sons did.

7

AFTER THE OTHER GUESTS DEPARTED, the three McGees and I stayed up until past midnight bringing each other up to date about ourselves.

Kate and the twins were well. Jason had come to Philadelphia to purchase machinery and equipment for a new grist mill under construction on a tributary of Sherman's Creek. Kate had been left in charge of overseeing the work of the building. But with all this business up in New England, Jason thought he might remain in Philadelphia to see what the new Continental Congress would do.

Ephraim had just completed his medical studies and was weighing an offer to go to Barbados as personal physician to a wealthy planter-merchant. And, Chris devilishly volunteered, Ephraim was in love with the daughter of his professor of medicine.

As for Chris, they were thinking of enrolling him in the College of Philadelphia. According to Ephraim, "He enjoys arguing so much, we figure he might read law later."

What was I doing in Philadelphia? Without naming names, I indicated that I was on sensitive business on behalf of the Massachusetts authorities, even though it meant risking the thriving business my partner and I were engaged in. I told no outright lies; I simply left out some facts and enlarged upon others.

All the time we talked, it was as if the ghost of Gerta were sitting in the corner, auditing and inhibiting our conversation. And although I longed to know, I'd be damned if I would inquire about her. At last Jason stretched, yawned, and suggested the boys take themselves off to bed.

After they had gone, he cleared his throat and said, "Writing you that letter about Gerta was just about the hardest thing I ever had to do."

"Receiving it wasn't exactly a pleasure," I replied.

"I suppose not. I reckon you'd like to know more about her."

"Whatever you want to tell me."

As it turned out, I would just as soon he hadn't told me. She and her husband had settled west of a crossroads called Charlotte. Their school was built, and they had a goodly enrollment, mostly the children of Ulster Presbyterians who had moved south from Pennsylvania. And they were expecting a child, according to Gerta's last letter.

I stared into the ashes of the fire without responding for so long that Jason finally put his hand on my shoulder.

I shook it off and snarled, "Why didn't you give me a chance to explain things? Why did you let her marry somebody else? I could have provided for her like a queen."

"You had several years to explain, and you kept silent. What were we to think? Besides, what was there for you to explain?"

First taking a deep breath, I told Jason everything, the full truth, right up to the time I received his letter.

"Poor Jerry," he said when I was finished. "You spent all those years thinking you had murdered the man."

"Yes, and you want to know something? Not once in that time did I ever regret his supposed death. Thinking him dead was better than picturing him as the living husband of my mother."

Taken aback by the vehemence of my speech, Jason shook his head and got a strange look on his face.

"I never told this to anyone, Jerry, but Kate was not my first choice for a wife. She had a younger sister, a fair-haired beauty. She promised herself to me but married another man while I was out in the Ohio country. This was before the Indian wars broke out. I settled for Kate, and now I am glad it worked out that way. She was the better girl by far."

He stopped to squint at his watch. "Look here how late it is. And I must be up early to see a fellow on business."

The next day Ephraim showed Chris and me around Philadelphia. He had been away when I returned from the sea to court Gerta, and I was as interested in observing my former student as I was in seeing more of the city. Just turned twenty-one, he stood about five foot nine and was slender of build with blond hair, Kate's fair skin, and deep blue eyes. His hands were slender with long fingers, almost like a girl's. As I was to discover later, he could perform miracles with those marvelously dextrous hands, even tie a knot in a thread with one hand. He had taken to dressing and speaking like a Philadelphian rather than the son of a backwoodsman. In many ways he was a stronger man than his father, only more sensitive and genteel. And I never knew a more intelligent person, even though I sometimes doubted his common sense.

At sixteen, Chris stood only an inch shorter than I. His hair was the same color as my chestnut thatch, but he had gray rather than my hazel eyes. Also, his complexion was fairer. But all in all, a stranger might have thought him my younger brother rather than Ephraim's.

Away from his father's control, Chris came right out and told me how sorry he was that Gerta had not been allowed to marry me.

Ephraim tried to shush him, but he would not until he had made it clear that he thought Gerta's Chester Peebles was "a self-important prig." He added, "And you ought to see him. He's barely taller than Gerta and he has already started going bald."

"Chris, now that is enough!" said Ephraim, thinking, I suppose, of my feelings.

"Well, it's true. And you ought to hear what he said about how"—the lad dropped his voice an octave and assumed an unctuous tone—"the British Empire is a great institution. It has brought civilization even out here beyond the mighty Susquehanna. I expect it to endure forever."

"Chris," Ephraim said sternly, "if you don't stop it, I shall tell Father."

"You mean Pa? I swan, Ephraim, you have started putting on airs so I hardly know you."

I placed my hand over Chris's mouth and shook him as I used to when he was a little boy, which gave Ephraim an opportunity to ask if I'd like to go calling with him on Miss Laura Mason. He suggested to Chris that he might prefer to return on his own to The White Swan, but the boy replied, "In a pig's eye! I want to see your precious Laura."

After promising to behave, he was allowed to accompany us to the Masons' three-story brick house near the edge of Philadelphia, on Sixth Street. Most of the houses in Philadelphia had been built in rows with common walls between dwellings, but this one had a sizable garden and a roof of slate rather than cedar shingles. I felt ill at ease in my rough seaman's garb.

A mulatto maid answered Ephraim's knock and admitted us into the drawing room, which was richly furnished with English sofas and chairs. A harpsichord occupied one corner, and on the walls hung several portraits.

In a few minutes a dark-haired woman with unnaturally stiff posture entered the room and greeted Ephraim without great warmth in an English accent. Ephraim introduced us to Mrs. Mason, who nodded and commanded us to sit.

It did not take me or Chris long to get a bellyful of Madame Mason and her English Tory views. I sat there biting my tongue while she expressed her indignation at the behavior of "those New England ruffians" and her dismay that even in Philadelphia "one hears shocking opinions expressed against Parliament by persons supposedly of gentle breeding."

Ephraim caught my eye and pursed his lips in a silent plea to me not to speak out. But the woman rattled on and on.

"And have you heard the latest? Benjamin Franklin—Dr. Franklin, as he likes to be called—returned from England but yesterday with his tail tucked between his legs, I should think. My cousin Alfred wrote about the tongue-lashing the fellow had to take before the Privy Council last year. Wouldn't or couldn't even reply to the charges of intercepting and publishing private correspondence to feed discontent. Well, let me tell you—"

"Mother, I hope you are not talking politics to our guests again."

There in the doorway stood a slender girl who looked as if she were made of glazed porcelain rather than flesh and blood. She was beautiful in a rather anemic way, but for my tastes seemed too remote. She looked as if a hearty hug would break her into a hundred pieces.

And that was how I first saw Laura Mason, daughter of the eminent doctor and medical professor Horace Mason. She allowed Ephraim a genteel peck on her elegant cheek and gave both Chris and me a curtsy.

We remained for tea and a brief recital on the harpsichord by Laura, who played surprisingly well. In fact, I was impressed by the evident strength in her arms and hands, which belied her delicate appearance. Although she was not my cup of tea, I could understand her appeal for Ephraim. I was enjoying our visit until her mother called a halt to the music and got tuned up herself about the effrontery of Americans to convene "an illegal congress." When she stopped to catch her breath, Ephraim pleaded another engagement.

Laura lingered behind with me while her mother pressed Ephraim about whether he would accept "my husband's offer" to visit Barbados.

"I must apologize for Mother's outspokenness, Mr. Martin. She was born in England. She and Father met when he went over there for medical studies. She has never quite adjusted to this country, I fear."

"Not to worry, Miss Mason. But you might want to tell her that I was at Lexington and that the reports of what the British soldiers did there are quite true."

She looked at me with momentary alarm and curtsied. "Thank you for your reticence, Mr. Martin."

Then with a bright smile she held out her hand. It was warm and strong. Ephraim wasn't such a bad judge of girls after all.

On our way back to The White Swan to meet Jason for dinner, Chris remained unnaturally quiet as Ephraim praised the skills and graces of Laura Mason. It seemed to me that he was in part infatuated with the idea of paying court to the daughter of his medical mentor, but I held my tongue except to ask, "Tell me more about this trip to Barbados. Who will you treat there if you decide to go?"

The name of the mysterious patient—Francis Bolton, *Sir* Francis Bolton—meant nothing to me at the time. Nearly eighty but still a bachelor, this Sir Francis was reported to be in marvelous health except for a chronic throat ailment about which he had come to consult Dr. Mason.

"Why doesn't Dr. Mason go to Barbados himself if Sir Francis requires such personal care?"

"Oh, Dr. Mason is much too busy here. Sir Francis asked that he send a protégé as a substitute."

"Well, are you going?"

"I can't decide. It would entail a handsome fee but also would mean being away for several months."

I began to get the idea. "And you don't want to be separated from Dr. Mason's daughter?"

"Exactly. Yet I need that money. It would go a long way toward establishing me in practice here."

Chris broke his silence. "La te da. Pa would help him set up shop out in Cumberland County, where doctors are really needed, but no, only Philadelphia is good enough."

Ephraim looked at his brother in disgust and asked me the question I had been dreading: "Well, what do you think of her?"

"A lovely girl. I doubt she would be happy on the frontier, however."

"Oh, I couldn't ask her to go there."

"Have you asked her to go anywhere? Spoken for her hand, that is?"

"I am trying to get up my nerve. But her mother is always hovering about, you know."

At The White Swan we learned that Jason had persuaded his merchant friend, a Quaker, to dine with us. A roly-poly fellow with white hair but a youthful face, the merchant was named Dogood Mackey. He had met the boys but had wanted to meet me and hear about Lexington.

At dinner, to Ephraim's chagrin Jason asked Chris what he thought of "Eph's sweetheart."

"Laura is sweet and pretty, but that mother of hers. It was all I could do to keep from telling her off when she made those remarks about Dr. Franklin."

"Chris, I wish I had left you with Father today."

"I do, too. Pa, it would have made you sick to hear what that woman said about Benjamin Franklin. You met Franklin once, didn't you?"

"Quite so. It was in 1754, at a conference he was attending in Carlisle with some Indian tribes from the Ohio Valley. I was passing through on my way west. He took time to chat with me, a stripling of nineteen. A wonderful man."

"I know, Father," Ephraim said wearily. "You have often spoken of it."

Oblivious to his son's boredom, Jason went on to praise the great Franklin for his many scientific and civic achievements.

Jason's Quaker guest had been listening to all this with a knowing smile.

"Does everyone here admire Friend Franklin so much?" he asked at last.

I nodded in concert with Chris's enthusiastic yes and Ephraim's more restrained "Indeed."

"And would thee all like to meet him?"

Mr. Mackey had been invited to a Sunday-afternoon reception at Franklin's home on Market Street. "Our assembly has appointed him to serve as an additional congressional delegate from Pennsylvania. He is eager to talk to all kinds of people to learn how they feel about these troubles. Thee may be the only folk there from the frontier and"—turning to me—"thee can tell him about what thee observed in New England. Don't think of refusing. And don't be shy with him. He is as common as an old shoe."

8

FRANKLIN'S BRICK HOUSE on Market Street was already crowded when we showed up in midafternoon. His wife, recently deceased, had built the house during his long absence as London agent for Pennsylvania and other colonies and as deputy postmaster general for North America. His daughter Sally and her English-born husband lived there at the time.

We had to elbow our way into the gathering room. There the great man sat beside the fire, his hair down to his shoulders, his stockinged calves thrust out in front, his eyes full of wisdom and his face full of understanding. He was peering over his spectacles at his guests as he asked and answered questions without a trace of self-consciousness.

He was telling how, during the second half of his journey, he had taken temperature readings of the ocean several times a day to determine the position of the Gulf Stream. Everyone listened almost reverently as he expounded his theories of how this warm current flowed northward "like a tropical river" and how sea captains were best advised to sail directly across it to reduce their travel time.

Someone asked how his voyage had gone.

"Swimmingly, sir. Swimmingly. We left Portsmouth, my grandson and I, on the twenty-first of March, and I never experienced a smoother passage. The sea was as calm as a millpond." He paused and looked over our faces. "But I find the waters back here much troubled by contrast." He shook his head and made a face of mock disbelief. "Whoever would have thought to see militia companies drilling throughout William Penn's city?"

"Three battalions of foot and one of horse already formed," one man said.

"So I hear."

What did he think about the outbreak of fighting?

"I am relieved that it was General Gage and not we who drew the sword. Certainly it was they who set the stage for this tragedy. What madness, to mix soldiers among a people already deeply irritated! I long have felt a deep anxiety that such a carnage might ensue from some trivial incident. But from all I hear and read, the provocation might have been deliberate."

Across the room a well-dressed, portly man wearing a wig hovered solicitously beside the chair of a birdlike old man who had white hair to his shoulders.

"Do you really mean to state, Dr. Franklin," the portly man said in a supercilious tone, "or anyway suggest that His Majesty's troops went out on a mission to incite rebellion? I was under the impression that their orders were to intercept certain materials of war illegally gathered in Concord."

Franklin fixed his eyes on the man. "Ah, Dr. Mason, I did say 'might have been deliberate,' did I not?"

I raised my eyebrows at Ephraim, and he nodded to indicate that this haughty man was indeed the father of Laura.

Franklin held up his hand to forestall an interruption. "You would have had to observe the deterioration of relations from across the Atlantic, as have I for the past decade, to appreciate why I make such a bold suggestion. I must say that if King George and a majority of Parliament had set on a deliberate course of provocation, they could hardly have chosen a better one than the one they have followed month in and month out."

Dr. Mason persisted. "My wife and I maintain a steady correspondence with friends and relatives in England, and while I am as concerned as any about our rights as Englishmen, still one can appreciate the government's point of view."

A rough-looking man in the plain dress of an artisan broke in. "What is their point of view? That they have the right to trample on our rights?"

The physician-professor pointedly ignored the rebuttal. Looking directly at Franklin, he replied, "As subjects of King George, do we not owe allegiance to His Majesty and some responsibility for financial support of the protection we enjoy from the crown?"

Franklin again held up his hand to stop the derisive uproar that Dr. Mason's remark caused.

"Please, gentlemen, let us not quarrel. There will be contention enough when our Congress convenes. I love England almost as much as America. It pained me to leave my friends there, but now that I am back in the city of my youth, my hopes are renewed. Here we are, thirteen colonies stretching from cold, rocky New England south to the warm climes of Georgia and west to the great Appalachians. This vast land, although it contains only some three million people—one-third the population of our mother country—is many times larger and potentially many times richer with our deep forests, fertile soil, and invigorating climate. Time is on our side. But do you know what gives greatest substance to my hopes?"

His audience remained silent, waiting for him to answer his own question.

"Our people. My British friends fail to recognize that we, or our ancestors, have inhabited this land for five generations, and that although we claim the rights of Englishmen, we are unlike them in many ways. As I look about this room I see members of the Society of Friends, Presbyterians, Lutherans, and—" He paused with a smile. "And here and there an Anglican such as Dr. Mason. I see men who earn their bread by the skill of their hands, as well as by the employment of their wits. But I see none who have inherited their positions." He shook his head with an air of sadness. "Nothing came closer to arousing my anger these past few trying months than to have the question of our rights argued before the House of Lords. Imagine a body of inheritors of legislative privilege daring to pass judgment on our rights as free men! It saddens me to say so, gentlemen, but England is an old, corrupt country. I am happy to be back in my new and uncorrupted native land, where men make their way by industry and merit."

He shifted his weight and grimaced. "I must apologize for my weariness. It is not from your company, I assure you. I am not feeling my best. Too much salt meat and not enough exercise on the voyage."

His son-in-law helped him to his feet. The meeting broke into separate conversations and arguments. Our Quaker friend made his way past Dr. Mason and toward Franklin.

Ephraim stopped to introduce us to Dr. Mason, who deigned to give Jason's hand a perfunctory shake but barely acknowledged the presence of Chris or myself. Judging by his flushed face, he had been much discomfited by the rude reception of his remarks, or perhaps he had been put off by his companion, the old man in the chair. This old gentleman had sat through the entire session without saying a word, yet his glittering dark eyes had missed nothing.

"Let me detain you a moment, Dr. McGee," said Dr. Mason. Then leaning deferentially over the old man, he said, "Sir Francis, allow me to introduce to you Dr. Ephraim McGee."

The delay irritated me. I was eager to meet the great Benjamin Franklin. Out of the corner of my eye I could see that the Quaker had his attention and was pointing toward us. And yet I was fascinated by the strange little man who arose to his full height—barely five feet, I would say—and took Ephraim's hand.

In a rasping voice, Sir Francis said, "So you are the young man Mason is trying to foist off on me."

Ephraim blushed and recovered to say, "Why, he has asked me if I were willing—"

The old man's skin was as swarthy as a Spaniard's and as smooth as a babe's. His face was narrow, with a sharp, curved nose and thin lips. In contrast to his snow-white hair, his eyebrows were dark and bushy.

"Well, are you willing?" the old man rasped.

"I don't know just yet, sir."

"When will you know?"

Ephraim looked helplessly at Dr. Mason, who had the grace to say "very soon, I should say, what Dr. McGee?"

"It will have to be soon. Wait, Mason, don't try to rush me off. I should like to meet other people. You, I judge," he said to Jason, "are the father of this young quacksalver. I missed the names of these other two young rogues. Would they be brothers?"

Ephraim patiently explained our identities. The old man took my brawny paw in his birdlike clasp and fixed his piercingly dark eyes on my face.

Now our Quaker friend was motioning for us to come and speak to Franklin, but the old man would not release my hand. He wanted to know why I was wearing a seaman's costume. He asked about my accent and then wanted to know my business in Philadelphia, at which Chris volunteered, "Jerry was at Lexington when the British massacred the militiamen."

"Oh, I should like to hear more about that. Well, young Dr. McGee, I sail for Barbados within the week. You will have to decide soon. You can find me at The London Coffee House. I see our garrulous host wishes to give you an audience."

By the time Ephraim and I finally got free of the old Barbadian, Franklin and Jason were deep into their reminiscence of the Carlisle Indian conference. Franklin did not pretend to remember meeting Jason, but he was much interested in his views.

"Will you be ready for war out there if it comes, as I fear it will?"

"We have a militia company, yes."

"Good riflemen, I trust?"

"Some of the best. And many of us served under Armstrong, as did I."

"Good, good. I tell you Captain McGee, it will require the greatest wisdom and forbearance on the other side of the Atlantic to stop this thing from becoming complete, open warfare. The King and his present advisers must realize that once it becomes that, the contest could go on for ten years or more."

He paused to hear our names, then took Chris's hand.

"I doubt I would live to see the end of a war with Great Britain, but you would my lad. And never fear the outcome. We shall prevail. This nation and this people have only begun."

At that, Jason told him about my having been at Lexington. Over the protests of his daughter, Franklin drew us into a small side room and pumped me dry of information. He was particularly interested in the condition of the New England militia and how they were being directed.

Some people think Franklin was a fraud, an opportunist who moved with the times. They say the same of me today. I regard him as a benevolent and wise old grandfather to us all. I left his house in a glow. He had made me feel proud to be an American. And he had given me a pride in myself stronger than ever, which of course is the gift of the master politician.

That pride was quickened two days later by an enormous military parade to welcome congressional delegates from some southern colonies. The McGees and I rode behind a mounted force of five hundred militia officers to meet the delegates six miles south. Waiting two miles from the city were all the militia units or "Associators," which had been drilling twice a day for the past two weeks. They escorted my fellow southerners along streets that were lined with more people than I had ever seen.

Still another great military display followed the next day, to honor delegates arriving from Massachusetts, Connecticut, and New York. By May 10, when the congress convened on the first floor of the State House, Philadelphia had been transformed into a war center.

It took me the better part of two days to deliver the sealed messages that had been entrusted to me by Dr. Warren, for he had instructed me to hand them over only in private and to inform the recipients that he wished a reply to be brought back to him by me.

While waiting for these responses, there occurred two events ultimately of great import for the McGee family and me.

First, Jason received a letter from Carlisle asking him to notify the proper members of the congress that Cumberland County was enrolling every able-bodied male into Associator companies to serve as a home guard and to provide a pool from which to draw soldiers for service elsewhere. And incidentally, would he head a company as he had during the old Indian troubles?

This news proved of great interest not only to Franklin but to other delegates. It led to talk of raising special companies of frontier riflemen for service in Massachusetts.

Chris was elated at this development. "Then I can enlist, too, can't I, Pa?"

A crushed look came over the face of my young foster brother when his father replied, "Over my dead body. You're coming back here for college, my boy. I don't want anything to stand in the way of your education."

The second development involved Ephraim—and ultimately me, even more profoundly.

He announced it breathlessly to Jason and me as we sat talking about the difficulty of financing the McGee grist mill.

"We sealed the bargain, Father. Sir Francis has persuaded me to come with him."

He went on to explain that the old man had sensed that Ephraim was troubled by devoting so much time to only one patient, however rich. He held out the incentive of improving the medical care of his two hundred black slaves while in Barbados.

"Then, before I had a chance to answer him on that score, he offered to double my fee. Double it, mind you."

Ephraim turned to me. "By the way, Jerry, Sir Francis wanted to know all about you—where you are from exactly, your family, and how you came to know us. He'd like you to tell him all about Lexington. If he does not hear to the contrary, he will expect you to sup with him at The London Coffee House this evening, alone."

"What the hell?" I said. "I have no plans for the evening, and I am always ready for a free meal."

9

SIR FRANCIS sat reading a newspaper at a corner table of The London Coffee House. He looked up, removed his spectacles, and fixed me with his penetrating stare.

"Sit down. Young McGee tells me you were at Lexington. How did you come to be there? He says you have some Red Indian blood. How did that happen? Your name is Martin, which is English, of course. Do you know aught of your English ancestry? And he says you were educated at William and Mary."

"Which question do you wish me to answer first?" I replied.

"What? Oh, you must forgive my manner. Here, I have written an agenda for our conversation. Most of the questions are listed. But first, what will you have to drink? Never mind about supper, I have ordered fish for us both. Brain food, you know."

Taken aback by this inquisitorial whirlwind, I simply sat down and looked at him.

He raised his thicket of eyebrows. "Well?"

"Madeira," I said.

"What? What?"

"You asked what I wished to drink. My answer is madeira."

He laughed and beckoned the barmaid.

Once Sir Francis realized that I was not to be rushed in my replies, we got on well enough for a while. Since my story of Lexington was so practiced by then, I told him that one first.

"Imagine," he said when I was finished, "militia daring to do battle with our regulars. You Americans are fools, but so is King George and most of Parliament. God knows what this will do to our trade. It causes me"—he stopped to cough and clear his throat—"causes me great concern. Confound this thing! It is like a frog in my throat. Mason thinks there is a cure, but I cannot wait while he observes the effects of his regimen and medication. No more smoking and less talking, indeed! I must return to Barbados. As you know, I am taking your friend McGee with me. No need to dwell on my health. Tell me about yourself."

I was amazed at the old fellow's perceptiveness. There was no escaping his questions. If you evaded one, he caught you with the next. All the while I felt that he was comparing my answers with what Ephraim had told him.

"Who first brought the name Martin to the shores of Virginia?"

"He was a doctor, so I believe, named John, and he arrived in the 1670s, judging from our land grant. He would have been my great-grandfather. His wife was half Indian."

"Know you aught else of him?"

"I remember my father saying he was a Quaker and that he may have come to America from England by way of the West Indies."

Sir Francis pondered this information, then shrugged. Just as I was about to ask why he was so interested in my ancestry, he went off on a new tack. "What did you study at William and Mary?"

Our conversation ran thus throughout our meal. By the time our port arrived, it seemed to me that Sir Francis Bolton knew more of my life than anyone other than Jason McGee. Although I was puzzled by his interest in me, I dropped my guard, seeing that he had covered all the questions on his agenda.

"I am curious about two other points," he rasped.

"What points, sir?"

"Why did you leave your home in Virginia and join Bouquet's expedition at so early an age?"

Later I would learn that this was his way—to save his most probing question for the end of an interview. Suddenly I wished that I had not accepted his invitation.

"With all respect, sir, that is a most personal and private matter and one that I do not wish to discuss."

He smiled. "Forgive me. I know that I sometimes overstep my

bounds. Then perhaps I should not ask my second question, either."

My back was up now. "You can ask it, but I may not wish to answer it."

"What is the purpose of your visit to Philadelphia?"

"Why do you inquire?"

"You have been observed asking for and handing over messages to certain members of this congress gathered here and, I am informed, are accepting replies of some sort, which I assume you will take back to persons in Massachusetts."

It took all my willpower not to flinch, but I managed to look into his eyes without a change of expression until he broke into a smile.

"Come, Master Martin. Or may I call you Jeremiah? Let us stop playing games with each other. It matters not a whit to me who has commissioned your visit to Philadelphia. But if you are returning soon on your horse—whose name, I believe, is Ned—I may have some employment for you. I should like you to carry some messages for me. The compensation would be most generous."

"You are English," I said.

"Barbadian," he corrected me.

"Well anyway, British, and I don't think I want to carry messages for you."

"Come, come, you are British, too, at least for the present. My messages are not official government documents of any sort. They are of a commercial nature. Look here, they are all written out and sealed in this very small packet. Your delivery instructions are written on this single sheet of note paper."

He slid the paper across the table, and I glanced at it.

"But these addresses are all in Boston!" I exclaimed.

"That is why I am willing to pay so very well. Oh come, Jeremiah, don't play the innocent with me. I know more about you than you think. And I shall not pretend with you, either. I care nothing for politics. I am neither Whig nor Tory. I support our empire, not out of a love for kings or queens or for church or state, but because of its network of trade."

"Trade, sir?"

"Damn it, young man, I was told you were bright! Commerce, banking, insurance, sugar, rum, molasses, barrel staves, pig iron, household wares, ships' stores, leather, the ships to transport the stuff, yes, and the money to pay for it. This silly business about taxation or liberty means naught to me. The thing that I dread about this gathering war is the interruption it will bring to our trade. And let me tell you this—only a fool thinks tis love that makes this world go round. It is trade, trade, trade."

He sat back as though exhausted from speaking so vigorously. I waited until he finished his fit of coughing.

"I don't see how I can do what you want. The British would regard me as a spy."

"Pish, tish. There is always a way for a bright, determined chap like you. I doubt you would be running half the risk you are running now in coming to Philadelphia openly, under your real name. After all, Virginia is not so far from here, is it?"

The ruthless old bastard had discovered that I was a fugitive from Virginia justice. Why couldn't Ephraim have kept his mouth shut?

In a flash, before I could decide how to react, he slid a small leather pouch across the table.

"Open it. Count them. All gold. All yours. You need only follow the instructions on the sheet of paper."

"And then what?"

"Why, if you find the assignment not too disagreeable and the pay not too niggardly, perhaps we may do other business in the future. And you may rest assured that that warrant from Virginia will never be served on you."

Without warning, without bidding me farewell, he arose and walked spryly from the room, leaving the money, the packet of sealed messages, and the instruction sheet lying on the table. I swept the items into my pockets and left the tavern.

My mind raced as I walked back to The White Swan. That clever old man had put his hooks into me. But if what he said was true, about the nature of the messages and his own views, what was the harm of following his instructions—after, of course, delivering the delegates' replies to Dr. Warren?

Entering the back door of The White Swan, I found the place deserted except for Liz Oliver, who was setting pewter plates about as if to get a jump on the breakfast work.

"Well, there is our Jerry," she greeted me saucily.

"Dear Madame Oliver," I replied. "Where is everyone else?"

"Captain McGee and his boys long ago retired." She smiled at me with her head cocked to one side. "I heard tell that you were to sup with that funny little man from the West Indies."

"You heard correctly."

"I hear tell, too, that he is quite the wealthy one. And he has been knighted."

"What you say is correct, as far as I know."

"Well then, what did you think of the gentleman?"

I was less interested in talking about Sir Francis at the moment than in the bountiful bosom of our tavernkeeper's wife. I have never gone out of my way to seduce a legally married woman. But there have been occasions when a wife put herself forward, as Liz Oliver was now.

"Where is your good husband?" I asked.

She tossed her head disdainfully. "Good for what?"

"I don't see him about."

"He is snoring his head off upstairs. He thinks he has to have ten hours of sleep a night. Can't think why he should be tired. Never does aught. No matter. Why do you ask about him?"

"Why, I am weary and thirsty. But I did not want to detain you should Master Oliver be waiting up." I said this with a sly smile.

"Well, I might be persuaded to share a mug of cider with you— on one condition."

"What's that?"

"You must tell me about this Sir Francis. What sort of person did you find him?"

More and more as we sat talking and drinking in the darkened taproom, my mind wandered from the little merchant king to this full-figured woman. But she plied me with questions, until finally I leaned over and kissed her square on the mouth.

She drew back, as if surprised. "Why, Jeremiah Martin. I was given to believe you were a Virginia gentleman."

"But I am leaving tomorrow for Massachusetts, where women as warm and generous as you are rare indeed."

"In that case, you should have another kiss."

Which led to another and another, until finally we found ourselves in a small pantry off the tavern kitchen in which were conveniently piled some sacks of grain. They made a good enough mattress. And Liz Oliver made a better than good enough companion.

There is an old saying that one piece is never missed from a sliced loaf. I was a most hungry young man, and the loaf was more than willing to share herself.

Afterward, she clung to me rather sadly, all sauciness gone from her manner, and said, "Jerry, you are a gentleman, and I know a gentleman does not boast of his conquests."

I smoothed her hair and pressed her closer. "Never fear. No one will ever know."

"Captain McGee, in particular."

"Why, in particular?"

"I admire him more than any man who has ever set foot in this tavern. And I would not want him to think ill of me."

I stepped back in amazement. "You are in love with Jason?"

She slapped my hand. "It is just that I admire him very much. Now, promise me you will not tell."

"I, Jeremiah Martin, do solemnly swear that I will never, ever breathe our secret to a soul, especially Jason McGee." I stopped. "Why did you allow me, when Jason is here in your tavern?"

"He loves his wife. Any fool can see that. Even though he first loved her sister, the man is devoted to his wife and family. And besides, I felt sorry for you—the way life has treated you, I mean. Come, enough talk. Are you man enough for another go?"

Only after I went to bed did it occur to me that Jason had said he had never told anyone else that he had settled for Kate after being spurned by her younger sister. Then I realized that Liz Oliver must have eavesdropped on the long conversation between Jason and me after the boys had left us.

No matter. I had been well enough compensated, both by Bolton and by Mistress Oliver. I slept the deep sleep of the well-satisfied, if not the innocent.

10

ON TAKING MY LEAVE of the McGees, Ephraim promised to write me of his experiences in Barbados. Chris unenthusiasticly promised that he would not disgrace his old tutor when he was in college. Jason clasped my hand long and hard as he said, "Jerry, our house and hearts will always be open to you."

As I mounted Ned and raised my cap in farewell, I noted that in the doorway of the tavern kitchen behind the McGees, Liz stood with a forlorn look on her face. Seeing my eyes on her, she assumed her usual saucy smile and blew me a kiss.

And so Ned and I headed north, across the Delaware by ferry. At my first overnight stop, at Princeton, New Jersey, I had to sleep on a straw tick in a room with a dozen other wayfarers.

I arose early, ate a hurried breakfast, and was saddling up Ned for another day's ride when a familiar-looking spotted horse pounded up the pike toward the tavern yard.

"Jerry! Jerry!" the rider called to me.

"Good Lord, Chris, what are you doing here?"

"I have been riding all night. I want to go with you. I want to get in on the war before the British surrender."

I tried threats, bribes, and appeals for the feelings of his family—everything—but the lad would not return to Philadelphia.

"I explained everything in a note. Gave it to Mrs. Oliver to hand over to Pa when he wakes up this morning. I promised to come back to college soon as we whip the British."

I felt sorry for Jason, losing two sons in the same week. But I relented and let Chris ride with me. The boy was good company, after all.

In our eagerness to reach the American camps, we rode without stopping on the last night of our hard journey north from Philadelphia. We neared Roxbury as the dawning sun was just lighting up the distant spires of Boston. Two militiamen suddenly stepped out of the bushes with cocked muskets and blocked the road. One was a dark fellow with a crossed eye; the other was fair-haired and stocky.

The blond militiaman seized our bridles, while his companion squinted down the length of his musket barrel at us.

"Who do you be?"

I explained that I had business to conduct with Dr. Warren and that my young friend was a recruit.

"And you have come all the way from Pennsylvania. What for?"

Chris piped up with, "I want to sign up before the British surrender. They are still in Boston, aren't they?"

"Surrender?" The fair-haired fellow pointed toward Boston Harbor. "See them ships out there? Them's British warships. And Boston is jam-packed with lobsterbacks. They're waiting for us behind breastworks, just about a mile down this very road, where it crosses the Boston Neck. Surrender, my ass! They'd love for us to attack them."

The cross-eyed man put his fingers to his lips. "Hold up, Jasper. How we know these two ain't spies? We supposed to shoot spies, you know."

I had assumed the pair were simply having some rough fun at our expense, but my blood ran cold at their jest. What if they should search me and my saddlebags?

"You wouldn't shoot a friend of Benjamin Franklin's," I ventured.

"Franklin? You claim to know him?"

"The two of us were in his home in Philadelphia only a few days ago. Were there to help welcome him back from England."

They hesitated and looked at each other. I pressed my advantage.

"Enough of this foolishness. Either take me to your own commanding officer, or else stand aside so we can proceed to Hastings House in Cambridge. We have not ridden all the way from Philadelphia to be toyed with."

Cross-Eye looked at Towhead and said, "T'ain't likely two spies would ride up along the main road in broad daylight, is it?"

Chris told me later that on the long journey from Philadelphia he had imagined the British army dispirited, hemmed in by an intricate ring of carefully constructed fortresses manned by superbly disciplined Americans and studded with great cannon. He was disappointed to see a jumble of huts, lean-to's, and unmatched tents and thousands of plain-dressed militiamen armed with an assortment of smoothbore muskets and fowling pieces.

From my viewpoint, the scene around Harvard Yard appeared even more chaotic than when I had left.

44

At first I barely noticed a newly painted wagon drawn by two matched bay horses and parked under a tree with militiamen thronged about it. But then I recognized Lovejoy Brown and saw that he was doing a brisk business selling cups of rum and mugs of spruce beer.

I waited until his customers had made their purchases before I approached him. He was so pleased to see me, he almost smiled.

Yes, nearly half the tents had been manufactured and delivered. Our sailmaker in Marblehead would keep making them as long as his canvas held out. "And you can see for yourself how well the drink goes. Oh, Jerry, I hope this war lasts forever! Here, have a cup of cheer to celebrate our success."

I introduced Chris and made the obligatory inquiries about the health of Mother Brown. Receiving assurances that she was "as well as could be expected," I finished my grog. Then we—Chris and I—rode over to Hastings House.

Dr. Warren was delighted to receive my packets of correspondence from Philadelphia. He was equally pleased by my eyewitness reports on the city's preparations for war. But when I started to tell him about my meeting with Franklin, he summoned the officious Harvard aide to request General Ward to join us.

It was a wonder to me that General Ward, overweight and unhealthy as he was, could be expected to command even a militia company, much less an army of over ten thousand. At any rate, he thanked me when I had finished my report.

"Mr. Martin has done us a great service, General Ward," Dr. Warren said. "We must compensate him for his trouble."

"There is one small favor which I might ask," I began. I explained that Chris, eschewing college to join in the war, had come without arms. This made very little impression on two men who already had a surplus of untrained troops on their hands until I had the wits to say, "And this young patriot is an excellent horseman and has a first-rate mount."

Dr. Warren looked at General Ward. "I should think that a mounted messenger might be of some use to us both, General."

Afterward, Chris complained that "I want to fight, not run errands," but I told him to shut up. This would give him something to tell his children and grandchildren someday.

For the next day or so I was busy attending to the business Lovejoy and I had created for ourselves. All the while as we were hustling up to Marblehead and back, that packet of Sir Francis's messages burned a hole in my pocket, as did the pouch of gold coins.

Why had I let that cunning old man manipulate me so? Of course, I could have just kept the money and burned the messages, but I had made a bargain with him; and also, there was that veiled threat about the Virginia warrant. It would be a simple matter for him to inform the Virginia authorities of my whereabouts.

Still, I did not relish the thought of sneaking through both our lines and the British lines to get into Boston. And even if I were to be accepted there as an envoy of the influential Sir Francis Bolton, how would I ever escape back to the mainland?

I thought briefly of bribing someone else to deliver the messages, but could think of no one I could trust who was clever enough. Some traffic still continued across the Boston Neck. Tories were allowed to pass in and patriots to depart—especially the latter. In fact, the British were forcing people of doubtful loyalty out of the city to reduce the demand on their dwindling food supplies. But I would be hard put to offer an excuse that would be equally acceptable to the Americans and to the British for both entering the city and departing from it.

At first blush, my plan seemed inspired. Very simply, after sewing the Bolton messages into my jacket lining, I approached Dr. Warren with a proposition to slip into Boston on a spying expedition for him and his Committee of Safety and to report on British strength in the city, the state of their morale, and their plans.

He eagerly accepted my offer. To avoid suspicion, I agreed to accept a modest payment for my services.

Almost immediately after leaving Hastings House, I regretted my rashness. By this time I was too well known in the American camps to try to pass myself off as a Tory desirous of taking up residence in Boston. Besides, I wanted to return with a clear reputation, if not conscience. What a mess I had got myself into! I considered rowing over in a boat after dark, or wrapping my clothes and Sir Francis's messages in oilcloth and swimming across the Charles, or bribing our pickets to look the other way while I dashed across the Boston Neck on foot. But each idea had its pitfalls; I could drown or be fired upon before I identified myself.

I was no closer to a resolution the next afternoon when I turned Ned over to Chris for the day and rode with Lovejoy to help deliver a wagonload of tents to General Thomas's militia in Roxbury. As we passed through the village of Brookline, the road was blocked by a mob of local citizens and militiamen who were gathered in front of a shop marked by the sign of a boot over the door.

We stopped and watched while their ringleaders broke the shop windows. As several females within screamed, they crashed through the door and dragged forth a scrawny little cobbler wearing a leather apron over his pot belly.

This fellow struggled with the desperate strength of a cornered rodent, but the bullies were too numerous and too strong for him.

A fat woman whom I took to be the cobbler's wife and four girls of various ages yelled their protests and tried in vain to free the poor man.

The ruffians lifted him onto a granite mounting block. Their leader, a great red-haired lout, held up his hand for silence.

"Alexander Turner!" he shouted. "We charge you with treason. What do you have to say for yourself?"

Most of the prominent and wealthy Loyalists of Massachusetts had gathered up their valuables and high-tailed it for Boston early enough to escape the patriot mobs. But many of the more stubborn or less well off remained in their homes until it was too late. This appeared to be the case with Alexander Turner.

The cobbler straightened his narrow shoulders and said in a clear, thin voice, "I was born in this house forty-five years ago. My father built this place as a young man. Many of you remember him. There wasn't a better bootmaker in Massachusetts. And I have followed his trade. I have repaired shoes for some of you when you lacked the money to pay."

"It's the truth!" his wife cried. "My Alex and me have never done a one of you any harm."

It was an exceedingly foolhardy thing to do, but I stood up in our wagon and shouted, "What is going on here? Why are you tormenting these poor people?"

The leader of the gang looked at me in surprise. "If it is any of your damned business, this man refused to fill orders for boots for the militia. He has called us rebels. We charge him to be an enemy of the people of Massachusetts. What do you say to the charges, Alexander Turner?"

The cobbler raised his chin and looked at our faces one by one, as if to shame each person in the crowd. Then he said with calm dignity, "If anyone in this assembly is a traitor, it surely is not I, nor my wife, nor my daughters."

"Answer the charges!" Carrot Top persisted. "What do you say to them?"

"I say hurrah for King George!" the cobbler shouted.

The cobbler's boldness gave the growing mob momentary pause. But then with an ugly roar, they seized the poor fellow and stripped him to his trousers. Someone had already warmed a bucket of tar. Others invaded the cobbler's living quarters at the rear of his shop and brought out two large pillows.

"Not my goose-down pillows!" the wife implored. "My grandmother gave me them!"

There is nothing humorous about tarring and feathering. The incident was all the more humiliating because it was carried out by neighbors and supposed friends of the victim in front of his wife and daughters.

47

The mob was too large and ugly-minded for me to deter them. I could not bear to stay and watch. Screams of "Dear Papa! They must not—" and "Unhand my poor husband!" faded behind us as Lovejoy and I continued on our way.

Near nightfall, we were just leaving Roxbury with an empty wagon and full pockets when we saw a most curious procession coming toward us from Brookline. Teams of bully boys were bearing the ends of a fence rail. On it straddled the cobbler, who now looked like a rumpled ostrich bird, with tufts of feathers covering his pitiful anatomy. Behind him labored a bony horse drawing a wagon that overflowed with chests and feather ticks and chairs—all the household goods of the family Turner that could be crammed aboard the rickety vehicle. Beside the wagon trudged the cobbler's wife and four daughters with tear-streaked faces.

In a flash I knew what to do. I waited until after our wagon had passed the cobbler on his rail; then I shook Lovejoy's hand and said, "Look after Chris and Ned for me. I'll be back in a few days."

Before he could reply, I jumped to the ground. It was easy enough to climb aboard the rear of the wagon without being seen by anyone but the mystified Lovejoy. To burrow down through all the feather ticks and sacks to the wagon floor was not so easy, but I managed it by curling myself around a bag of long-unwashed garments.

It was only two miles to Roxbury and another mile beyond that to the British lines. With every turn of our wagon's wheels, my decision seemed more and more foolhardy. I could barely breathe, and I dared not make any noise. I thanked God that at the American lines the militia took the word of the Brookliners that the traitors were carrying nothing that would benefit the British, and they did not search the wagon. They let the cobbler dismount from his rail, and the wagon headed down the road toward the British lines.

After we had gone a little way, however, the wagon stopped. The cobbler yelled back toward his tormentors and former neighbors, "Hurrah for King George! Hurrah for King George! Down with all traitors!"

As the wagon continued along the flat, muddy road, the cobbler's wife called him a fool and blamed him for their calamity.

"All you had to do was say you lacked the leather or were too busy," Mistress Turner said. "But no, you had to tell them you were against the uprising!"

"That's not fair, Mama," one of the daughters said. "You are just as much to blame. You have always acted as if you were better than other people. They all had it in for us."

"Shut up, Amanda!" a second daughter rejoined. "You always take Pa's side in everything."

The bickering continued until I heard an English voice cry, "Halt! Who goes there?"

"Loyal subjects of Good King George," the cobbler replied.

I could see a glimmer of lantern light through a crack in the wagon bed. This was followed by an imperious bellow: "What's going on here?"

"Another damned lot of refugees, sir," said another voice.

Suddenly the bellow turned into a chuckle, and the chuckle into laughter. Taking their cue from the officer, other soldiers joined in the laughter.

"He looks like a gawdamned white turkey!"

I felt almost as sorry for the cobbler during this British derision as I had felt when the mob was breaking his windows and stripping him of his clothes. It stopped only when the wife burst into tears and called them "unfeeling brutes."

It was pitch dark by the time the wagon creaked along Orange Street over the mud flats of the Neck and onto the cobblestones of Newbury Street. It was no trick to slide out the back of the wagon without being seen. I hid behind a tree long enough for the cobbler and his family to fade into the darkness of Marlborough Street ahead; then I took a deep breath to clear my lungs from the stench of stale laundry and cut across Winter Street toward the Common.

How Boston had changed since Lexington and Concord! The streets were jammed with Loyalist refugees and British soldiers. The Common was as crowded with tents as the Harvard College yards across the Charles. Whereas on my last visit to Boston, the British uniform had been treated with scorn, now soldiers marched about as if they owned the place.

I walked along Treamont Street past King's Chapel, skirted Beacon Hill, and made my way to Hanover Street. Then I turned off onto Friend Street, which led downhill to the inlet that had been dammed up and turned into a body of water called the Mill Pond. There it was, the sign of The Green Dragon, which Bolton's instructions called for me to visit first.

PART TWO

1

FROM PREVIOUS VISITS to Boston, I knew that the hulking two-story tavern, a former mansion overlooking the so-called Mill Pond, had been a gathering place for Bostonians who opposed British oppression. But as I discovered more and more, this was a different Boston from the one I had known before.

The great taproom of The Green Dragon was packed with uniformed British officers. It was all I could do not to flee the place. How would these arrogant fellows have reacted if they had known I had fired at them and their troops on the road between Concord and Lexington and had been supplying the rebels with tents and blankets? I glanced at the faces of the civilians in the room and satisfied myself there was none present who might recognize me. Finally I nerved myself to ask an impudent-looking barmaid where I might find a Mr. Halbertson.

"Expect he's retired."

A small coin was enough to pry from her the location of the room where he might be found. I refused her offer to accompany me. My heart in my throat, I climbed the stairs to the second floor and walked down the hall to a rear corner room.

No one answered at first.

A louder knock elicited a booming "Who's there?"

"I wish to speak to Mr. Reuben Halbertson."

"This is Mr. Halbertson, and I am in bed. What's your business?"

"I have a message for you, sir."

"Well, leave it with the man downstairs, and I will read it in the morning."

"My instructions are to give it to you personally."

"Instructions from whom?"

"From Sir Francis Bolton."

The bed creaked. There was a great shuffling about inside. A light appeared under the door, and the floorboards within complained. The door opened. There stood an enormously fat man wrapped in a dressing gown and wearing a nightcap. He raised his candle so that its rays illuminated my face.

"Sorry to disturb you, sir, but he said—"

Before I could finish, the man took me by the elbow and drew me into the room.

"Keep your voice down," he said as he closed the door. "Here, here. Sit."

He pointed me to a chair drawn up to a large work table that was covered with papers and proceeded to light three candles in an ornate silver stand.

"Well, now, what's this message?"

I removed my coat and fumbled in the lining. Then I drew out the packet of messages that had weighed so heavily on my person since I had left Philadelphia. I handed him the letter marked with his name.

He broke the seal, unfolded and flattened the letter, and drew from the table drawer a small book. Then I saw a sight that chilled me. The letter had been written in some sort of code. How would I ever have explained coded letters on my person if I had been searched, no matter by which side?

The fat man frowned and chewed his lips as he looked back and forth between the letter and his code book. I sat there sweating as if it were a sultry night in midsummer.

When he finished, he regarded me with what I took to be satisfaction.

"Well, Mr. Jeremiah Martin, I am pleased to make your acquaintance."

He reached across the table and took my hand in his blubbery paw.

"How did you make your way into Boston?"

I saw no harm in telling him at least part of the story.

"Sir Francis knows how to pick 'em," he said when I had finished. "That is one of his great advantages—he understands human nature like nobody I ever encountered. Well now, let's pour you a drop of port, and then we'll see if there can be found a place for you to sleep. Would put you up with me, but I am told that my snoring would wake the dead."

Halbertson was able not only to commandeer a tiny dormer room for me on the third floor of The Green Dragon; he also caused the barmaid to bring me up a supper of boiled potatoes and salt fish with a chunk of coarse bread and mug of good strong ale.

The barmaid looked at me appraisingly after she set her tray on the tiny table in the room.

"Ain't just anybody gets treated like this in Boston these days. Food and drink's hard to come by. So's a room all to yourself. You must be somebody important."

Her air of familiarity and curiosity annoyed me.

"Not really."

"Well, Mr. Halbertson says anything you want, I'm to provide it."

She had a good enough figure but a muddy complexion and a sort of squashed nose. My session with Liz Oliver had occurred long enough ago that I would have been tempted, had I been less weary and apprehensive.

"I will let you know if I require anything else." I dismissed her in my most patrician manner.

She left. After wolfing down my cold supper, I fell upon the narrow bed and slept until the sun was well up the next morning.

Reuben Halbertson presented a far less rumpled appearance at the late breakfast we shared than he had the night before. Wearing a brown wig, he was dressed in a long coat of the best broadcloth and a shirt with lace cuffs. His ample calves were stockinged in hose of top quality, and his feet were clad in patent-leather shoes with silver buckles.

There were fewer British officers at breakfast than had been present the previous night, a fact for which I was grateful.

Halbertson wanted to know more news from Philadelphia. I gave him as little information as I could without plain-out telling him to mind his own business. His manner was irritatingly proprietary, as if he now owned a piece of me.

I wasn't about to give open offense to a man who by snapping his fingers could have me arrested. So I enjoyed my porridge and eggs as best I could and asked to be excused.

"You have other errands to run for Sir Francis, I know."

That word *errands* galled me, but I smiled and nodded. Then I went out into the winding, crowded streets of Boston.

Boston has long boasted a peculiar intellectual and commercial vitality, but for my part I found the people contentious—as did the British—and rather too cold and sarcastic for my tastes. As I made my way to the second address in my set of instructions, I thought about the contrast between Philadelphia, with its wide, straight streets and its easy-going but industrious populace, and this city crammed onto a small peninsula with twisting, narrow alleys and steep slopes. But I must admit that the awkwardness of my position in Boston somewhat colored my opinion.

As I walked along Brattle Street, British soldiers jostled me or crowded me against the wall several times. I was hardly in a position to shove back. Thence onto King Street and along Cornhill, I came at last to the address on Water Street.

"Ask for Madame LaFontaine," my instructions read.

The house was a narrow wooden structure squeezed between a tavern and a counting house. The door was freshly painted, and the brass knocker looked as if it were polished daily.

Fearful that I might offend some grand lady and a bit ashamed of my rough appearance, I tapped lightly. As I stood waiting for the door to open, two British officers strode past. One looked at me and said, "Bit early in the day, ain't it, Yankee Doodle?"

I ignored the bastard and knocked more forcefully. I stepped out onto the sidewalk and looked up at the two second-floor windows. The blinds were drawn.

I applied the brass knocker more vigorously. The window directly above the door opened, and a woman with a shiny black face looked down at me. "We closed. Come back later."

"I have a message for Madame LaFontaine."

"Madame, she sleeping. Don't want no messages."

"Tell her it's from Sir Francis Bolton."

"Him? I tell her, but she ain't gonna like it."

It seemed an eternity passed before I heard footsteps inside the little house. The black woman, dressed in a housecoat, opened the door. "You can wait in the parlor."

It must have cost a fortune to furnish that one room alone. The drapes were of rich velvet, and the carpets outdid anything my feet had ever trod upon. The furniture was upholstered with the finest fabrics.

The black woman, who at close range was rather pretty in a pouty, impudent way, boldly looked me up and down. "Maybe you better not sit on that chair," she said. "Try this one." She pointed to the only plain wooden chair in the room and left.

A clock ticked away on the mantel. I could hear British voices shouting in Water Street, and I wondered whether I dared try out my rough French on this Madame LaFontaine. Then I heard footsteps on the stairs in the hall, and finally in the parlor doorway stood a tall woman with glistening dark hair, pale skin, and brilliantly black eyes. In the subdued light, she could have been any age from thirty to fifty.

I stood up and grinned. Her stern look gave way to a faint smile. "Monsieur."

54

"Madame." I bowed. "Allow me to introduce myself."

She opened the drapes for light and read her message, which I judged was uncoded. When she finally looked up, her eyes sparkled, and there was a genuine look of welcome on that queenly face.

"So you are Jeremiah Martin, and you come from Virginia, and Sir Francis thinks you are a young man of great promise. Here, stand in the light and let me see you more clearly. You are not as young as I first thought. How old are you?"

"Twenty-eight my last birthday."

"And not married?"

"No, Madame."

"But a man of some experience, if my judgment is not wrong."

Normally it is not easy to embarrass me, but this woman was unsettling. I must have blushed, for she laughed.

"Well, now Jeremiah Martin, my old friend Sir Francis says I am to look after you while you are in Boston. I am to make your visit as pleasant as I can. Have you a place to stay?"

She frowned at my mention of The Green Dragon. "I suppose that great swine Halbertson put you up there. I don't know why Sir Francis places such trust in that great sack of guts. By the bye, have you no clothes other than those?"

I explained that I had come into Boston on short notice.

"Good enough. I shall expect you to return here at five o'clock this afternoon. You may use my private bath, and I think some of the clothes of my late husband might be, shall we say, pressed into service. Then you will be required to remain for dinner."

I tried to worm out of the invitation, but she would not accept a refusal. When I capitulated, she took my hand and curtsied. "I should have been devastated had you refused me. Now, I expect that Sir Francis has loaded you down with errands."

There was that damned word *errands* again. I was too tongue-tied to protest, however.

By midafternoon I had seen, on Sir Francis's behalf, a Scotsman in his ships' chandler's office on Boston's famous Long Wharf, an attorney with an office overlooking Faneuil Hall, and the chief clerk of a shipping office on Fish Street. The Scotsman had showed neither curiosity about nor generosity toward me. He merely asked if he was to send Sir Francis a reply. When I said no, he wished me a good day and returned to his ledgers. The attorney was a slyer sort. He tried several approaches at prying information about myself. I gathered that Sir Francis had not told him very much about me in his letter. The chief clerk was a worried little man—and who could blame him, with the port closed except to British warships?

"Well, Sir Francis says you know something of the sea. Are you looking for a job?"

I declined, thanked the man, and went out into the sunlight. I felt both relieved at having delivered the messages and apprehensive about how to gain information that would be useful to Dr. Warren.

2

WHEN I RETURNED to Madame LaFontaine's establishment at five o'clock that afternoon, the black woman opened the door at my first knock.

"We expecting you. Follow me."

I heard voices coming from the parlor, but she led me past its closed door, up the stairs, and down a long hall to a rear room that contained a great tin tub filled with water. Cloths and a razor had been placed in front of a mirror. And across a chair lay a man's waistcoat, breeches, shirt, and stockings.

"Madame LaFontaine, she say you to wash yourself and change your clothes. She tell me to clean your old clothes." She held her nose.

That bath felt wonderful. I washed myself from head to toe and, after debating with myself, scraped off my beard.

The shirt and waistcoat were long enough but a bit tight across the shoulders, and the breeches were a trifle large in the waist; but all in all, I turned out well enough.

Downstairs I hesitated outside the parlor door. I could hear unmistakably British voices within. For a moment I was tempted to tiptoe through the front door and make my way out of Boston as best I could. My life would have turned out very different if I had obeyed that impulse.

"Well, go on in. She expecting you." The black woman was standing behind me.

I opened the door. Inside three men in British uniforms were talking to a group of pretty young women.

Madame LaFontaine arose and took my hand. Turning to the officers, she said, "Gentlemen, let me introduce Mr. Jeremiah Martin. He is an assistant to Sir Francis Bolton, here in Boston on business. Captain Featherington, Major Tuttle, and Captain MacDougal."

I was trapped. With only a few words, this elegant woman had put me in one of the most difficult spots I had ever experienced. What could I do but shake hands all around? The officers looked me up and down and proceeded to ask questions about where I had been, how I had got to Boston, and so forth.

Well, in for a penny, in for a pound. I told them no outright

56

lies, but neither did I disclose all the truth. Questions about the length and nature of my relationship to Sir Francis, I coyly dodged. As to my own background, I told them about my long time at sea and then made it appear that I was in the general mercantile business. During this ordeal I spoke softly, even shyly, and I expressed relief at being away from rebellious areas. The officers treated me in the condescending way that the British often assume in talking to Americans. Except for Major Tuttle, who kept his eyes on me, they soon grew bored with this dull colonial and resumed their own conversations again, which had to do with a clash between American militiamen and a party of their soldiers who had been sent to confiscate a store of hay on nearby Grape Island. Although they didn't say so directly, I deduced that the militia had chased them away.

Meanwhile, the women in the room had also gone on with their own conversations. Now Madame LaFontaine said, "My girls are most eager to meet you, too. Mr. Martin: Abigail, Francine, Mollie, and Arabelle."

I looked closely at the girls. One was a brunette, one a blonde, one a redhead, and one had chestnut hair like my own. Each was well dressed. Each was pretty in her own way. But there were no last names. Then I realized what sort of madam this Madame La-Fontaine was.

Except for the obligatory toast to the King, I barely touched my wine at dinner, and I listened closely to the Britishers' talk. Madame LaFontaine apologized for offering nothing better than roasted chicken, but the officers expressed surprise and gratitude that she had been able to set so good a board under Boston's straitened circumstances. There certainly was no reason for her to apologize for the china and silverware on which the food was served; nor for her young ladies, who had been well trained to smile and agree with whatever was said to them.

By the time port was served, I had learned the name of every regiment in Boston and its strength. Dr. Warren probably knew all this from other sources, however. But when they speculated over whether Gage would sally forth either to fight or to seize advantageous high ground on the near mainland, my ears perked up, even though I was distracted by the pug-nosed redhead across the table, the one called Mollie.

Madame LaFontaine managed the evening with finesse. She watched the face of each man. She knew how to stir a conversational pot to keep the talk going. Twice she frowned at one of her girls to stop some minor breach of manners.

She ended the dinner in a businesslike but graceful way. "Gentlemen, since most of you are busy officers of the King, perhaps we should dispense with formalities. As is our custom, I will assign you your partners for the remainder of the evening. Major Tuttle, if you will follow Arabelle. Captain Featherington, Francine. . . ."

As each girl's name was called, she arose and held out her hand for her officer. Then only Mollie and I were left.

I had never been in a fancier brothel. Mollie turned out to be a skilled practitioner of her trade. With women of her training one can't be certain, but if she was only feigning passion, she would have made a damned fine actress—aye, and one with a varied repertoire that she seemed determined to demonstrate for me. It was a grand place for romping but a poor place for sleep. Finally, long after midnight, we declared it a tied contest, and I lapsed into exhausted sleep. I awakened at dawn and eased myself from under the weight of Mollie's well-shaped leg. I tiptoed down the hall to the washroom, where I was pleased to find, beside a most welcome chamberpot, my old clothes spread on a drying rack. My shirt was still damp, but I wore it anyway. I reached the front door undetected, only to find it locked.

I turned and slipped down the hall into the kitchen. The back door opened into a small walled garden. I sat down on the kitchen stoop and put on my shoes, then lifted the bar on the gate in the wall and stepped out into a narrow alley.

I would have enjoyed the pleasant morning air, but I was troubled by the fact that Madame LaFontaine had stripped away my disguise. Perhaps I could find a way to slip out of the city as a rebel outcast. I would be able to provide Dr. Warren with confirmation of British troop strengths and the general condition of affairs in Boston. But my escape would have to wait until dark.

I made my way back to The Green Dragon and my little room on the third floor. There I stretched out on the bed and napped to recover from my long contest of lovemaking with Mollie.

I was awakened by a rough hand on my shoulder. Reuben Halbertston loomed over me like a Falstaff.

"I waited up until near midnight for you. Where were you?"

I mumbled something about attending a dinner.

"Dinner? Let me guess. You were at the establishment of that notorious whoremongress, that so-called Madame LaFontaine. Madame, indeed! She is no more French than you or I. You ought to be ashamed of falling in with that wicked woman."

"She speaks well enough of you. Why do you blackguard her?"

"Never mind that strumpet. Get dressed and come with me."

"Where? What for?"

"Down to Long Wharf. A ship has just anchored in harbor. She has brought over three generals and a fresh lot of soldiers."

That was how I came to be present at the arrival on American soil of three major generals who would play important roles in the war. I watched William Howe, Henry Clinton, and "Gentleman

Johnny" Burgoyne debark from the longboat that brought them and their baggage to the wharf from their warship, the *Cerebus*. England had sent three of her supposedly best soldiers. As I learned later, they had left Spithead two days after Lexington and Concord, ignorant of the outbreak of fighting until brought up to date that very morning by a Boston Harbor pilot.

Constructed mainly from rubble left by Boston's great fire of 1711, the Long Wharf stretched like an extension of King Street from the shoreline several hundred yards out into the harbor, where it terminated in a T. Warehouses and offices cluttered one side of the broad wharf; the other side was now thronged with civilians and soldiers. A magnificent carriage waited to transport the three generals to Province House, which General Gage occupied as military governor. Men cheered and women waved their handkerchiefs. Soldiers saluted as the coach moved slowly through the crowd along King Street. You would have thought the British were celebrating a great victory.

"Well," I thought to myself, "I have something to report to Dr. Warren after all."

As the throng moved past the State House and turned into Cornhill, I heard a shrill voice rise above the hoarse cheers of others.

"Hurrah for King George! Hurrah for King George!"

Sure enough, there were the little cobbler, his wife, and their four daughters in tow following the carriage with looks of idiot delight on their faces. Even though I had shed the beard I had worn when watching their humiliating treatment back in Brookline, I wanted to take no chance of their recognizing me now. Besides, I had seen enough. As the others followed the carriage on to Province House, I turned in the other direction, toward The Green Dragon. I thought this would be a good time to slip out of Boston, while every eye was on the three newly arrived generals. But damn it, there was Halbertson puffing along at my elbow.

At The Green Dragon nothing would do but that I join him in a toast to the King and listen to his thirdhand report of what General Burgoyne had supposedly said when he learned that Gage had allowed five thousand of the King's soldiers to be hemmed into a narrow peninsula by an armed rabble: something to the effect, "We'll have to venture forth and make a little elbow room for ourselves."

I ached to get free of the man and to figure out how to escape to the mainland. But over mugs of sour ale, Halbertson was waxing verbose over the prospects of an early end to the uprising, "now that we have three of our best generals on hand." He also interrogated me about my plans. "Expect you may want to join Sir Francis in Barbados."

"Perhaps."

"Well, I shouldn't be in a great hurry. If I were you, I would stick around and see the fun when we break out of this city and thrash the rebels."

"Yes. That would be most interesting to see."

Halbertson regarded me closely for a few minutes, then leaned across the table.

"Martin, I know you are merely a courier for Sir Francis. Yet I have discerned in you a certain reticence and adaptability that would do credit to the most discreet of"—he puffed out his cheeks as he searched for the words—"let us say confidential agents."

"Oh?" I said.

"Yes, and I perceive that although you are an American, you are no rebel. Yet you would not have been able to move so freely twixt here and Philadelphia were you known as an outspoken supporter of King and Parliament."

"I have never been much for politics," I said.

"Nor I. My role is simply to serve the interests of Sir Francis Bolton in Boston and surrounding areas. I was born in this country, as were you; I lived in this establishment when it was thronged every night with plotters against the King. I still live here now that it is frequented by officers of that same sovereign. I am a realist. Facts are facts. No matter what certain rapscallions such as Samuel Adams and John Hancock and Dr. Joseph Warren may think, we are still a part of the British Empire. Don't you agree?"

"I suppose so."

He weighed my less-than-enthusiastic response, then plowed ahead.

"At that dinner at Madame LaFontaine's establishment, there was a certain Major Tuttle."

"I think that was his name."

"You made a favorable impression on Major Tuttle."

"I am glad to hear it."

"He has been making inquiries about you."

Concealing my growing alarm, I asked, "What sort of inquiries?"

"Whether you might be willing to perform a service to your King, a service of a most confidential nature."

Uneasy at the trend this conversation was taking, I kept quiet as he regarded me through half-closed eyes.

"Major Tuttle wonders whether you might be willing to undertake a mission on behalf of Good King George."

"You mean spy work? No, thank you. Spying is a dirty business, and dangerous, too. I have no wish to be hanged."

"The pay would be generous."

"I don't need money that badly."

"It would earn you the favor of the government, and I am sure that Sir Francis would mark the act down to your credit."

I very nearly informed Halbertson that I despised the British and

60

their King and did not give a damn for the good opinion of Sir Francis Bolton. Then it occurred to me that this might be a test, or even a trap.

"What would be expected of me?"

"Come with me, and you can ask your questions of Major Tuttle for yourself. Come, 'twill do no harm to hear his proposition."

So that great tub of lard practically dragged me out of the tavern to a rear door of Province House. Before I knew what was happening, he had us past the sentry and through the crowd that had gathered on the ground floor to greet the newly arrived generals. He escorted me up the backstairs to a small office. There Major Tuttle sat with his feet on his desk reading a London paper, one I judged to have been brought over on the *Cerebus*.

He looked up at me with the same skeptical eye I had noticed at Madame LaFontaine's dinner.

"Ah, Martin. There you are. Quite recovered from last evening, I trust?"

Halbertson explained that I had an aversion to spying but officiously added that I was eager to be of service to "our King."

I could have murdered the meddlesome fool. Tuttle cut him off with an explanation of what the British wanted of me: to cross over the Charles, ascertain the exact strength of the militia and the state of their supplies of arms and ammunition, and return to Boston with the information.

Dumbfounded, I asked, "When? And how?"

"This very night. The sooner the better. Have no fear. We will deliver you across the Charles."

Suddenly I felt as though a great weight had been removed. My problem of returning to the mainland was solved, and I would be paid in the bargain.

3

MY ESCAPE FROM BOSTON occurred that very night, and it was deceptively easy. The Charlestown peninsula had become a no-man's-land after the British, with amazing short-sightedness, withdrew all their troops across the Charles River to Boston following their debacle on the road back from Concord. Major Tuttle provided me with a cockleshell and appointed a crew of His Majesty's sailors and a large boat to tow me over in the dark to Mouton Point. He gave me a password and instructions on how to conceal the little boat and its oars in the grass to facilitate my anticipated return.

At first, as the crew began rowing into the darkness, I congratulated myself. I had fulfilled my foolish obligation to Sir Francis Bolton, and I had gathered valuable information for Dr. Warren. The British would not be happy when it dawned on them that they would realize no benefit from the money they had given me, but who cared?

When we landed, I turned the cockleshell upside down in the knee-high grass. It was simply a matter of walking a mile across the peninsula over the Charlestown Neck, and I'd be home free—or so I thought. It was dark. Why had I not thought to bring a lantern? Why had I not insisted that the British row me up the Mystic River, closer to my destination?

I settled my cap about my ears and groped my way toward the barely discernible contour of the highest point on the Charlestown peninsula, the height now so well known as Bunker Hill. From across the Charles, this end of the peninsula had appeared to be a generally upsloping meadow, almost parklike, but it was not. I tripped over low stone walls, stepped into holes, nearly lost my shoes in sticky clay, yes, and stumbled over the debris of an old brick kiln. And at every uncertain step I was assailed by bloodthirsty mosquitoes.

Of course, this was the same ground over which the British would advance in their attack against Breed's Hill in just three weeks—but that is getting ahead of my story.

I felt my way for only a few hundred yards of this morass until I reached a rail fence; then followed it until I barked my shins against a low stone wall. To hell with it! I could wait until morning to continue. So I made my bed in the deep grass of the fence corner. By curling up with my seaman's jacket collar protecting my ears and my cap over my face, I blunted the assault of those voracious mosquitoes and managed to lose consciousness until the dawn and the bells of a British ship awakened me.

I sat up and looked around me. Off to my left was Breed's Hill and ahead, nearer the Neck, was the higher Bunker Hill; to my right was the Mystic River; to my left rear was the village that gave the peninsula its name, Charlestown; and behind me, across the Charles, was Boston. I arose, took a long, salutary piss, and decided that even in the daylight there was a better way to reach my friends than climbing over fences and walls and stumbling over old piles of cow dung concealed by the deep grass.

I cut over to the steep bank of the Mystic River. The tide was out, exposing a narrow beach six or eight feet below the grassy brink. Down I slid to the water's edge, and lo and behold, I found myself a regular highway of sand leading to the mainland.

So none the worse for my experience, except for scores of insect bites on my hands and face, I walked along that beach for about a mile, to where the peninsula narrowed to the Neck. There I climbed the Mystic's bank and set my feet on the muddy road to the mainland.

The challenge of "Halt, who goes there?" from a Connecticut militiaman came as a most welcome greeting.

At Hastings House, Dr. Warren's eyes never left my welted face as I described the arrival of Generals Burgoyne, Clinton, and Howe. He laughed when I told him that Burgoyne reportedly said the British would come across the Charles to gain "elbow room." But he was all seriousness during my account of the speculation that General Gage might decide to seize and fortify high ground on our side of the Charles.

For more than an hour he pumped me for details, and when he felt he had learned all he could, he stood up and shook my hand.

"You are an extraordinary fellow, Martin," he said. "You have performed a noble service for your country."

Lovejoy Brown grumbled at my unexplained absence, "leaving all the work for others to do, as is your usual way." Chris wondered at my now-unbearded and mosquito-ravaged face. But our business continued to prosper. Lovejoy and I rented a cow shed from a local citizen to use as a warehouse for our rum and articles of trade and as a barn for our horses. We put several of our tents together to form one large shelter and slept there next to it. I put myself to sleep at night by counting up the money we had accumulated and reliving my pleasant sojourn with Madame LaFontaine's Mollie.

We provided Chris with a cot in our oversize shelter. I enjoyed his artless accounts of his errands for General Ward and the other militia officers. He provided a welcome contrast to Lovejoy's sour disposition. One Sunday he rode up to Marblehead with us to check on our tent supplier; there even Mother Brown succumbed to his youthful charm.

At this time I gave little thought to the compromising position into which I had allowed myself to be maneuvered. I was now a candidate for hanging by whichever side discovered my duplicity first. But what the hell? I was now back within our own lines. Major Tuttle had not given me all that much money. Dr. Warren did not know all that I had been up to, but I had done him and the patriot cause a useful service. And in conducting my patriotic duties, I was making Lovejoy and myself a small fortune.

By the second week of June, however, the pace of our money flow slackened. More and more militiamen were taking off for home to tend their crops and resume their trades. Nothing was happening that seemed to require their presence, and their families and occupations needed them. But these departures seriously reduced the number of men on whom General Ward and Dr. Warren could rely in case the British did bestir themselves. With fewer customers and with many of the basic needs of those remaining now satisfied, our supply business faltered. In fact, I had just about concluded that the time had come for Lovejoy and me to sell our enterprise and invest our capital in a sloop or schooner when Chris galloped up to our tent to report that Dr. Warren wanted to see both Lovejoy and me.

"What about?" I asked.

"He didn't say, but a fellow from New Hampshire slipped out of Boston with information about the British that seems to have stirred everyone up. Even old General Ward acts excited."

At Hastings House, Dr. Warren appeared fatigued and worried. He came directly to the point. The militia needed as many spades, picks, and axes as we could obtain. We would be paid a good price in gold. Were we interested in providing these digging instruments "as soon as possible?"

Indeed we were interested, I said.

"Good. Now, Martin, I'd like a private word with you."

Once Lovejoy was out of the room, Dr. Warren lowered his voice to a whisper.

"There is one string attached to this project."

"Why, sir, if it is the price, surely we could negotiate that."

"There is a price, but it is one you must pay."

He settled his intelligent gaze upon my face as if trying to look into my brain. I grew uncomfortable.

"Price, sir? I don't understand."

"I need you to return to Boston."

My first foray into British-occupied Boston had been brought about by Sir Francis Bolton's manipulation of my greed and by my fear of being turned over to the Virginia authorities. This time I would be going out of loyalty to Dr. Warren and, yes, out of love of country and my growing dislike of the British.

But I could explain nothing of this to Lovejoy or Chris.

Lovejoy was reluctant to venture alone out into the countryside with our wagon and team to buy up spades and picks and such. I told him simply to shut up and follow my instructions, which were to play upon the patriotism of farmers and their wives to sell us their implements at the lowest possible price. As for my own plans, they were a private matter between Dr. Warren and myself.

"I just hope you won't go disappearing again as you have done twice before."

"I, on the other hand, would like very much for you to disappear while the sun is still high enough for you to do some trading before dark."

Off he drove, grumbling about my cheekiness.

As for Chris, he said that he'd be glad to look after Ned during my absence. Later, near sundown, I suggested that we ride out to the Charlestown peninsula.

The pickets watching the Charlestown Neck knew us and let us pass their lines with no questions. Chris and I rode past the remains of a small redoubt that the British had thrown up the day after Concord and Lexington. We rode to the top of Bunker Hill, which looms up a good 130 feet above the Charles River and provides a grand view of the entire Boston area.

We sat on our horses and surveyed the scene. Red and yellow light from the setting sun was reflected from the spires and windows of Boston across the Charles and from the masts of the several British ships anchored in the river. Chris pointed beyond the Boston Neck and Roxbury toward Dorchester Heights.

"That's the place General Ward really wants us to fortify. But General Thomas says he has barely enough men to cover Roxbury and make sure the British don't attack us across the Boston Neck."

"I can see that artillery over there could play merry hell with their ships," I replied. "That hill looks right down on Boston Harbor."

"Since we don't have proper artillery and since General Thomas has so few men, Dr. Warren and General Ward decided the next best thing would be to take possession of this hill. Otherwise, we hear, the British will cross over and seize it. And they have plenty of artillery."

Chris suddenly stopped talking and a hurt look came over his face. "You aren't listening, Jerry."

"What?" I asked. "Oh, sure, I heard every word. I was just wondering whether your hat would fit me."

He handed me his tricorn, and as I had hoped, it was a good fit.

"Chris," I said, "I have a favor to ask of you."

"Anything, Jerry. What do you want me to do?"

"Follow me."

We rode down to the edge of the Mystic and there exchanged clothing. Except for a half-inch difference in sleeve lengths, his blouse and coat fitted me well, as did my shirt and sailor's jacket him. He asked no questions then, nor when I asked him to exchange his breeches for my bell bottoms.

I handed him Ned's reins.

"Jerry, I think I know what you are up to."

I simply looked at him.

"I think you are doing spy work for Dr. Warren. I think you are going to cross over to Boston."

"Chris, it is none of your business."

"Well, I just hope you don't get yourself hanged."

I seized him by the lapels of my old jacket and growled, "Just you keep your mouth shut, or I'll have you hanged."

He grinned. I pulled my sailor's cap down over his eyes and gave him a playful punch in his rock-hard belly. Then I slid down the steep bank to the edge of the Mystic and walked along the sand toward Mouton's Point. It was dark by the time I reached the spot where my cockleshell still lay in the long-unmown grass.

4

I ROWED QUIETLY out into the water of the Charles, just outside the circles of light cast by the lanterns of each British ship. It was my plan to land at the base of Copp's Hill, but I had failed to consider the tide, which was running out faster than I had thought possible. Sweating like a horse both from the exertion of rowing and from simple fear, I was swept right past North Battery and into Boston Harbor. At this rate, I would end up at sea in a boat meant for calm waters. I cursed my luck and bad judgment. As my cockleshell passed Clark's Wharf, it took all my willpower not to cry out for help.

The Long Wharf loomed to my right. I maneuvered the boat to make the bow face the outgoing tide. By manipulating the oars furiously, I worked my fragile craft around the end of the wharf and, at painful last, into the calm, shallow waters of its lee, closer to shore.

Safe at last from the fiendish tide, and exhausted, I bent my head forward, my arms trembling, and let the cockleshell drift. I could hear voices along the waterfront. A horse and carriage rattled along the cobblestones. I picked out a dark stretch of shore and eased the boat for it. I was beginning to think that my luck had returned when someone shouted, "Halt! Who goes there?"

I leaned down to present a lower silhouette and applied my oars more vigorously.

"Stop, or I'll fire!"

It was on my tongue to cry out "Friend! I have the password!" when the soldier's musket flashed and a bullet carried Chris's tricorn right off my head and into the water.

Acting by instinct, I cried out as if in pain and fell into the water on my back. Then I put my feet against the stern and thrust the cockleshell out of the shadows and back into the square of light cast by the guard's lantern.

The water was shallow, barely above my knees. The sentry could not see me as long as I crouched. In a great uproar, people came rushing out of taverns along the waterfront to inquire about the shooting.

"There's the boat right there!"

"See where's the bastard as was in it. I must of hit him!"

Grateful for the covering noise, I waded as fast as I could without revealing my location and was able to reach the shore a hundred yards away from where the sentry had fired.

Now some of the braver spectators were thrashing about in the water around the cockleshell.

"Here's his hat!"

"To hell with his hat! He should be floating about somewhere."

More lanterns appeared around the sentry. I removed my shoes and darted behind the cover of two hogsheads.

"Maybe you didn't hit him after all."

"Somebody look along the edge of the water that way!"

I knew then how a hare feels when a pack of hounds comes baying in his direction. Where could I take refuge? Or would I be better off to stand up and identify myself?

Suddenly, I thought of Madame LaFontaine's establishment. It was over on Water Street, not far from my hiding place. It would be impossible to reach her front door without being seen, but I remembered that her house backed up to an alley. With no more thought than that, dripping water and carrying a pair of wet shoes, I darted like a desperate rabbit across the street toward a dark gap in the line of lighted houses facing the waterfront.

"There he goes!"

Another sentry fired his musket, and the bullet ricocheted off a brick wall ahead of me.

With speed born of terror, I ran up the dark alley. The mob took a few moments to collect their wits and soon came clomping along behind me. They were not close enough to see me in the dark, but they were noisy enough to arouse the curiosity of people whose houses lined the alley. I stopped beside a water cistern to catch my breath.

A woman raised a window I had just passed and cried out to the mob, "I just heard someone run by here!"

Two shots rang out—from a pair of pistols, judging from the sound. I bolted from my hiding place. The woman shouted again, "There he goes! Up the alley!"

I ran madly, thoughtlessly, desperately and gained a few yards on the booted feet that followed me. Ahead of me the alley opened into a well-lighted street. In my condition, with a howling mob behind me, I would be trapped.

Thank God—there was the brick wall with its door opening onto the alley. No—not opening, for the damned thing was locked! I tried to break it open with my shoulder but only made a racket that brought someone to the upstairs window. With a burst of strength and energy I did not know I possessed, I leaped high enough to get an arm over the top of the wall, then one leg over, and finally I dropped into the garden.

"Who out there?" a woman cried.

I looked up and recognized the black maid who worked for Madame LaFontaine.

"Quiet, for God's sake! It's me, Jeremiah Martin!" I whispered out as loudly as I dared.

In a moment the mob went galumphing past the gate.

"Wait! Look here! It's a pair of shoes—and they're wet!" I heard.

"That's why the bastard can run so fast," sounded a voice that had to be an officer's. "He's barefoot. Here, try this gate!"

Now I blessed the person who had barred the door.

"Break it down!" the officer shouted. "No, not all of you. You, you, and you—run to the street and see if he went that way. Now, shoulders to this confounded gate!"

The back door of the house opened, and out walked Madame LaFontaine carrying a lantern. She walked right past me, as if I were not there in her plain view, and called out in an imperious tone, "What in God's name is going on out there?"

"Looking for a spy, ma'am. Please open up and let us search."

"Indeed, I will not open my door! There is no spy here."

"Well, we found his shoes right here beside your gate."

"That may be, but there is no one in this garden but myself and my maid. Malinda, have you heard anyone pass?"

"Yes, ma'am, somebody did just run up the alley. They was running fast and breathing hard. Wondered what was going on."

"Damn it, we shouldn't have wasted time here! Run ahead and raise the alarm. We can't let him get away!"

Madame LaFontaine waited with her lantern until the sound of their feet could be heard no more. Then she turned the light on me and said, "Welcome back, Jeremiah Martin."

I have always been an adaptable creature. Thus, I reentered Madame LaFontaine's house as if it were my home. And indeed, I was made to feel most welcome.

Once again, the maid, Malinda, laid out clothes, the very same ones I had worn before, only this time in the kitchen. Madame LaFontaine excused herself "to look after my guests," and I proceeded to dry myself off under Malinda's unabashed stare.

Overcome by uncharacteristic modesty, I turned my back as I completed my toilet. When fully dressed, I turned to face her again, and she was still staring.

"You must be some kind of conjure man. That fool girl Mollie ain't stopped talking about you since you was here. And I never seen the madam go out of her way to help nobody like she has you."

"I suppose I'm just lucky. By the way, who is here tonight?"

"Some of them redcoat officers, as usual. Oh, you don't need to look like that. We ain't gonna tell them you here." She laughed. "Wish you could have seen yourself hunch down beside that wall. You looked like a man about to be hanged."

"I might have been, had you not helped."

Her habitual expression of scorn melted. I pressed my advantage by asking her questions about herself.

She was born in Boston. Her mother had been set free by her wealthy owners when Malinda was a little girl.

"I ain't never been no slave," she declared. "And I ain't never sold my favors to no man. I a honest woman."

When had Madame LaFontaine come over from France? "France? She just a girl born in London. When she forget herself or have too much wine, she talk just like one o' them Cockney soldiers you hear on the street."

Had she always been in this business?

"Lord, no. She been an actress. To hear her tell it, she a good one. In London, sure, and other places in England. Oh, I heard her entertain officers with what she call her recitations. Shakespeare and that stuff."

Then why the French name?

"Oh, she got in with this old man from over there in France. He bring her and what she call this company over here to put on plays. They try Philadelphia first, but them Quakers down there close them down, so they come on up here to Boston. They did all right, I reckon, until all the troubles start and the British send these soldiers in here. Well, the Monsieur, as she use to call him, he up and die. Leave her with nothing but a pile of debts. Madam, she figure her actresses, they giving it away anyhow. Why not forget the acting and sell it? So she buy this house, and she set up business."

"If the Monsieur left her in such bad shape, how did she buy this house and furnish it so?"

She pursued her lips and nursed her secret for a long moment, then said at last, "The money, it come from this old man that visited Boston from down the West Indies someplace."

I was balked from hearing more about Bolton by the reappearance of Madame LaFontaine. She explained that Mollie and the other girls "and their beds" were occupied, but that, "seeing your exhausted state," I was welcome to her bed for the night. I protested, but she was adamant, explaining that she could occupy a couch in the drawing room.

Too weary to protest, I followed her upstairs to a huge, opulently furnished room. She set the candle on a bedside table and suggested that I make myself comfortable while she fetched me a nightcap.

I slid my naked and aching body between real sheets. Madame LaFontaine soon returned with a goblet.

"It is a special mixture of wines and brandy. Mulled. 'Twill make you sleep like a baby."

She stood beside my bed while I drank the brew. I had never tasted anything quite like the syrupy liquid. It was sweet at first, but had a faintly bitter aftertaste.

"Drink it all, Jerry," she said.

She took the cup, bent over and tousled my hair, then snuffed out the candle and slipped from the room.

A burst of sunlight on my face brought me back to consciousness. Madame LaFontaine, fully dressed, every shiny black hair of her head in place, opened the blind. There at the foot of the bed stood Malinda with a tray bearing coffee, toasted bread, and poached eggs.

"You slept well, I trust?"

"Very well, except I had the wildest dreams."

"You were very tired and overwrought. Are you hungry?"

"Ravenous."

"Then eat. We will return with suitable clothing."

After I had eaten, I lay abed trying to sort out my recollections of the night. I suspected that the drink the woman had given me contained more than mere spirits, but I could not be sure.

When they returned, Malinda carried a sort of shallow chest and clothing that appeared to have been rescued from a ragbag.

"Jeremiah Martin, how would you like to go promenading with Malinda and me this fine afternoon?"

"I don't think so."

"But you would like the opportunity to see what the brave soldiers of our King are up to. And as his loyal subject, you should be keenly interested in their precise plans for dealing with the ugly rebellion that has broken out."

This was said with a knowing smile.

"Yes, but you don't understand—"

"I understand that you think it unwise to go abroad in daylight under your own name and in recognizable form. But suppose you were invisible?"

For a moment I thought my nightmares had returned—or that this woman was a witch.

"No one is invisible."

"Well, let us say that you were disguised in such a way that no one would take any notice of you."

"Sure, but what are you getting at?"

70

"Malinda," she said. "Set the box here on the bed. And you, sir, sit up. Come, come, don't be modest. We've both seen naked men before."

The three of us—Madame LaFontaine, Malinda, and I—made a strange trio as we left the house on Water Street and proceeded along Cornhill. Carrying a parasol, the madam was dressed in her elegant best, complete with lace bonnet. Malinda wore an apron and a kerchief over her head. And then came I, Jeremiah Martin, looking most unlike one born of a landed Virginia family. The two women had spent more than an hour staining my face and hands a sort of mulatto brown and dyeing my reddish beard black. They had stuffed cotton under my lips to make them appear Negroid. And from a trunk the madam had brought out a kinky wig, which she said was last worn by the Monsieur when he played Othello.

Malinda had instructed me in how to walk. "Not like that. Walk humble. And don't look nobody in the eye. Here—you too tight. Gotta walk loose, like you don't own nothing in the world, so you got nothing to lose. Now here, you carry this basket of food for us ladies. And walk two steps behind us."

The women were still trying to stifle their merriment even as we walked along Union Street. At the sight of Reuben Halbertson coming out of The Green Dragon, I ducked my head. Bolton's agent raised his hat and nodded contemptuously to Madame LaFontaine but seemed to take no notice of me. Our promenade continued past the Old North Church and on to Copp's Hill. There we found a battery of twenty-four-pounder cannon that had been newly emplaced on the edge of an ancient burying ground.

The young captain in command of these formidable guns seemed flattered at the interest an elegant lady showed in his weapons. He assured her that they could hurl their missiles all the way to that high hill over there on the Charlestown peninsula. Yes, ma'am, he missed England, but he didn't mind. No, he wasn't worried about the Americans across the river.

"Sure, they've proved they can shoot from behind trees and walls. But I'd like to see what they do in a real fight out in the open, with artillery and bayonets. I wager they'd never stand up to cold steel."

The young officer, who looked to be but little older than Chris McGee, was rewarded with a raisin muffin from my basket.

Throughout most of the afternoon, I followed the two women from one end of Boston to the other, from Copp's Hill clear back to the Common and even out to the Neck, to where the British had erected a strong redoubt covering this, the only land route into the city. The madam asked the very questions I would have asked of officers we met along the way and rewarded them with her raisin muffins. On our return from the Neck, in front of Province House, she halted and called out to a cocky-looking chap with epaulets on his shoulders.

"You are General Burgoyne, are you not?"

"Indeed, madame, I am he."

She introduced herself and informed him in the process that she had once played on the London stage and how impressed she was that the King had sent over a man who was not only an able general but a gifted playwright.

Burgoyne acted stiff at first, but he unbent under her flattery.

They chatted a bit about common acquaintances in the theater; then she put her hand on his arm and asked in a confidential tone, "Tell me, what do we propose to do about that rabble across the river? Surely, with you on hand we will not suffer ourselves to long continue in this humiliating posture."

"Ah, madame, how right you are! Before the week is out, I expect we will have taught those impudent chaps a lesson. We have more than enough force to accomplish our purpose. Indeed, we should count it a blessing that so many of the rebellious-minded in that population are gathered in one place. That enables us to smash them all at once and put a quick end to this rashness."

"And you think it will be accomplished soon?"

"Very soon. 'Tis simply a matter of deciding at which point to strike."

"Do you not fear that they will move against us first?"

"Impossible! They have hardly any artillery and no ships. We hold all the cards."

Madame LaFontaine assured General Burgoyne that he had greatly relieved her fears. She offered him the services of her "young ladies" in case he should wish to produce a play while in Boston.

I cannot recall all the military intelligence I overheard that afternoon, but by the time we returned to the house on Water Street, my head was spinning. Much of my confusion sprang from the puzzling actions of this Madame LaFontaine. She was a clever and devious woman, to be sure. What was her motive?

At that point, none of the girls of the house knew of my presence. To keep them in ignorance, the two women instructed me to wait outside the garden gate while they entered the front door. After a few minutes Malinda led me into the kitchen and, with the door barred, lit a candle and proceeded to scrub the stain from my face, neck, and hands.

She found this far more humorous than I did.

"What you act so sour about, Mister Jeremiah Martin? Many's the time I wished I could scrub myself white."

With no inkling of the consequences of my decision, I declined her offer to shave off my regrown beard. I was back in Chris Mc-Gee's old clothes when Madame LaFontaine, holding a note, entered the kitchen. She notified Malinda that "Major Tuttle sends his regrets. Reports there is some sort of alert. Now, Malinda, if you would allow our guest and me to have a word in private. And no eavesdropping, either."

She barred the kitchen door behind Malinda and turned to face me.

"So? Have you learned all you need to know?"

"I think so. Except for one thing: Why have you gone to such risk and trouble on my behalf?"

"I am not altogether certain. Maybe it's spite."

"Against the British? You are English yourself."

"Oh?" She raised her eyebrows. "Malinda has been talking out of turn, hasn't she? Well, it is true. I am London born and bred. I grew up without a father. I have had to claw my way out of poverty. Yes, I hate the British—or anyway, those who run the country. Them and their arrogant ways."

"Come, Madame LaFontaine. You entertain their officers."

"Yes, and make them pay for the entertainment very, very dearly."

"You are an American sympathizer, then?"

"I would not go so far as that. But I am against tyranny."

She paused, and for a moment a look of pain passed over her face.

"Also, I am a realist. Quite frankly, no matter what that ass Burgoyne says, I don't see how England, for all her military might, can contain this rebellion. Sooner or later they will have to leave. In such a case, I should like Dr. Warren and others to know that I was of assistance to one of their spies."

"I am no spy."

"Do not pretend with me, Jeremiah. You are worse than a spy. You have become a double agent."

Suddenly I grew angry. "That wine last night—you drugged me!"

"The experience was not unpleasant, I trust."

"But I could be hanged if you told about me and Dr. Warren."

"Or if I told Dr. Warren about you and Major Tuttle. Oh dear, what a pickle you have got yourself into!"

"Could you not be hanged if Major Tuttle were to learn that you helped a spy gain information?"

She laughed. "So we must trust each other, *n'est-ce pas?*"

I frowned. "There is something I don't understand. You work for Francis Bolton, and yet—"

"No. I am his business partner, just as you have become."

I let her remark pass. Something more pressing was on my mind.

"Look, since you know all about me, tell me, how can I get back to the mainland with what I have learned?"

"There are ways. If you would shave off that disgusting beard, I could disguise you as one of my girls. We might tell Province House that you were made pregnant by one of their officers and suggest that you be sent to the mainland to avoid a scandal. Or I could pass you off as a sailor who has come down with smallpox. They'd be delighted to send you through the lines to the Americans. . . ." She continued with a half-dozen ingenious ideas. I marveled at her cleverness.

"But I need to return tonight."

"It is not possible until tomorrow. Besides, there is a price attached."

"What price?"

She smiled and winked. "A price that can only be paid by your remaining the night."

Before I could answer, she had blown out the candle and was leading me out of the kitchen and into the darkened hall.

5

THAT TRULY MEMORABLE night ended abruptly at about 4 A.M., just as I was about to drift back into a delicious languor. The windows of the bedroom rattled, and I heard the boom of several cannon firing at once. I sat up in bed. Again the room shook.

I freed myself from Madame LaFontaine's arm and threw on my clothes (or rather Chris's). I reached the door before she could ask where I was going.

Forgetting all else, I ran toward the sound of the firing. It stopped as suddenly as it had started at about the time I reached Union Street. Boston looked like an anthill that has been kicked over by small boys. As dawn broke over the city, half-dressed British officers came boiling out into the streets, shouting for their sergeants. People in nightclothes stood befuddled on doorsteps. I ran on until I reached Copp's Hill.

In response to my questions, the sergeant of the crew of one of the twenty-four-pounders replied, "Bloody rebels throwed up a redoubt over on yon hill. The *Lively* has been giving them a few broadsides."

Even without a spyglass and with the sun not yet fully up, I could make out fresh mounds of earth—not on Bunker Hill as I had expected but on the lower and much nearer Breed's Hill. Below us, down in the Charles and the mouth of the Mystic, the several Brit-

74

ish warships were signaling back and forth to each other as they shifted their positions to bring the new fort within better range. As I had discerned from my intelligence-gathering tour the day before, it was a formidable fleet. The *Lively* carried twenty guns. Then there was the sixteen-gun sloop *Falcon,* the *Symmetry,* a transport armed with eighteen cannon, and the twenty-four-gun frigate *Glasgow.* If this were not force enough, the British could call upon the mighty *Somerset,* which lay at anchor with her sixty-four cannon near Hancock's Wharf on the other side of the town, plus two so-called floating batteries, not to mention the twenty-four-pounders there on Copp's Hill. To oppose this collection of mighty guns, the Americans had but a handful of puny cannon served by a set of ill-trained poltroons.

I made myself agreeable to the gunners by offering to fetch them a bucket of birch beer from a nearby tavern. So they allowed me to hang about "so long as you stays out of the way," as the sergeant, a pudgy little Cornishman, put it. At around 8 A.M. the *Lively,* having re-anchored off Mouton's Point, reopened fire on the new fort, which, I now could see, encompassed a sizable square atop Breed's Hill. About an hour later, crews of the twenty-four-pounders brought their ponderous weapons into play as well. It was thrilling to stand atop a small tomb with my hands over my ears amid the belching roar of the big guns and the shouts of their crews and look down upon the bombardment. Had I not been so aware that fellow Americans were in danger, it would have made a pretty sight, the way the ships' guns flashed and smoke billowed and geysers of earth sprang up around the fort.

My new-found friend, the gunnery sergeant, lent me his spyglass while he helped his crew relay their gun. I made out a party of militiamen who were using, I supposed, tools procured by Lovejoy as they threw up a long breastwork stretching from the fort toward the Mystic. Hundreds of others milled about back on Bunker Hill, acting rather more like spectators than warriors.

Speaking of spectators, as the morning wore on the entire populace of Boston made its way to the western side of the peninsula to watch the grand show from atop rooftops and from upper-story windows of houses. By late morning all the British ships—including the awesome *Somerset*—and the Copp's Hill battery were booming away at the Americans in the fort and behind the new breastwork, while the floating batteries bombarded the narrow Charlestown Neck to discourage reinforcements from joining the militia on the peninsula.

The pretty village of Charlestown had been abandoned by its inhabitants since Concord-Lexington. Some American militiamen had infiltrated its streets and were sniping away at British ships, but I consider that a poor excuse for what the British did. The crews of the twenty-four-pounders loaded their guns with "carcasses" and deliberately fired these incendiary shells into the village. Ships joined in with red-hot cannonballs until fires had sprung up throughout Charlestown. So much for British chivalry.

In the course of time I learned from Chris and others that General Ward had chosen three Massachusetts regiments—some eight hundred men under Colonel William Prescott—to carry out the expedition that touched off all these fireworks. The members of the expedition had assembled on the Cambridge Common to hear a long-winded prayer by the president of Harvard College and then about dark had set out in the company of the army's chief engineer for the narrow Charlestown Neck, where they were met by about two hundred Connecticutters and my old friend Lovejoy Brown with his wagonload of digging tools. After much discussion, the officers decided that, rather than Bunker Hill, they would fortify the lower Breed's Hill, six hundred yards nearer Charlestown and Boston. Working like beavers from midnight until daylight, the Americans had constructed a 135-foot-square fort, complete with firing steps and moat.

Later, after daylight illuminated the terrain, they had hurriedly thrown up that long breastwork that stretched from the fort toward the Mystic.

Various British generals came to Copp's Hill to peer across to Breed's Hill, first Gage himself and later Clinton, Howe, and Burgoyne. Burgoyne danced up and down and clapped his hands with delight at the spectacle of the burning village and the flashing naval guns. By late morning it was obvious that the British intended to do far more than hurl cannonballs at the militia, for Howe disappeared to muster troops for an expedition and Gage departed for the better view he could obtain from the belfry of the Old North Church.

Here let me pause and pay tribute to the greatest victims of the American War for Independence. I refer to the rank and file of our enemy, the long-suffering, ill-used, doggedly brave British regulars. For the most part they are scrawny, low-bred little fellows from the slums of London or the most poverty-ridden hills of Wales and Scotland. They are often flogged by their sergeants. They are underpaid and underfed. But as they demonstrated that day and in many another battle of the American war during the next six years, they are as tough and brave as their officers were stupid and callous.

Seeing a fleet of large naval barges converging toward the North Battery Wharf, I deserted my observation post on Copp's Hill. I went down to the wharf to watch the British soldiers of the light infantry and grenadier companies of each of ten regiments—the same units that had been sent out to Concord—line up in close ranks. It was a warm day. Each soldier was dressed in heavy wool trousers and jacket, and each carried a full knapsack with other heavy accoutrements, including a "Brown Bess" musket with a fixed bayonet and full cartridge boxes. It is no exaggeration to say that most of those troops were carrying the equivalent of their own body weight.

Down into the barges they went, packed in so close that they had to stand to leave room for the sailors to man the oars. As these so-called flank companies—about six hundred men in all—departed, regular companies of the Fifth and Thirty-eighth Regiments marched up to the wharf and awaited their turn at the boats.

I returned to Copp's Hill with a fresh bucket of birch beer for the sweating gunners. What a pretty sight those naval barges made as they moved across the Charles to the stately rhythm of the sailors' oars! To the left, smoke from the burning houses and other buildings of Charlestown created a huge dark backdrop. All across the mouth of the Charles and the Mystic lingered clouds of white smoke from the ships' guns.

The barges disgorged their heavy-laden redcoats near the very spot I had landed with my cockleshell and then turned back toward Boston to take aboard still other soldiers. I longed to find some way to pass on to Dr. Warren the information I was now picking up with great ease. Major General William Howe was crossing with the second wave of troops to direct an attack on our fortifications. More than fifteen hundred men and a battery of six-pounder field guns were to be committed to the assault; several hundred more lobster-backs—the Forty-seventh Regiment and the First Battalion of Marines—were standing by in case they were needed. I consoled myself with the thought that our commanders could see for themselves pretty much what the British intended to do.

Across the Charles, General Howe took his time, as if he meant to awe the Americans by the very deliberateness of his preparations. Part of his force marched over little Mouton's Hill and casually sat down to eat their midday meal in easy view of the militia.

By 3 P.M. I could see that all was ready. Some three hundred light infantrymen were lined up along the shore of the Mystic in ranks of eight. As for the grenadiers, after they helped manhandle the battery of six-pounders across a marshy field to within range of the American fort, they arranged themselves into a long rank, backed up by a second rank of two regular regiments. Three other regular regiments massed to the left, nearer Charlestown. The flank companies had been supposed to sweep around the fort and breastwork to the north while the other troops bypassed Charlestown and assaulted the main fort.

As it turned out, the British had brought over shells meant for twelve-pounder rather than six-pounder cannon and had to send back for proper ammunition. Meanwhile, they opened the action by peppering the breastworks with grapeshot—a waste of gunpowder.

The real action of that bloody afternoon began along the narrow strip of sand that separated the waters of the Mystic from the steep bank. Even from Copp's Hill I could make out a pile of stones across the beach as the light infantry, with a shout that carried across the Charles, began advancing, their bayonets flashing.

From my distant vantage point, I could not see Stark's New Hampshiremen crouching three deep behind their hastily constructed stone breastwork; nor could I discern the two white aiming stakes that they had driven into the sand about fifty yards from their muzzles. What I saw as the front rank of the light infantry—men of the Royal Fusiliers—neared the stone barricade was a flash of musketry and billow of smoke. In less time than it takes me to write these words, a second row of muskets fired.

The beach was suddenly littered with red-coated forms. But men from the next company pressed forward, and a third volley cut them down like the proverbial scythe slicing through rows of wheat. Then, with scarcely a pause, our first rank fired again.

I would not have thought it possible for militiamen to load and fire so rapidly. Again and again fresh redcoats rushed along the beach and into that marvelously disciplined and destructive point-blank musketry. And then, in an instant the British all turned around and were running, yes, running back toward their boats, leaving behind a body-strewn strand.

Apparently the steep bank of the Mystic spared the grenadiers the sight of this carnage that was occurring as they advanced through the knee-high grass. Followed closely by a rank of regulars, they moved ponderously, like a red-coated juggernaut. I watched them stumble over the same obstacles that had so frustrated me a few nights before. They halted to take down a rail fence, moved on in a now-crooked line, and then became further disarrayed in crossing a stone wall. As they were heading, only the men on the left of the line were to go up against the breastwork. The others, it appeared, were to sweep around the American fortifications and isolate them from Bunker Hill.

While the decimated and demoralized light infantry huddled about their boats on the beach, the grenadiers passed the remains of an old brick kiln and mucked their way across a bog. Not only did these big fellows all carry full packs, they were walking uphill and were further burdened by their heavy, peaked bearskin helmets.

A spatter of musketry broke out along the breastwork without great effect as far as I could tell. But it was a different story after the rest of the long front line broke ranks to cross a rail fence. They had just reformed on the other side and were moving forward again when suddenly all along their front there burst a perfect inferno of musketry. It began with a single mighty crash and then rattled on like hail falling on a roof. The grenadiers returned a single uneven volley. Then, losing all semblance of order, those strapping fellows, the pride of the British army, turned tail and lumbered back down the slope, carrying with them the second rank of regulars. I had to choke back a cheer.

What had happened was that several hundred brave Connecticut men under the command of Captain Thomas Knowlton had volunteered to slip down from Bunker Hill during the British bombardment and turn a long stone wall topped by a low rail fence into a concealed breastwork by covering it with clumps of long grass. The British had played right into their hands—or should I say into the deadly fire of their muskets?

The gunnery sergeant reclaimed his spyglass to survey the scene. "They have slaughtered our grenadiers!" he exclaimed.

Again, it was a struggle for me not to cheer when we observed the left wing of the British advance falter before sharpshooters' fire from houses in Charlestown long before it reached the main fort atop Breed's Hill.

But the battle was far from over. The grenadiers quickly formed up again, their packs still on their backs. Then, joined by the survivors of the light infantry companies, up the slope they advanced once more, at the same deliberate pace as before, over the forms of the dead and wounded from their first attack. Just as they had before, the Americans behind that long stone wall arose and laid down the same sort of furious but steady fire. The British stood their ground long enough to get off a couple of volleys. For a moment it appeared they might be about to drive home a bayonet charge; but no—they once more broke and fled back over the bodies of their dead and wounded to escape that merciless American musketry. Meanwhile, the other wing, having cleared the snipers out of Charlestown, advanced toward the fort but turned back without going up directly against its high wall.

Availing myself once more of the sergeant's spyglass, I studied the entire Charlestown peninsula, from the charred ruins of the village, to the soldier-strewn slopes of Breed's Hill, to the American fort, and finally to Bunker Hill, where far more militiamen skulked than there were down on the firing line.

In retrospect, each side made a serious mistake at this point. The Americans did not reinforce the fort or the breastworks, and the British did not make a new landing on the Neck behind Bunker Hill. Instead the British sent additional troops directly across the Charles, until Gage had transported over a third of his forces, some 2,300 men.

Except for the constant bombardment of the ships, there came a long respite. Then, reinforced and seemingly more determined than ever, the British got back into formation, only this time in column rather than lines. As my gunnery sergeant said, "Bloody bastards have come to their senses and shed them silly packs."

By now the British fieldpieces had received their proper ammunition. They banged away at the breastwork from close range in a way that drew cheers of admiration from my nearby twenty-four-pounders' crews.

Between blasts from these guns, the rat-a-tat of drums could be heard, beating out the signal for a resumption of the slaughter.

There the stupid, fearless British fools moved out again in what may have been the grandest spectacle of the entire war. Gage from his observation post in the church belfry, I from atop my tomb, and the thousands of soldiers and civilians who watched from rooftops—none of us could have appreciated the suffering that already had taken place across the river or the greater horror that was about to occur. Count on it—anyone who thinks that war is grand has never experienced it personally or observed it at close hand.

This time the assault concentrated on the fort atop Breed's Hill. From the fort and the breastwork there opened a perfect storm of musketry. Under it the heads of the British columns melted away, only to be replaced by redcoats stepping smartly forward over their fallen comrades. Right up to the deep ditch this advance carried, right up against three sides of the fort. The British columns, converging into a giant, formless mob, hesitated there briefly and fired off first one volley, then another. A cloud of white smoke obscured my view briefly. I waited for the deadly American musketry to resume and for the British to fall back once again. But no, by God— the defenders' return fire was only a sputter! We had run out of ammunition. The British gave a mighty roar of rage and frustration and went surging up the steep face of the fort and over the top.

After talking to survivors on both sides, I now know what a bitter, bloody struggle took place inside that fort. British bayonets were thrust against militiamen, who wielded their muskets like clubs or hurled stones. One of the brave Americans who fell in that fort was Dr. Warren. He had got up from his sickbed in Cambridge to take his place with his fellow Americans. And one of the many British who fell in that final assault was Major Pitcairn, the marine officer who had commanded the light infantry at Lexington Common.

The surviving defenders of the fort and the breastworks would have been massacred or captured en masse had it not been for Captain Knowlton and his men behind the stone wall. Although they were not involved in the final defense of the fort, they served as a rear guard for their fellow Americans, firing from behind one position long enough to delay the British, then retiring to the next wall and repeating the process. But by the end of an hour, the last

American had departed the Charlestown peninsula. I could make out the red of the British coats swarming atop Bunker Hill, yes, and many a quiet form dotting the grassy meadows in front of Breed's Hill.

Little more than half of the men Gage sent across the Charles that day came out of the battle alive and unwounded. They won the victory, if by winning you mean that they carried our positions and ended up in possession of the Charlestown peninsula. But what a price they paid!

Quite forgetting my own precarious situation, I went down to the Long Wharf to watch the barges that had carried over the confident troops return with the wounded redcoats. Carriages, chaises, wagons, and carts lined up clear back to King Street waiting to convey the groaning, suffering soldiers to makeshift hospitals that had been set up in places such as the almshouse and various factories and churches about the city. Officers on the landing yelled for help, and without thinking, out of simple humanity I lent a hand lifting my maimed enemies into these conveyances. The dead and wounded at Lexington after the massacre there and even what I saw after bloody Bushy Run paled by comparison with this scene. Grown men screamed in agony. Some cried out for their wives and mothers, and others pleaded for someone to put them out of their misery.

A young lieutenant who had been shot in the stomach cried out in pain and called me a clumsy fool when I lifted him from a barge. Suddenly he coughed and vomited blood all over my chest. By the time I reached the chaise that was to have received him, his moans had ceased and his head had fallen back.

An army doctor looked into his open eyes and said, "Waste no more time on him. Lay the body over there against the wall."

I was helping a grenadier who had been shot in the leg hobble across the wharf when someone called, "Jerry, is that you?"

There was Madame LaFontaine with Malinda and Mollie and her other girls. They wore plain frocks and carried pitchers of water.

At the sight of the blood on my jacket, the madam turned pale and cried out, "Oh, my dear, what happened to you?"

I assured her that I was not wounded, that I had been helping the grenadier.

But the look of concern remained on her face. "Should you be out in public like this?"

"What else can I do?"

"Don't let Tuttle see you! And come back to our house when you are through. Promise?"

"He'll not be looking for me in the midst of all this."

Throughout the long night I labored on that wharf, working until I was blind with fatigue. Barge after barge arrived, bearing the fruits of General Howe's foolish assaults. It had all looked so grand, so romantic from a distance. Now we were dealing with the reality of a war.

By dawn I could hardly stand, much less carry another wounded soldier. My coat and blouse were soaked with blood.

I accepted the thanks of the British surgeon I had been helping and stumbled up King Street toward the only refuge I knew, Madame LaFontaine's. Along the way I passed several public buildings that had been turned into hospitals. From within I could hear the screams of men as surgeons probed for bullets or removed mangled legs and arms. Had I been less weary, I would have yielded to my impulse and gone in to help. But I turned off King Street into Levert's Lane. Only a few steps to go, and I would be on Water Street and safety.

I stood aside for a rickety wagon, drawn by a scrawny horse and surrounded by a squad of British soldiers, to pass. On the wagon lay several groaning redcoats. Leading the horse was the little cobbler I had seen tarred and feathered in Brookline.

The procession stopped.

"You there, fellow! Are you wounded?" the cobbler called out.

I looked at the gore glistening on my jacket.

"No, I have been helping carry the wounded."

He peered at me closer.

"You look familiar. Don't I know you?"

A chill ran down my back as I replied, "Can't think why you would."

The sergeant in charge of the escorting squad interrupted. "Let's get on with it. We've no time for social visits."

To my relief the cobbler turned his back and led his horse on toward Water Street. I wiped the sweat from my face and fairly tiptoed on to the doorway of Madame LaFontaine's establishment. It was like being home again. I mounted the steps and applied the knocker. A second-floor window opened.

"Jerry, my love, you have come back!"

"Yes, let me in. I am worn out."

The window slammed shut. I waited while keys were turned inside and bolts drawn. The door opened, and there she stood in a nightgown, her hair down over her shoulders. I felt like falling into her arms.

She frowned, I supposed at the sight of the dried blood that caked my front.

"Who have you brought with you?" she asked.

I turned and saw at the foot of the steps the cobbler, along with the sergeant and two British soldiers carrying muskets.

The cobbler pointed his finger at me. "Ain't you the fellow that watched them traitorous bastards tar and feather me?"

I shook my head.

He turned to the sergeant. "It's him, all right. Him and another fellow was in a wagon. Loaded with rebel tents, it was. My wife and daughters will remember him if you don't believe me."

Nothing Madame LaFontaine did or said could persuade the sergeant not to drag me off to Province House and into the presence of Major Tuttle himself.

PART THREE

1

BOSTON'S PUBLIC PRISON-COURTHOUSE stood on Queen Street facing down Brattle. I got to know that dismal place better during the next few months than ever I had wished to.

There within its thick, dark walls I passed many miserable days. The story I told when brought before Major Tuttle that next day was a simple one, and I stuck to it. I had followed Tuttle's instructions; I had spent several days nosing through the American camps and had learned that they planned to occupy the Charlestown peninsula. Thereupon I had crossed the Charles in my borrowed cockleshell, only to arrive too late for my information to be of any use.

There were some gaps in my account, but Major Tuttle, with the battle an accomplished fact, would have accepted it—except for that blasted cobbler. He identified me not only as having been in Brookline but as a supplier of the American Army. I admitted that I might have done a bit of profiteering. No harm in that; it had been before I came into Boston and accepted the assignment from Tuttle. Perhaps, said Major Tuttle, but he would have to keep me confined and in chains until he had time to look into my case further.

Meanwhile, the British went on with the gruesome business of cleaning up from their costly victory. Church bells tolled throughout the days after the battle to mark the death of officers. Past the jail there flowed a constant traffic of wagons and carriages that had been pressed into service as hearses. The large attic room in which I was confined soon became filled with Americans captured during and just after the battle. Most were wounded, and some were in dreadful shape. I kept my mind off my own trouble by helping tend these suffering fellows. They got precious little help and much abuse from the British. Sad to relate, few of my fellow prisoners survived their delayed medical treatment and the niggardly rations and the bullying of our jailor, a great Tory oaf named Cunningham who singled me out for the most humiliating duties, such as emptying the slop pots for our fetid quarters.

I passed part of those dreary hours inquiring about the battle from the Americans jammed into that steamy top-story room with me. They understood that I was being held as a suspected spy for their side, and I said nothing to disabuse them of the notion, so they talked freely while I kept my own counsel. The fact that I was forced to wear leg and arm chains further played upon their sympathy. One of my fellow prisoners had been trapped in the fort and stabbed in the thigh by a bayonet. He told me of Dr. Warren's joining them and of seeing that wise and noble man fall with a bullet in his brain during the final assault.

By the end of the summer, most of the Americans imprisoned with me had died. And with all food supplies from the mainland shut off, there was little enough to eat for those outside the prison. Inside, we counted ourselves fortunate to be served twice a day a sort of swill brewed with potato peels, with an occasional crust of bread made from unhusked wheat. Once a week we were treated to the luxury of half-spoiled fish. Every day that the British left me there to rot, on no formal charges, embittered me more against our so-called Mother Country.

One of our guards, a pleasant Irishman, would slip us an extra ration when our chief jailor was not looking. It was from him that we heard of George Washington's appointment as commander-in-chief of the American armies and later of the arrival of several companies of riflemen from Pennsylvania and Virginia. It was he, too, who told me one day that a sloop had just arrived from Barbados with a cargo of molasses and rum, and that a fresh lot of prisoners was to join us that very October afternoon.

There were five of them. Two had somehow survived the amputation of their legs by British surgeons and had recovered enough to be removed from hospital. Two others—unwounded, elderly men—said they had been too slow to escape the British when they surged up over Bunker Hill. They had been pressed into service as male nurses at one of the British hospitals. Now, the wounded having all died or healed, the British had no further use for them. And then there was one chap, a Bostonian, who said he was accused of trying to pass information to the American army.

Throughout my imprisonment I had kept my mouth shut about my activities on either side of the Charles. By contrast, the purported spy seemed to go to considerable pains to advertise his patriotic sentiments. He then questioned each person in the room about his loyalties and the circumstances of his capture.

"Was with Knowlton behind the stone wall," one of the old men said. "Couldn't run as fast as the other fellows."

One of the amputees explained that a spent cannonball had crushed his foot late in the day of the battle. And so on around the room this busybody went, saving me for last. "And you—I see no signs of wounds on you. How long you been in this hellhole?"

"Long enough," I replied,

"Were you in the battle?"

"Not exactly."

"Where were you then?"

The fellow was grating on my nerves.

"Ask me no questions and I'll tell you no lies," I replied.

"Take no offense. I judge you to be an American. I only hope that you're not here under charges of spying, as I am. They have threatened to hang me, you know."

"And are you a spy?" one of the old men asked.

The fellow turned coy and lowered his voice. "Well now, I wouldn't want to say. I have done my bit of service to our cause, and that is as far as I'll go. Here now, we must keep up our courage. Join me in cheering for George Washington and the Continental Congress. Hip, Hip—"

A weak *hurrah* arose from the throats of a few.

The fellow continued with a proper harangue about the rightness of the American cause and the perfidy of "our British persecutors." I considered cautioning him against speaking out so plainly and loudly, but he was acting such a fool that I decided to let him learn of Cunningham's cruelty firsthand.

All the while he was talking, this patriot walked around and around the low-ceilinged room peering into our faces. He stopped in front of me.

"Your accent is not from this region."

I merely looked at him.

"And yet you seem familiar to me."

I wanted to strangle him, but I said nothing.

"Wait. It has just come to me. I saw you several weeks ago leaving The Green Dragon. You were wearing a seaman's garb, and you were in the company of a notorious British agent, a fat man named Halbertson."

He turned to face the others. "Do any of you know aught of this man?"

One young chap, whom I had nursed during our first days together in the prison and who remained too weak to do more than sit up, spoke. "I know that my own brother could not have treated me more tenderly. I would have died without his help and care. He is a Christian and an American. That is all I want or need to know about him."

"Yes, yes; but is he not charged with being an American spy?"

"We have assumed so," another of our original prisoners said. "The British have treated him most severely."

"Yes, yes. But if he really were a spy, they would have hanged or shot him by now, surely."

"See here," another prisoner said. "What are you getting at?"

"I suspect this fellow of having been planted here. I say he is a British, not an American spy."

Without thinking, I arose and seized the man by his jacket lapels. Through clenched teeth I growled, "Lay off, my friend, or you will regret it."

He showed no trace of fear as he replied, "Then let us hear you deny that you are in league with the British."

"I am no spy of any sort."

"Which side are you on, then?"

"I am an American."

"That is no answer. Are you Whig or Tory? Tell us straight out."

One of the old men joined in. "It's a plain enough question. Why don't you answer it?"

"Yes," another prisoner chimed in. "We have left you alone, thinking you one of us. But now that the matter is out in the open, why not declare yourself?"

"He doesn't answer because he is a British spy. That is it."

Before I could mount any kind of defense, the newcomer had stirred up my fellow prisoners into a mob that would have tarred and feathered me if they could. I grew furious, first at my tormentor and then at the others, including those I had nursed back to health. Two of the stronger men tried to seize my arms, but despite my chains, I flung them off.

"Keep away. You are making a dreadful mistake."

"No mistake. He's a Tory. He's our enemy."

Foolishly, heatedly, I blurted, "Not true! I was at Lexington. I was a friend of Dr. Joseph Warren. I provided a good part of the army with tents and blankets and—"

"It's a lie! You must have been working for the British, or you would not have been in their company."

"No, I was working for the Americans."

"Do you swear it?" one of the old men asked.

"I swear it."

The provocateur smiled and folded his arms. "Guard!" he called.

The door swung opened, and there stood Cunningham and Major Tuttle.

Major Tuttle shook the hands of the supposed American spy and the two elderly gentlemen. "Congratulations," he said. "You have done well. I have been wanting to break that one down for months. He is all yours, Cunningham."

Whatever remote feelings of affection I might have felt for the English were dissipated during the long, excruciating night that followed. Cunningham and two redcoats took me to a far corner room of the basement, stripped off my filthy blouse, tied my hands high over my head, and whipped me, first with straps and then with a cat-of-nine.

After a taste of each, Cunningham called a halt and gave me a chance to confess.

Gritting my teeth against the pain, I said. "Nothing to confess. I have told all there is to tell."

"You liar," he said. And to drive his point home, he smashed his fist against my chin.

I would have sold my soul to Satan to have the chance to meet this ogre on equal terms. I cursed him, which earned me a blow that knocked me senseless.

They doused me with water, and I came to with my knees slack and my arms nearly pulled from their sockets by my unconscious weight. I blinked the water out of my eyes and straightened up.

Tuttle stood in front of me now. "Look here, Martin, you are a brave, stout fellow. I don't want to have to bring Cunningham back in here. We heard what you said in there. We know you were spying for the rebels. Well, maybe you were caught in the middle. Saw a chance to make a bit of coin from both sides. That was it, wasn't it?"

"Go to hell!"

"Come, come. I thought you were smarter than that. We've got the goods on you. You told an entire roomful of people that you were working for Warren. So why not sign a paper telling just what you did? Don't force me to bring Cunningham back in here."

"I came to Boston to deliver messages for Sir Francis Bolton, and you recruited me to spy for the British. That's all."

"Yes, but what about your relationship with Dr. Warren?"

"I sold him some tents and blankets for the militia."

"But what about Lexington and Concord?"

"I merely observed those battles."

He looked into my eyes for a long while, then said, "One more chance. Will you sign a statement admitting your guilt?"

"Never! I refuse to say another word. Go to hell!"

He turned and called for Cunningham.

I held out until nearly dawn. By that time my back was crisscrossed with long, deep lacerations. The blood ran down my backside and into my shoes. Both my eyes were swollen shut, and my jaw felt as if Cunningham's fist had broken it. I passed out more than once and each time was brought to with a bucket of cold water. Each time there stood Tuttle, offering me a fresh opportunity to escape my torture by signing a paper saying I had spied for the Americans.

About 4 P.M. they forced my mouth open and poured a cupful of croton oil down my throat. The results not only created a boiling turmoil in my guts and a stinking mess down my legs, they robbed me of all dignity. So when Tuttle returned with handkerchief to his nose and a look of disgust on his face to ask if I had come to my senses and was ready to sign my confession, I said, "Lead me to your goddamn paper."

They unchained my arms and legs and allowed me to strip off my filthy clothes. After sluicing me down with cold water, they provided me with a cloth and some rough workman's clothing and shoes.

Tuttle set an inkwell and pen in front of me. There I sat, my blouse sticking to my still-bloody back, my bowels aching. I was stripped of all dignity with no friend to advise me; no one cared one whit whether I lived or died. I had been brought about as low as a person could be. As I reached for the pen, I glanced at the face of Major Tuttle. It bore an expression of triumph.

"Sign there, Martin. There's a good fellow."

I looked at him again, and this time he was smiling. It was a sort of smirk, mixing contempt with triumph. That did it. I let out a growl like that of a cornered bear and swept the document and inkwell to the floor.

Tuttle stepped back, his look of victory replaced by one of alarm. I arose shakily.

"I am an American! I demand a trial with a jury!"

"Don't be a fool, Martin. Sign that paper, and I may get you off with a prison term. You're guilty as hell and you know it. I would hate to have to turn you back over to Cunningham."

At last, in exasperation he had me thrown into a solitary cell in the basement with orders that I was to have only bread and water.

Cunningham opened the door of my cell two days later. I assumed he had come to take me before a firing squad. I still thought so when a squad of soldiers carried me out and placed me in a cart.

It had been early summer when first I was dragged through the front door of the prison. Now the leaves along Treamont Street and on Beacon Hill were turning, and there was a chill in the air. The people along the streets looked gaunt and shabby. The sight of yet another prisoner drew no attention.

The cart stopped in front of Province House, and I was half-carried into the front hall. Before I could take it all in, I was ushered into the presence of General Thomas Gage, commander-in-chief of the British forces in America and Royal Governor of Massachusetts. Speaking from hindsight, he was the man who touched off the American Revolution by sending soldiers out to Concord and other high-handed actions.

I had observed him from a distance on Copp's Hill the morning of the battle. Now, at close hand, I could see that he was a slender fellow with a long nose and a melancholy expression, caused perhaps by a recently received order to turn over his command to General William Howe and return to England.

Tuttle, his face as red as a turkey's comb, was standing in Gage's office.

"You are Jeremiah Martin, I believe," Gage said.

"Yes, I am," I mumbled through swollen lips.

"And you are employed by Sir Francis Bolton."

"I delivered some messages for him, yes."

Tuttle spoke up in a low even voice, as if he were fighting to control himself. "I tell you, sir, this man was spying for Dr. Warren. We have his confession."

"A confession? In writing?"

"No, not in writing. But I have witnesses who heard him admit it."

Suddenly it felt as if a ray of sunshine had burst into the room. My mind cleared in a flash, and I declared, "He tried to trick me into saying I spied. But it was a lie! He even had me tortured and tried to make me sign a written confession, but I refused because I am innocent. I demand a trial by jury!"

Tuttle shot me a look of pure hatred.

I pressed my advantage. "He enlisted me into his own spy service. I risked my life to seek out information in the American camps, and after I returned he threw me into prison!"

"This fellow is the most arrant liar I have ever met," Tuttle said. "You cannot believe a word he says."

Gage cut him off. "That may be your opinion, but I have known Sir Francis Bolton for many a year, and he seems to hold this Jeremiah Martin in higher esteem. He has sent a letter asking me, if possible, to locate this fellow and send him back to Barbados on his sloop, which has just delivered us a much-needed lot of molasses and rum."

"Sir," Tuttle said, "this man is an American spy. I am convinced of it. He deserves to be hanged."

Gage shook his head. "You *think* he was an American spy. But both you and he admit that he was a British spy. Perhaps he was both. Who knows? Indeed, who cares? I know only that he is an agent for Sir Francis, and that my old friend wishes him to be delivered back to him in Barbados. Oh dear, I hope that his appearance will improve on the return voyage. I should hate for Sir Francis to see him in this shocking condition. Really, Tuttle, I wonder if you did not go too far with this young man."

Again Tuttle sputtered, but Gage cut him off with a faint smile. "See him down to the Long Wharf, where Sir Francis's sloop *Charlotte* is tied up. Deliver him to Captain Fitzgerald. Send along a new suit and shoes. Well now, Master Martin, there is an end to your difficulties. Awfully sorry about the misunderstanding. Don't feel too hard toward Major Tuttle. Sometimes we grow overly vigilant in our zeal to do our duty, what? Pity I did not receive Sir Francis's letter sooner. It would have saved you some discomfort and Major Tuttle a deal of trouble. But all's well that ends well. Do give my very best regards to Sir Francis, will you, Mister Martin? The sloop sails at noon. Bon voyage."

2

As his final act of revenge, Major Tuttle dismissed the cart that had transported me from the jail to Province House and—accompanied by a squad of soldiers—forced me to march down King Street to the Long Wharf. At every step of that Golgothan path he berated me as a traitor and a fraud. Twice I stumbled and fell, which afforded him the pleasure of assisting me to my feet with a vigorous kick.

Far out toward the end of the Long Wharf, he called a halt and stood before me with outthrust chin.

"You're lucky this ship came before General Gage leaves and General Howe takes over. God help you if you ever set foot in Boston again."

"What's going on down there?" a squat man with an orange beard called from the quarterdeck of the sloop.

"On General Gage's instructions, I am to deliver into the custody of Captain Fitzgerald this scoundrel who goes under the name of Jeremiah Martin."

"I am Fitzgerald. Bring the fellow aboard."

The soldiers stood aside, and I got a better look at Atticus Fitzgerald. He was dressed immaculately, in the style of a British naval captain *sans* insignia. He reminded me of a small red rooster.

But it was not Fitzgerald that held my attention; it was the ship he commanded. I would have fallen in love with the *Charlotte* at first sight, even if she had not represented my deliverance from hanging. Just as a petite, coiffured beauty stands out in a roomful of disheveled women, so did this exquisitely crafted sloop make the other vessels tied up to the Long Wharf that October morning look frumpy.

I soon learned that she had been built to Bolton's specifications the previous year by master craftsmen in Bermuda. From her high, curved stern, set with small glassed windows, she stretched seventy-five feet to an ornate bow graced by the carved bust of a beautiful woman. She measured twenty feet across at her widest point. A commodious, raised quarterdeck occupied more than a third of her aft section. In front of that, on the main deck, was lashed a long boat. The single towering mast was seated well forward of midships, and her boom stretched clear past her stern. And beyond her bow protruded a long bowsprit.

Captain Fitzgerald waited with his arms folded across his chest as my trembling legs carried me over the gangplank.

"So they found you. No gear? You look like a man who's been keelhauled. Don't know what the old man wants with the likes of you, but I'm glad I can deliver him the goods, damaged though they be. What's that?"

Tuttle explained again that my wrists were to remain bound until we were at sea and that he would leave two soldiers on the wharf to make sure I did not jump ship.

So, aching in every bone and too weak to stand, I leaned against the mainmast of that immaculately kept vessel while the crew completed the complicated business of readying her for sea.

About half the *Charlotte*'s dozen sailors were black and, judging from their accents, of Barbadian birth; the others sounded like Irishmen and Cockneys for the most part. Fitzgerald shouted his orders with a Dublin lilt. Befuddled though I was, it did not take me long to recognize that he was a most unlikable man but that he knew how to run a ship. Evidently the crew feared and maybe even hated him, but they did his sarcastic bidding without a murmur.

Having gone unfed since eating my portion of jail swill the previous day, I grew fainter as the morning wore on. My back hurt, and my head ached. I sat on the deck and put my forehead on my bent knees. I was vastly relieved at escaping both prison and the gallows, yet I felt a curious dread about what lay before me.

I raised my head at the sound of a female voice from the wharf. It was Malinda, Madame LaFontaine's maid. She wore a scarf over her head and carried a cloth-covered basket. The soldiers were telling her they would not permit her to board the ship; she replied that it was not their vessel but Sir Francis Bolton's. Then Captain Fitzgerald entered the discussion. He too denied her admission but in the end compromised by allowing me to come to the rail to talk.

"You done got youself into a big mess," she said.

"Actually, I think I'm getting out of one."

"Well, Madame, she had been worried about you. She want to come down to say good-bye, but she think it look bad to old Tuttle."

"It is all right, Malinda. I understand."

"She say to tell you good-bye and say she hope you meet again. She say take good care of youself."

"Tell her I thank her—for everything."

"And she say to give you this."

She held out the basket. The two soldiers moved in before I could reach out. She refused to surrender the basket to them. At last Fitzgerald took custody of it.

"Ain't nothing but some ointment for his back and something to eat and drink."

The captain raised the cloth for a perfunctory search, then handed the basket to me.

The aroma of fresh-baked bread and meat made my mouth water.

"Tell Madame LaFontaine that I shall never forget her or her kindness," I said.

Fitzgerald ordered me to carry my basket up to the quarterdeck so I would be out of the way of his crew as they swung the giant boom into position and raised the fore-and-aft mainsail. Then the pilot came aboard, and they cast off.

I sat on the quarterdeck hatch in front of the tiller and, despite my bound wrists, managed to stuff my mouth with bread and chicken. The ship's cook, a black Bajan with massive chest and forearms, took pity on me and uncorked one of the bottles of wine. On an empty stomach, the wine quickly went to my head. I turned around and watched the hills and spires of Boston grow smaller and smaller. I should have been filled with great happiness over my escape, and indeed I was relieved, but as we hove to off Castle William Island and waited for a boat to come and take off our pilot, a feeling of gloom fell upon me. It struck me that I was leaving not just Boston but my homeland, America. Although no longer a prisoner of the British, had I not become the captive of the architect of my recent troubles, Sir Francis Bolton?

Captain Fitzgerald reassumed control of the ship. He ordered the square-rigged topsail to be hoisted, and with a brisk quartering breeze he set a course for the helmsman. Then he came over and scrutinized me as if I were some sort of captured animal. I was about to enlarge my hatred to include him when he asked, "Do you play chess, Martin?"

"A little. Why?"

"Do you snore?"

"Not that I know of."

"Do you mind snoring?"

"I am a sound sleeper. Why do you ask?"

"I've been turning it over in my mind whether to put you in the fo'csle or to give you a bunk in my cabin under the quarterdeck."

"It is up to you, sir," I said. "Either way, I am very weary."

He had the first mate unbind my wrists and show me to my bunk in his cabin. The ocean swells rocked me to sleep so soundly that it was the next morning before I awakened.

There were times during those next six weeks when I regretted my decision to bunk in Captain Fitzgerald's cabin rather than in the forecastle with the crew. He did indeed snore, yes, and he talked in his sleep as well. And he ground his teeth. I never grew so weary of anyone's company as that of Atticus Fitzgerald. Besides all that, he was an abominable but dogged chess player. I had to work hard to lose an occasional game, for he would not let me stop playing until he had won. Although he rarely wasted a word in directing his crew, he never stopped talking to me except when he was pondering his next chess move.

Still, let it be said that he was a competent captain, and I learned much from him about sailing, Sir Francis Bolton, the crew, the *Charlotte*, and, yes, Atticus Fitzgerald himself.

Just as I thought, he had been born in Dublin, of an Irish father and an English mother. While still a lad, he had gone into the British navy with hopes of eventually winning command of his own ship. After twenty years he had still been only a lieutenant, and it became obvious even to him that his lack of formal education barred him from further promotion.

Judged by his chess playing and by the paucity of his reading material, he was a man of pedestrian intellect. He was stubborn and painstaking and on the whole unimaginative. He showed passion only when he talked about the *Charlotte*. From him I learned the details of her construction, including the fact that Sir Francis had gone to the considerable expense of having her bottom sheathed in copper as a defense against barnacles and sea worms.

He spoke of the sloop's characteristics as a dull but fond husband might praise the talents of an accomplished wife.

The frigate on which Fitzgerald had served in the navy had called at Bridgetown three years earlier. There he had met Bolton and disclosed his disillusionment with the navy. The old man signed him into his own service by telling him of his plans to have a sloop tailor-made to carry light cargoes and messages between Barbados, other West Indian islands, and North America. He needed a disciplined seaman to oversee the construction, sign up and train the crew, and take command of the vessel. So he got himself a captain who was as loyal as a dog.

Growing increasing bored with the captain, I began to make friends with the crew, especially with the black cook, Cato, who was kind enough to apply Madame LaFontaine's ointment to my lacerated back. Observing my growing popularity among the men, Fitzgerald sarcastically suggested that I might prefer to sleep in the forecastle rather than in his cabin. I got the hint and eased off on fraternizing with his crew.

My hatred for things and persons British still festered long after

I left Boston, but it took only a week or two for me to recover physically. After that I pitched in and helped steer the *Charlotte*. Off Cape Hatteras I lent a hand at hauling down the mainsail during a brief storm. Captain Fitzgerald helped me brush up on my navigational skills. On the whole, the time passed agreeably.

One morning I awoke to see a bluish lump on the southern horizon. By noon the *Charlotte* had drawn near enough to the north headland of Barbados that I could make out houses through the captain's spyglass. Throughout the afternoon, as the vessel tacked back and forth against an easterly trade wind, I could see more and more clearly with the naked eye that, far from the jungle I had imagined, Barbados appeared to be nearly void of trees. The terrain rose from the palm-lined eastern coast in a series of long, terracelike plateaus, every foot of which seemed to be planted with sugar cane, right up to the dominating peak, marked on Captain Fitzgerald's map as Mount Hillaby.

I was surprised, too, by the number of windmills I observed on the island and by the numerous ships anchored in the broad waters of Carlisle Bay. Nor was I prepared for Bridgetown. What a bustling place it was! Its houses and other buildings looked as handsome as those of Philadelphia. But the damp heat was something else. Even though the sun was beginning to set, I was soaked with sweat by the time the long boat put me and Captain Fitzgerald ashore.

The dock at Bridgetown was thronged, mostly with planters garbed in long linen coats, wide-brimmed straw hats, and boots and carrying short whips. Others were dressed in dark suits, like the merchants and lawyers they turned out to be, plus a sprinkling of Negroes and quite a few ragged, barefoot poor whites with sunburned complexions.

Captain Fitzgerald and I were surrounded by this polyglot crowd, all clamoring for news from America and demanding to know what cargo we had brought back.

"Jerry! Jerry! Over here."

From the rear ranks of the crowd, Ephraim McGee was waving his hat and jumping up and down to attract my attention.

3

THE SKIN on his nose peeling and his hands a nut brown, this was a new and healthier Ephraim McGee than the one to whom I had said good-bye in Philadelphia six months before.

"I didn't think they could possibly find you," he said. "By the way, this is Ibo. He's been with Sir Francis since childhood."

A plump shiny-faced Negro, dressed in a short, white robe and wearing a sort of fez, bowed and said in a squeaky English accent, "My childhood, not his." Then he added with a giggle, "I am most sincerely pleased to make your acquaintance. The master has spoken often of you."

Ephraim explained that they had sighted the *Charlotte* from Bolton Hall around noon as we were tacking our way south, "but it took you so long to get here we'll have to take lodgings for the night."

The Bow Bells, on Bridgetown's Broad Street, was a first-rate establishment, and we enjoyed an excellent supper there, marred only by the tiresome presence of Captain Fitzgerald. But even if we had been alone, it would have been difficult to converse, what with the stream of planters and merchants stopping by to pump us for news from Boston.

Fortunately, Ephraim had booked a separate room for Fitzgerald. In the privacy of our own shared room, I brought him up to date on my misadventures and trials of recent months.

"And you really think they meant to hang you?"

"If your Sir Francis's letter had not arrived in the nick of time, the world would now be shut of Jeremiah Martin."

"He is not *my* Sir Francis!"

Taken aback by his uncharacteristic vehemence, I could only say, "Oh?"

At first Ephraim was reluctant to talk, but I kept after him until he confessed that he had learned to despise Sir Francis Bolton and wanted desperately to return to Philadelphia and claim his precious Laura Mason. "But that calculating, cold-blooded, avaricious old man is practically forcing me to remain here in Barbados," he said.

With feigned piety, I expressed surprise that he harbored such feelings toward a poor old invalid.

"Poor?" he snorted. "He has as much wealth as any person I know, and yet he must always press for more. He can be gracious and even superficially kind, but it's always for a selfish purpose."

I suggested that Ephraim was exaggerating. That touched off a fresh tirade.

"You say General Gage himself ordered your release? You can bet your last farthing that sometime in the past Bolton did something to put Gage in his debt."

"Whatever the obligation, it has benefited me. Look here, Ephraim, it is unlike you to dislike anyone so much."

"Bolton is more Machiavellian than Machiavelli himself. He uses people, Jerry."

The hour was late, and frankly Ephraim was beginning to bore me with his harangue. To get him off the subject, I asked why the old man had gone to such lengths to bring me back to Barbados.

"He seems to have developed a peculiar personal interest in you. He has pumped me dry for information about you and your family."

"Is he some sort of pederast?"

"His only passion is for wealth and power over people. But he seems more than usually interested in you."

I lay awake long into the stiflingly hot night puzzling over what Ephraim had said.

The next morning, after a good, English-style breakfast, Ibo brought the carriage around, and the four of us, including Fitzgerald, set out for Bolton Hall, which overlooked the western coast of Barbados about ten miles north of Bridgetown. The road led us up a slope to a long plateau that afforded us a grand view of Carlisle Bay and Bridgetown. From there, Ibo drove our two smart gray horses past mile after mile of canefields in various stages of growth.

We had Negroes and plantations a-plenty in Virginia but I had never seen so many black slaves as labored away here, in close ranks under the hard eyes of armed and mounted overseers. It was bad enough to be a slave even under an owner as kind as my late father, but I could see that Virginia would have seemed a paradise to the hard-driven Africans drudging away in those Barbadian canefields in the merciless heat.

At last, we turned off onto a palm-lined lane that led to a massive, two-story house built of coral stone and surrounded by a deep veranda. Sir Francis himself waited on the front step. He welcomed me warmly and ordered Ibo to find me a hat so that "our young doctor friend can show Master Martin around our humble estate while Captain Fitzgerald and I conduct a bit of business."

With 350 acres of reddish, coral soil, a windmill, a furnace room, and large curing shed, Bolton Hall was a veritable sugar factory, operated by 200 blacks. Many of them, according to Ephraim, were descended from slaves owned by the first Bolton on Barbados, Sir Francis's grandfather.

The truth of Ephraim's grievances against his employer were revealed on that tour of the plantation. First we stopped at the so-called Negro Yard, two long lines of huts situated several hundred yards "downwind" from the great house. I commented on the orderliness of the settlement and the generally healthy appearance of the slaves.

Ephraim snorted. "Of course they are healthy. It makes economic sense to keep them well. That is why the old man employs me. But let them show the slightest resistance to his will—well, I'll tell you, just after I arrived a fine strapping slave went on a hunger strike. Refused to eat or work. Bolton wanted to mate him with a young female, but the fellow had fallen in love with a wench at the next plantation. The overseer wanted to flog him into submission, but Sir Francis simply called in a slave dealer who was buying up a cargo to ship to Jamaica."

We got even closer to the truth when we visited the curing sheds. There hundreds of conical "pots" of sugar stood about for the molasses to seep into a drain pipe. A tall, lean white man with sky-blue eyes and iron-gray hair was supervising the crew, who were emptying sugar from the cured pots into a hogshead.

"Mr. Ramsay," Ephraim said, "this is my long-time friend, Jeremiah Martin. Mr. Ramsay is the overseer."

Ignoring my presence, Ramsay said in a Scots accent, "No reason Portia can't return to the fields, is there? Been two weeks since her bairn was born."

"You know Sir Francis agreed they should have a month off."

"Ye're pampering them."

"No, Mr. Ramsay, it is an investment in good health."

Ramsay walked away, muttering to himself.

"There goes an example of Bolton's hypocrisy and machinations," Ephraim whispered. "Ramsay was captured at the Battle of Culloden as a youth some thirty years ago. They 'barbadosed' him—exiled him out here. Bolton bought his indenture. Found he was clever but distraught because he had left a sweetheart back in the Highlands. So Bolton sent back for the girl. Ramsay married her and was made overseer. Today he'd jump off that windmill if the old man asked him to."

Ephraim paused, then continued with tears in his eyes. "And he'd flog a black slave who loved someone as deeply as he loved his lassie. See, there's the injustice. You can buy another fieldhand for only twenty pounds. Mustn't go too far catering to their wishes, or you'll give them notions. As Bolton puts it, 'Better to sell a bad actor off to Jamaica now and then. You get money with which to buy a replacement, you get rid of the problem, and it serves as a good example for the others.' That incident alone was enough to sour me on life in Barbados."

To draw Ephraim out even more, I defended Bolton by suggesting that, after all, he had done the Scot a great favor.

Then the full truth emerged. It seems that after the incident of the lovesick slave, Bolton had asked Ephraim to extend his one-year contract and stay to continue his medical supervision of the plantation. In an effort to break down Ephraim's resistance, he had proposed to use his influence to persuade Dr. Mason to allow Laura to marry.

"And he even offered to provide for her transportation out here. That was when I told him that I could never be purchased as he did Ramsay. Things have been very cool between us since."

Back at the mansion, I endured one last meal with Captain Fitzgerald. Then he departed to sea after tidying up the *Charlotte* from her Boston voyage.

During the month that I remained at Bolton Hall, Sir Francis Bolton barely spoke to Ephraim, but he spent hour after hour talking to me. Whatever Ephraim had prescribed for him, his voice was less raspy now, and he coughed less than he had in Philadelphia.

I was both repulsed and fascinated by the old man. Unlike Captain Fitzgerald he had the ability to sense when he was starting to wear thin. He would halt in midsentence and suddenly solicit my opinion on a matter or ask yet another question about my family.

The old man arose at dawn and went straight to writing letters and laboring over his account books. Often after breakfast a lawyer or merchant from Bridgetown would appear, and there would follow intense conversation about shipments of sugar or insurance questions on ships. He would dispatch his letters back to Bridgetown with these visitors, eat a light midday meal, and nap for half an hour. In the afternoons he conferred with Ramsay about the plantation and normally read a book or played a game of chess with Ibo. He was delighted to learn that I played the game.

"Good, good. Ibo is a competent player. Taught him myself, but he is too cautious. It will be good to try someone with a different style."

Sir Francis was a far better player than Atticus Fitzgerald. I advanced to the attack right off. We traded a knight for a bishop. He avoided my rash challenge to swap queens, absorbed my assault, and in about half an hour checked me.

Ibo came out onto the veranda with glasses of wine laced with honey. Sir Francis allowed the African to stay and watch our second game.

Having learned the old man's style, I played more conservatively. The game ended in a draw after more than an hour. Sir Francis complimented me upon my flexibility of play.

We played again the next afternoon. This time Ibo looked on with a sandglass to limit our moves to three minutes each. Sir Francis moved quickly to the attack, placing his pieces without hesitation. While I pondered my moves, he drummed his fingers on his chair arm and talked to Ibo. I found this disconcerting. He won that game.

I asked for an immediate rematch, and Sir Francis granted it with the understanding that we not "waste so much time between moves."

I swallowed my irritation and feigned an opening attack, then pulled back and castled. Thereafter I played a deliberate game in which I frustrated his every attack. And while he pondered his responses, *I* talked to Ibo. Standing behind his master's chair, Ibo grinned and nodded at my impertinence. I fended off the old man's final attack and put his queen and a rook into a fork with my knight. Ibo put his hand over his mouth to keep from laughing. As I reached over to claim Sir Francis's rook, the old man coughed and crossed his legs so that one of his knees upset the board, spilling the pieces all over the floor.

"What a pity," he said. "Forgive my clumsiness. Well, another day perhaps."

But we played no more chess. Thereafter our time together was spent in conversation.

He barely touched on my activities in Boston until after I had been at Bolton Hall for more than a week. One evening as we sat on his veranda watching the sun sink into the Caribbean, he turned to me and said, "Fitzgerald tells me that you were under suspicion as a spy for the rebels. Said they were ready to hang you when he appeared with my letter to Gage."

"They did accuse me of spying."

"Come, come. Don't evade. Tell me the truth of the matter."

So I repeated the story I had spun for Tuttle, namely that I had sold supplies to the Americans but that I had entered Boston solely to deliver his—Bolton's—messages. "Before I knew it, I was trapped into working for this Major Tuttle."

"Whether you are telling me the whole truth or not, Jeremiah, you are a resourceful fellow. Now that you are safe from hanging, what do you propose to do with yourself?"

"I would return to America if I had anyone there to return to."

"You like money, don't you."

"I would rather have it than not."

"And you are both adaptable and tenacious. I can see that from your chess. Admirable qualities."

"I have been forced to be so, sir."

"Yes, well, these are traits one rarely finds in a person who is both young and physically robust, as you are."

"What are you getting at, sir?"

"You met Halbertson in Boston. He is one of my many agents. But I have no one person on whom I can rely to coordinate my business affairs. A trustworthy person to help me with my correspondence and, when the occasion demands, to represent me on voyages of a confidential nature. After all, I'm not getting any younger. How would you like to serve as my personal secretary?"

I was so surprised that I could only stammer, "You know, sir, that I am an American. I can never be anything else."

"Oh, come, you are going to disappoint me as your young physician friend has? For all his intelligence, he is a naïve fool. He has spurned my patronage. I have nothing but contempt for such posturing piety."

"Allow me to think about what you propose, sir."

"Oh yes, think about it. By the bye, Fitzgerald thinks well of you. Have never known him to like anyone before. You have a way with people—no doubt about it. And brains and ambition, too, if I'm not mistaken. By all means think it over. Think it over."

I went to bed with my head reeling after that conversation in the soft Barbadian night. What if I should refuse the old man? He could have me shipped back to Boston in chains if he chose. I had no other employment. Maybe, I told myself, just maybe the King would come to his senses and make peace with America. In Barbados, at any rate, I heard little sentiment for strong British prosecution of the war. In fact, the war caused the island to suffer from the interruption of her trade with North America, which was the source of most of her basic supplies and an important market for her sugar, rum, and molasses.

Ephraim was so indignant at hearing Sir Francis's proposal to me that I wished I had not told him. He grew even more agitated when he realized that I was considering the old man's offer. His self-righteousness irritated me so that I lashed back at him. "That's easy for you to say, you little prig! You have a family and a profession awaiting you back in Pennsylvania. I have nothing and nobody."

I checked myself when I saw a hurt look on his face.

"Come, Ephraim, let us not quarrel. Just don't be quite so hasty in judging people who have lived through very different experiences from your own."

He said, "All the same, Jerry, I hope you will spurn his offer. My year's contract will expire next June. Let us return to America together. Laura has many friends in Philadelphia. There is sure to be just the right wife for you there, and plenty of opportunity, too."

The following day Sir Francis arose early and left by carriage to confer with the Royal Governor in Bridgetown. Bored with myself and the plantation, I asked Ibo if he would like to play a game of chess.

There followed a two-hour match that ended in a deadlock. I expressed surprise at his skill.

"You think because I am black, I have no mind?" he said, then giggled as if to remove any sting from his remark.

"No, but Sir Francis said you were little challenge to him."

Ibo looked at me slyly and said, "Perhaps I do not wish to challenge my master overmuch. It would hardly be politic."

I regarded his plump countenance with new respect.

"You have been with Sir Francis for many years?"

"He bought me in Africa when I was scarcely weaned, from an Arab slave dealer on the Gold Coast."

"Your English is flawless."

"Why should it not be? Sir Francis taught me the language. And

I have visited England more than once with the master. It is a grand tongue, don't you think?"

I had guessed from the timbre of his voice and from his plumpness that he was a eunuch but restrained myself from questioning him on that score.

"Do you like the master?" he asked.

"I find him fascinating."

"That is not the same thing."

"Do you like Sir Francis?" I asked him.

"Like you, I find him fascinating. He treats me well. My life has been—still is—most interesting because of him. So I devote my life to his comfort. What choice do I have?"

"What if you had remained in Africa?"

"I would not live so well as I do here, certainly. But I would have a wife, perhaps several wives, and many children. I would be a man."

His eyes turned cold and his face seemed to harden with these bitter words. He bowed low and left me on the veranda. I was still pondering what he had said when Sir Francis's carriage appeared in the lane. I went out to meet him and tried to help him climb down, but Sir Francis pushed my hand away and entered the house without speaking.

He remained in a black, uncommunicative mood throughout our supper. I did not learn what was bothering him until that evening, when he summoned me to join him on the veranda for what had become a ritual of watching the sun set. Even then I had to ask him if anything was wrong.

"Is anything right? This bloody war has become a blasted nuisance. Here we are with our first decent sugar harvest in three seasons, and now there is talk of shipping delays until we can arrange convoys to England."

"Why is that, sir?"

"Danger of privateers."

"But I have heard of no privateers in these waters."

"Not yet perhaps, but if this war drags on, you will. Already the insurance rates will have to go up. That will benefit my insurance interests in London, of course."

"Then you have nothing to worry about."

"It's more than that. The army in Boston wants this island to send them food."

"And will you?"

"The governor wants to very badly. It would make him look good in the eyes of London. But planters who sit in our Assembly here are of a different mind. They fear a slave revolt if we cut back rations."

"There seems to be food aplenty."

"There is for the present. But with no more coming in from your accursed country, we will soon run out unless we switch from growing cane to growing foodstuffs."

"And that upsets you."

"It certainly does not please me to think of diverting a considerable part of our land to feed slaves whose purpose is to produce sugar. It's bad economics. Yet eighty percent of our population are slaves, and they must be fed."

"Pardon me for saying so, sir, but it seems to me that as this plantation is but one of your many interests . . ." I paused, thinking I might be going to far.

"You are perceptive. I live here because it is my home. My real financial interests lie elsewhere. This is where I was born, where my grandmother came to settle as a girl from England over a century ago. She was the bride of the cavalier who first worked this land as a white slave in bondage to a Cromwellian planter. I cannot abandon this plantation."

He went on to tell me that the planters were in an uproar over reports that a delegation of British officers was expected soon from Boston to impress livestock and foodstuffs for Howe's besieged army. "The governor has sent back exaggerated reports of our food reserves. As always, the planters—who already despise the governor—want to hoard their supplies."

"What position will you take, sir?"

"I should like to hear your advice, young man."

I thought furiously, then took a deep breath and replied, "Well, sir, when one sees a thing is inevitable, often the best course is to swim with the tide rather than against it."

"What are you getting at?"

"I assume the army will send agents here, and they will take what they need for your soldiers in Boston no matter how your planters whine and complain. But really, sir, I don't know enough of your local politics to advise you on specifics."

We said our good nights. The next morning he invited me to join him on the veranda for breakfast.

"I lay awake late last night pondering your advice, Jeremiah. I am thinking of arranging a cargo of sheep and cattle and other foodstuffs and shipping it up to Boston on my own. I will contribute some of my own livestock, and I will buy what I can from other planters. If I pay enough, they will sell, never fear."

"Will the army cover your costs?"

"That does not matter. We can make it up on the return voyage."

He went on to outline a plan to send the cargo over to Boston in the *Charlotte* and then have the vessel stop off in Philadelphia to pick up wheat and maize to be brought back to Barbados. Where, in his words, "We'll sell it for more than enough to pay for the army's cargo. I will make a cash profit, but more important"—he chuckled—"I will have demonstrated once again my devotion to our glorious empire."

I reminded him that since the *Charlotte* was considered a British vessel, she would hardly be allowed to anchor in American-held waters.

"She will be a British vessel when she enters Boston. On her return, there is a way to turn her into an American craft temporarily. Here, pull your chair closer. We must not be overheard."

4

OVER RAMSAY'S OBJECTIONS, Sir Francis had half the sheep, cattle, and pigs on his plantation rounded up and driven down to Bridgetown. With the help of a factor in the town, he purchased dozens of barrels of salted fish that had originally come from Canada, plus a quantity of the flour and corn meal that the assemblymen had protested they had so little of. He paid premium prices, but he was depleting the island's food reserves so that he would receive even higher prices for what he would bring back from America under his complicated scheme.

Because he did not know what was up and observed me working so closely with the old man, Ephraim practically stopped speaking to me. I sometimes caught Ibo staring at me as though in reproach. At the end of the week, with the cargo all put together, Sir Francis and I visited the office of a lawyer on Bridgetown's narrow little Swan or Jews' Street to order certain papers drawn up. The lawyer was a slight, sandy-haired chap with a very English accent. His eyebrows went up—as did mine—when Sir Francis referred to me as his personal secretary. He had not mentioned that post since our talk on his veranda three weeks before, but I let it pass.

The lawyer observed that Bolton was putting much trust in his "young American friend."

"I will have him under bond, never fear."

"Quite so, Sir Francis. I have never known you not to protect your flanks."

On our carriage ride back to Bolton Hall for my final night at the plantation, Sir Francis once again raised the subject of Ephraim.

"He is an excellent physican but a fool nonetheless."

I saw a glimmer of hope for Ephraim. "Do you wish him to return to America with me?"

"No!" he said with rare force. "He made a bargain to remain here until next June—let him live up to it!" Then his voice softened. "I offered to persuade my old friend, Dr. Mason, to allow his talented daughter to come out here and marry him. The young fool spurned my generous offer."

"If I may be so bold, Sir Francis, I think Ephraim regarded your offer as an attempt to place him in bondage."

"Nonsense! It would give me great pleasure to have a young, attractive couple about Bolton Hall. She is a lovely girl. Have you met her?"

"Yes, briefly. She is an accomplished pianist, too."

"So she is. I have heard her play."

He remained quiet until our carriage neared the lane to Bolton Hall.

"You have noticed the portrait in my drawing room."

"Yes. It is of your grandmother."

"Indeed. That painting was made on behalf of her second husband, a physician, when she was in her midthirties. I do not remember my late mother. My grandmother, who was by then a widow, reared me. She retained her beauty into her old age."

"It is a an excellent portrait," I said, although in truth I had paid little attention to it.

"Quite. Tomorrow, when the morning sun comes in, open the blinds and look closely at the portrait. See if you do not discern a resemblance to Laura Mason."

I promised to do that; then I added that if he did not mind my saying so, he might be better served if he allowed Ephraim to return to America and authorized me to bring back another young physician to take his place.

His voice cracked like a whip. "Never! I always live up to my contracts. Let him learn to do the same. Do not interfere." Then as our carriage stopped and Ibo jumped down to hold the horses' reins so we could dismount, he put his hand on my arm and whispered, "However, you would place me forever in your debt if you were to find the means to deliver a message from me to Dr. Mason and if you were to help me persuade her to come out here and join our headstrong young physician—as his bride. I think he would not be so eager to leave my employ then, do you?"

Appalled by the old man's connivance, I replied, "Ephraim is so unpredictable, I really cannot say."

The next morning, as Ibo was harnessing the carriage to carry us down to Bridgetown, Ephraim came up from the Negro yard to bid me a rather frosty farewell. I ignored his hand and, turning to Sir Francis, said with an ironic grin, "Could Dr. McGee not ride with us?"

Without enthusiasm, the old man replied, "If he wishes."

I turned and winked at Ephraim, who I could tell was at the point of saying he did not want to go.

In Bridgetown, Sir Francis and I left Ephraim at the Bow Bells

106

while we returned to the lawyer's office to sign the bond and other agreed-upon papers. Then we all three went down to the dock, where a disgruntled Captain Fitzgerald was herding Sir Francis's livestock onto the straw-strewn deck of the *Charlotte.*

The barrels of fish and sacks of grain had been stowed below-decks, Fitzgerald reported. "The crew is ready. With your permission, sir, I'd like to sail at first light tomorrow morning."

"I have no objection. Now, take this." He handed the captain a packet of papers sealed in oilskin. "You will deliver your cargo to the Long Wharf in Boston. Make your visit there as brief as you can. You will find further instructions in this packet that you are not to open until after you have departed Boston Harbor. Follow them to the letter."

That evening over dinner at the Bow Bells, Sir Francis was as expansive as Ephraim was glum. A crowd of admiring planters gathered to hear the old man voice his opinions on many subjects, including what he called the hypocrisy of American opposition to taxation "while still crying for British protection against savage Indians and the French."

As my mother might have said, I remained "as wise as a serpent and as silent as a dove." I suspected that he was testing my loyalties.

Ephraim sullenly excused himself for bed. Sir Francis and I sat up with his Barbadian friends until nearly midnight. When I ordered a pint of mild ale as a nightcap, he reminded me to be ready at dawn, saying that he wished a final conversation with me just before we sailed. When I went up to bed, Ephraim was asleep.

The old trick that I learned in my Indian days worked. Around 3:30 A.M. my near-to-bursting bladder awakened me. I pissed out the window into the adjoining alley and then shook Ephraim awake.

I tried every argument I could think of to overcome his objections. Of course he wanted to return to America, but he had signed a contract that did not expire for six months. No, he refused to slip out of the tavern and stow away aboard the *Charlotte.* That would be dishonest. Of course he longed to see Laura Mason.

"Well, you're a damned fool to let yourself be held here against your will."

"I will not say what I think if you are to allow yourself to be used by Sir Francis Bolton," he said with a prissiness that infuriated me.

"To hell with you, Ephraim!" I whispered. "You will see who is used and who is not. You can stay here and rot for all I care."

If he had not made me so angry, I would have told him of Sir Francis's effort to enlist me in his scheme to bring Laura Mason back from Philadelphia, but I doubt if that would have changed his mind. Well, he had made his bed, and he insisted on remaining in it there in the Bow Bells. Sleep was out of the question for me. So I said "good night and good-bye" in a savage tone and stomped out of the room to spend the rest of the night brooding in a chair in the tavern's common room.

Ibo was surprised to find me there at dawn.

"Isn't Dr. McGee joining us?"

"We said our good-byes last night. He prefers to sleep in."

"If I would not miss him so, I would wish that he were going with you. He is not happy here."

"I know, Ibo."

"But you will return?"

"I am under bond so to do."

"You say *under bond*. I hope that you do not wind up 'in bonds' like me, without your freedom or your manhood."

"What do you mean?"

"Sir Francis thinks I was too young to remember. But my manhood, or rather my potential for manhood, was not taken away from me until after he saw me in that Arab's slave pen. He struck a bargain to buy me only after one requirement had been met."

There were tears in his eyes.

"Why do you tell me this, Ibo?"

"I have overheard your talks. He wants you to serve him."

"And you think I should not?"

"No man should decide how another is to spend his life. I would counsel you only on one point. Do not let yourself be gelded by him or anyone else."

I cannot explain why this advice so deeply offended me.

"It is none of your business," I snapped. "But there is little danger of that happening."

"Ibo, you scoundrel!" Sir Francis called down the tavern stairs.

Ibo's voice turned soft, but his shining eyes remained fixed on me. "The spirit can be gelded as well as the body. Dr. McGee understands that, I think." He cleared his throat and dropped his gaze. "You will repeat nothing of what I have said to the master, I trust."

I assured him that our talk would be kept in confidence.

"Good. When you return, at least I will have someone with whom I can play chess—on equal terms, I trust."

"Ibo, you lazy rascal!"

"Coming, master."

Holding Ibo's arm, Sir Francis walked down to the dock with me. The eastern sky glowed yellow and gold. Her main deck teemed with pigs, sheep and cattle as the *Charlotte* sat low in the pale green water. As we drew nearer, the peaceful scene was disturbed by a barrage of Captain Fitzgerald's shouted commands to his scurrying crew.

On the dock, Sir Francis drew me aside.

"You understand what you are to do?"

"Indeed so, sir."

"I trust you also understand the consequences of failing to carry out what you have agreed to do."

"Consequences, sir? Have we not signed formal contracts?"

"So we have. About Miss Mason. I have been thinking. You have my permission to purchase a harpsichord for Bolton Hall, if you are successful in persuading her to return with you." He paused and added with a wink, "Perhaps you should mention that intent early in your negotiations with her."

"That is an interesting idea, sir. And most generous, too."

"It would be a joy to hear music at Bolton Hall again, and to see a beautiful young woman about the place. Bye the bye, did you observe the portrait of my grandmother, as I suggested?"

"Sir, I forgot."

"Pity. Well, let us hope we can compare her in the flesh with the picture. Here, Jeremiah, take my hand. Godspeed. Don't fail me, lad. I am counting on you. Hey there, Fitzgerald—I'll expect you back by spring! Bon voyage."

During the six-week voyage to Boston, I took special pains to learn every detail of the *Charlotte's* construction and handling. Pleased by my interest, Fitzgerald taught me many tricks of sailing and navigating. The mate resented the attention paid me by the captain and the way I ingratiated myself with the crew, especially Cato, the powerfully built cook, and Herbert Gwin, the Cornish-born bosun, but that did not deter me.

Of course, the weather grew chillier the farther north we sailed. A bone-chilling northeaster kept us stymied off Nantucket for two days. By then the feed for the livestock was gone, and the half-frozen animals were bleating, lowing, and squealing with hunger. At last the storm blew itself out. We cleared Cape Cod and drew close enough to Boston late in the day to see Castle William. Fitzgerald ordered a sea anchor put out, and bundled against the unaccustomed cold, everyone tried his best to sleep—all except me. I volunteered to stand the early morning watch. Through that night, I debated whether to proceed with a scheme on which I had been working ever since we left Barbados and even before.

I reflected long and hard on the words of the noble Shakespeare: *There is a tide in the affairs of men, which, taken on the flood, leads on to fortune; omitted, all the voyages of their life is bound in shallows and miseries.* Surely my life had been too long bound in the shallows and miseries of Boston Harbor. I'd be damned if I'd allow myself to be carried back into that accursed port. And I was haunted by Ibo's final words to me: *Do not let yourself be gelded.*

As dawn neared, I slipped onto the deck and barred the hatch to the forecastle, where the crew slept. Then I pried open the locker where Fitzgerald kept half a dozen muskets and a like number of pistols, together with balls and powder. I loaded two pistols and stuck them in my belt. The other weapons I hid in the galley under the bunk of the still-sleeping Cato.

The better to accommodate our cargo of livestock, the captain had moved the longboat from the main deck and suspended it over the stern from davits. As quietly as I could, I lowered the boat into the choppy water. Its keel just touching the surface, there it swung, thumping against the stern of the *Charlotte*.

Then I took a deep breath and shouted for Captain Fitzgerald. He came up from his cabin in his stocking feet, minus his trousers and wearing a knit cap.

"What in hell's name is going on?"

"The boat has slipped its lashings. Look there."

He bent over the rail and swore vengeance on the bosun for his carelessness.

"By the way, captain," I said. "Are you a strong swimmer?"

"I swim well enough," he said. Then turning to face me, he demanded, "Why in the hell are you asking a stupid question like that? Fetch the bosun. I'll make him pay for this! Here, why are you carrying those pistols in your belt?"

"Oh, look there, sir! Over the rail, at the bow of the boat. What is that?"

"I don't see anything."

"Bend over a bit more. Is it a hole in the bow of the boat?"

Leaning far out over the rail with his backside skyward, he made a ridiculous sight. It was a simple matter to grasp his ankles and dump him into the water. He came up blubbering and shouting for help. I took hold of the ropes and lowered the boat completely into the water.

The mate came racing up to the quarterdeck to see the cause of the uproar, a blanket about his shoulders.

"The captain fell overboard," I said.

"Well, for Christ's sake, save him! He'll die in that cold water."

"Do you swim?" I asked.

"No. Why, the boat is in the water! What's going on here?"

By now the captain had a good grip on the boat's gunwales. Seeing the mate, he shouted, "That goddamned American bastard pushed me overboard. Arrest him!"

The mate was a skinny, solemn fellow. He turned toward me and looked into the barrel of one of my pistols. By now some of the crew had been aroused by the shouting and were hammering at the barred hatch leading up from the forecastle. Cato came forth from his galley bunk. I whipped the second pistol from my belt and ordered him to stand against the rail with the mate.

"The fellow has gone mad," the mate said. "Seize him!"

Even if he had not been facing two cocked pistols, I don't think Cato would have obeyed. He detested the mate, as did most of the crew.

Down in the water, still clinging to the boat, the captain continued his vain commands for my arrest and his rescue. The hammering on the forecastle hatch grew louder.

Cato demanded to know if I had lost my senses.

"I am in full command of my faculties—and of this sloop," I said. "Now, put that ladder over the rail and assist our mate in climbing down into the boat. Careful—he doesn't swim."

"You will hang for this," the mate said.

"Why in hell doesn't somebody throw me a line?" the captain shouted. "I'll have you all keelhauled!"

"Over the rail, or I'll shoot," I said to the mate. Then to Cato, "Help him down the ladder, or you'll find yourself in the water with a ball in your belly."

Cursing me as a bloody American rebel and reminding me of the penalties for mutiny, the mate climbed down into the boat and pulled the apoplectic captain out of the icy water.

"You want to join them or stay here and follow my command?" I asked Cato. He grinned and said, "Why Captain Jerry, sir, it look to me like you got the quarterdeck."

I freed the ends of the ropes from the davits and cast them into the boat. Then I ordered Cato to fetch the captain's uniform and some blankets from his cabin.

"It is only a couple of miles to Castle William," I said to Fitzgerald. "You and the mate are sturdy fellows. The exercise will keep you warm."

The captain yelled once more for someone to seize me and bring him back aboard. I threw his clothing down to him. He stood in the boat and shook his fist at me.

"Listen close to me, Martin," he said through chattering teeth. "I will see you hanged as a pirate, I swear it! If it takes me the rest of my life, I will make you pay for this!"

"Better start rowing," I said.

My next move was to retrieve the sloop's weapons from under the cook's bunk. I brought them up onto the quarterdeck, where I loaded and primed each. When all was in readiness, I told Cato to unbar the forecastle hatch and stand aside.

As soon as the first crewmen popped out, I fired a pistol, which sent them scrambling back inside. Then I called for Gwin, the bosun, and three other crewmen to step out. I threatened to shoot anyone else who dared show his face. After the four men I had designated appeared, I ordered Cato to rebar the hatch.

"Now, the four of you come closer and attend well what I have to say."

They made their way through the livestock and stood at the foot of the ladder up to the quarterdeck.

"This ship is now mine. Sir Francis Bolton has sold it to me. I have a signed bill of sale. I have discharged Captain Fitzgerald and the mate. If any one of you does not wish to serve aboard this vessel, speak now, and I am sure Mr. Fitzgerald will make room in his boat. Stay with me and follow my commands, and you will be richly rewarded."

They looked at each other and then back at me.

"Meaning no offense, sir," Gwin said, "but anyone could say they owned this sloop."

"Do you read?"

"Well enough to get by, sir."

I drew papers from my coat pocket and held them up. "You are welcome to examine this bill of sale."

Then before he could reply, I added, "By the way, you'll be expected to serve as mate. Do you think you can handle the duties?"

"I know as much of sailing as that fellow ever did," he said, pointing toward the boat. "Probably more."

"Good. Who would you like to take your place as bosun?"

He looked at the three others and pointed to a tall mulatto.

"Good. Now, how about the four of you joining me on the quarterdeck? We'll just keep your mates confined until we have time to sort out what to do with them."

On the way into Marblehead harbor, I laid all my cards—or I should say papers—on the table with my new mate. There it was in writing—a bill of sale from Sir Francis to me for one seventy-ton sloop named the *Charlotte* and a copy of my promissory note for two thousand pounds given him in exchange.

"But this bill of sale provides that the sloop be returned to Bolton if payment be not made within six months," Gwin said.

"Quite true, but meanwhile I have title."

With the help of Cato and our three loyal deckhands, Gwin helped me sail the *Charlotte* north to Marblehead. It wasn't easy with so few hands, but by midafternoon we had worked our way north around Nahant Point and into Marblehead's commodious and welcome harbor.

Once ashore, I found a local farmer who was willing to feed and shelter our emaciated livestock for a few days. The crewmen of the *Charlotte* were another matter. Nobody wanted them ashore. I could not be sure of their loyalties. So I removed the weapons from the vessel, together with charts and sextant, and left Gwin and Cato in charge aboard while I went ashore.

112

Mother Brown came to the door of her cottage in answer to my knock.

"Well, look who it is. Back like a bad penny."

"So I am, Mother Brown. Where's Lovejoy?"

"Where's Lovejoy? Well you might ask. You whose fault it is that my poor son has taken to drink."

Lovejoy's room stank like a pigsty. He was drunk all right, passed out cold. I poured water in his face and slapped and pinched him. His breath was as foul as a latrine, and his face as bristly as a hog's back. Finally, I propped him up and was able to pour some of Mother Brown's muddy coffee down his gullet.

He opened one eye, then the other.

"That you, Jerry?"

When it finally dawned on him that I was back, he wept. It was the first time I had ever seen him show such emotion.

5

WITH GREAT RELIEF I learned that Lovejoy had not, as I feared, spent the money we had earned selling tents and rum. In fact, he had not bothered to collect payment for the tools he had provided the militia to dig the fortifications on Bunker and Breed's Hills.

"Ain't the same down there at Cambridge," he said. "That damn fool Washington has messed up our business. They pay with paper money, backed they say by Congress. And the tyrant rations the amount of spirits you can sell. I gave it up. What happened to you anyway, Jerry? Thought either you had gone over to the British or else they had hanged you."

God bless him, he had not disturbed our cache of gold and silver coins under the hearthstone of his mother's cottage. It came to only about five hundred pounds, a far cry from the two thousand pounds required to make the *Charlotte* legally—if not ethically—mine.

From Lovejoy I learned that Chris McGee had joined an expedition of volunteers under General Arnold to march north against Quebec.

What about Chris's father, Jason?

"He was still in camp last time I was down there. Them riflemen are a bunch of hell-raisers, though. Old Washington has had his hands full trying to keep that lot in line. Some of the worst of them went off to Canada, but them that stayed here is bad enough."

The man who had owned half of the ketch that Lovejoy and I lost to the British was a Salem merchant named Philemon Tubsworthy. He had washed his hands of Lovejoy and me, blaming the loss

113

of his craft on our carelessness. So when I went around to offer him the opportunity of buying our cargo of livestock, salt fish, and flour, he said sourly, "Hell no, Martin. I'm not interested."

Tubsworthy was a chubby fellow with bulging blue eyes and normally a kind enough manner. I couldn't blame him for feeling uncharitable toward Lovejoy and me, although he had known the risks involved in our smuggling scheme.

So I thanked him and started for the door. "Wait," he said. "Whose pretty sloop is that you brought into harbor?"

I explained that it was mine. He was skeptical. I told him I didn't give a damn whether he believed me or not. I had bought her. He expressed curiosity over my source of funds. I told him that was none of his business. He wanted to know what I intended doing with "this vessel which you claim to own." Ignoring his sarcasm, I said I was thinking of reentering the shipping business.

"Ah, Martin, that is dangerous work, as we both know from our experience with the ketch," he said. "And with this war on, it is becoming more so."

"Well, the *Charlotte* is just about the finest sloop I ever laid eyes on. I should hate to lose her. She cost me dear."

"What would you take for her?"

"Not a penny less than three thousand pounds, if I were to sell her at all, which I have no intention of doing."

He pressed me for more details about her size and specifications, which I provided in an offhand way. His eyebrows went up when I said she had a copper-sheathed bottom. Would I allow him to inspect the vessel?

"Perhaps, after I return from Cambridge."

"What business do you have down there?"

"A patriotic mission. Now, if you'll excuse me, Mr. Tubsworthy, I must be on my way."

I had feared when I found Lovejoy drunk that he might have sold off Ned and our team of draft horses. But no, they were being maintained in good style by a local livery stable. What a ludicrous sight our procession down to Cambridge made! I rode good old Ned. With Lovejoy driving, our team of horses drew our wagon loaded with flour. Our farmer friend followed with another wagonload of salt fish, and his sons herded our livestock. It took us all day to lead this menagerie down to the north bank of the Mystic River, in sight of the hills and spires of Boston.

While Lovejoy and the farmer settled the livestock down for the night, I crossed the river on the ferry and inquired of the pickets who challenged me where I might find the camps of the Pennsylvania riflemen.

Jason's company of William Thompson's Pennsylvania rifle battal-

114

ion had taken possession of a Tory's abandoned barn. My old friend himself was squatting in front of a campfire gnawing on a johnnycake with some of his men when I rode up in the winter twilight. We shook hands and pounded each other on the back and talked away at a furious rate. First I told him about my incarceration in Boston, then of some of Ephraim's experiences in Barbados, leaving out our bitter leave-taking. Jason told about the rapid march he and his men had made from Pennsylvania to Cambridge the previous summer.

"And Chris has gone off to Quebec?"

Jason got tears in his eyes. "I didn't want him to go without me. They said I was needed here, but I think it was because of my age and my leg." He lowered his voice. "Some of our fellows have got out of hand. When we first showed up, everyone marveled at our long rifles and our marksmanship. Now they complain that we waste powder sniping at British warships and that we incite the lobsterbacks to bombard us. Right now two of my best shots are in irons for stealing chickens and assaulting the provost's guards sent to arrest them. The high and mighty Washington is trying to turn us into an imitation of the British army."

Jason scrounged up a blanket, and I found myself enough straw to make a bed in the barn loft. Before dropping off to sleep, I told Jason about our cargo and asked who was in charge of procurement for the army.

"That would be Colonel Mifflin from Philadelphia."

"Do you know him?"

"Certainly. He was in the Pennsylvania Assembly. I'll take you over to see him in the morning."

Thomas Mifflin, Washington's quartermaster general, rode out with me. After inspecting our animals and foodstuffs, he agreed to take them off my hands—but at a fraction of what they would have brought from the British, just a few miles away across the Charles. I told him to make the promissory note to "Francis Bolton of St. James Parish, Barbados." What the hell! If I wasn't going to get much for the stuff, it might as well go to Sir Francis. I have always been a fair-minded fellow. While I was at it, I asked and got another note from Mifflin to compensate Lovejoy and me for the tools he had provided to fortify Bunker and Breed's Hills the previous June. After all, there are limits to one's generosity.

Over the next few days I gained a new appreciation for George Washington. I perceived many improvements in the American situation. Our fortifications had been increased and enlarged. Men no longer came and went as freely. There wasn't so much open drunkenness or foul language. The mob of militiamen was slowly but surely becoming an army.

During my visit in our camps, several exchanges of artillery took place across the Charles. Little damage was done by either side, but it was plain to see that we were woefully outgunned. Jason said this imbalance was expected to be corrected within a few weeks; Washington had dispatched Colonel Henry Knox to Fort Ticonderoga over on Lake Champlain with orders to haul back the considerable store of artillery captured from the British there the previous May.

From what I could hear, the British were having a lean time of it in Boston. They could have used Sir Francis's cargo.

I had seen George Washington the previous May in Philadelphia, where he served as a delegate to the Second Continental Congress. It would have been hard to miss him, tall as he was and dressed in the blue uniform of a colonel of the Virginia militia. I saw him again around Cambridge several times, and I must say the gentleman had a noble bearing as he rode about with a stern look on his face. He was a far cry from fat, lethargic old General Ward.

Some people don't appreciate the handicaps Washington overcame, first to create an army and then to preserve it. I'll grant that he is no brilliant tactician, but he is a superb leader, even though Jason and many others did not realize it at the time.

And Washington is a more astute military and political strategist than many people on either side appreciate. He understood the advantage the British had with their great fleet. They could move an army across the ocean and land at any point they wished. They could choke off our supplies from the outside world. They had disciplined, trained soldiers. What did we have? A great mass of independent-minded militia and a vast territory, void of manufacturies, except shipyards.

Before Congress authorized a formal navy, Washington created a temporary one of his own. He commissioned a fleet of New England schooners to harass British shipping. I gave passing thought to volunteering the *Charlotte* for such duty. Today I am mighty glad I kept those thoughts to myself.

When I observed how much sickness there was in the American camps, I regretted all the more my failure to persuade Ephraim to return with me. Hundreds of men were lying about with mumps or smallpox in the several large houses that had been turned into hospitals. Far more men succumbed to disease that winter than had fallen to British bullets and bayonets around Breed's Hill. The militia's regimental surgeons were more a nuisance than a help. The army needed experienced, professional doctors like Ephraim. But out of a misdirected sense of honor, that knucklehead had chosen to remain on Barbados. And *he* had warned me not to get caught in Bolton's web!

My business in Cambridge concluded, I rode back to Marblehead and found Tubsworthy suspiciously eager to talk to me.

This shrewd Yankee had taken the liberty of inspecting the *Char-*

lotte in my absence. And as I soon discovered, he had taken another step.

He did a a lot of hemming and hawing before he showed his hand. Finally I said, "Mr. Tubsworthy, I am a busy man. Just what are you getting at?"

"I am getting at making you a rich man, Jeremiah."

I figured he wanted to make an offer to buy the *Charlotte*. The three thousand pounds would give me enough to pay off Sir Francis—however much against his will—and leave a thousand pounds for myself. But no, he had something quite different in mind.

"I have not always lived in such comfortable circumstances as I do now, Jeremiah. I was a young fellow, just turned twenty-one and newly married, back during our war with the French. I got rich during that war, Jeremiah, and do you know how?"

I shook my head warily.

"Privateering. I mortgaged my widowed mother's farm and borrowed money from my wife's father to purchase an interest in a schooner. We outfitted and armed her. Hired a captain and crew, and she proceeded to take three French prizes off Nova Scotia on her first voyage. Made enough right off to discharge my loans and buy an interest in a second vessel. By the end of the war I had accumulated what seemed to me at the time a fortune, but there are greater fortunes to be made in *this* war. At first I thought the British would put this uprising down in quick order. This fellow Washington is making a difference, however. And our Congress down in Philadelphia appears to be pulling the colonies together better than ever I dreamed. Don't mistake me, Jeremiah, I am no Tory. I am a wait-and-see fellow. Well, sir, I have waited, and what I see is a long war and for sharp fellows such as you and I, a profitable war."

"Where do I come into all this?"

"It takes a lot to get into privateering. It takes money, which I and certain friends in Salem and Beverly have. It also takes time. We must build craft specially for privateering. Even now we have our shipyard orders in for several narrow-beamed, sharp-hulled schooners, with masts and rigging to carry a heavy spread of sail. But time can be money in this case. Now, you have a sloop to which you claim ownership—"

"Which I do own," I corrected him.

"And which you have in port with a goodly crew aboard. And you have in Lovejoy Brown as good a sailor as ever I have seen, when sober."

"When sober, Mr. Tubsworthy? I have never seen you drunk."

"Don't jest, Jeremiah. This is a serious proposition."

"Then please make it and quit beating around the bush."

"I propose that we outfit your pretty sloop and send her out as a privateer to operate against British shipping."

117

"*We*, Mr. Tubsworthy? How do you figure in all this?"

"It will take money, more than you may think, to fit your vessel for this duty. You would need a spare set of sails and rigging. And you'd need to arm her with at least six four-pounders, plenty of powder and shot, and a score or so small arms of all kinds. And you'd have to post bond with the Massachusetts Provincial Congress to procure a proper letter of marque."

"Letter of marque? What for?"

"To avoid being hanged by the British as a pirate if you should be captured. Make no mistake, there is risk both of money and life, but the riches to be reaped—ah, they are marvelous."

He explained that the captured British vessels would be brought into port and sold as prizes, with the proceeds to be split fifty-fifty between the owners and the crew.

"How much of a crew?"

"A large one. From talking to your Cornishman, I'd say you've got your first mate already. And a good part of your present crew may want to sign when they hear they can earn more in a year than they would during the rest of their lives."

He went on to explain that the half of the prize money reserved for the crew would be parceled out in shares, "eight for the captain, four each for the sailing master, first mate, and surgeon. Oh yes, you'll need a surgeon. Then two each for your prize master, carpenter, gunner, bosun, steward, cook, and sailmaker, with their mates receiving one and a half shares. Then one share goes to each seaman. And if you have any lads under sixteen as powder monkeys or such, they would get a half share each."

"Exactly how many men would we need?"

"More than you may think, because, you see, after capturing a vessel, you have to spare enough hands to sail your prize into port and guard the prisoners."

For more than an hour, Tubsworthy lectured me on the fine points of privateering, of the business end, that is.

"I don't have a captain," I said when he stopped for breath.

"Come, come Jeremiah, don't play modest. You can handle men. Of course, you don't know the fine points of navigation or sailing, but you've got Lovejoy. Make him your sailing master. And that Cornishman will serve well enough as mate. Don't worry about the rest of your crew. There are plenty of good sailors eager for jobs these days. But you'd better grab them fast."

I was nearly ready to agree to Tubsworthy's scheme. But then I asked, "What will we do about a letter of marque?"

His answer was to grin and hold up a sheet of paper.

That was when I learned that while I had been down at Cambridge, that Yankee son-of-a-bitch had gone before the Massachusetts Provincial Congress at Watertown and procured a letter of marque that gave him or parties he might designate the power to take enemy prizes and bring them into port for sale. He had even filled in the name of the vessel as the *Charlotte*.

"There," he said. "You have the sloop. I have the license to operate the vessel."

The look on his face resembled Major Tuttle's look when he thought he had broken my spirit and that I was ready to sign a confession of spying for the Americans. Nobody had beaten me or dosed me with croton oil now, true. I just did not like that smirk. So I told him I would have to sleep on his proposition.

Out of his mother's hearing, I sought Lovejoy's advice. He listened to my proposition with his face aglow. When I finished, he clapped his hands and said with enthusiasm, "By the Almighty, Jerry, let's do her!"

"Do what? Join up with Tubsworthy?"

"No. We don't need him. Let's do her ourselves. Why make that butterball any richer?"

Herbert Gwin was harder to win over. Before he would abandon his loyalty to King George, I had to tell him the story of Lexington and Concord, get him drunk on rum, and help him figure out how much money he could earn. With Cato and the mulatto bosun, Toby, it was just a matter of promising them that they would be free men.

Tubsworthy's face reddened and the corners of his mouth turned down as he listened the next day to my refusal of his proposition.

"I've made you a generous offer. What's the matter? Are you afraid?"

"Did you sail on any of those privateering voyages that made you so rich?"

That struck a nerve. His face turned a shade darker, but he kept his voice steady.

"You mentioned taking three thousand pounds for your sloop. I will pay it, half in gold, a note for the remainder."

"I'll give you a hundred pounds in gold, plus these notes from the army, for that letter of marque," I responded.

"I'd sooner throw it in the fire."

I made another suggestion as to how he might use his piece of paper and walked out onto the Marblehead waterfront, still a free man. The sight of the *Charlotte* riding elegantly at anchor in the harbor further buoyed my spirits.

"Mr. Martin!"

I turned around. Still holding his letter of marque, Tubsworthy was standing in the doorway of his office. "Let's talk a bit more."

He offered to sell the letter of marque to me for five hundred pounds, the same amount Lovejoy and I had saved from our trading. I countered by raising my bid to a hundred fifty. He pointed out that his services as an agent might be useful and lowered his price to three hundred pounds in gold. Neither of us would budge until it occurred to me to offer him ten percent of our prize money.

"How about a ten percent interest in the sloop as well?" he responded.

"No. Ten percent of the prizes taken and sold under the letter of marque that you have fraudulently obtained from the Provincial Congress."

"What do you mean, fraudulently?"

"You are not an owner of the *Charlotte*. You were not when you applied for this letter, and you are not now. What will the delegates think when I inform them of this fact, when I apply for my own letter of marque for this same vessel?"

He slumped onto an office stool, a deflated, beaten man.

"Ten percent of all prizes taken by the *Charlotte*," he said.

"No, ten percent of those prizes taken by her under this particular letter of marque. And you must serve as our agent with the prize court and such. Take it or leave it."

"Done," he said. "You are a hard man, Jeremiah."

"You have nothing to complain about, Philemon," I replied. "You are being well compensated for a mere piece of paper."

Lovejoy and I spent a lot of time and money equipping the *Charlotte* for sea. She had to be cleaned from stem to stern, and extra sail had to be laid in. By hook and by crook, we obtained a new stock of small arms. Ideally we should have had six or eight four-pounder cannon, but the only gun to be found was a two-pounder swivel gun left over from the French war. Lovejoy hired a crew of carpenters from a local shipyard to turn out six wooden replicas. Painted a shiny black and mounted on real gun carriages, they looked authentic enough.

Most of the Charlotte's old crew were willing to sign on as privateers. When word got around that we intended to go a-privateering, we soon signed up a score of sturdy local seamen.

Going back to Cambridge to visit Jason, I learned that his two Pennsylvania riflemen had been court-martialed and ordered to leave the American camps. They were brothers named McClintock, of Ulster stock. Each claimed to be a champion sharpshooter. It was a simple matter to sign them as Gentlemen Volunteers, eligible for one share each of our prize monies.

Jason was worried about Chris off in Canada and about whether Ephraim would return from Barbados safely. Also, he was concerned about Kate and the twins back in Sherman's Valley. He was bored by the inactivity in the American camps, but not so bored that he wanted to sail with me.

As Lovejoy went about purchasing supplies and helping me interview applicants for places on our crew, he became a changed man.

120

I was amazed at his grasp of the business of privateering. He knew just what we would need and in what quantity.

At last our money was all spent. We still lacked some vital supplies, such as a complete change of sails and a battery of cannon, but we were in good shape for a short cruise. Some of our berths were unfilled, most notably those of surgeon and chief gunner. But since we carried no cannon and I had no intention of fighting without them, we were ready to go a-hunting.

"Except for one thing," said Lovejoy. "You have got to give the crew a good rousing speech. It is always done."

While Philemon Tubsworthy, Lovejoy's old mother, and a score of other locals watched from the Marblehead wharf, I assembled our crew on the main deck of the *Charlotte*. This was the moment over which I had tossed and turned all the previous night. I stood on the quarterdeck looking down into that assortment of faces, some black as pitch, others lily white or pink, and many of hues between these two extremes. All were turned up toward me as their captain. A feeling of powerlessness and dread came upon me. I had not delivered a public speech since my brief stay at the College of William and Mary. And I had never been a ship's captain. Lovejoy's mother had warned that we were biting off more than we could chew, "which is his usual way." I had replied, "With all our money spent, Mother Brown, we have bitten off more than we dare *eschew*." Neither she nor her son had got the joke.

I took a deep breath and gripped the quarterdeck rail to steady myself. It wouldn't do for that lot to see their captain's knees shaking.

"Men," I began nervously, "we are about to depart this harbor under a letter of marque to seek out and capture vessels sailing under the flag of Great Britain, a nation with which our own people are at war. There is great danger in what we are about to undertake. Blood may be shed. The work will not be easy. Success is by no means assured. If any man here wishes to change his mind, now is the time to speak up."

I paused. Seeing or hearing no one speak, my anxiety lessened, and my thoughts became better focused.

"Your silence lends your assent. You all know who I am. I own this vessel, and I am also your captain. You all know the man beside me. He is Lovejoy Brown—Mr. Brown to you, henceforth. He and I have sailed around the world together. He has forgotten more about sailing than most of us will ever know. As sailing master, he is my second in command. You are to obey an order from him as if it came from me. Also here on the quarterdeck is Herbert Gwin, who will be our mate. Mr. Gwin aided in the construction of this sloop in Barbados. Like many aboard this vessel, he was not born in America, but he has my confidence and trust, and you must give him yours."

I went on to introduce each of the twenty-five men, calling them by name with a bit of background about each. I concluded by asking if there were any questions.

A young fellow from over Salem way raised his hand. "These cannon here ain't real. What if we get into a fight?"

"We don't plan to take on a warship. If our Quaker guns don't convince a merchantman, we have plenty of small arms aboard, not to mention our swivel gun. And we've got two men here with fine Pennsylvania rifles. They can knock a captain's hat right off his head at two hundred yards."

They laughed at that but grew serious when one of the McClintock brothers questioned the absence of a doctor.

"Look on the bright side," I said. "We don't have to set aside the usual four shares for a ship's surgeon. That means more for each of us. Except for accidents or illness, why should we need a doctor? I can set a broken arm as well as any quacksalver."

I asked Lovejoy to speak. His discourse was to the point. "No liquor on this cruise. Do what you're told. Rough weather, always keep one hand free to save yourself. I'll never ask you to do anything I won't do myself. I ain't much for speaking. I'd rather show you than tell you. Like Jerry—I mean Captain Martin—says, I have sailed around the world, as a bosun on an East Indiaman. I have skippered a trading ketch. And I have worked as deckhand, gunner's mate, and what have you aboard a privateersman from this very port back in the sixties. Some of you may have signed up for the money. You'll likely get plenty. As your sailing master, I am entitled to four shares. Let me tell you something, though. I'd have signed on for this cruise just as quick for a seaman's wage. By God, men, you're in for more fun than you'd ever dream. There ain't nothing like privateering. You'll soon see what I mean."

One of the Pennsylvania riflemen let out a shrill cry, which was taken up by the rest of the crew. Cato clapped his hands and laughed. The other Bajans slapped each other on the back.

I jumped to the wharf, shook Tubsworthy's hand vigorously and before she could defend herself, gave Mother Brown a hearty hug and a kiss.

PART FOUR

1

BEATING OUR WAY against a contrary wind, we took most of the afternoon to work the *Charlotte* out of Marblehead Harbor. Finally, with Nahant Point off our starboard bow, we set light sails and headed south in a choppy sea under a chill gray sky.

To the amusement of the veteran sailors aboard, both our backwoods brothers became seasick. Lovejoy remained on the quarterdeck with the helmsman throughout the first night. He lectured the suffering sharpshooters on how to conduct themselves should we get into a fight. At daylight he resumed his instructions, this time with the entire crew, putting them through drill after drill. This was a new Lovejoy Brown. He was no longer a landbound drunk, no more an old bachelor tied to his mother's apron strings; not a trace of his former hangdog expression remained. He ran that crew ragged as he had them put on and take off sail, change courses, and practice lowering and raising the longboat. By the time Cato had their boiled potatoes and salt beef ready at noon, their tongues were hanging out.

The wind died down during the afternoon, and that night we lay to just out of sight of land. Lovejoy slept well, leaving Gwin in charge of the quarterdeck. The next morning came more drills. The Pennsylvania riflemen recovered enough from their seasickness to complain that they had not signed up to become common sailors.

"Well, we didn't sign you up to sit about on your arses to be waited on," Lovejoy told them. "If you want to eat aboard this vessel, you'll damn well turn to like everybody else."

In truth, I could not much blame them for their feelings. The *Charlotte* was as snug and seaworthy a sloop as ever sailed those waters, but it was a bad time of year to be cruising in those parts. It was cold.

On our third day out, we spotted a sail on the eastern horizon, and I called all hands on deck. A muffler around his face and his cap pulled over his ears, Lovejoy climbed with spyglass into the crow's nest.

"Can't make out what she is, but she's headed this way," he shouted.

We shortened our sail and hovered about until he cried, "She's a brig! Looks like a merchantman."

"She armed?" I asked quietly when he returned to the quarterdeck.

"Can't tell yet, but we ought to be ready just in case."

Lovejoy and I had agreed that in such situations, I would fight the ship and he would sail her. So I selected the greenest of our crew to man our wooden cannon, leaving the more experienced hands free to maneuver the sloop.

Lovejoy mounted to the crow's nest again and yelled down the report, "She's flying British colors all right!"

At that we replaced our new thirteen-stripe flag with our old British ensign and headed for our prey.

At about a half-mile, Lovejoy brought us about, shortened sail, and maneuvered the *Charlotte* to a course parallel to and windward of that of the two-masted square-rigger now closing fast with us.

I looked her over from stem to stern and agreed that she was unarmed. At about two hundred yards, we put on a bit more sail, and I ordered that our swivel gun fire a shot across her bows.

The brig hove too and allowed us to come alongside. I raised my speaking horn to my lips and hailed her. The captain identified her as the *Frome* out of Bristol and demanded, "Who the hell are you?"

When I told him we were the *Charlotte* out of Bridgetown, Barbados, he asked what we wanted.

"We want to examine your papers."

"Go to hell!" he shouted.

Whereupon I ordered my riflemen to send three balls whistling through his rigging, which they did, and I followed up by bellowing, "Starboard battery! Run out your guns!"

My lads put on a convincing performance of sweating and straining. Lovejoy ran us right up beside the brig, close enough so that I could have hit the captain with a pistol ball.

"You have no right to stop me!" the fellow shouted.

"Light your linstocks!" I yelled to my gun crews.

My boys made a great show of obeying this command, which I followed with, "Prime your touchholes!" and, "Lay your pieces!"

The other captain huddled with his mate and bosun. By that time we could have slaughtered everyone on the quarterdeck with our smoothbore muskets.

"Ready your pieces!" I shouted. "Take aim!"

"Don't fire!" the other captain cried.

Lovejoy took that as his signal to order grappling hooks thrown over the brig's rail. We rolled back our "cannon" and closed the gunports. In short order we had drawn the two vessels alongside each other, and a band of my most disreputable-looking crewmen scrambled over and took control of our prey.

The captain nearly wept when he discovered that he had been taken by a mere sloop operating under a Massachusetts letter of marque. He was heavy laden with a mixed cargo of food, muskets, blankets, and tents intended for General Howe's army in Boston. After blackguarding me as a pirate, he fell to cursing the British navy for not sending along an escort.

"Well, I am your escort now," I said.

So that was our first catch, and a damn good one she turned out to be. We left the *Frome* in the custody of Tubsworthy to be libeled and sold, and we set sail again. This time we ventured to within ten miles of Castle William and lay to throughout a moonless night. We awakened at dawn to see a frigate bearing down on us from the direction of Boston. We loitered about thinking she would be another easy catch until a cloud of smoke from her bow and a cannonball skipping toward us across the waves identified her as a British warship.

Lovejoy went into frenzied action, screaming orders to hoist our mainsail and swing the boom around to catch the wind. Our crew scrambled about, stumbling over each other; I stood helplessly on the quarterdeck as the frigate swept toward us under full sail. At last we got our spritsails out and our square-rigged topsail up. The *Charlotte* shuddered as her mainsail caught the wind. The frigate fired a second round from her bow gun. We surged ahead. The frigate gained on us for a few minutes, but we finally caught our wind, so to speak, and maintained a distance of about a half-mile.

The frigate doggedly kept up the chase until near noon. Lovejoy edged the bow of the *Charlotte* closer and closer into the wind until she was within four points of the direction from which the stiff breeze was blowing. Although this maneuver slowed us down, it forced the cumbersome square-rigged frigate to tack. She finally gave up the game with a broadside that came nowhere near us. Just for the hell of it, I had my marksmen double-load their rifles and put holes in our pursuer's sails.

Lovejoy leaned against the quarterdeck, exhausted.

"Too bad we don't have real cannon," I said. "We might have taken ourselves one of King George's own ships."

He looked at me in disbelief. "We're damn lucky we aren't carrying real guns! They wouldn't have been enough to match theirs. And the extra weight would have slowed us down so that the whoresons might have caught up with us. We were lucky, that's what we were, Jerry."

The next day we cruised north until we sighted a ketch, which we overhauled with ease. She was a fisherman out of Halifax. I wasn't sure she was a legitimate prize, but we decided to let the court settle the question and so herded her and her irate crew into Marblehead Harbor.

On our next foray, up near the tip of Nova Scotia, we picked up two more fishing vessels. When we returned to Marblehead, we found the place in an uproar over three pieces of news. Paine's diatribe *Common Sense* had been published a few weeks earlier in Philadelphia, and copies were in circulation locally. In my view that little pamphlet of less than fifty pages did as much as Lexington and Concord to shove America toward Independency. " 'Tis time to part," wrote Paine. "Everything that is right or reasonable pleads for separation." I liked what Paine wrote so well, I read it aloud to members of my crew, including my Bajans, who incidentally were showing increasing signs of homesickness.

The next piece of news concerned the success of Henry Knox's expedition to bring captured British artillery three hundred miles over difficult country from Ticonderoga to Cambridge. Much of it heavy stuff, these guns had been placed all about Boston, giving Washington a real throathold on the British.

The third news was that Congress was considering issuing its own licenses for privateering.

The price brought by our captured brig and its cargo was not quite as large as I had hoped. When I questioned Tubsworthy about this, he said the vessel and cargo had been auctioned off to the highest bidder as soon as possible after legal condemnation by the prize court. I dropped the subject with him but obtained records of the sale and showed them to Lovejoy.

"The son of a bitch is up to his old tricks," he said. "I should have warned you."

The winning bid had been submitted by an old friend of Tubsworthy, a prominent Salem merchant. I said I saw nothing wrong with that as long as the auction was an honest one.

"This one wasn't." Lovejoy pointed out that only three bids had been made for the ship and that two of them had been from obscure people. He named several prosperous ship owners who should have entered bids but did not.

"Two to one, they are in bed with Tubsworthy. Look, he told you he and others had gone in together to build privateers. That same lot ganged up and entered a joint bid that's about half what she should have brought."

I decided to bide my time and remain silent for the present. After all, I had no proof.

By now it was well into March. I left Lovejoy in charge of reprovisioning the *Charlotte* and paid a visit to the American camps around Cambridge. I arrived there the morning after a violent storm had swept over the area. Everyone was in a joyous uproar. Our newly emplaced cannon had been bombarding enemy positions across the Charles nightly. Although Washington's army had shrunk considerably with the termination of most militia enlistments at the end of '75, he had signed up more than eight thousand men for longer terms as "Continentals." Morale and excitement were running high because Washington had caught the British off guard by occupying and fortifying Dorchester Heights, a hilly peninsula from which our guns dominated Boston Harbor and its entrance.

"We first thought the British would cross over and try to drive us off as they did at Breed's Hill, but it don't look like they will now, not after the way that storm scattered their ships and boats," Jason McGee said. "In fact, reports are flying about that they may be getting ready to abandon Boston. Give it up. That would end the war, I should think."

"Well, if the war is ending, why do you look so sour?"

There was pain in his eyes as he replied, "It's Chris. I'm worried sick about the lad."

"I heard the expedition to Quebec ran into trouble."

"Big trouble. We hear they attacked the city in a snowstorm at night. General Montgomery was killed, Arnold wounded, and our little army nearly got wiped out. If anything has happened to that boy, Kate will never forgive me."

I took his hand. "Remember what you said to me at Bushy Run when the Indians were whooping all around us and I was so scared I nearly shit in my breeches?"

He shook his head.

"You said, 'Nothing is ever as bad as it seems.'"

"Well, that is not much comfort to me now."

"Actually, I found it of damn little use then." I waited for his grin and added, "Seriously, Jason, Chris is a tough chap who can take care of himself. Like me, he leads a charmed life."

After a vain attempt to persuade Jason to sail with me, I said good-bye to my old friend, and to the sound of cannonfire from our batteries and those of the British, I turned Ned's head back toward Marblehead.

127

As I have written earlier, intelligence—advance information, if you will—can be a mighty valuable commodity. And I had two pieces of it that would be valuable for my new business. But were they true? Was my business agent, Philemon Tubsworthy, really feathering his own nest at my expense? And were the British really planning to vacate Boston?

My first question was answered by Lovejoy soon after I returned to Marblehead to resupply the *Charlotte* for another cruise. His face an angry red, he stormed onto the dock.

"That Bristol brig we captured—they have renamed her!"

"What business is that of ours?"

"They've changed her from the *Frome* to the *Deborah*. You know who Deborah is?"

"Nor do I care."

"You ought to. That is the name of Mrs. Tubsworthy. I told you not to trust that lardbucket!"

It took but little investigation to learn not only that the vessel had been renamed but that the Massachusetts Provincial Congress had issued her a letter of marque. This meant she would be competing with us for prizes and crewmen.

Even without the resentment I now felt against Tubsworthy, I could not have fallen asleep easily that night. As I lay in my captain's bunk and the *Charlotte* gently rocked in rhythm to an occasional swell, I heard the rumble of cannonfire from down Boston way. More and more I was hearing talk of Independency for America. What about independence for myself? Wasn't it time I declared myself independent of sharpsters like Tubsworthy and old Sir Francis Bolton?

The next morning, without consulting Lovejoy I enclosed our letter of marque with an explanatory note and hired a local to deliver the sealed package to the Provincial Congress. Then I wrote another letter to Philemon Tubsworthy in which I thanked him for his backing and informed him that I was terminating our agreement, had returned our letter of marque to the authorities, and was taking the *Charlotte* back to sea as a cargo vessel.

As he was not in his office when I called round, I left my letter with his clerk.

Making sure all my Bajans were aboard, I ordered Lovejoy to make ready for a swift departure. He complained about such short notice but turned to and got us in proper trim to slip out of the harbor on an afternoon tide.

We were only a few hundred yards from the wharf when Lovejoy pointed back and said, "Ain't that Tubsworthy waving his hands and yelling?"

"It sure looks like him."

He peered through his spyglass. "He's waving a piece of paper.

Wonder what he wants."

"Probably just wants to say good-bye. Steady on your course."

And then I waved my handkerchief toward the wharf and made what can only be described as an obscene gesture in the direction of Master Tubsworthy.

2

A FITFUL NORTHWESTERLY WIND bore us south. Without a letter of marque I was not eager to encounter other vessels, but as night drew near, we saw to our amazement a veritable forest of masts and furled sails off our starboard bow moving in the direction of Boston.

Lovejoy thought it might be a fleet of British ships delivering a huge, fresh expedition to crush Washington. I wasn't so sure. The British had to know that the American army had become too formidable a force under its new commander-in-chief to be overcome so easily. Whatever the reason, there the ships were. We had to avoid them.

I set a westerly course and let the *Charlotte* run before the wind through the night. I was awakened at first light by shouts of "sail ho" from the deck. Racing to the door of my cabin, I saw a large three-master looming not a mile off our starboard bow. She was flying British colors, and her decks were jammed with people.

Out of curiosity more than any design, I let the *Charlotte* loll along so the stranger could come closer.

If she carried cannon, I could not make them out. But to discourage any aggressive intent, I had our crew open their ports so that the muzzles of our Quaker guns showed. And then I ordered them to raise our false British colors.

A cheer went up from the crowded decks of the ship.

We lowered our mainsail and let the other vessel draw to within hailing distance.

She was the *Severn Queen*, bound from Boston for Halifax, the captain informed me.

"Why so many passengers?" I shouted.

"Haven't you heard? We're evacuating Boston."

As far as Lovejoy knew, we still had our letter of marque. In his view the *Severn Queen* was a fat prize, ours for the taking. He clapped his hands and ordered the *Charlotte* to close with the British transport.

"No," I said.

"Why the hell not? She ain't armed. And even if she was, her captain wouldn't risk all them people. Look there at the women. Even some children. There's bound to be plenty of Tory gold aboard her."

I shook my head at him and cupped my ear to hear what the other captain was saying. Something about needing an escort. Were we available?

I let Lovejoy bring us to within a few yards of the other ship, whereupon we both lowered our mainsails, leaving just enough canvas aloft to maintain headway.

"If you want to come aboard, we can talk about the proposition," I called to the other captain.

His deckhands obligingly hurled a monkey's fist over our forward rail. To it was fastened a small line, which in turn was connected to a heavier one. The same procedure fastened our sterns together. In a few minutes we were snugged up against each other, the sides of our delicate sloop against the looming sides of the great transport.

I looked up into the broad, bewhiskered face of the captain. In a Midland accent he said, "I've got two hundred loyal civilians with their personal belongings aboard. We're quitting Boston, letting the bloody rebels have the stinking place. We got a lot of sickness aboard, and I can't see waiting about until the navy is ready to escort us up to Halifax. I see you're well armed. From Barbados, are ye? Well, we'd pay you for your time if you'd care to escort us. Ye could pick up a good cargo in Halifax to carry home. What do ye say?"

This was more than I had bargained for. The ship would have made a grand prize, but to take her without a letter of marque would be piracy. And then there were all those people. I looked at the faces lining the rail, peering down at us. Wouldn't it be a grand joke to play on the British to accept a generous payment for escorting their refugees to Nova Scotia?

"Bring your papers and your first mate aboard, and let's discuss the matter."

A rope ladder was thrown over their side, and the captain was descending it when suddenly someone yelled from the bow of the vessel, "Wait! It's a trap! I know that scoundrel."

Major Tuttle was waving his hands and shouting to attract the attention of the captain, who paused midway down the ladder.

I drew my pistol from my belt and pointed it at his ample backside. "Come on down, Captain, if you don't want a ball up your arse."

He lowered himself onto our deck and demanded an explanation. By way of reply, I ordered Lovejoy to run up our true colors, and then I informed my prisoner that we were a privateer operating under a Massachusetts letter of marque. Whether this was an outright lie or merely an out-of-date truth, what does it matter? All's fair in love and war.

130

We stayed lashed up against that transport for nearly an hour. With the captain a prisoner in my cabin, I demanded and got a complete list of their passengers. Sure enough, on it was the name of Major Tuttle.

After a show of bluster and threats, the other captain composed himself and asked resignedly, "Well, you have got us. What do you propose to do with us?"

Lovejoy cackled at this question. Rubbing his hands together, he said, "What are we going to do? Listen to him! A full-size ship. By God, she'll bring thousands of pounds. She's the biggest prize ever I seen taken. He'll soon find out what we plan to do. Now see here, Jerry, let's quit this beating about the bush and get under way before the British navy catches on to our game."

Ignoring Lovejoy, I said to the British captain, "This fellow Major Tuttle. Call him to come aboard. We can discuss an arrangement under which you might proceed with your passengers to Halifax under parole, as it were."

He refused until I threatened to put a prize crew aboard his ship immediately and run her directly into Marblehead.

I have to hand it to Tuttle. An out-and-out coward might have hid in the hold or tried to disguise himself, but in answer to the captain's command, he manfully climbed down the rope ladder and came into my presence.

He looked me in the eye without flinching, leaving it to me to speak first.

"Well, Major Tuttle, what a pleasant surprise to meet you again."

"What is your business with me, Martin?"

"I merely wanted to look into the face of an old acquaintance once more. To inquire after his health."

"My health is fine."

"No constipation, I hope?"

His face reddened, but he kept his voice steady. "I have no complaints of any kind. So you've turned pirate. I should have hanged you when I had the opportunity."

I might have sent him back up the ladder unscathed if he had not made that remark.

"Seize him," I ordered my Pennsylvanians. "Strip him to the waist and bind his wrists in front."

Tuttle's expression of arrogance started to fade.

"Have we a cat-o'-nine-tails?" I asked Lovejoy.

"Of course not." He drew me aside and whispered, "Jerry, have you lost your mind? You can settle with this fellow in port! We're taking a chance loitering about here with all them British warships on the horizon."

"We have plenty of rope. Bring two lengths. Cato, you take one, and I'll take the other. Oh yes, bring out our medicine kit as well."

The other captain spoke up. "What is going on? This man is an officer of King George. You will have to answer for any mistreatment."

"You believe that mistreatment of prisoners should not go unpunished?" I asked the captain.

"Decidedly not."

"How about you, Tuttle? Do you agree?"

"Go to hell, Martin!"

Cato appeared with two stout lengths of line and Lovejoy with our medicine kit.

I drew out a bottle of castor oil and held it in one hand and a rope in the other.

"Which would you prefer, Tuttle? One hundred lashes or a dose of oil?"

He shut his mouth and glared at me.

"If you do not speak, it will be both."

He looked over my shoulder as if I did not exist.

"Cato, help this gentleman kneel to receive his punishment."

The giant Negro lowered Tuttle to his knees. Ah, it was sweet to see that haughty British officer shivering bare-waisted in the chill March wind! His lips and ears turned blue, and his arms were puckered with goose pimples. Despite his best efforts, I am sure, he trembled and his teeth chattered.

"We'll take turns, Cato. I'll strike first, then you. After thirty lashes, if he is still conscious, we'll douse him with water and lay on the next thirty. Ready?"

"Wait." Tuttle's face bore an expression of pure hatred.

"What is it?"

"I'll take the oil."

And so he did, a good quarter of the bottle. I would have poured it all down his throat, but I figured we might need some for the crew.

He was kneeling on our deck and gagging in full view of the refugees aboard the transport, when Lovejoy called out, "Sail off our starboard bow! It's a frigate, damn it!"

So it was, and it was flying the British flag and carrying more guns than ever I would want brought to bear on me. So I ordered Tuttle's hands unbound and let him climb back up the ladder. Then I shook hands with the British captain and thanked him for his trouble.

"You wanted an escort. Here comes one. Hurry now, sir, or we'll have to take you with us."

Cursing me for a damn fool and his crewmen for their slowness, Lovejoy took a cutlass and hacked the lines binding us to the transport in two. I let him take over the business of seeing our sails raised. As the wind bore us away from the transport, I saw no sign of Major Tuttle. How sweet it was to take revenge upon such a foe!

It was no great trick to elude the approaching frigate. We ran out to sea for an hour or so, and then I set us on a southerly course once more and explained my actions to Lovejoy. He grumbled at my rashness in relinquishing our letter of marque, although he saw my point in cutting our connections with Philemon Tubsworthy.

Two days later, Cape May appeared on the horizon. We entered the mouth of Delaware Bay and dropped anchor near the village of Lewes and waited for a boat to bring out a pilot. Borne along on an incoming tide and a favorable wind, we passed from the broad waters of the bay into the river itself. The river curved north around Wilmington and thence past Mud Island, on which had been erected a low earthen fort. Finally, there in the rays of the late afternoon sun gleamed the spires of Philadelphia.

Since we had no cargo to discharge, we passed the docks and dropped anchor above the city. I ordered Lovejoy to keep our crew aboard ship, then paid our pilot his fee and rowed him ashore in the *Charlotte*'s boat. The city had changed little in the year since I had visited there. At the harbormaster's office I reported what I had learned about the Boston evacuation. Within minutes the word had spread, and I was hemmed in by dozens of people asking me questions. After an hour of this ordeal, I broke away and made my way along the waterfront, south to The White Swan tavern.

Liz Oliver was in the act of chastising a servingmaid for slovenliness when I entered the taproom.

"Be not too hard on the poor girl, Mistress Oliver," I said.

She whirled in indignation at this intrusion. Then her mouth dropped open, and she hurled herself into my arms. Remembering her dignity, she quickly drew away and gave the maid one final warning to change her ways.

"Ah, Jerry, I never thought to see you again. Have a mug of our best beer and tell me where you've been."

I spun her a good yarn, which she interrupted to inquire after Captain McGee and his sons.

I then interrupted her to inquire after her husband.

"He's well enough. Went out to Germantown this afternoon to buy provisions."

I raised my eyebrows. "Would you have room for a lodger for the night?"

"We're crowded at the moment. You'd have to share a room."

"Is the pantry off the kitchen not available?" I asked with a smirk.

She slapped my hand and leaned close to whisper, "You did not ask with whom you would have to share a room."

I grinned. "But Master Oliver?"

"I said he had gone out to Germantown." She paused and added, "Overnight."

That woman treated me well that night, better than I deserved. I was hungry for good cooking, and she saw that I got the best her kitchen could provide. I was hungry for love as well; after her other guests had retired and the tavern doors had been barred for the night, she gave me the best she had to offer in that department as well. No furtive coupling on grain sacks in a kitchen pantry this time. No listening out for the possible approach of a husband. Ah, the sweet luxury of that plump, tender woman's body given and taken freely in her own feather bed! She was as hungry as I, or acted so.

We awakened near dawn and talked in low tones.

"You seem different, Jerry," she said.

"How so, my darling Liz?"

"More practiced, I would say."

I wondered if my experience with Madame LaFontaine could have made that much difference but passed off Liz's comment with, "A hell of a lot of practice you get on a sloop with twenty-five cut-throat sailors."

"Maybe that is it. You are in command of your own ship. You act more masterful."

At dawn's first light, she turned me out of her room. "Must set a good example for my kitchen help, you know."

Later, after breakfast, I made my way to the Pennsylvania State House. There I discovered that sure enough, the Congress was considering the issuance of privateering licenses. It would be a while before they ironed out the details. But the members with whom I talked were far more interested in my news about Boston than in privateering. It did my popularity no harm at all to bear such welcome tidings. In fact, it took all morning before various delegates were finished with questioning me.

As I was departing the State House, a ragged lad caught my sleeve and inquired if I might be Jeremiah Martin. I nodded, and he presented me with a note that he said was from Mr. Dogood Mackey.

It took me a moment to connect that curious name with the genial Quaker merchant friend of Jason McGee, the man who had introduced us to Benjamin Franklin. His note reminded me of our meeting, said he had learned that I was in port with a sloop, and requested that I drop by his office on Front Street at my earliest convenience.

Now, the Quakers of Philadelphia have always been a canny lot, trading as they do on their well-deserved reputation for honest dealing. But they were much divided over the issue of war. Some thought it wrong to oppose the King by force of arms; others thought it wrong of the King to bring arms to bear against his subjects. Rare indeed, however, is the Quaker businessman who is not willing to discuss an opportunity to make a profit and scrutinize it carefully by the lamp of his Inward Light.

Dogood Mackey greeted me with great warmth. He listened to my account of my adventures since we had parted with his head cocked to one side and a slight smile.

"And thy sloop has a copper bottom? Seventy tons, thee says? And thee bought her from Francis Bolton? A good experienced crew, thee says? Well, with all these resources, what brings thee back with empty hold to our fair city?"

Mackey was one of those unusual men who both merit and inspire one's trust. I could not bring myself to deceive him, so I told him the full story of our privateering in New England waters.

For a presumably peace-loving Quaker, he knew a great deal about the business of privateering and about Congress's feelings on the matter.

"They are talking of requiring a bond of five thousand pounds for a vessel of under a hundred tons. Twice that for larger craft."

My heart sank at this news.

"There is talk, also, of requiring each privateer to recruit landsmen to make up at least one-third of its crew. The Congress fears that the competition for experienced sailors would inhibit recruiting for the navy they have authorized, thee sees."

As Friend Mackey went on relating some of the likely restrictions Congress would place on privateering, I began to wish that I had not been so hasty in returning my Massachusetts letter of marque and severing my arrangement with Tubsworthy.

"Thee seems downcast," the Quaker said.

"All these regulations," I said.

"Congress does not wish to unleash bands of pirates upon the sea lanes. The business has to be regulated, and strictly so. If it were not, I would wish to have nothing to do with it."

Suddenly my ears perked up.

"You mean you are interested in privateering? You, a member of the Society of Friends?"

"It is a form of business, and of patriotism. Someone will do it. So to answer thy question, yes, if there are severe penalties for barbaric conduct, I might be interested in playing a quiet role. I am a patriot, Friend Martin. We cannot match the strength of the British navy ship for ship. But privateering, regulated by law, could do much to even the odds. Stay in touch with me until Congress has reached its decision on this matter. Meanwhile, let us keep this conversation between thee, me, and the gatepost. I would be turned out of meeting if my interest were advertised. Now, tell me about Boston. Have the British abandoned the city for certain?"

3

I WAS NOT EAGER to visit the Masons, but thought I should for Ephraim's sake. After getting my whiskers and hair trimmed by a barber and brushing my clothes, I made my way to the spacious brick home I had visited the year before.

Laura herself answered my knock.

"Why, it is Mr. Martin! Where's Ephraim?"

"Ephraim is fine. He sends his regards," I began.

"Laura, who is at the door?" It was the voice of Dr. Mason.

"Father, you remember Jeremiah Martin."

"What is he doing in our house?"

"Why, he has come with news from Ephraim—"

"He has come to Philadelphia as captain of a privateering vessel that has been preying upon His Majesty's shipping! He is no better than a pirate! I will not have him in our house."

"Father! How can you be so rude?"

"The news is all about town. He has got possession of one of the boats of my friend Sir Francis Bolton and has been committing depredations against British ships. He has come to apply for the approval of Congress to continue his piracy. Away from my house, sir, and never darken my door again!"

By now Laura was in tears.

I bowed to Laura, then turned and strode away from the house.

During the next few days, Dogood Mackey kept in close touch with Congress's Marine Committee as its members worked, mostly in night sessions, on the privateer question. During that time our friendship and my respect for him grew. He was a wise and good gentleman. Unlike Bolton, he did not try to manipulate me. He spoke his mind frankly and expected others to do likewise. There was no pretense about him. His forthrightness made me feel guilty at withholding my entire story from him.

Over supper one evening at The London Coffee House, he fixed me with his kindly eye and asked why I seemed troubled. I blurted out the truth about my dealings with Sir Francis and my spying activities in Boston—everything, right up to my revenge upon Major Tuttle.

He listened without comment until I stopped for breath.

"Fascinating," he said. "Thee has been caught in a web, it would seem. Well, we must consider how thee may extricate thyself. Might I be allowed to see the bill of sale for thy sloop and the copy of that promissory note?"

He put on his spectacles. As he read, a broad smile spread over his face.

"Francis Bolton has outwitted himself. He set the price too low. Once Congress passes its privateering bill, that sloop will be worth far more than two thousand pounds. Oh, this is delicious! The old fox thought to ingratiate himself with the British army and do a bit of war profiteering, using thee as his cat's paw. Still, and meaning no offense to thee, it is strange that he would take such a risk with one he knew so slightly."

"What should I do now?"

"The decision is up to thee, Friend Jerry. From what thee says, he has not scrupled to put thy life in jeopardy for his own purposes. Yet he has placed unusual trust in thee. To what end?"

"I suppose he reckons that he holds the whip hand over me."

"And so he does—with one hand. But with the other he extends the carrot of financial preferment. I find this quite inexplicable."

"So do I. And sooner or later, word of my privateering will reach him. Even if it did not, I can't very well return his sloop to him with no cargo."

"Ordinarily, I would counsel thee to abide by the spirit of thy understanding rather than by the letter. But one does not deal with Francis Bolton in ordinary ways. Indeed, I have avoided any transactions at all with him. He is far too slippery for my tastes."

"I had thought to pay him the stipulated two thousand pounds and keep his sloop. But then I would have no letter of marque. I lack the means to post a five-thousand-pound bond, not to mention to buy cannon and recruit new crewmen."

"Yet, thee has a capital resource greater than mere gold, unless I am very wrong. Thee has youth, and boldness, and wit. I mislike the small traces of deviousness I perceive in thy character, but I can see that circumstances have forced thee into behaviors perhaps not natural to thy nature."

"I have always played fair and square with those who have done so with me."

"Jason McGee thinks highly of thee."

"I am glad, but where is all this leading us?"

"It is leading us to an arrangement in which I would sign the bond for thy privateer's license and direct thee to persons who might assist thee in equipping thy sloop as needed."

Remembering my experience with Tubsworthy, I restrained my eagerness.

"What share would you expect for this backing?"

"I prefer not to own any share. I could lend thee money for cannon and other equipment, but that would be contrary to my conscience. However, I can put thee in touch with persons who feel otherwise."

I wrung his hand so hard that he winced.

Back to The White Swan I fairly skipped, whistling and snapping my fingers and, yes, wishing that Phineas Oliver were still in Germantown. Oh, this was news to be celebrated long and lustily in bed with a luscious partner! But no, the proprietor himself was presiding at the bar when I arrived. I don't know whether he suspected anything between his wife and me. He seemed surprised to see me and said he hoped I had been shown proper hospitality. I assured him that I had.

The best Liz and I could manage that night was a hasty romp in the pantry after Oliver had gone off to bed. Afterward, as she buttoned her dress and straightened her hair, she said, "My, you are the randy gentleman tonight! What has got into you?"

"Oh, I feel like a new man. I have received a bit of good news today. But you act glum. What has got into you?"

She looked at me wryly and gave me a playful punch. "A randy gentlemen with some good news, wouldn't you say? Tell me your news, Jerry, please. I am low in spirits and could use a good boost."

On April 3 of that crucial year 1776, Congress adopted a bill authorizing privateers to "by force of arms, attack, subdue, and take all ships and other vessels belonging to inhabitants of Great Britain, on the high seas." As Dogood Mackey had wished, article six of the act provided that anyone guilty of killing, torturing, or maiming prisoners in cold blood should be "severely punished."

I had no objections to this or the other articles except number eight, which specified, as Mackey had warned, that "one third, at the least, of your whole Company shall be landsmen."

By that time I was beginning to wish I had no landsmen at all in my crew. My Pennsylvania brothers had gone ashore with their rifles and, roaring drunk, had put on a demonstration of marksmanship on Toby's Wharf. They had been arrested and thrown into jail. I could have bailed them out but thought it wiser to let them stay there, where I could find them when time came to sail. Now, to meet this congressional requirement, I would need a dozen additional landsmen. I considered and rejected the idea of riding out to Sherman's Valley to recruit some less rambunctious riflemen. But that would take two or three weeks. Instead, I placed an advertisement in *The Pennsylvania Gazette*, with interviews to be conducted at The White Swan.

What a motley lot of applicants appeared! A lad with a harelip, a free-born mulatto with one eye, a near imbecile, several farm boys, and several of what I judged to be runaway apprentices—they came in droves and stood about on the street while Lovejoy and I talked to them one by one inside.

Lovejoy went into what I at first thought needless detail, describing the hardships of a life at sea and the dangers of privateering. He also demanded to see their hands and to feel their arm muscles.

"Have ye ever done a day's labor in your life?" he asked one soft mama's boy, who then burst into tears at being rejected. Of another, whose complexion seemed sallow, he asked where he had been in jail and for how long.

Only those who passed his harsh scrutiny first were treated to my description of the spoils that lay in store aboard a privateer and how the shares were to be distributed.

By the end of the second day, we had our twelve recruits, mostly young fellows, but also several older, tougher chaps. Lovejoy took them out to the *Charlotte* for their first visit aboard a real ship. Dogood Mackey accompanied me to the Marine Committee to post my bond and help me secure my "letter of marque and reprisal."

After that we had a long, heart-to-heart talk in which he advised me on several points. At the end of our conversation, he gave me a letter of introduction to be presented to one Jan de Windt, the governor of the Dutch island of St. Eustatius, and another to Abraham d'Balboa, whom he identified as a Jewish merchant in Oranjestad.

Back at The White Swan, a letter was waiting for me. Liz Oliver watched from behind the bar while I broke the seal and read the following words from Laura Mason:

> Dear Jerry:
> I am much distressed at the way in which my father treated you at our house. My parents have suffered much in recent months, but that hardly excuses his rudeness to you. I pray that you will find it in your heart to forgive him.
> It further distresses me that you were not given the opportunity to give me news of Ephraim. Would it be too much of an imposition to ask that you write a note telling me about his situation in Barbados?
> I hope that this cruel war will end soon and that there will be no more animosity between neighbors.
> > With all good wishes, Laura Mason.

Liz waited until I had finished writing a reply to Laura before she asked, "You'll be leaving us again soon, Jerry?"

"Yes."

"You wouldn't be needing a cook aboard your ship, would you?"

"We have a cook."

She smiled sadly. "Pity. You'll be back, I hope."

"Philadelphia is our home port."

"Phineas has gone out to Germantown again."

"Overnight?"

She smiled and winked.

At dawn the next morning, instead of turning me out of her bed, Liz drew me close and wept on my shoulder.

"Life's not fair," she sobbed.

"How so?"

"Because you are a man, you can come and go as you please. You can love where you want to love. Look at me—I was married off too young to a man who can imagine nothing better than to own a tavern. And I am trapped! That dullard could go off and join the army or sail with you, but not me."

One thing I have learned is never to agree with a wife's criticism of her husband. Nothing is surer to make her defend him.

"He is a good provider," I said. "And I never saw him mistreat you. Is there anyone you'd rather be married to?"

She dried her tears and put her face against my neck. "Yes, and you know him very well."

I took this as a compliment to myself. Some response seemed to be called for. "Too bad he is not the marrying sort."

"Oh, but he is! That is just the trouble."

I propped up on one elbow and disentangled our legs. "I don't understand."

"Captain McGee has a wife, as you well know."

Crestfallen, I said, "Oh," as I lowered my head beside hers.

She wiped her eyes and said with forced cheerfulness, "Well, here now, you'll be taking your leave today. Let's give himself something to remember on those long nights at sea."

After a good breakfast, I gathered my clothes and gave Liz a lusty kiss. I might have felt more sadness if she had not made that remark about Jason McGee. Whoever thinks he understands women deceives himself.

I had arrived at the wharf where our boat was tied up before I remembered the two riflemen still in jail. They cursed me roundly for leaving them there so long. When I made as if to walk away in anger, they promised that never again would I have cause to complain of their behavior if only I would secure their release and take them with me.

They got another severe lecture from Lovejoy when we reached the *Charlotte*. A pilot was already aboard and eager to guide us down the Delaware.

I took a long last look at Philadelphia and shouted, "Up anchor!"

4

SURELY THE MAN WHO FALLS closest to being in command of his own fate with freedom to come and go as he chooses and—within limits—to do as he pleases, surely that man would be the captain of a privateer operating under legitimate papers against an enemy who deserves no more mercy than he shows.

That is what I thought as I stood on the gently lifting and falling quarterdeck of the *Charlotte* on a fine April day as we skimmed along with a light cargo and a full crew southward past the Virginia capes. Down on the main deck, Lovejoy Brown was swearing away at the awkward landsmen we had signed on at Philadelphia. My Pennsylvanians were running through their gun drills with our make-believe cannon. Under the galley awning, Cato was peeling potatoes and singing a Bajan lovesong in a pleasant baritone. The sea was just as I liked—deep blue with a moderate swell rolling in from our compass heading, south by southeast. No sails were in sight anywhere. My carnal appetites had been slaked by Mistress Oliver. My faith in human nature had been restored by Dogood Mackey. I had in my possession as genuine a license to privateer as ever one could ask, with promises of financial backing available in St. Eustatius, or "Statia," as it was commonly called. I had an adventuresome task before me and an intriguing decision to make.

Lovejoy complained about a dozen things—not the least of them the stupidity and awkwardness of our recruits—but he was never happy without something to protest. I refused to allow his constant fretting to rub off on me.

Our luck held for the next two weeks. We hit a line of squalls near the Bahamas. The experience was good for our green crew, although one chap nearly got washed overboard when a wave surged over the side of the *Charlotte* as we were coming about to a new course. One of our riflemen and an old salt from Marblehead nearly came to blows over a card game. This gave me a grand opportunity to deliver a blistering lecture to the entire crew. At Lovejoy's suggestion, I banned gaming until we made port. I might have been justified in flogging both the quarreling parties, but I could not bring myself to inflict such punishment on free-born Americans.

Several times we sighted sails, but in each case I changed course to avoid an encounter.

Except for an occasional tropical rainstorm, the farther south we sailed, the calmer grew the weather. Despite Lovejoy's gloomy attitude, it was a happy, easy cruise. We passed between the Virgin Islands and St. Maartens and beat our way against a brisk trade wind through the eastern Caribbean. We worked our way eastward between St. Lucia and St. Vincent and headed south once more.

Finally one morning, with Barbados's Mt. Hillaby a speck on the northern horizon, I ordered a reversal of course so that we could sail northward again with the wind off our starboard quarter. The native Bajans onboard became more animated the closer we drew to their native shore. By the time the sun had dipped into the Caribbean, we were near enough to make out Fort Needham, which guarded the entrance to Carlisle Bay.

With only the light of a half-moon to guide us, I turned the helm over to Lovejoy and told him to deliver the *Charlotte* into a bay just south of Speightstown. We dropped anchor in the dark. I summoned Cato to my cabin and explained my mission to him. With his assistance and the use of some charred wood from his galley, I transformed my countenance into that of one of his own race. Then, barefoot and with a scarf tied about my head and two loaded pistols in my belt, I had our boat lowered into the water. Cato and I got in, and he rowed us ashore.

We dragged our boat across the beach and into the underbrush, then took our bearings on the moonlit outline of Mt. Hillaby. We headed inland and upward along a wagon track.

I swear that Cato could see in the dark as well as a cat. He even had a feline ability to return to his home. Had I undertaken that mission alone, I would have blundered off in the wrong direction and ended up anywhere but in the lane leading into Bolton Hall. By that time I had come to regret going barefoot. I stopped beside an old slave graveyard to catch my breath and get my bearings. Off to our right, we could see the dying cook fires of the Negro yard and hear the voices of the slaves as they settled in for their night's rest. Ahead of us, candlelight showed through the windows of the great house.

Thanking my stars that Sir Francis despised dogs, I took Cato's hand. We crept into the yard and then through a side garden to the cook house at the rear of the main building. I could hear a high-pitched voice singing.

"It is that eunuch, that Ibo," Cato whispered.

We sneaked to the kitchen window, and sure enough there was my old chess partner puttering away at some dish while the cook slept in a bunk beside the fireplace. I tapped lightly on the window-sill. Ibo froze and looked up.

"Who is there?"

He recognized my voice at once, but when he opened the door and saw my blackened face, he stopped and seemed at the point of raising an alarm. Cato seized his arm, swept him out into the darkness, and placed his great paw over his mouth.

"Quiet, Ibo," I whispered. "It is all right. I want you to do something and do it quickly without asking questions."

Cato and I waited under the huge fig tree in the kitchen yard while Ibo went into the great house.

After several minutes, I grew restive. Telling Cato to remain where he was, I crept past the kitchen and up to the lighted window of the drawing room. I reached out my hand and fumbled for the windowsill to steady myself. Damn it to almighty hell! I had forgotton that under each window of Bolton Hall, there was planted a cactus or thorny hedge to discourage peeping Toms. My arm and side stung as though a hundred bees had assailed me, but I dared not cry out. I ground my teeth against the pain and peered through a crack in the shutters.

There sat the old man himself, hunched over a table, wearing his spectacles and holding a book. He was dressed in a nightgown, and his shoulders were draped with a shawl. I half wished I could go in and talk to him. He had caused me much misery since our introduction in Philadelphia a year before. But he had brought a measure of excitement and opportunity into my life that I had never dreamed of. What would happen if I were to extricate myself from that damnable thorn bush and walk right into the room and announce that I had returned with the *Charlotte*? No, damn it, I had gone too far for this. This was British soil, and Bolton, for all his cynicism, was a loyal supporter of the King. There could be no turning back.

The old man looked up from his book.

"Who's there?"

I held my breath.

"Ibo? What's going on? Who is in the hall?"

"Only me, master."

"Well, where is my pudding? Where is Dr. McGee?"

"I go and fetch your pudding, master."

On tender feet and with burning arms, I slipped away from the window and back to the shadow of the bearded fig tree beside the kitchen door. There by the light of the moon, I made out the slender figure of Ephraim standing next to the great bulk of Cato.

It took him an agonizingly long time to accept that it was I who stood before him. To stop his torrent of questions, I put my hand against his lips.

"I have come to take you away, to rescue you."

"I don't need anyone to rescue me. Besides, I have another month before my indenture expires."

"What difference will a month make?"

"My agreement specifies that I remain a full year from the time of my arrival on Barbados and the payment of one hundred pounds at the conclusion of the term."

"Damn the hundred pounds. I'll make it up to you. Is there anything you need to take? Medical kit, or whatever?"

"I have an entire trunk of valuables. All my books and notes on my observations of tropical diseases. I refuse to steal away into the night like a guilty thief."

Dear God, I hated to do it, but I could not afford to stand there arguing with that impossible prig. His precious honor was at stake, but my equally precious life was also at serious risk. Taking care to use just the right amount of force, with my hand wrapped in my head scarf, I drove my fist against Ephraim's chin. He went down like a calf under a butcher's sledgehammer. I tied his hands behind him and gagged him securely.

"Do you think you can carry him until we are out of earshot?" I asked Cato.

He lifted Ephraim's limp form across his massive shoulders and grunted. "I can carry him all the way to the boat, Captain."

As we passed the drawing-room window, I could hear Sir Francis complaining to Ibo about the texture of the pudding he had brought from the kitchen. I prayed that Ibo would keep his mouth shut.

At the slave cemetery, Ephraim recovered consciousness. I had Cato set him on his feet, and in as few words as possible I explained to my young doctor friend what I intended to do.

He shook his head and tried to force his words past the gag.

"You have a choice, Ephraim," I said. "Either walk along peaceably, or I will clout you on the jaw again, and Cato will have to lug you the rest of the way. You don't want to make unnecessary work for him, do you?"

We reached the beach, and Cato dragged our boat back into the water. Ephraim turned and ran toward the trees, but I brought him down with a fairly gentle tackle and carried him back to the boat myself.

Back aboard the *Charlotte,* I left Ephraim's gag in place while our crew raised anchor.

Lovejoy Brown did a masterful job of navigating the *Charlotte* that night. The water was calm and the winds light, but he did exactly what I required of him. That was to tack back and forth to the south so that by the time the sun rose, we would be in a position to sail into Carlisle Bay. Lovejoy thought it madness to take ourselves into a well-fortified British harbor while carrying a congressional letter of marque, but he followed his orders to a T. As we passed Fort Needham on our right, a gun boomed a challenge. We fired our swivel to the left, signaling our peaceful intentions, and we dipped the British colors under which we now sailed. By that time I had scrubbed the black from my face and had changed into my best clothing. Ephraim was locked away in the first mate's cabin. We dropped anchor away from the other ships in the harbor. Once again our boat was lowered into the water, and Cato rowed me ashore.

It took some fast talking on my part to convince the harbormaster that there was no need to inspect the *Charlotte* right away. I would keep the crew aboard ship, and he could come out that afternoon to look us over.

What cargo were we carrying?

"We are traveling in ballast. Boston has been evacuated. We thought it prudent to return home quickly."

"We learned two weeks ago that Boston was evacuated. Where have you been since mid-March?"

I winked and put my finger beside my nose. "That sloop belongs to Sir Francis Bolton. He wouldn't want me to discuss details with anyone but himself now, would he? By the way, some of my men were naughty back in Boston, and their punishment is to remain aboard ship for a full day after reaching harbor."

After fending off other questions from the hangers-on about the docks, I walked over to Swan Street and asked to see Bolton's lawyer. His clerk said he wasn't in but would be arriving at any moment. Damn that pettifogger's eyes—he did not appear for nearly an hour, a very anxious hour for me, which I spent worrying about what, if anything, had been relayed from Boston about my seizure of the *Charlotte* and our failure to deliver the livestock and food-stuffs to the British army. With sweat dripping from my brow and soaking my jacket, I fended off the clerk's questions until at last the lawyer arrived, smelling of brandy and very much surprised to see me.

"Sir Francis has been beside himself with concern about his sloop. We must send a messenger up to Bolton Hall forthwith. No, better, I will hire a coach, and we'll drive up there together. Did you bring in a good cargo of American foods, as you were supposed to?"

"Wait. Let's not disturb Sir Francis just yet. As for cargo, I have brought back something far more valuable than salt fish and cornmeal."

I made it appear that I had a quantity of gold aboard the *Charlotte*—which of course I did. The lawyer leaped to the assumption that this was money brought out of Boston. I winked and nodded, then leaned forward in a confidential manner.

"I dared not bring so much gold ashore. I should like very much for you to come out to the *Charlotte* with me. Inventory what we have. I'll treat you to a bottle of good madeira while we count the loot."

The lawyer instructed his clerk to postpone his other appointments for the morning, and within minutes he was tripping along in his white suit and broad-brimmed hat down to the dock. Cato rowed us out to the *Charlotte*. The lawyer wanted to know why our crew was not ashore and why there were so many strange faces among them.

"We picked up some loyal Americans along the way," I said as I hurried him into my cabin.

145

With a bottle of madeira on the table and a glass at his hand, I brought out all the gold and silver that I had accumulated from the sale of the prizes we had taken off the New England coast.

Now, this is a curious thing to me. That little lawyer had no legitimate interest in that money, and yet it might have been his own from the way his hands trembled and his eyes shone as he inspected and counted each coin and noted it on a sheet of paper—all this between glasses of madeira.

"Did you bring out no jewels, no plate?"

"Just money, gold and silver, as you can see. How much do you count there?"

"I make it out to be four thousand, two hundred fifteen pounds, six shillings, and four pence."

I picked up three gold guineas and put them in his hand. "I think that a suitable and well-earned reward to compensate you for deserting your office on such short notice and taking all this trouble, don't you?"

He hesitated. He acted as if he were about to give it back, but I closed his fingers over the gold and told him to consider it a gift from me. He put the coins in his vest pocket, and I poured him another glass of madeira.

"Now, sir, while I have your attention, I should like very much to review these documents you helped Sir Francis and me to prepare."

I laid out the bill of sale and the promissory note, together with a copy of Sir Francis's letters of instruction to me and to Atticus Fitzgerald.

"Captain Fitzgerald." The lawyer raised his head. "I don't see him. Where is he?"

"Alas, I have dreaded telling you this. The poor man fell overboard."

"Lost at sea? My God, how did that happen?"

"He was inspecting a boat that had slipped its lines, and he lost his balance. Please, I can't bring myself to discuss it just now. These papers—you remember them?"

"Of course. I wrote them, didn't I?"

"They transferred title to the *Charlotte* to me on the understanding that within six months I would pay to the order of Sir Francis Bolton the sum of two thousand pounds, is that not so?"

The lawyer began to look suspicious. "That is what the documents say, but of course our understanding was that you would return the sloop with a cargo of staples to Sir Francis."

"Where are the documents stipulating that understanding?"

The lawyer stood up, his face suddenly red.

"Look here, Martin, what are you getting at?"

The lawyer had counted the coins into piles of a thousand pounds each. I moved two of those piles closer to him.

"The note specifies that the money must be paid to Sir Francis Bolton or his agent. You are his agent. I am hereby paying to you, on his behalf, the sum of two thousand pounds."

"That is preposterous! It is his own money."

"It is my money. It is none of your concern how I came by it. I want a receipt, and I want you to sign this note as paid."

"I would die first," he said, and started for the door.

I seized his collar and flung him into his chair.

"You speak of dying. That is exactly what will happen to you if you do not do as I tell you."

"You are bluffing! This is a British port—don't forget that."

"You have three choices: accept the two thousand pounds and give me a receipt or sail with us to St. Eustatius, where I will deliver payment to authorized persons there to be held on Sir Francis's behalf. Or if you prefer, we'll toss you overboard and let you swim the half-mile to shore."

"You can't treat me like this. Release me and let me return to my office."

I went to the door of the cabin and shouted, "Attention, all hands! Bring the ship's boat aboard. Up anchor, and prepare to sail. On the double."

The lawyer's face turned ashen.

"This is duress. It is highly illegal."

"Would the arrangement Sir Francis made with me stand the scrutiny of a court of law? Look, we can argue the fine points on the way to Statia. Or you may wish to swim ashore. I hear that in the old days slave ships used to throw their dead cargo overboard to the sharks in these very waters. Do they still do that?"

"I will sign only under protest."

"You can explain that to Sir Francis. I expect you'll require an additional fee for your trouble. Would a hundred pounds do?"

I got my receipt. I gave him a canvas bag containing two thousand pounds in sound gold coins. We lowered the ship's boat into the water. Just before he climbed into it, I said, "Give Sir Francis my respects, and tell him he can keep the boat. And by the bye, tell him Dr. McGee is sailing with us. Oh yes, give him this also. It is a letter of credit from the American army for the livestock and foods he shipped off to North America."

Then I turned to our crew and called out. "Many of you are from this island. If you wish to remain here, you may join this gentleman in the boat. But if you wish to continue with this ship as crewmen, I can promise you much adventure and possibly great rewards. How say ye?"

Several of my blacks, the mulatto bosun included, raced to the ladder and jammed down into the boat with the lawyer. I looked into the faces of the others. Cato grinned at me.

"We gonna stick with you, Captain Martin," he said.

"Fine. Cast off that boat. Up anchor."

My business completed, we set our mainsail and headed back into the Caribbean. The *Charlotte* was mine, and I had the papers to prove it. I felt very much as if the entire world had likewise suddenly become the property of Jeremiah Martin.

5

I NEVER KNEW Ephraim McGee to show such anger as he did off the northern point of Barbados after I had untied his hands and freed him from the mate's cabin.

At first he glared at me, refusing even to speak.

"Now, Ephraim," I said, "let us shake hands and sit down as friends. I have much to tell you."

He crossed his arms and turned his back.

"Look here, don't you realize what a risk I took coming to Bolton Hall in the dead of night to rescue you?"

Still no reply.

"It is a pity you aren't speaking. I have but lately come from Philadelphia. And while there I paid a visit to Laura."

He walked away and looked out the rear window of the cabin.

"I saw your father in Cambridge earlier. He was much concerned over Chris, over his safety. You see, Chris went off on an expedition with General Arnold to Canada."

He half turned his head at that, then looked away again.

I squelched my urge to plant a healthy kick to his backside and said with feigned calmness, "You know, Ephraim, that year I lived at your house, I remember that you got yourself into a pout over some trifling matter. Chris and I threw you down and tickled you until you wet your breeches. Do you remember that? Shall I call Cato to help me treat you so again?"

He remained motionless until I started for the door.

"Mama was right about you," he snarled. "She said you were shifty and self-seeking. Too clever for your own good, she said."

"I was clever enough to get you off that island."

"My time was nearly up. I did not need the help of a renegade to regain my freedom."

I swallowed the impulse to punch him on the jaw again and said with forced sweetness, "You may have a point. But I need your help, Ephraim. I need it badly."

"What sort of help?"

"First, let me give you the news about your father and Chris. Here, sit."

"Very well, but don't play tricks on me. Tell me the truth straight out, without embroidering the facts. What is this about Chris? And who is General Arnold?"

I brought him up to date as quickly and directly as possible, including the fact that Dr. Mason had ordered me out of his house.

"Do you think Chris might have been wounded or taken prisoner?"

"Many who went north with Arnold were. The general himself was wounded in the assault on Quebec."

"And Laura did not appear well?"

"I would say tired. Her family have been harassed by overzealous patriots. Incidentally, Ephraim, she is a lovely girl. You are a lucky man."

He got tears in his eyes, but suddenly his face hardened again.

"I heard you talking to Bolton's lawyer. You have pulled another of your sharp deals, haven't you? You got title to this ship by underhanded methods."

"You are wrong, Ephraim."

"Please don't insult my intelligence with lies."

"You are wrong when you call the *Charlotte* a ship. She is a sloop and one of the finest."

"Ship or sloop, it means nothing to me."

"Oh, but it does. We have no ship's surgeon. It is customary for a privateer to set aside four shares of prize monies for the surgeon. I need you to serve as surgeon of the *Charlotte*. And it is important that you call your craft by its right name."

He flared up again at that. "So that is why you abducted me from Bolton Hall? I have no wish to participate in legalized piracy!"

"You sound as pompous and self-righteous as your prospective father-in-law," I replied. "Look, Ephraim, like it or not, we are at war with Great Britain, which has the mightiest fleet in the world. It would take years for us to build a comparable navy. Privateering is the only answer. I have a legitimate license, and I have a bought-and-paid-for sloop. So please preach me no sermons. Don't decide about my offer for a few days, if you like. First though, in case you feel any regrets about leaving the service of Sir Francis Bolton so abruptly, let me tell you what that old conniver asked me to do to keep you in his employ."

He listened closely as I told him of how Bolton had asked me to try to persuade Laura to return with me to Barbados.

"You didn't broach the subject to her, did you?"

"Her father threw me out of the house before I could speak about anything."

"And he really wanted you to bring a harpsichord back? He is a devious old man. A sad, lonely, and thoroughly corrupt person. He thought he could enslave me as he did Ramsay, his overseer, by importing the girl I love."

149

"And he thought to enslave me by making me his personal secretary and involving me in his schemes."

"But are you not as much a schemer as he? After all, you got possession of his ship—I mean sloop—by questionable means."

"Questionable means of his own concoction. He simply fell into his own trap. Dogood Mackey himself said so."

"What has Mr. Mackey to do with all this?"

I told him about my letters of introduction to persons in Statia and the five-thousand-pound bond.

He shook his head and, for the first time, half grinned. "I'm sorry I repeated what Mama said about you. In all fairness, I should tell you Father's reply. He said you were like a cat. He said you had nine lives and always landed on your feet."

"Your father is the best friend I ever had, Ephraim. Now, about this surgeon business. Why don't you wait until after we have stopped at Statia before you give me your answer? All I ask is that you don't say no just yet. Take your time. Get to know the crew. And the *Charlotte*. The old man named her after his grandmother, you know. He told me Laura reminded him of his grandmother."

Ephraim stared out the window for several moments before he spoke again. "Much as I despise that selfish, grasping old man, still I pity him. He wanted a young couple and music about him at Bolton Hall. I disappointed him, I know. I would have preferred to depart his employ with dignity. He will be even more disappointed when his lawyer tells him what you have done. You may have gained yourself more than a sloop, Jerry."

"What is that?"

"A powerful, cunning, and implacable enemy."

"I am not in the least concerned about him anymore. He is out of my life for good. Let us dismiss him from our minds. Here, examine the charts of Statia, and I'll let you in on my plans to help the American cause and make a bit of profit for ourselves in the bargain."

I had never been to St. Eustatius, but I understood it to be a Dutch-owned island in the Leewards group, situated between St. Maartens and St. Kitts. Our chart showed it was about two miles wide and a bit over five long. Dogood Mackey had explained that the canny Dutch long ago turned it into a major exchange post for the various nations engaged in trade with the West Indies. "A crossroads between Europe, Africa, and both South and North America," he had called it, adding that "you can buy or sell anything you want in that place."

Even so, I was quite unprepared for what I found on what should have been just another obscure dab of land along the edge

150

of the Caribbean. Near noon, we sighted the serrated rim of the volcanic cone that dominated the southern end of Statia—"the Quill," as it was marked on our chart. In late afternoon we sailed into Statia's anchorage, which lay in a shallow bay along the eastern shore in the shadow of the island's chief—indeed, only—town, Oranjestad.

I was amazed at the number and variety of ships anchored in what seemed to me a very poor excuse for a harbor, merely a two-mile indentation in the shoreline. And I was further amazed by the jumble of buildings that lined the shore. Some were obviously warehouses, but others appeared to be offices, and some even commodious houses. All these structures had been erected at the base of a long cliff, the top of which was occupied by the town proper, complete with fort, churches, and houses.

A black peddler in a small rowboat eagerly accepted our offer (and fee) to row Ephraim and me to the long stone wharf that lined the shore.

I had never been in a busier place than that so-called "lower town" of Oranjestad. The narrow street was jammed with rough sailors, workmen of all colors, clerks in their shirt sleeves, and elegantly clad gentlemen, not to mention women of varying colors who were behaving in an unvaryingly coarse manner, much to Ephraim's embarrassment.

We walked from one end of the street to the other, observing the warehouses, sail lofts, chandlers' stores, grog shops, bordellos, shipping offices, and counting houses that occupied every square foot of the long, narrow strip between sea and cliff.

Having completed this tour, I inquired of a pasty-faced fellow lounging in an office doorway where we might find Governor de Windt, for whom Mackey had given me a letter of introduction.

"You'll have a hard time finding him. He died last year. Johannes de Graaff is the governor now. Richest man in the island—and the meanest."

"What about Abraham d'Balboa? I hope he is not dead, too."

"You'll find him up in the Jewish part of the upper town, just two doors from their synagogue. What are you here for? Is that your sloop that just came in? American, aren't you? And riding empty, I'd say. Looking for a cargo, maybe?"

"Maybe. Thanks for your help. How do we reach the upper town?"

"Unless you sprout wings, you'll have to walk up the path like everyone else. Or take the cart road, but that's longer."

It was a steep climb up a hard-packed incline that ran diagonally along the hundred-foot-high bluff. The upper town offered a pleasant contrast to the lower. A fort with a battery of rusty cannon looked out over the anchorage. The streets were wide and uncrowded. I asked a half-grown Negro the way to Abraham d'Balboa's house.

A wall of hewn coral surrounded the narrow two-story house. The gate was locked and my knocking drew no response. At least Ephraim and I shook the gate vigorously and shouted, "Anybody home in there?"

We heard the doorway to the house open and footsteps in the yard.

A man's voice spoke in a language that I neither understood nor recognized.

I kicked the gate and said, "Abraham d'Balboa?"

"What do you want with him?" the voice asked in heavily accented English.

"I want to talk to him about a business matter."

"Don't you know that our sabbath is about to begin? There is not time to talk business. You will have to return on Sunday morning, or Monday if you are a Christian, I suppose."

"Never mind religion. I was given your name by Dogood Mackey of Philadelphia."

There was a long pause. Then a woman's voice called from the house, and the man answered her in Dutch.

"You know Mr. Mackey?"

"He is an old friend. I brought a sloop into your harbor."

We heard bolts being slid back, and at last the door opened enough for me to see the dark face of a middle-aged man dressed in a silken robe and wearing a curious sort of tasseled fez. Jet-black hair hung down to his shoulders. Equally black eyes, full of intelligence, looked first at me and then at Ephraim.

"It is only an hour before the sun goes down and our sabbath begins. I am to read the service at our synagogue tonight. You may have half the time that remains to me. Come in quickly, and do not waste words."

The house, richly furnished with colorful rugs and ornate tapestries, smelled of freshly baked bread and roasting chicken. The man led us through a dining room with table already set and candles lit to a small office at the rear of the house. A heavy-set, blond woman watched us as if disapproving our intrusion.

"You have a letter from Mr. Mackey?"

I handed him the missive. He looked carefully at the seal, then broke it and, without spectacles, read it quickly. When he looked up, it was with an expression considerably less austere and suspicious.

"Mr. Mackey is a fair-minded, honest man. You are fortunate to have gained his good opinion. This young man you have with you—he does not look old enough to be a physician."

152

Before I could intervene, Ephraim recited his training and recent experience.

At the mention of Bolton, d'Balboa grew agitated. "You were physician to that one?"

Sensing that we had stumbled onto a dangerous subject, I stepped in quickly. "Ephraim placed himself under contract to Sir Francis, but it was not a happy relationship between them. He is glad that his indenture has ended and that he is free to join me. I count myself lucky that he has agreed to join our ship's company."

I ignored Ephraim's glare.

"Abraham," the woman called from the kitchen.

I looked up and saw beside the woman a girl with dark, waving hair that hung far below her shoulders. She had a curved nose and deep-set eyes. She put me in mind of a Mediterranean version of Gerta McGee.

D'Balboa arose. "My wife and daughter lose patience with me. Our time grows short. I think I know what it is you require, but our business will have to wait. To avoid offense to our Dutch Christian brothers, I do not conduct business openly on Sunday, but I will be at home to talk if you should wish to confer then. Or if your religious scruples interfere, return on Monday. Either way, we will have time to consider possibilities. Shalom. Thank you for coming."

He ushered us out his gate and back into the bustling world of trade and finance.

The black boatman offered to row us back to the *Charlotte*.

"I have a better proposition. Let me buy your boat."

The next day was, of course, a Saturday. I left Ephraim to conduct sick call for our crew while Cato rowed me to shore once more. I shouldered my way through the lower town's human swarm and made the steep ascent to the upper town. There it was a simple matter to obtain directions to the Governor's office, which was maintained in a two-story house with a steep, tiled roof and a second-floor veranda facing the sea.

At first the clerk in the entry room, a young Dutchman, tried to turn me away.

"But I have a letter of introduction for the governor."

"Give it to me, and I will present it to him when he is not so much occupied."

Since my letter was addressed to the former governor, now deceased, I was reluctant to surrender it.

"Has the governor any visitors at present?"

"I don't see that is any of your business."

"Either you will go and tell the governor that I wish to see him, or I will proceed on my own and shall inform him of your officious rudeness."

The clerk turned scarlet. At last he rose indignantly and said, "I will see if he will receive you. I doubt very much he will."

The clerk came back down the stairs and said churlishly, "If you will be very brief, the governor can spare you a moment."

I mounted the stairs to a pleasant room that opened onto the second-floor veranda. A dark-haired man with a large nose and broad forehead looked up from the papers on his desk. He did not bother to rise.

"So, you haff a letter for me."

"Yes, it is from Dogood Mackey of Philadelphia."

He frowned. "Am I to know this person?"

I took a deep breath and plunged right in, "Why yes, Governor de Windt. He said he had known you for many years. Here, let his letter speak for itself."

The man stood up. "I am not de Windt. He is dead. I am Governor de Graaff. You should have learned that before you pushed your way in."

I thrust the letter into his hands.

"Forgive my ignorance, but I am the owner of a fine sloop with papers from our Congress itself, and I think it only right that you should read the letter since the former governor cannot. I am most terribly sorry to learn of his death."

"We all must die sometime."

He left me standing while he read and reread the letter.

"This Dogood Mackey thinks well enough of you. You want to buy supplies here. Our harbor is full of cargoes to be bought and sold. We take no side in your controffersy with your motherland. English, American, French, Spanish, or Dutch—all are free to buy and sell here." He paused and smiled ever so slightly. "Naturally, we cannot permit such things as arms and ammunition to be brought here openly, but otherwise you will find we giff you no problems. Fill up your sloop with whatever you haff the money to buy. Bring back whatever you wish from North America. You will find a market for it here. We Dutch have a saying, 'Chesus Christ is good, but trade is better.' "

He laughed. "They call us the Golden Rock. We take no sides, we trade with everyone. You are a clever fellow. Not many can get past Pietr downstairs. You did not really think de Windt was still governor, did you?"

"Mr. Mackey thought so when he wrote that letter."

"It does not matter. Who else did you bring letters for? I like to know what goes on here."

"I have a letter of introduction for Abraham d'Balboa."

"Ah so, one of our good Jews. There are many here of his tribe. We welcome them. They are good for business. Clever race. Almost

154

as clever as the Dutch, aha. How much did you pay for this sloop you own?"

"Two thousand pounds," I blurted out without thinking.

"*Mein Gott*, so little! Who was so foolish as to sell her at that price?"

I smiled and bowed. "Ah, Governor, there are some things which are to be kept to oneself."

"So, so. Now begone and spend your money."

6

I SPENT the rest of the day with Lovejoy surveying the wares available to us in that vast emporium called Oranjestad.

Spare sails, medical supplies, sextants and other navigational instruments, silks, laces, perfumes, rum, wines of every sort, molasses, various fruits, coconuts, monkeys and parrots, paint, tar, shoes and hats—everything a sailor could wish for himself or his lady friends was for sale along that strip of strand.

By evening I had been made a hundred propositions in a half-dozen different accents by everyone from sail merchants to prostitutes. And at least three merchants had asked if I wanted to sell the *Charlotte* herself. I was kept busy far into the night finding and ferrying our crewmembers back to our sloop. They arrived in various conditions of drunkenness. Ephraim had to bandage several wounds. It was midnight before I got to sleep.

The next morning I climbed the path to the upper town, accompanied by the bell tolling in the tower of the substantial Dutch Reformed Church just south of the fort. The people streaming toward the church made an interesting contrast with the rough throng milling about at the foot of the cliff. Several sedan chairs passed, carried on the shoulders of slaves and occupied by older women. Younger ladies walked under the protection of colorful parasols. The men for the most part were dressed in fine, dark broadcloth.

I proceeded under the already boiling sun to the Synagogue Path and stopped at the gate of Abraham d'Balboa. This time he responded to my first knock at his garden gate. He led me into his house and back to his office, whose deep windows were opened wide to catch the morning breeze.

His daughter served us coffee in gold-rimmed cups. I tried not to stare at the girl as she moved gracefully about the room, her eyes averted, her feet making hardly a sound.

"Thank you, Rebecca," her father said. "This is Mr. Martin. He is an American."

I arose and bowed. The girl finally looked directly at me, and I noticed that her eyes were a curious sort of greenish hazel. She nodded and withdrew, leaving us to talk business.

"So, I hear that you went to visit the governor."

"Why, yes. How did you learn that?"

"For all its busy trade, Statia is a small place. Words gets around. Was he civil to you?"

I laughed. "Just barely. But he assured me my money would be welcome here."

"Ah, that de Graaff. You are fortunate he took any notice of you at all. Owns a quarter of the land here. Has some three hundred slaves. His word is law. He has the island council in his pocket. What is the English words for him—*imperious*?"

"And overbearing and very sure of himself."

"Well, I have no complaint to make of him. He treats me and my fellow Jews with tolerance. As long as we don't get too big. As long as we keep in our place and make ourselves useful, we are safe here. The Dutch are good businessmen. Very practical people. I should know—I married a Dutch woman." He paused and looked at me until I grew discomfited by his gaze.

"You did not tell me your sloop was once the property of Sir Francis Bolton of Barbados."

"You did not ask me. And besides, we had very little time to talk."

"If we are to do business together, I must know everything. I do not like to play in the dark. How came you by the sloop?"

After I had finished my story, he smiled. "You have a receipt from his lawyer and a canceled promissory note?"

"And a license from our Continental Congress."

"What is it you need here?"

I drew from my pocket a sheet of paper listing everything Lovejoy and I felt the *Charlotte* required to fit her out as a full-fledged privateer.

He raised his eyebrows and pursed his lips. "You want eight six-pound cannon."

"Indeed, I do. But the governor told me weapons and ammunition are contraband."

D'Balboa winked. "He has to say that. It is a sensitive matter, but not impossible. Let us see how much all this is coming to."

I drank the powerful coffee and admired the speed with which he manipulated his abacus.

He came directly to the point and offered to provide me with everything on my shopping list—cannon included—for a promise to repay him at ten percent interest within one year. To secure the loan, I was to give him a mortgage on the *Charlotte* herself.

I wasn't born yesterday. I knew that he would be making a profit on each item provided me, but even so it was a risky investment for him. What was to prevent me from sailing back to North America and conducting my privateering out of Philadelphia or Boston? Where would he be if the *Charlotte* were lost in a storm or captured by the British?

"Why do you hesitate?" he asked. "If you think my terms too severe, you are welcome to shop about elsewhere in Statia to see if you can do better. I will leave my offer open for three days to give you time to make your inquiries."

"No, actually, I was wondering that you would extend such generous credit to someone you met just two days ago."

"You come recommended by Dogood Mackey. He has trusted you enough to post a five-thousand-pound bond in Philadelphia. You have a fine sloop with a copper bottom and a good crew."

He paused to sip his coffee. "Last but not least, it would give me a big satisfaction to see Francis Bolton bested, even humiliated, for I despise the very name of that man."

I was taken aback by his vehemence.

"Why is that?"

"He is an enemy of my people. He loses no opportunity to thwart us in Barbados and elsewhere, even back in London, where he has enormous influence. He has driven more than one of my friends to the wall for no other reason than his hatred of Jews. It will give me exquisite pleasure to see his own ship used against him. Can you understand my feelings perhaps?"

Abraham d'Balboa was as good as his word. Nearly everything we needed was promptly delivered to the *Charlotte*. All I had to do was sign the receipts.

I was beginning to think we would not get our cannon and ammunition, however. But near dusk a couple of days later, a heavy-laden ketch propelled by oars drew alongside the *Charlotte*, and a man asked me in a French accent if I was Jeremiah Martin.

When I acknowledged my identity, he said, "I have your order for ballast material ready for delivery."

"Ballast? I ordered no ballast."

"That is odd. I have crates here consigned to you by Monsieur d'Balboa for eight units of bronze ballast, each weighing twelve hundred pounds, and five hundred six-pound weights—oh yes, and six chests of tea, comprenez-vous?"

Lovejoy whispered to me. "Jerry, you damn fool! He's talking about our cannon."

We had to light lanterns and rig up a crane to shift the guns from the ketch to the *Charlotte*. It took an hour of backbreaking labor, but at last the eight gun barrels lay on our deck. They had been beautifully fashioned by French artisans and decorated with fleurs-de-lis on their breeches.

The cannonballs and tea chests, which contained gunpowder, followed. I asked the Frenchman if he wished a receipt for this "ballast." He bowed. "No receipt is desired. I wish you good hunting."

As the ketch drew away into the darkness, Lovejoy clapped his hands and did a half-jig.

"By God, Jerry, you have brought it off! Now we're really in business."

Before we sailed the next day, I returned to shore and ascended to the upper town for a final conference with my Jewish partner. Pausing at the top of the cliff to catch my breath, I watched a frigate approaching the anchorage. As she drew nearer, she dipped her flag and fired a gun. The fort overlooking the anchorage was manned by a motley lot of employees of the Netherlands West India company. It took several minutes before they managed to fire an answering blast and dip the Dutch flag waving over the fort.

I was pleased to see the frigate anchor to the north, a good mile from the *Charlotte*.

In his office D'Balboa explained to me the procedures by which we were to dispatch captured vessels and most of their cargoes up to Philadelphia for condemnation and sale there.

"Items which may be of special value you can bring into Statia. You will not want to overburden your sloop with cargo, however. Attempt no captures within sight of Oranjestad. Bring no British prizes into this place, or you will upset a hornet's nest. Just last month a British frigate pursued an unarmed American brig into our road and hauled it over to St. Kitts. It was an illegal act, for we are a neutral port. Our governor has protested the action. There is talk of closing our anchorage to British warships under any circumstances. Oh yes, you must be careful to take no neutral vessels, especially Dutch. I employ a Dutch agent who will store at least part of your cargoes and find buyers for them."

"Why can't you handle the sales yourself?"

"It is better to do this through a Dutchman. Leave this poor old Jew in the background. Don't worry. The agent is a cousin of my wife. He does as I tell him."

By the time I got back to the wharf, where Cato was waiting with the boat, the frigate had anchored and a longboat was being rowed toward shore. I joined the crowd gathering to watch.

Suddenly I felt as if someone had struck me in the chest. What in the name of holy heaven was Captain Atticus Fitzgerald doing in St. Eustatius?

I whirled, drew my cap over my eyes, and hurried to our boat. Within half an hour we had our anchor up and were under way to begin our first cruise, armed with eight fine French cannon and a congressional license to privateer. Oh yes, and a fully manned crew, including one especially well-educated surgeon, who had agreed to set his scruples aside long enough to give privateering at least a small try, with the understanding that he was doing so out of patriotic motives and not for pecuniary gain.

PART FIVE

1

D'BALBOA HAD WARNED me that the vigilance of the British fleet to stop the flow of gunpowder and lead to the rebelling colonies was increasing. So we avoided contact with all sails while our crew got used to handling the *Charlotte* now that she carried nearly five tons of cannon on her main deck, which caused her to sail a trifle top-heavy.

I enjoyed teaching our greenhorns how to load and fire our lovely French weapons. Throughout the first day, I had them run through their drills over and over, without ammunition, until they learned just how to respond to my commands. "Cast off lashings. . . . Bring up powder and ball. . . . Remove tampion. . . . Raise gunport. . . . Clear touchhole. . . . Sponge your weapons. . . . Load powder. . . . Ram shot. . . . Prime your pieces. . . . Run 'em out. . . . Ready, aim, fire!"

They learned always to place their cartridges and balls to the windward of their pieces, to stand clear of the rear of the gun carriage as the gunner brought his lighted linstock to the touchhole ("Think of it as a mean-tempered mule who likes to kick"), and various little tricks I remembered from watching Bouquet's desperate artillerymen in the West.

Toward the end of the second day, I let the powder monkeys bring up powder and balls from the hold, and we fired off two broadsides. My crews danced around the deck slapping each other on the back and exulting in the smell of real gunpowder.

"Let's spend no more time on drills," I said to Lovejoy. "It is time to start hunting."

"Wait until they come up against British navy gunners. They'll learn about handling guns the hard way. Your boys are too slow. You ain't explained what to do if a charge don't go off or if a ball gets wedged in the tube and has to be drawn out. They ain't learned how to pack a proper cartridge, neither. Every man should know the job of every other for when somebody is wounded. They need to know how to board and how to repel boarders. You always want to go off half-cocked."

"We can keep training while we look for prizes."

"When we make a capture, we got to get it back to Philadelphia. And that will require a prize crew."

"We have forty-five men. A half-dozen good fellows could sail a sloop like this, for instance."

"Ours ain't all good fellows by a long shot, not yet. And at least one of each prize crew has to be able to navigate. I've picked out five of our men to start learning how to use the sextant and azimuth."

I and my gun crews spent several impatient days until Lovejoy was satisfied that we were ready. At last I could give the order. Flying our false British colors, we set our course for the Barbuda Channel.

Around noon on our third day of searching, we spotted the sail of what turned out to be an unarmed Bermudian snow, under British flag, on her way from Bristol to deliver naval stores to the royal dockyard on Antigua.

Taking us at our word that we were a Barbadian sloop en route to Bristol ourselves, her captain hove to and engaged in a friendly conversation, telling us all about the situation in England. "Everybody is in an uproar about the American war. Insurance rates have gone up. They're preparing a big expedition to go over and put down the rebellion for once and all. Bugger the Americans, I say! What are you carrying, anyway?"

"Eight bronze six-pounder cannon and a light cargo of powder and shot," I yelled back across the hundred yards of choppy water that separated our vessels.

At that I ordered our gun crews to open their ports and run out our loaded but unprimed French pieces so that our Bermudian friend could see sunlight glistening on their muzzles. As soon as this was done, I called for our British flag to come down and our American flag to be raised.

The other captain shouted for his crew to raise their sails.

Ephraim touched my elbow. "Jerry, this will be murder! They are unarmed!"

Lovejoy took the linstock from one of our gunners' hands and touched off the priming powder. The six-pounder boomed and jumped back against its restraining ropes. I could hear the shot slam into the side of the snow. After the smoke had cleared, I saw the other captain looking at me in disbelief.

"Fire two!" Lovejoy bellowed and, without taking aim, lit the priming powder in the touchhole of a second gun. The ball ripped through the rear sail just above the quarterdeck.

The captain waved his arms at us, then shouted to his crew to leave off raising the mainsail.

I forced him to launch his longboat and bring over his ship's papers. She was the *Elizabeth*, registered to owners in Hamilton, Bermuda, and her manifest indicated a rich cargo of bales of canvas, lines, caulking materials, tools, medicines, and much else that would be even more welcome in Philadelphia than in Antigua.

The captain adopted an ingratiating tone as he presented his documents. There was much sympathy for the American cause in Bermuda, he said. Some of his friends in the islands had been instrumental in arranging for the abduction of a great supply of royal gunpowder in response to requests from George Washington. He also pointed out that since a vast armada of British ships carrying thousands of soldiers, including many German mercenaries, was about to descend on American shores, it would be in my best interests to let him proceed unmolested.

"I thought you said 'Bugger the Americans.' "

"That is just an expression. I meant no offense."

I said I hoped it made his capture less galling to know it had been done by a Barbados-built craft. He said he didn't give a damn where we were built. "I am a ruined man all the same."

"You can't be blamed for surrendering an unarmed vessel to one armed to the teeth, as we are."

"You don't understand. I refused to pay the premium for insurance on this voyage. Thought the rates too high. My owners will have my skin when they hear of this."

While this was taking place, Lovejoy put together a six-man prize crew to sail the *Elizabeth* off to Philadelphia. The sea was too choppy to allow us to lash up against the other craft, so we sent their boat over to bring her crew aboard us. While Lovejoy and his prize crew were taking charge of the *Elizabeth*, I had the Bermudian crew assemble on our deck. I gave them a little talk about what the British had done to make America rebel, including a colorful account of Lexington and Concord. I went on to tell about the joys and rewards of privateering.

I ended up with two volunteers to stay aboard the *Elizabeth* and help our prize crew and two to accept half-share berths aboard the *Charlotte*.

Lovejoy was pleased by this arrangement. He withdrew one of our crewmen from the *Elizabeth*, and he appointed as prizemaster a seaman we had signed on in Marblehead, a young married man who had been miserably homesick. We transferred part of the ship's cargo to the *Charlotte* for our own use, together with much of the food, and sent the *Elizabeth* on her way north.

The next day we rowed the Bermudian captain and most of his crew to a quiet beach on Antigua and got away as fast as we could.

We painfully beat our way north for two days to get clear of the Leewards and changed to a westerly course. With the trade wind off our larboard quarter, we raced for Grand Turk island. Skulking about one day under a merciless sun, we spotted two sails, but on Lovejoy's advice did not give chase. "They are riding empty, headed into Cockburn Town. Let's wait and catch one loaded."

The next morning our lookout cried "Sail ho!" A three-master was coming out of harbor, riding low in the water. We turned north and coasted along, waiting for her to draw near. Then, having the advantage of the wind, Lovejoy edged us closer.

"Damn it, Jerry, she's armed! Here, look for youself."

I could see only two guns, one forward and one aft, but they looked to be nine-pounders at least.

So I gave the command for battle stations. Our gun crews loaded their pieces and stood by.

Lovejoy let the bark come even with us. At a distance of two hundred yards, he gave me the signal to begin the fun.

I ordered our forwardmost larboard gun to put a shot across our quarry's bows whilst we hoisted our American flag.

Instead of hauling down her sails, she responded with a blast from her forward cannon. The ball sailed right over our heads and splashed to our windward. Then the bastard put his helm over and turned to the northwest, the better to catch the wind, and defiantly gave us a shot from her aft gun, which hit the water so near, the spray splashed our quarterdeck.

Lovejoy swore and ordered all sails up. The chase was on. Although the bark was heavy laden, she had an advantage with her square-rigged forward and mainmasts and a brisk following wind. Her aft gun gave her a further edge, which they exploited by hurling balls with impunity, knowing we could not bring our guns to bear in that position and at that range. The best we could do was to double-load the old swivel and put our marksmen to work from our crow's nest.

Now we could read the name of the bark painted across her stern. She was the *Bulldog* out of Liverpool, and she was aptly named. I prayed that one of those nine-pound balls would not strike our single mast. One shot came close, punching a hole through our topsail. Our Pennsylvanians thought they hit a sailor on the other side, but that did nothing to slow down the *Bulldog*.

The next shot from the bark's aft gun passed between two of our gun crews and smashed right through my cabin. At a range of only a hundred yards, the blow made the *Charlotte* shiver from stem to stern.

I yelled up to our Pennsylvanians, "A gold crown for every one of their gun crew you hit!"

Lovejoy made a slight change in our course so that we could draw even with the bark. We gave them first one and then another broadside as we passed her on a slightly diagonal course that carried us away from the *Bulldog*. As the smoke cleared, I could see that part of the bark's railing had been torn away. Both of her guns could fire at us now. I found the situation uncomfortable but was cheered by our marksmen's claim that they had just bagged a gunner.

Lovejoy and I conferred hastily. "Jerry," he said, "this ain't getting us anywhere. Them nine-pounders gives him the edge on us at this range and with this following wind. We got to close in on him, and fast, too. Now here's what we got to do. . . ."

I had our gun crews change from solid shot to grape, and we raced ahead of the *Bulldog*, out of range from her infernal long guns. Then, with several hundred yards of lead, Lovejoy ordered our boom reset and our helm put over to bring us back on an intercepting course. It was a tricky maneuver for an unbalanced sloop carrying every inch of sail that could be crowded on. First I feared we would capsize; then, with the wind once more on our larboard quarter, I feared we would ram the *Bulldog*. But no, Lovejoy was too good a sailor for that. He sailed us right across the bow of the bark. My larboard battery sprayed her rigging with grape. We were barely clear when Lovejoy once more shifted the boom and put the helm over, so that we headed back toward the north-northeast. Again I thought the *Charlotte* would tip over; but no, she righted herself and drew even with our prey—not quickly enough to cross her bow, but close enough for me to get two broadsides of grape into her from my starboard battery, and close enough, too, that every spare hand could pepper her decks with small-arms fire.

Lovejoy screamed at me to have our larboard battery load with solid shot again. As soon as this was done, he pointed our bow toward the *Bulldog* in a maneuver that once more convinced me he meant to ram. Instead, we crossed behind the bark by less than a cable's length, and my larboard battery slammed four good solid shots into the stern.

Lovejoy pounded me on the back and shouted.

"Has she struck?" I asked.

"No, but she will! You shot away her rudder. She has no choice now."

It took a moment for the other captain to realize why his ship no longer responded to the helm. Down came first his colors and then his sails.

For a man who had put up such a stubborn fight, the captain turned out to be mild-mannered. He even complimented me on my superior seamanship. Lovejoy beamed when I gave the credit to our "superb sailing master."

I had expected to find the *Bulldog*'s decks ankle-deep in blood. But their only casualties were a gunner who had taken a rifle ball in the thigh, a cabin boy with a splinter of wood in his shoulder, and a bosun with a split scalp and concussion caused by a pulley brought down by our grapeshot. Ephraim was able to patch up these casualties during the time it took Lovejoy to organize a prize crew and me to determine that the *Bulldog* was loaded with several tons of precious salt, produced from the saline ponds of Grand Turk.

We lay alongside the *Bulldog* throughout the night while our carpenters, working with theirs, fashioned a new rudder. It was a crude affair, and it was the devil's own job to remove the shattered one and position the new one. The next morning we nearly broke our backs transferring the *Bulldog*'s two nine-pounders onto the *Charlotte*. The work was completed by noon the next day. Off the *Bulldog* went with Herbert Gwin in charge. Once she was on her way, we sailed the *Charlotte* close to a break in the reefs around Grand Turk and rowed our complacent captain and his crew to shore.

The two nine-pounders made an impressive addition to our armament. Fortunately, our sloop had five gun ports on either side, so we put one of our new weapons in the middle port on the larboard side and one on the starboard side.

We spent the next week tacking westward against a stubborn trade wind. Off Puerto Rico, we hailed a full-rigged ship flying the Spanish flag. One look at the swarthy complexions of the crew and a brief conversation with the captain convinced me she was not fair game. Off St. Maartens, it was the same story with a Dutchman on her way in to Statia. The captain gave us a bit of interesting information, however. He had learned that the British were growing nervous about the privateering situation and planned to organize convoys to haul the yearly sugar crop from their West Indian islands back to England.

"What is your cargo?" I yelled across to him.

"Tea!" he cried back. "We carry plenty of tea! Plenty of good stuff made in France. You want to buy some?"

I declined but thanked him. We had enough "tea" at present to serve our cannon.

Lovejoy was downcast by our lack of prizes and by the news about the British convoy plans. "We can't make no money this way," he said. "Perhaps we should be operating back north again."

"Not yet," I replied. "Look, we've sent back two good prizes. Our boys are getting right proficient. Perhaps it's time to tweak the lion's tail."

2

"IT'S MADNESS, Jerry," Lovejoy said. "We'd be taking a terrible risk."

"Look," I replied. "The British men-of-war are out searching for American and other ships carrying contraband, right? So while those hounds are off baying in the fields and woods in search of the fox, Old Reynaud will sneak right into their henhouse and grab a plump fowl or two off the roost."

"What makes you so sure there'll be that many ships?"

"You heard the Dutchman. The sugar harvest has just ended. There are sure to be ships loaded or being loaded with sugar. If we wait much longer, they'll gather themselves into a convoy with escort and sail out of our reach."

"But why St. Kitts?"

I swallowed my frustration and explained for the third time. "First, it's a big British colony and it grows lots of cane. Second, it's not far from this point. Third, it's the next island to Statia, so we can duck back into Oranjestad and safety. Fourth, the time is right."

I could have taken a high-handed tack and simply ordered Lovejoy to shut up and direct us on a course to St. Kitts, but I did not want a half-hearted sailing master on a mission that would require his best skills. I finally won him over by promising that once we had completed our raid on St. Kitts, we would retire to Statia for refitting and recruiting. And to assuage both him and Ephraim, I promise to at least consider the possibility of hauling a cargo of ammunition up to Philadelphia.

St. Kitts—or St. Christopher, to call it by its right name—lies a mere seven miles to the southeast of Statia. More than twenty miles long, it is shaped like a chicken's drumstick; the capital, Basseterre, and its harbor are situated on the lower western coast, where the island becomes narrow. As I learned later, the planters of that mountainous island were as hypocritical a group as ever drove slaves under a tropical sun. While they and their governor objected mightily to the Dutch selling ammunition to Americans, they played a considerable role in Statia's trade, using their neutral neighbor as a depot for exchanging commodities and goods with whoever had the money to pay—all this in violation of British policy.

Cato knew these waters well. He served as pilot as we beat our way south to the channel between St. Kitts and her southern neighbor, the smaller island of Nevis. At dawn, after a night of treading water, we crowded on all sail and set a brisk course west. En route, we loaded our ten cannon and covered them with canvas, both to conceal them from view and to protect their charges in case of rain.

Under a blazing noon sun, with an oversize British flag flying from our topmast, we made our appearance at the entrance of the harbor of Basseterre.

"Good God Almighty!" Lovejoy exclaimed as we rounded the point and saw the masts clustered at anchor. "There must be twenty of them at least!"

We took in sail. As we eased our way closer, I scrutinized the sugar fleet through my spyglass, much as a wolf sizes up a herd of grazing deer. I did not want to take a worm-eaten tub that we would have to constantly pump to keep it afloat. Nor did I want even a first-rate vessel, unless it was loaded with hogsheads of valuable sugar.

Only one of the craft was under sail. She was a sloop-rigged cutter, almost as long as the *Charlotte* but lacking our raised quarterdeck. A cannon boomed from her deck as she approached us.

I ordered our swivel gun fired in response and dipped our British colors.

She was a smart-looking vessel and smartly handled, too. She drew nearer, and Lovejoy swore when he determined that she was a Royal Navy vessel.

"How many guns?"

"I make out six. Damn it, those fellow will know how to handle themselves! I shouldn't have let you talk me into this."

"Be quiet. Let me do the parlaying."

The cutter slacked off her sail, and the captain demanded to know who I was.

In my best imitation of an English accent, I told him we were the *Charlotte* out of Bridgetown.

"We have been sent to pick up a load of sugar and escort a convoy across the Atlantic."

"We were expecting a frigate. Are you armed?"

"We carry eight six-pounders." I thought he might become suspicious if he knew about the two extra nine-pounders.

"Well, anchor over there between that brigantine and that bark. We're on our way for a short patrol. Come over for a drink when we return this afternoon. Meanwhile, the harbormaster will want to see your papers and all that. He's as nervous as an old woman.

Worried about privateers, you know."

Lovejoy, with his usual skill, slid us right into place midway between the two vessels, which lay on the outer edge of the anchorage area. The bark was the larger and better-looking craft, but I could see from the way she rode that she was not yet loaded. The brigantine sat low in the water. As it turned out, the former vessel had just arrived from London, and the latter had been in harbor for a month.

We dropped anchor and looked all around the harbor. How I would like to have had a fleet of American warships at my command! We could have swept that harbor clean. There were sloops and snows, barks and brigs, brigantines and barkentines, square-rigged three-masters—vessels of every description and condition. The distant wharves swarmed with men loading hogsheads onto lighters. I truly did feel like a fox in a henhouse.

We went straight to our work. I armed six prize crewmen with pistols, and we rowed past the unladen bark to a new-looking schooner that appeared to be loaded.

The solitary man on the quarterdeck said the captain and most of the crew were ashore.

We had come to help convoy the fleet. Could we inspect this handsome craft?

His reward for giving us a grand tour of the schooner was to be seized and tied up, along with two other crewmen.

That done, I rowed back to the *Charlotte*. Lovejoy ordered the anchor raised and let us drift right up against the loaded brigantine. Her crew shouted warnings that we were about to collide. Minutes later, we bumped against her side, and I led a surge of cutlass-bearing men over her rail.

To save time, Lovejoy cut the brigantine's anchor cable. Leaving a second prize crew behind, we scrambled back aboard the *Charlotte* and headed for the harbor entrance. Behind us the schooner had her sails up and was making good headway.

Just for the hell of it—and to Lovejoy's exasperation—I had first our starboard and then our larboard batteries fire off broadsides.

"We're celebrating, you dull old seadog!" I said. "We've pulled off a grand coup, and you want to complain about a few pounds of gunpowder?"

All seemed in splendid order as we cleared the harbor of Basseterre. Our captured brigantine, rigged as she was with square sails on her foremast and fore and aft on her main, was not as fast or maneuverable as either the *Charlotte* or our captured schooner. But she was sailing well enough as night fell. We headed away from St. Kitts on a south-southwesterly course with the trade wind just abaft our larboard beam. We decided to sail far enough south that we could tack back on a north-northeasterly course between Nevis and Antigua, with the trades off our starboard beam. Then, when we got our two prizes safely out into the Atlantic and on their way to Philadelphia, the *Charlotte* could duck back into Statia for a well-deserved rest.

Leaving Lovejoy to pace the quarterdeck and fret, I fell asleep quickly. I awakened at dawn to the sound of rain spattering the *Charlotte*'s decks.

Going topside, I found Lovejoy in his oilskins, drinking coffee and peering at the horizon astern.

"What's up?" I asked.

He pointed to a sail several miles away.

"I can't make her out in this rain, but she appears to be following us."

"Want to let her catch up? Might be another prize."

"We got prizes enough as it is. I wish we'd left the brigantine in St. Kitts."

The rain squall passed to the west and soon obscured the sail. Once more in the sunlight, with a moderate sea and a steady breeze, Lovejoy fired our swivel gun and raised a signal flag from our topmast to order a course change for our little fleet.

He shifted our mainsail boom to catch the trades on our other side and brought us about to our new north-by-northeast heading. The schooner crew responded smartly, but the men on the brigantine floundered for half an hour trying to bring that cumbersome vessel about to her new heading. Lovejoy let the *Charlotte* lag close enough for him to shout instructions that they furl their square sails and rely on their fore and afts to make the course change.

By the time all this had been accomplished, the skies were clear again. The schooner was half a mile ahead, but the brigantine was laboring along, barely making headway.

Lovejoy was in a bad temper over such poor seamanship when our quartermaster yelled, "Sail ho!"

There our mysterious friend was again. She had changed course to match ours. We sent a man aloft with a spyglass.

"It's that British cutter, the one what was at St. Kitts!" he yelled down.

Lovejoy flew into a rage. He was all for recovering our prize crew from the brigantine, setting her afire, and sailing on to freedom with our schooner.

"Don't be silly," I said. "That cutter has only six guns to our ten. She'd make a lovely prize."

"Don't you be silly," he replied. "She can sail as close to the wind as ourselves. Her gunners aren't greenhorns like ours. Besides all that, she has plenty of men to sail her and fight her. We're down to twenty-five hands. Even if you cut back to two men to the gun, that leaves me only five to sail us."

"We can fire only one broadside at a time. Give me three men for each of our five larboard guns, and you'll have ten to handle ship. We can whip their asses. Just think what it would be to capture a Royal Navy cutter."

I purposely drew out the argument until it was too late for us to recover our men from the brigantine. Now we would have to fight, or sacrifice both the prize and the crew. I designated our gun crews, had them load both batteries, delivered a hortatory address, and then stood with crossed arms while the cutter closed the distance between us.

I wished there were a way to penetrate the mind of the other captain as he bounded after us. His best strategy would have been to race ahead and catch the schooner, put a handful of his men aboard her, and turn back to intercept us. We might have fled at his approach, which would have made it a simple matter to recapture the brigantine.

His other choice was to fall upon the *Charlotte*, try to sink or capture us, and recover the two prizes at his leisure.

Lovejoy took the tiller while I made sure we had cartridges and balls in place beside the cannon and that the Pennsylvanians were ready with their rifles. The cutter swept closer and closer. Her gunports opened, and the muzzles of her three starboard guns slid out.

One thing about Lovejoy Brown: He might argue and naysay in advance of an undertaking, but once in the midst of it, he held nothing back. He had the advantage of being to the windward of our adversary. The cutter was fast, but not fast enough to work around us to seize the weather gauge.

Had the other captain known his advantage in manpower, he could have fallen back and quickly recaptured the brigantine before giving battle. But no, he seemed hell-bent to make a fight of it right off. So we let him draw closer and closer until I could see the expressions on the faces of his crew.

He had come almost even with us to a distance of a hundred yards when I ordered our swivel gun fired across his bow and our American flag raised.

Then with trumpet to my lips I bellowed, "Ahoy there! Furl your sails and come to!"

"What did you say?" came back the incredulous reply.

"Strike your colors, or we'll blow you out of the water!"

Even at that distance, I swear I could see the other captain's face turn an apoplectic red.

"Fire!" he screamed.

Three clouds of smoke billowed from the Britisher's starboard gunports, and three cannonballs splashed in the water around us.

"The nine-pounder only!" I cried. "Fire!"

Our big gun made a satisfyingly deep roar, but its ball sailed over the heads of our adversaries and into the sea beyond.

Faster than I would have thought possible, they gave us another broadside. One of their balls struck our boat, showering our deck with splinters. A Bajan crewman cried out in pain. Ephraim helped the man belowdecks.

I waited until our nine-pounder had been reloaded before giving the order to reply with a full broadside "and keep firing at will, fast as you can."

That became the pattern of the fight. The better-drilled British fired broadside by broadside, in unison. We gave them one blast of five guns the first time, and thereafter our crews kept up a ragged fire, one at a time.

Once during my cruise aboard the East Indiaman many years before, I witnessed a desperate fight between two sailors in a Bombay dive. For the better part of an hour they gouged and bit and choked and struck blows, all with a deadly air of determination rather than with blazing anger. Finally one fell to his knees exhausted, leaving the other barely able to stand. It was hard to tell which had won the fight.

So it was between the *Charlotte* and that British cutter. Lovejoy kept us to the windward, although there were several opportunities for him to put his helm over and either cross the cutter's bows and rake her with our overworked larboard battery, or cut behind and batter her stern with our starboard guns. I lost track of time as I raced from one end of the deck to the other, now helping carry cartridges handed up by our powder monkey, now helping a wounded man into Ephraim's waiting arms, ever exhorting our gunners to load faster and aim better. I grew deaf from the roar of our guns and hoarse from shouting. My nose ran, and my eyes smarted from the gunpowder smoke. The cutter's balls smashed into our hull, tore through our canvas, and shrieked so close to my head that I actually felt their wind. Our men stood to their guns well enough. As the fight wore on and they gained confidence, our rate of fire increased.

Up on our quarterdeck, Lovejoy stood with one hand on the tiller and the other waving a pistol, looking like an ecstatic Viking warrior.

Suddenly there came a lull in the fighting. As the smoke cleared, I looked across at our adversary. His forward rigging was in shreds. One of his guns had been knocked off its carriage, and his men were frantically wrestling a replacement from the other side.

Our captured schooner was sailing well ahead of us, as if our fight was no concern of theirs. The brigantine's crew had fallen even farther behind. Lovejoy and I held a hurried conference. We agreed that now, while the cutter had only two starboard guns in action, was the time to take drastic measures. We sent our riflemen up to the crow's nest and had our gunners swab out their overheated cannon and double-load them with chain and bar shot. I adjusted the quoins under the breeches to elevate our muzzles and gave our gunners their new orders.

The British crew were just manhandling their other gun into position when Lovejoy put his helm over and narrowed the distance to a stone's throw.

One of our gunners called out, "Now?"

"Not yet!"

Without waiting for orders, our Pennsylvanians opened up with their rifles from aloft. The cutter replied with a ragged volley of small-arms fire. Closer and closer Lovejoy crowded the cutter. Our riflemen fired again, and this time I saw their helmsman drop to one knee and grab his side. Before their captain could seize the tiller, the wind had pushed the cutter's bow away from us so that our guns now bore on her starboard quarter.

Lovejoy nodded. "Fire!" I shouted.

Our five cannon fired in unison. A cheer went up from our gunners. One of our bar shot struck the point where her mainsail boom was joined by a collar to the mast. The mainsail flapped as uselessly as a housewife's sheets on a clothesline. The cutter lost headway.

Lovejoy circled the Britisher twice, giving us the opportunity to hurl shot into her from both larboard and starboard batteries. We amused ourselves thus until our brigantine waddled past us.

Lovejoy and I debated whether to stay and harrass the cutter until her captain surrendered.

"What's the good of capturing her? We can't sail her without making repairs," he said. "We can't board her. They've got more men than us. We have the advantage, but the more we pound her, the less of a prize she becomes. We'd better quit while we're ahead."

I was all for continuing until we sank the cutter or she struck her colors. But then a very weary Ephraim came up from his surgeon's bay in the hold to report that one of our landsmen had just died of a head wound and that two of the seven wounded men he had treated were in serious condition.

"Haven't we had enough bloodshed for one day?" he asked.

I looked over at the cutter. Her casualties must have been at least as heavy as ours. I considered the burden her wounded would cause us and the time it would take to repair her boom. Lovejoy was right. She wasn't much of a prize anymore. So I ordered all our crew to stand at attention by our rail in honor of the brave captain and crew of that cutter. Then we dipped our colors and fired a blank broadside. Having paid tribute to a valiant adversary, we resumed our course.

As we edged our way cautiously along the southern coast of Nevis, I helped Ephraim patch up our wounded, one of whom had lost a leg below the knee and another a hand. That was a sobering experience—to see the suffering of men who had responded to my own appeals to join up for adventure and profit. I was even more sobered by the sight of our dead landsman. He was a fair-haired, baby-faced lad who had spent much of his spare time writing in a diary. His eyes were open, as if he could not believe what had happened to him. I had our sailmaker sew up a shroud, and we tenderly laid him in it with a cannonball at his feet. Again I assembled the crew on the main deck and delivered a brief speech praising the fellow's bravery under fire. After leading the men in the Lord's Prayer, I nodded for them to slide the weighted shroud into the sea.

Then I turned our men to patching up the poor *Charlotte*. Fortunately for us, the cutter had not been stocked with bar or chain shot, so our rigging had suffered only from round shot. Besides smashing our boat, these had punched several holes in the larboard side of our sloop and had carried away part of the roof of Cato's galley. It pained me to see these scars of battle on our elegant lady, but war is war. On the whole, I thought, we had come out ahead.

Once in the Atlantic we bade our prize crews adieu and headed the battered *Charlotte* back for Statia. On the way, I sorted through our dead landlubber's effects and found his diary. The poor lad was far better educated than I had realized, and he had the soul of a poet. Many of his entries described the beauty of the sea and sky and the wonder of the changing weather and the excitement of sailing and of shore leave in St. Eustatius.

One of the older men had taken him to a Statian brothel. He wrote of his disgust with himself after that visit and of his fears that he had contracted a disease and God's displeasure.

But I was most touched by his descriptions of his fellow crewmen aboard the *Charlotte*. He had been fascinated by Cato, whom he called "an ebony giant with the kindest heart that ever beat in black or white breast." Ephraim was "our brilliant young surgeon, somewhat aloof in his dealings with his fellow men, but dedicated to their welfare." Lovejoy was "a stern, relentless old denizen of the sea who knows how to sail this lovely vessel as does a skillful horseman know how to ride a spirited steed.

"As for our captain, Jeremiah Martin, he hails from Virginia. He knows how to lead and manage men as well as Mr. Brown knows his seamanship and navigation. He is a lively fellow of some thirty years, I judge. He has the knack of inspiring you to do better than you think you are able. He is reputed to have Indian blood. Although some of my mates call him Chief Big Wind behind his back and make light of his abilities as a sailor, I consider him a brave and forthright gentleman and would follow him to the death."

Chief Big Wind indeed! Of course, that had been written before our raid on St. Kitts and our battle with the cutter, but still it stung. I considered showing at least part of the diary to Ephraim but decided against it. Instead I tied the ledger with twine and put it in with the boy's personal belongings, to be returned to his parents at their farm near Chester, Pennsylvania.

3

As USUAL, the roadstead under the Statian cliffs was crowded with ships. As Lovejoy brought us into harbor, I swept my spyglass across the bay and was vastly relieved to see no sign of Fitzgerald's frigate or any other British man-of-war.

On the shore, word of our exploits spread quickly. The lower town was thronged with American sailors, many of whom wanted to buy a drink for the captain and crew of the sloop that had so impudently twisted the lion's tail. It was with difficulty that I extricated myself from well-wishers and climbed the cliff to Oranjestad's upper town.

While his wife and daughter eavesdropped from the kitchen, Abraham d'Balboa listened with glistening eye to my account of our cruise.

"A snow, a bark, a schooner, and a brigantine, all in one cruise— not to mention cargoes of ships' stores, salt, and sugar. Very good, indeed," he said.

"And if we had had more men, we might have brought in a Royal Navy cutter."

"Perhaps it is just as well you did not. You would have gained no cargo, and you would only have caused the British to hate you more than they already do."

"I was not aware that their feelings toward me were any worse than they are toward any other American captain."

"At least one Englishman bears you a special hatred. Do you know a Captain Fitzgerald?"

"Indeed, I do. But he is no Englishman. He is Irish."

"He is the newly commissioned commander of the British frigate that came into harbor the morning you departed. 'Tis said the man nearly had a stroke when he learned you had been here. He says he reentered the King's service expressly to capture you. Why does he bear you such enmity?"

I told him about dumping Fitzgerald into the water and about his inordinate affection for the *Charlotte*.

"So you have made an enemy both of Sir Francis Bolton and of his captain."

"So it seems. But they can't reach me here, can they?"

"I think not. Governor de Graaf has banned British warships from entering Statia's harbor. You will have to be very careful outside our waters to avoid this Captain Fitzgerald. He wants very much to see you hanged, they tell me."

"He will have to catch me to hang me."

He smiled and turned toward the kitchen. "Wife, daughter, set another plate for supper. We have a hero to be honored. Feed him well, and perhaps he will tell us about his great sea battle."

We spent the next two weeks getting the *Charlotte* back into fighting trim and recruiting replacements for our prize crews, for the unfortunate farm boy who was killed, and for the man who lost his leg. For the most part, the American vessels in port were merchantmen come down to exchange tobacco, wheat, barrel staves, and such for ammunition, rum, ships' stores, and other items no longer available from Britain. Some of the American ships were operating under letters of marque, which permitted them to capture enemy vessels, but in general they were too lightly armed to take a prize of much size.

Recruitment of replacements had been a great worry to me. To my amazement and pleasure, so many crewmen from American tubs applied for berths on the *Charlotte* that it took most of my time and Lovejoy's to interview them. Part of our appeal was monetary, of course: a share in the prize earnings of a successful privateer could be worth more than they would receive in a lifetime as deckhands on an ordinary vessel.

Within a week, I heard reports that the *Charlotte* had captured the entire sugar fleet of St. Kitts and in the bargain had sunk a British frigate. I gave up trying to repudiate these idiotic rumors.

So it was that when the repaired, reprovisioned *Charlotte* set sail again, we had a full crew of sixty men, so many that we had to convert our hold into sleeping quarters. And in necessary violation of the congressional quota of one-third landsmen, nearly all were experienced sailors. They were a boisterous lot. It was all Lovejoy and I could do to handle them.

Keeping our distance from occasional sails on the horizon, we angled our way northwest. After several days of patrolling just out of sight north of Grand Turk, we picked up an unarmed barkentine carrying a goodly cargo of salt. Off we packed our prey to Philadelphia with a prize crew and headed westward again to try our luck in the sea lanes beyond Barbuda.

After two days of fair sailing against the trades, we lost our breeze and became becalmed. The sea turned an oily, greenish color, its surface smooth, despite occasional swells. Aggravated by the oppressive heat and the inactivity, the mood of the crew turned ugly. Twice I had to threaten to knock heads together to stop quarrels. The men lost their appetites. I overheard one of our new recruits say he wished he had remained with his cargo vessel in Statia.

"It's this damned weather," Lovejoy said. "I don't like the feel in the air."

To break the tension, I let our men stretch a net beside the *Charlotte* so that those who knew how to swim could show off their skill. Lovejoy scorned the sport. He claimed that men made better sailors if they could not swim, but I joined in the fun, going so far as to dive under the keel of the *Charlotte* and bob up on the other side. Even Ephraim joined us. Later, as night drew near, I issued an extra ration of rum and joined the lads in a round of singing.

I awakened at first light with an uneasy feeling. A whining wind had come up, a wind that seemed unable to make up its mind as it rose and died first from one direction and then from another. I joined Lovejoy on the quarterdeck to watch the sun appear amid an eerie, deep-red glow off our starboard quarter. Lovejoy pointed astern to the mare's-tail clouds high in the western sky.

"Don't like the looks of this at all," he said.

The sea had resumed its deep blue color and lost its unnatural smoothness. The swells now ran higher and came more often, hoisting first our stern and then our bow as they rolled past, as if in flight from some distant enemy. By noon the wind had settled down to a steady gale from the north. The *Charlotte* lunged through the white-capped waves like a spirited steed. A film of thin cloud obscured the sun, so that Lovejoy was unable to shoot his usual noon azimuth.

After the men had eaten their midday meal, he took me aside and proposed that we "batten everything tight as a tick."

I did not share his alarm. After all, I had been through rough North Atlantic weather when the wind had pierced me to the bone and the waves had come up like small mountains. But it occurred to me that the crew would be better off to have something to occupy them, so I agreed. To my amazement, Lovejoy ordered that our ten cannon be dismounted and lowered into the hold. This was backbreaking work, made all the more difficult by the great swells now rocking the *Charlotte,* but once the job was done we rode with better balance. Then we triple-lashed the gun carriages to their stay rings.

While all this was going on, Cato cooked up extra pots of rice and beans and stacks of johnnycake. Then he had to extinguish his galley fire.

To keep me out of the way, I suppose, Lovejoy asked me to go through the hold and crew's quarters and make sure that every-thing below was tied down. When I came back on deck, the western horizon was obscured by a bank of dark clouds touched with shades of orange and green. Deep within this ugly mass, as though ema-nating from some colossal furnace, I saw intermittent pulses of lightning. A steady growl of thunder rolled across the water.

A squall swept over the ship. I took the helm to permit our quar-termaster to fetch his rain gear. It was all I could do to hold the tiller steady against the mighty surges of the sea upon our rudder.

Lovejoy was everywhere, hectoring the crew as they went about their tasks. He had them run several lifelines at waist level across the deck and along the rail. He was dissatisfied with the way our boat had been lashed down and made the bosun redo the job. He took down our mainsail, swung the boom amidships, and tied it down securely.

Now we were running with only our topsail and jibs. It seemed as though we were being propelled by the motion of the sea rather than by the wind howling through our rigging.

By the time the quartermaster returned, I was exhausted from clinging to the tiller. I remained to help the fellow hold us on our westerly course. The squall passed, but soon a light, steady rain be-gan falling. Lightning flashed closer and closer, and the thunder sounded like a distant cannonade.

The clouds became thicker as they spread directly overhead. To the west I saw a line of gray puffs speeding toward us. Lovejoy sent four men aloft to take down our topsail.

By late afternoon the western sky had become so thick with clouds that you could hardly see. Lightning zigzagged as though the gods of sea and weather had gone mad. The sea became so rough that it was difficult to keep one's footing on the quarterdeck. The *Charlotte* rose and plunged like a creature gone wild. The wind shrilled through her rigging, and our timbers groaned from the pounding of the white-foamed waves.

Cato came up to relieve me at the tiller so I could confer with Lovejoy in my cabin.

"Look a-here, Jerry, we're in for a bad night of it, and make no mistake."

"It is a bad one, all right," I said. "But we've been through storms before."

"You ain't never been through a hurricane."

We were interrupted by a bosun come to report that the wind had snatched away our jib sheets. The *Charlotte* was at the mercy of the storm.

Lovejoy left me in the cabin feeling helpless and useless. He groped his way forward across the rising and plunging deck to su-pervise our deck hands in putting out a sea anchor. But before they could complete this work, a huge following wave crashed in the glass windows of our officers' cabin, drenching me with water.

With the sea anchor finally out, the wind blew the *Charlotte* around until the line grew taut and she was headed about with her bow toward the huge waves.

Gigantic bolts of lightning now crashed around us, and the rain fell as if poured from enormous buckets. Up one wave the *Charlotte* would climb and then violently descend the reverse slope. By now we had lashed our tiller into a fixed position and ordered every man belowdecks. We could only pray that the sea anchor would do its job and keep us headed into the waves. It would have been suicide to go on deck.

In the cabin, water leaking from the quarterdeck extinguished our candle. Ephraim and I clung to the center post to keep from being tossed against the bulkhead. The lightning broke all around us, illuminating our cabin so brightly that I could have read a book by it. The wrenching timbers of the sloop cried out like a woman in prolonged labor. Never had I felt so helpless, so awed by the blind force of nature.

Sometime around midnight, the wind subsided and the rain let up. Lovejoy took advantage of this lull to come back to the cabin to tell me that he was putting out a second sea anchor and that our ship's boat had been carried away.

The eye of the hurricane soon passed. The wind rose again, and once more the rain gushed down upon us. The *Charlotte* went through yet another ordeal of battering and twisting and turning. By dawn, however, the worst of the storm was over. The sea still ran heavy, but we had survived.

I ventured out on deck. Our bowsprit had been snapped off. The galley had been swept away, as well as our boat. A good section of our rail was stove in. In general, however, the *Charlotte* appeared to have come through like the champion she was.

Later in the morning, Lovejoy called the crew on deck for muster. All answered to their names. Their faces were drawn from lack of sleep. Lovejoy rationed out a cup of rum for each man. He appointed work details to pump out the holds in one-hour shifts while the rest of the crew dried out their bedding and slept. We left our sea anchors out and our sails furled.

By the next morning, the weather had returned to normal. Still lying to with our cannon remaining in the hold, we were making repairs to our rail and tightening our storm-loosened rigging when our lookout sighted a sail on the northern horizon.

Lovejoy sent a lookout aloft with a spyglass. A chill ran down my back when he shouted down that the vessel was a schooner flying British colors. We were unable either to run or to fight. Our bowsprit was gone, and there was no time to raise our mainsail. Even our small-arms ammunition had been soaked by the waves. All we could do was stand about and listen to our lookout's reports as the schooner bore down upon us.

"She's armed all right. I count eight cannon and four swivels. . . . They're not in uniform except for fellow on the quarterdeck. . . . Sails are in good shape. She looks like a new ship."

As the schooner drew nearer, we could see that she rode high in the water and that, just as our lookout reported, she seemed to be newly constructed.

At about two cable lengths' distance, she fired a shot across our bow and to my soul-felt relief replaced her British colors with a thirteen-stripe blue and white flag.

"She sure looks American," Lovejoy said. "I just hope it ain't a trap." So we raised our true colors.

The sea was calm, with a moderate swell. The other craft drew close enough for us to talk to her captain. My apprehension faded when I heard his New England accent. His schooner was the *Liberty* out of Philadelphia. He was operating under a congressional letter of marque, and this was his first cruise. We both put fenders over our sides, and he let his vessel drift against ours. Then we snugged up against each other, our larboard side against their starboard. I went aboard to get better acquainted.

They had left Philadelphia two weeks earlier. The captain told us the amazing news that the Continental Congress had declared the colonies free and independent of England. He had a copy of the official declaration. I interrupted our conversation to tell our crew, who greeted the news with cheers.

The captain then gave me additional and less encouraging news. "The British are not through with us, not by a long shot. They have sent over a hundred ships to New York Bay, and God knows how many soldiers, many of them hired in Germany. Last word we had was they have taken Staten Island and that more ships and soldiers are on their way. Make no mistake, Martin—this is a real war now."

He was captivated by my account both of our exploits and of the hurricane. He bombarded me with questions about conditions in the Indies. I gave him all the information I could.

Finally, he asked, "What can we do to help you?"

It cost me considerable pride to respond, "You can escort us back to St. Eustatius."

4

IT TOOK more than a month to repair the damage done by that vicious storm. Replacing the *Charlotte's* bowsprit, stern windows, and railing was work enough, but we found that her stern post had been splintered and several of her ribs split by the pounding of the murderous waves. It cost me a fortune to buy the precious timbers and hire Dutch artisans to make these tedious repairs.

By the time we had her once more in fighting trim, several of the men we had sent back as prize crewman on our earlier captures—the Cornish-born Gwin among them—returned from Philadelphia aboard a cargo vessel. They brought along enough money in the form of bills of credit to pay off Abraham d'Balboa's loans. Gwin also brought the alarming report that Washington had been beaten on Long Island by an immense British army and had escaped to Manhattan by the skin of his teeth.

At the time, I did not fret over this news. After all, my circumstances were good. I was free of all debt, with a refitted sloop and fully manned crew. Venturing forth in November, we captured an ancient Liverpool brig on which I would not have wasted a prize crew had she not been carrying a valuable cargo of shoes and other manufactured goods. We then ducked back into Statia, recruited additional men, and on Christmas Day set out again, this time into the Atlantic. After several days of patrolling east of Barbuda, we spotted a score of sails on the eastern horizon. As it turned out, this was the sugar fleet that had been in port at St. Kitts the previous summer, returning with bulging holds full of enough treasures to make a privateer's mouth water.

We bent on all sail and set a course to intercept them. I called our crew to general quarters and ordered our cannon loaded. Lovejoy and I swept our spyglasses over the approaching convoy to select our target.

I was rubbing my hands in anticipation when a sail broke away from the mass and headed our way. Even a landsman could have seen that she was a warship, a frigate who looked as if she might carry twice our number of guns. I was all for turning tail and outrunning her to the west with the wind abaft. The frigate would not desert her convoy for a long pursuit, I reckoned.

To my astonishment, the normally cautious Lovejoy set us on a heading of south by southeast, a course that carried us across the path of the convoy and that allowed the frigate to draw uncomfortably close before she gave up the chase. The convoy plodded past on its southerly course while we hung about on the horizon until twilight.

When I questioned Lovejoy's tactics, he replied, "Look at it from the standpoint of nature. A wolf, he don't just run away when a shepherd comes after him with a gun—not if he wants to eat. What does he do? He takes cover just out of reach and lets the flock pass. Then he sneaks up behind and pounces on one of the slower animals. He don't attack the shepherd at the head of the flock or one of the strong rams. No, he takes a lamb or a tender young ewe.

Now, if we had run before the wind, sure we would have got away faster, but it would have been the devil's own job of beating our way back against the wind. This way we have the advantage."

It was rare for Lovejoy to speak at such length and so metaphorically. I acknowledged the wisdom of his reasoning.

The next day, with the trades off our larboard beam, it took us until midafternoon to pick up the sails of the fleet once more. I was at the point of ordering our men to stand to their cannon when Lovejoy intervened.

"Look a-here, Jerry," he said. "Last thing we need is a drawn-out fight. We know there's at least one frigate, and there may be more. The sound of our guns would bring them down on us. Now, look close at the ships straggling along at the rear. Chances are they don't know about yesterday's chase. We can make this sweet, simple, and fast."

Two vessels lagged well behind the convoy. Keeping a sharp look-out aloft for the frigate, we crept closer and closer.

I complained, "At this rate, it will be night before we catch up to them."

"I know," said Lovejoy. "Just you have your boarding party out of sight but ready."

The sun was nearly touching the horizon by the time we drew within hailing distance of a brig displaying the name *Elspeth* across her stern. She was a broad, slow old thing, riding low in the water. Her captain stood on the quarterdeck, his speaking trumpet in hand. Our British colors flying, I waved at him. Lovejoy maneuvered us close enough for me to call out, "Ahoy, *Elspeth*! Do you need help?"

"No!" he yelled. "We're a little overloaded. Who are you?"

I shook my head and cupped my hand over my ear as if I could not hear. Meanwhile my boarding party huddled close against the starboard rail behind closed gunports.

"Louder, please!" I called. "Do you need help?"

With the wind to our advantage, we were half a length behind the brig now. A few more minutes, and we could lay a broadside into her. Lovejoy scanned the convoy ahead to see if any warships had spotted us. I stood on tiptoes to satisfy myself that the brig carried no cannon.

"I say, who are you? What do you want?" the other captain called.

I turned to Lovejoy as if to ask whether he had heard.

"Wait until we are alongside," he muttered.

With that, he put his helm over. He slid the *Charlotte* right up against the brig so adroitly that I swear we scarcely felt the impact.

"Boarders away!" I yelled.

A hail of grappling hooks flew over the *Elspeth*'s rail. My marksmen fired off their rifles. The helmsman of the other vessel went down. I fired my pistol in the air and commanded the other captain, "Strike your colors!"

Their crew went scurrying about for small arms. Her captain took an enormous pistol from his belt and fired it at me. The ball passed so close I felt its breeze against my cheek. Our men scrambled over the side. A grand melee broke out as their crew fought back with belaying pins and pistols.

I leaped from our quarterdeck to the *Elspeth*'s main deck and knocked down a stout English sailor. Then I mounted the ladder to their poop, waved my unloaded pistol, and bellowed, "Surrender!"

Her captain merely looked down at me.

"Do you strike?" I demanded.

Until the instant before he fired, I did not see the small pistol that he had concealed in his left hand. At first I thought the man had struck me in the ribs with his fist. I stopped on the top step and looked down at my side, then up again just as he was swinging the larger, empty pistol in his right hand. He was a big fellow, and it was a very heavy weapon. I had never been struck such a blow. The last thing I remember was falling backward, down, down, into a black whirlpool.

The faces of two Ephraim McGees hovered over me.

"Where am I?"

"In your bunk aboard the *Charlotte*."

"What happened?"

"You took a bullet in the chest and a blow to the head that would have killed an ox."

I tried to sit up, but my head ached and my chest throbbed so that I cried out. Twin Catos materialized to lower me back upon my pillow. The faces swam before my eyes and then disappeared into a red haze.

It was dark when I awoke again.

Twin lanterns glowed on my table.

"Where are ye?" a double image of Lovejoy was saying. "Where ye belong, in yer own bunk. . . . What happened? We have took our best prize yet. That old brig was loaded to the gills with gunpowder, medicine, lead bars—you name what they need in Philadelphia, and it was in the hold of that tub. Here now, you lie easy, and I'll fetch Dr. McGee. You'll want to thank him. Saved your life, he did, when I was ready to make your shroud."

Ephraim made me lie still while he explained that the captain's pistol ball had penetrated my chest muscles and broken the rib over my heart. "Fortunately the bone deflected the ball."

He held up a flattened piece of lead.

"It was your skull that worried me. Fractured, it is. You've been unconscious for two days. The fall you took off the ladder did you no good, either. Your left collarbone is cracked. Otherwise, you're in good shape."

"Why are there two of you?" I moaned.

He shook both his heads. "Lie easy, Jerry, and don't fret yourself. All you need is a long rest and some of Cato's chicken stew. We confiscated a coop of chickens from that brig, you know."

Later I learned that Lovejoy had been so incensed at the brig's captain for wounding me that he had sent him off to Philadelphia in irons.

5

I BARELY REMEMBER our trip back to Statia. My double vision had cleared up by the time we arrived at that familiar anchorage, but I was too weak to leave my cabin. A concerned d'Balboa came out to visit. I was too weak to protest when he insisted that I be transported ashore to his home to be cared for by his wife and daughter.

Those next two or three months were among the most difficult of my life. Abraham d'Balboa and his family could not have been kinder. They lodged me in a small room at the rear of their house, next to his office. An outside door led to a small garden shaded by a giant palm. As my strength returned, I spent more and more of the cooler parts of the days sitting under that great tree and trying to sort out my situation.

My frame of mind was already low when another of our prize crews arrived from Philadelphia bringing more bills of credit but also bearing bad news. Washington had barely escaped entrapment at White Plains and had fled across the Hudson, abandoning New York and its strategic harbor to the British.

I remained very weak. My head often ached so that I could not concentrate. I spent most of my time worrying about the American cause, reflecting on my life, and daydreaming.

Mistress D'Balboa was as matter-of-fact and humorless as she was kind. She remained a regular communicant of the Dutch Reformed Church. Her husband was equally faithful to his Jewish faith. On Friday nights and Saturday mornings I heard his voice rising above those of his fellow Jews two doors away at the little Honen Dalim synagogue. Their daughter attended Friday-night services with her father and on Sunday mornings marched off to the Dutch Reformed Church with her mother.

The girl was shy with me at first, but as I began to feel better, I set out to charm her. My motives were as pure as her morals. She was a serious-minded, well-read little girl who wrote surprisingly good poetry and who was an eager listener to my expurgated reminiscences. At that time I was more than twice her age, so my interest in her truly was avuncular. She was fascinated by my tales, but her eyes seemed to flash even more brightly at the appearances of Ephraim, and many of her questions concerned "the young doctor from America."

As time dragged by, I became increasingly irritated with Lovejoy. The old seadog, who had shown such valor and quick good judgment in our recent adventures, could not be persuaded to take the *Charlotte* out on his own.

"It is costing us money to keep her idle in harbor," I said.

He countered with this excuse and that until I wrung from him, "It's just plain bad luck to sail without your captain."

"For God's sake, you dunderhead, you have forgotten more seamanship than I will ever know! And you have Gwin back now!"

"You don't understand. Things ain't the same anymore. I been talking to other privateers. The British are on to our game. They've took two of our privateers just since you been laid up. And one of them was that schooner that helped bring us in after the hurricane."

"The British will be there whether I am aboard or not."

"Just so. We need you to fight the ship while I sail her. Our days of easy captures is over."

"For God's sake, anyone with an ounce of grit can fight! It's mostly bluff anyway."

"Our days of winning with bluff are over." Suddenly Lovejoy got tears in his eyes. "Jerry, I'm just plain afraid without you. The responsibility is too much."

Put off by this unaccustomed compliment, I replied simply, "In that case I had better hurry and get well."

By this time I had recovered my strength enough that I could walk about Oranjestad's upper town during the cool early morning. Standing on top of the cliff, I liked to look down on the lower town and observe with amazement and wonder as all those men bestirred themselves to begin yet another day of buying and selling, loading and unloading, paying and receiving, all because two years earlier at a little village in Massachusetts a band of British soldiers had fired upon a motley lot of American militiamen. How long would this war go on? It seemed plain to me that we stood little chance of beating Lord Howe's mighty army of British regulars and Hessian mercenaries in open battle. The best we could hope for would be to exhaust the patience of our foes. But we could not give up. If the British won, they would surely grind their heels even harder into our faces. They would hang or imprison great men like Washington and Franklin and, yes, lesser ones such as Jeremiah Martin. Even if I escaped hanging, the wealth I had accumulated would be confiscated. Bolton would repossess the *Charlotte*. Like it or not, my future had become intertwined with that of my native land. Dizzy and weak as I still was, I could not remain inactive any longer.

Ephraim was aghast. "You need more time to recuperate!"

Lovejoy saw my point. "If we don't sail again soon, we might as well sell the sloop and close up shop. Our chaps are leaving us in droves to sign up with other captains."

I was still debating the matter with myself when the most disquieting news ever arrived from Philadelphia. Six weeks earlier, a day after Washington's much-depleted army had abandoned New Jersey and slipped across the Delaware with the British on their heels, the Continental Congress had pulled up stakes and taken refuge in Baltimore. Was the game really up after all? Well if so, by God, I would have one more go at the British.

I gathered what was left of our crew—only about thirty men—and slipped out to sea before dawn one February morning. I made a great show of taking the helm, but the effort taxed my strength so much that I had to go lie down in my cabin. My stomach grew increasingly queasy, and my eyesight became blurred. My condition grew worse and worse. I was convinced that I was dying and sent for Ephraim.

I told Ephraim that I had committed many sins in my life. I confessed in particular not only to the sins of the flesh but also to those of pride and covetousness. I forgave his sister for marrying another man and instructed him to give part of my estate to her, dividing the rest between himself, Chris, and Lovejoy.

Ephraim told me to stop my babbling and let him examine me. He was holding a candle and looking down my throat when all the remains of Mistress D'Balboa's scrumptious dinner of the previous night came surging up from my stomach. Ephraim stepped back with a disgusted look on his face and my vomit all down his shirt-front. He called for Cato to bring fresh water and cloths.

He laid me flat on my back and took my pulse.

"You feel better now, don't you?"

"A little."

"Still think you are dying?"

"I know I am."

"Still sorry for all the people you have gulled in your misspent life? Still crave their forgiveness?"

"Yes."

"You want me to forgive you for entrapping me into this job as ship's surgeon?"

"I didn't entrap you," I said weakly.

"A dying man should be especially careful not to lie."

"I am not lying."

"Neither are you dying."

"What do you mean?"

"For heaven's sake, Jerry, you are just seasick. That knock you took on the head unsettled your sense of balance. Clean him up, Cato, while I go and change this shirt."

By afternoon I felt much better. By the next morning I had my sea legs and stomach back again. We sailed north to Anguilla, thinking we might intercept a cargo of salt off that dry-bones island. Several vessels were anchored off the west shore. We got our hopes up, but as we drew nearer we discerned that one of the vessels was a British frigate. We turned north again, toward the Atlantic, until we were sure the cruiser was not giving chase, then headed southeasterly to nose around Antigua.

En route to that busy island, we overhauled an ancient French three-master. Her captain reluctantly hove to and give me a tongue-lashing for interfering with a neutral ship. An examination of his papers convinced me that his vessel was indeed French and that her destination was Guadeloupe.

I'd be damned if we'd return to Statia empty-handed. So we continued on our southerly course clear down to the north coast of Barbados.

Off Speightstown, in view of Bolton Hall, we hauled in a fishing ketch manned by a half-dozen Negroes, among them one of the original crew of the *Charlotte*. He seemed glad to see me and Cato. The ordinary inhabitants of Barbados—the slaves and poor whites—had fallen on hard times, he said, with no food coming in from North America and shipping from England slowed down by the necessity of convoys.

What about Sir Francis?

"Oh, the master, he be gone to England. Ibo, he go with him. Wish they had took old Ramsay. He drive the poor black man hard. We'd starve if we couldn't fish."

I looked at the pile of flying fish in the ketch, then at Lovejoy.

"They need them worse than us, I reckon," he said.

We released the ketch and then, on devilish impulse, I ordered our cannon double-loaded and raised to their maximum elevations. Ephraim tried to talk me out of it, but I would not be deterred from firing two broadsides in the general direction of Bolton Hall.

It was a silly gesture. We were a good mile and a half from the plantation. An earthen fort, manned presumably by militiamen, got their cannon in action in time to take credit for chasing us away.

We hit some rough weather as we headed north again, intending to try our luck around Dominica and Montserrat. My seasickness returned with a vengeance, and with it my headache and blurred vision. I was made a prisoner of my bunk and of my bleak thoughts about my own fate and my country's.

187

Reluctantly I decided that we should return to Statia.

Within minutes of our arrival, my depression was dispelled by the news from America.

The British had not captured Philadelphia after all. On the contrary—on Christmas Eve, Washington had slipped across the Delaware and taken more than a thousand Hessian prisoners at Trenton, then a few days later he had repeated his triumph by whipping British regulars in open battle at Princeton. It had become the Britishers' turn to withdraw across New Jersey, thereby lifting the threat to Philadelphia. Congress could now reconvene there.

The Americans who now thronged Oranjestad's lower town were still celebrating the news.

Ephraim and Lovejoy joined me in reporting to Abraham on our fruitless cruise. He had received other accounts confirming our impression that the days had passed when a mere sloop could accomplish much as a privateer. Not only had the British put more cruisers on guard and organized a convoy system, they had taken to arming ordinary merchantmen. And we could no longer depend on the gullibility of captains.

"You need a larger, better-armed vessel," Abraham said.

"Spoken truly," Lovejoy said. "What we need is a stout topsail schooner, rigged to outsail even the *Charlotte*. Something that handles smart, that can sail close to the wind, and that can carry a hundred or more men."

It took a while for me to recover my sense of balance. During that time the D'Balboa family once more put me up in the little room near their garden. Ephraim was a frequent visitor. He enjoyed the companionship of the family as much as I did. And they liked to entertain him, especially Rebecca. She had lost her reticence with me. My teasing made her laugh. But she grew very quiet in Ephraim's presence, hovering about and drinking in his every word and gesture.

I twitted him about robbing the cradle. He turned red and protested that I was imagining things, and besides there could never be a woman for him other than Laura Mason.

During this period I received many offers to sell the *Charlotte* outright. Without the burden of her ten guns, she would have made an excellent smuggler. Also, many colonial agents and Dutch merchants approached me with offers for us to run contraband cargoes up to Boston or Philadelphia. My heart still lay with privateering, but I was frustrated by the difficulties imposed by the increased British vigilance. To venture forth at best would yield small gains and at worst would bring disaster. We needed a new, larger vessel, and quickly too, for our crew kept dwindling.

The question in my mind was, should we take the *Charlotte* out for one more cruise in the hope of capturing a grand prize with which to finance our new craft? Or should we load up with gunpowder and lead to be hauled off to Philadelphia for resale at a huge profit?

My mind was furiously working over our situation one day as I elbowed my way through the mass of humanity in the lower town. I blundered into a great, fat fellow clad in white linen and wearing an enormous straw hat.

"Pardon me, sir," I said, and started to step around him.

The man moved so as to block my path. "Pardon? Did you say pardon?"

My vision still was none too good. The sun was in my eyes, and his face was shadowed by that great hat. I put my hand to my forehead and squinted.

"Indeed, sir, I did apologize. Did you not hear me?"

"You have done much to apologize for, I should say."

Thinking the man wanted to pick a fight, I was about to tell him to go to hell when he took off his hat and I found myself staring into the florid, round face of Reuben Halbertson.

I stepped away from him in inexplicable panic. He put his hand on my arm in a conciliatory way.

"So, Jeremiah Martin. I have been looking for you since I spotted the *Charlotte* yesterday. I thought our paths might cross again. I have been making inquiries about you. Fallen in with Hebrews, I hear. And making gallows bait of yourself, too, giving battle with His Majesty's vessels, illegally using the property of others. Oh my, you have been a naughty young man. Sir Francis is disappointed in you. You have betrayed him, and he is hurt."

"What in the hell are you doing here, Halbertson?"

He assumed a shocked expression. "You add insult to the injury you have done us. My, my, your rudeness is shocking. You are old enough to know you play a dangerous game."

"This is neutral ground, Halbertson, and you know it. What are you doing here?"

"I am doing business here, just as you are, only my business is not piracy."

"Is is still double-dealing and entrapment? Playing cat's paw for old Bolton?"

"Come, come, Jeremiah, be not so harsh in your judgments. I should like to talk to you—in private."

"I don't want to talk to you. Talking to you got me into a hell of a mess in Boston. I wish I had never lain eyes on you."

I flung his hand off my arm and turned away.

"Wait, Jeremiah. I have something—"

I thrust my way through the crowd to get away from his loathsome presence.

189

Abraham listened to my tale of this encounter with great interest.

"I would assume that Bolton wishes to establish himself here in St. Eustatius and he is doing so through Halbertson. A goodly portion of the sugar and molasses in warehouses here belongs to West Indian subjects of King George. Statia is a great convenience for them, especially now that you and your privateering brethren have become such a danger. They can deliver their produce to Statia, collect their bills of credit or manufactured goods in payment, and leave it to French, Dutch, or Spanish ships to do the hauling across the Atlantic."

"I understand all that," I replied. "I just don't understand why that tub of guts wanted to talk to me privately."

It would be a long time before I learned the purpose of Halbertson's desire for a private talk. But our meeting stimulated me into action. I immediately set about arranging for a cargo of gunpowder and lead to haul back to Philadelphia. While this was being done through Abraham and Lovejoy, I returned aboard the *Charlotte* and stayed there until the time came to sail.

6

WE SAILED out of Statia, past the high-cliffed shores of Saba, and cleared the Virgin Islands easily enough, all the while keeping a careful eye out for British cruisers.

On the afternoon of the second day out, we spotted the sails of a three-master on the southern horizon. Assuming we had passed the area patrolled by the British, I was all for turning back to investigate, but Lovejoy would have none of it.

"We're carrying too much cargo," he pointed out. "We would have trouble catching a vessel with that much spread of sail."

It was true that the *Charlotte* was sailing sluggishly under her heavy burthen of lead and powder, but I liked the idea of bringing a large prize into Philadelphia.

"She might be loaded heavily herself, which would make her easy to take," I pointed out.

"Which would mean she might be an American carrying cargo like ourselves, in which case we would only waste our time."

"But if she is not American—" I began.

Lovejoy broke in, "That would mean she most likely is armed and would fight. We'd be asking for trouble with all this gunpowder we're carrying. Why can't you ever let well enough alone, Jerry?"

I put my spyglass to eye again, but the distance was too great for me to make out more about the ship.

Ephraim put in his oar. "What Lovejoy says is true, Jerry. And

190

besides, it's near sundown. Dark will come before you could intercept her."

I thought nothing of it at the time, but Gwin was hanging about listening to our debate. Since he was our second mate, I asked his opinion.

"Oh, I'd have a go at her if I was you. Nothing ventured, nothing gained, I say."

"Good man, Gwin," I said, and clapped the Cornishman on the shoulder. "Spoken like a true American. If she is still in sight in the morning, we'll take a closer look at her."

Lovejoy glowered at Gwin and went off grumbling to himself.

My plans to turn back and encounter the three-master were frustrated during the night by high winds. By the next morning the seas were running heavy, and it was raining. The storm continued for several days, shoving us along to the northeast at a rapid pace but requiring that all our crew's attention be given to raising and lowering the sails to Lovejoy's exacting standards.

There was little for Ephraim and me to do in such weather. We spent most of the time in our cabin reading, playing chess, and talking. Ephraim was bubbling over with plans to claim his Laura and start his medical practice.

What about the war?

"If what we hear is true, Washington has got the British holed up in New York. The danger to Philadelphia is past. Peace should follow soon."

"But what if it does not?"

"I have done my bit for America, serving aboard this sloop."

I could not resist asking what Dr. Mason might think about having a privateer as a son-in-law.

"Oh, he'll come around. Besides, I am not a privateer. I am a noncombatant."

His priggishness provoked me to say, "Oh, then you'll not be wanting your shares of our tainted money from our prizes when we get to port."

"If you feel I have not earned my shares . . . Oh, why do you try to plant a thorn in my bosom like that, Jerry? With or without your money, with or without Dr. Mason's consent, I propose to marry Laura. We have waited long enough. I can support her, have no fear. What about you? What will you do when we return to Philadelphia?"

Thinking of Liz Oliver, I replied, "You're better off not knowing."

Actually, Ephraim's question planted a thorn in *my* bosom. I envied him his dream of marrying the girl he loved and establishing his medical practice. What did I have? A sloop. A large quantity of bills of credit. Ephraim longed for peace, but I was glad the war

191

was dragging on. My ambition was to buy a larger, better-armed ship and take ever-larger prizes, partly out of greed and partly out of a still-unsatisfied desire for vengeance against an enemy that had punished and humiliated me. Perhaps if I too had had someone to love and who loved me and some peaceful occupation to consume my attention, I would have been as happy as Ephraim. On the other hand, as some have said of me, I am a perpetual malcontent, never satisfied with the status quo, always searching for something new.

By the time the storm blew itself out, we had passed the Bahamas. Onward we plodded north until Bermuda lay off our starboard bow, onward until one midday came the cry, "Sail ho!"

One of our keen-eyed Pennsylvania riflemen was the first to sight the sails off our larboard quarter.

Lovejoy took a spyglass aloft and came back to the quarterdeck swearing. "If my eye don't deceive me, it's that same three-master we spotted just before the storm."

Lovejoy was all for bending on extra jibs and putting distance between us and the ship. Ephraim, in his zeal to return to Philadelphia, agreed.

"What do you think?" I asked Gwin.

"Meaning no disrespect to Mr. Brown, sir, it seems to me a cowardly thing to run away. I can't see the harm of looking her over at closer range. And I think I speak for the crew when I say they'd welcome a fat prize, if she should prove not to be one of ours."

Gwin was usually such a close-mouthed fellow, I was surprised by this loquacity.

"No jibs," I said to a furious Lovejoy. "Take down our topsail. We'll let her catch up with us."

"Look here, Jerry, you made me sailing master—"

I was fed up with my old comrade's naysaying. "But I remain captain and owner of this sloop! And I say we slack off and look that vessel over!"

"You say you are captain and owner. If you wish to take the advice of your second mate over mine, why don't you make him your sailing master?"

Before I could reply, Lovejoy had stomped off the quarterdeck and gone below.

"Very well, Mr. Gwin," I said. "Give the order to bring down the topsail."

Without thinking, I put my sharp-eyed Pennsylvanian in the crow's nest to keep us apprized of the progress of the other vessel. It did not occur to me at the time that a seaman, versed in the nomenclature of ships, would have been a wiser choice.

"What colors does she fly?" I called out.

"None as I can see."

With ourselves practically dead in the water, the other ship was closing fast.

"How many crewman does she carry?" I yelled.

"Not many. Maybe half a dozen."

"Is she armed?"

"Can't tell. She has canvas over her rails."

I paced the quarterdeck, trying not to think of Lovejoy sulking below. I was sorry to humiliate him in front of our crew, but damn it, he should not have defied me like that!

"She is raising colors," our lookout reported.

Except for the usual creak of timbers and splash of waves, it was as quiet as a cathedral on our deck. Then the shout "She's American!" rang out.

"There you are, sir," Gwin said. "One of ours after all. Shall we take down our mainsail and let her draw alongside?"

"Not just yet. Let's make sure."

The other ship was a good sailer. She closed the gap between us rapidly. As she drew closer, I examined her through my spyglass from stem to stern. She was a smart vessel, all right, a sharp-hulled frigate with clean lines.

Still I saw nothing amiss. I figured that, like us, she was headed for Philadelphia or Boston. Thank heaven Cato brought me up a cup of coffee to the quarterdeck and that I offered him a peek through my spyglass.

He peered for a long while. When he handed me the instrument, he was frowning.

"Captain Jerry, did you take notice of the little man at the wheel?"

"No. Why?"

"He has a beard, and he is not wearing a cap or hat."

"What are you getting at, Cato?"

"The others have no beard. Only he is wearing a coat."

He shook his head and said, "That man do put me in mind of Captain Fitzgerald."

I focused the glass on the man at the wheel and cursed my stupidity.

Ignoring Gwin, I screamed at our crew to raise the topsail and bend on all jibs. I shoved our helmsman aside and took the tiller myself.

Ephraim demanded to know if I had lost my senses. What was the matter?

"The man at their helm—it's Fitzgerald. That's a goddamn British frigate!"

It took a moment for our extra sails to catch the wind. If we had not been so heavy laden, we could have outrun the frigate even though she had a strong following wind just right for a square-rigger.

Any doubts of the identity of our pursuer disappeared when her American colors came down to be replaced by the Union Jack. A cannon in her bow boomed. A spout of water sprang up behind us. The race was on.

I considered making a fight of it. But I gave up the thought when our adversary removed the canvas from his rails and ran out his guns. There were at least twenty-four of them. And her decks and rigging now swarmed with sailors.

Seeing that we would be overtaken in a straightaway chase, I ordered our boom shifted and put the tiller over to set us on a more easterly course. The frigate was taken by surprise but soon adjusted. But the best I could do was to maintain the distance between us.

Again her bow gun boomed, and a shot landed nearby. It concerned me to have to run to the east, away from Philadelphia. I considered turning back into the wind—that is, reversing our course—but that would have exposed us to a full broadside. Besides, I did not trust my seamanship for such a maneuver. Damn Lovejoy Brown. Why didn't he quit pouting and come to my rescue? Well, he had his pride, and I had mine. I remained at the tiller until dark. Each time the frigate began gaining on us, I shifted course. And so went the chase until dark closed over us like a welcome blanket on a cold night.

I called the crew to gather around, and I gave them our instructions for the evening. Gwin was all for continuing to run before the wind, but I overruled him. I gave orders to change back into the wind on a north-by-northwesterly course and threatened to keelhaul any man who showed a light or spoke above a whisper. At that, I turned the quarterdeck over to Gwin and went below.

The cabin stank like a pigsty. Yes, Ephraim whispered, Lovejoy was passed out, dead drunk.

"He drank a full bottle of the vile stuff, you know. No, I couldn't find anymore about. It's a wonder he is alive."

I went to sleep not caring whether Lovejoy Brown lived or died. I dreamed that I was back at my home in Virginia and that my stepfather was trying to thrash me, all the while shouting, "You damned scoundrel! You have betrayed us! I will kill you for this!"

Ephraim was shaking me.

"Jerry, Jerry! Wake up! There's trouble topside."

Above us on the quarterdeck was a fearful thumping about and sounds of angry cries. Without dressing, I raced topside. In the glow of a forbidden lantern, two figures were locked in battle, one—Lovejoy—swearing and calling for help, and the other—Gwin—fighting silently.

Cursing them both for damned fools, I covered the lantern and caught each by the back of his neck.

"Stop it! You'll have the British on us. What is going on?"

"He is a goddamn traitor," Lovejoy said in a breath so sour it made my eyes smart.

"You are a drunken fool!" I raged at Lovejoy. "You gave up your post! You have no business on the quarterdeck anymore."

"You are the fool, giving command to a turncoat! The son of a bitch was signaling the British. I came on deck for a piss and caught him red-handed."

"He lies!" Gwin said. "He brought the lantern topside, and when I rebuked him, he set upon me."

By now Ephraim and Cato had joined us on the quarterdeck. I ordered Lovejoy and Gwin to shut up and looked over the stern at the faint outline of the horizon. A light flashed—once, twice, three times quickly. There was a pause, and it reappeared for several seconds, like a question mark at the end of a sentence.

I told Cato to summon all hands on deck. When the entire sleepy, grumpy crew was assembled, I ordered Gwin put in irons and asked Lovejoy what he thought we should do.

What time is it?"

"Just past midnight."

He held up his hand to test the wind. He looked back over the stern. The frigate repeated its signal.

"Take down all sail and put out a sea anchor," Lovejoy said. "That is what I would do if I were sailing master of this sloop."

I was torn between wanting to punch the old seadog on the jaw and wanting to hug him.

7

WE LAY TO quietly in the dark. All our sails were lowered, and every voice was stilled. I cannot say for certain just how close the frigate came to us, but we could hear the voice of a bosun crying out orders and the rattle of pulleys against her spars and masts. I held my breath until the sounds faded, then smiled at the thought of Fitzgerald puzzling over the disappearance of his signals and blundering on into the night. We lay thus until the first glimmer of dawn. Then Lovejoy ordered our mainsail raised and our course set once more for Philadelphia.

"We can have a galley fire now, can't we, captain?" he asked me sarcastically. "I need coffee."

Gwin denied his duplicity until I searched his seabag and found a folded paper on which were written instructions for signaling.

Then I stood him before the crew and tied one end of a long line about his ankles. I ordered six of our stoutest fellows to "stand by to keelhaul this traitor."

The Cornishman broke down and cried. In the privacy of my cabin he sobbed out a confession. He had remained loyal for more than a year not to the American cause but to "you, captain."

What had made him wait until now to turn coat? After all, I had entrusted a prize to him. Instead of sailing it back to Philadelphia, he could have turned it in at Bermuda and collected a fat commission.

"Oh, I never done it for the money."

"Do you love King George so much, then?"

"I love my wife and my children."

Then the full story came out. Halbertson had got hold of him in Statia. Gwin, a fisherman back in Cornwall, had been exiled to Barbados for smuggling. There Sir Francis Bolton had recruited him for the *Charlotte* by sending subsistence money home to his family. Halbertson had threatened to have his family transported if he did not cooperate. That threat, coupled with a promise of a hundred pounds in gold and pardon from his exile, had turned him into a traitor.

"And you were willing to see this sloop captured, your shipmates imprisoned?"

"I love my family very much, captain."

"All the same, you are a scoundrel to betray the trust I placed in you. If you had told me, I could have done something to help. Goddamn it, you're a rotten traitor."

I was at the point of striking him when he said quietly, "Begging your pardon, sir, but did you not betray the trust of Sir Francis when you took possession of this sloop?"

I lowered my clenched fist and looked at Ephraim. He had his hand over his mouth, and his eyes were averted.

I lacked the heart to hang Gwin as I had the right to, or even to flog him as his crewmen expected me to. Instead, I tied his hands behind him and lashed him to our mast, leaving him exposed to the weather and to the insult and gibes of his shipmates.

The discovery of a traitor and our near capture by Fitzgerald shook my confidence, but as we neared the north of the Delaware, thoughts of profits to be made and praises to be enjoyed danced in my brain, and I regained my normal cockiness.

A fog bank lay off the Delaware coast as we approached. With no breeze astirring, we sat becalmed on the fringe of the cloud bank throughout one day. The fog began lifting the next morning, gradually nibbled away by a nice southeasterly wind. We raised our sails and felt our way toward the entrance to Delaware Bay.

There it was off our larboard bow—Cape Henlopen. To the

north the fog still hovered over the entrance to the Delaware, but we were in sight of home. I ordered our larboard nine-pounder fired off as a signal that we needed a pilot. Despite the lack of response, we sailed on our northward course, deeper into the remnants of the fog.

I meant to run the *Charlotte* up the coast far enough to put us even with Lewes, then drop anchor and wait for the fog to lift and for a pilot to guide us up the river to Philadelphia. Lovejoy was the first to spot the outline of a ship's masts just up ahead. Taking her to be an American, like ourselves waiting for the fog to lift, I sailed the *Charlotte* close enough for my shout to carry. "Ship ahoy. Who are you?"

"The *Mary Jane* out of Boston. Who do you be?"

Without hesitation, I called back, "The *Charlotte* out of Philadelphia. Ain't this fog a nuisance?"

There was a long silence; then, "You want to come alongside? You can tie up with us and wait."

Again without thinking, I shouted back, "Fine with us! We'll put out fenders."

Now the stern of the ship loomed above our quarterdeck. I put our helm over to bring us closer and ordered our mainsail lowered. The sea was calm except for a shallow swell. We let the current carry us up to within spitting distance of the ship. Their crewmen appeared as shadows along the rail. One of them swung what I took to be a monkey's fist around his hand. It came sailing over our forward rail.

"It's a grappling hook!" Lovejoy cried.

Another and another were hurled onto our deck and dragged tight to bite into our rail.

"Raise the mainsail," Lovejoy screamed. And to my amazement, he seized a cutlass and raced along the rail, slicing the lines that held the grappling hooks.

The Dublin-tinged accent of my nemesis, Atticus Fitzgerald, roared across the narrow distance separating our vessels. "Strike your colors and come to, or we'll blow you out of the water!"

Our sail was only half-lowered, so we still had some headway. I hurled myself at the tiller to turn our bow away from the frigate. The *Charlotte* sluggishly veered away.

"I have been stalking you for weeks, Martin!" Fitzgerald called from his quarterdeck. "You can't get away. Come to, or we'll pound you to pieces!"

I leveled my pistol at his ghostly outline and fired. There was a great clatter aboard the other ship as they opened their gun ports. With the British scrambling to bring their guns to bear on us and ourselves frantically raising our mainsail and shifting our boom to get away, every second became precious.

From the deck of the other vessel there first burst a storm of small-arms fire. Their bullets sang around our heads like a horde of hornets. We were too close for them to bring their cannon to bear against our hull and deck, thank God, but that did not stop Fitzgerald from ordering a broadside. The force of the twelve muzzle blasts nearly swept me off my feet. Their balls whooshed over our heads, all except one, which struck our mast high up. Our topsail fell to the deck, covering poor Gwin with canvas.

By the time the British had reloaded, Lovejoy had got our mainsail up and we had sailed almost past the frigate. Now only her most forward guns could be brought to bear on us. But they blasted away again anyway. One of her balls grazed our stern, sending a shower of splinters across our quarterdeck.

We could hear the sounds of pandemonium on the larger vessel as her crew simultaneously brought up her anchor, raised her sails, and fumbled with their guns.

I did not need Lovejoy to tell me that with our topsail gone and loaded as heavily as we were, the *Charlotte* could not outrun the frigate, not in a straightaway race. But that did not stop him from telling me so anyway.

"Then what in the sweet name of Jesus are we to do?"

"We could double back to the south. We can still sail closer to the wind than them bastards. They'd have to tack back and forth to follow."

"No, damn it, not only would that carry us back to sea, it would mean passing once more under his guns."

So we sailed on for a mile or so until we made out the now-raised sails of the frigate coming up fast astern of us like a ghost bent on vengeance. Then we turned east into Delaware Bay.

For the *Charlotte,* it was just a matter of shifting our boom and putting over the tiller. As Lovejoy hurriedly and in my view needlessly explained, for Fitzgerald's square-rigged frigate, it was quite another matter.

"The wind is from the southeast. He is on an east-by-northeast heading. To bring her back to the south-southeast, he'll have to swing her through the wind's eye. That means he's got to slack off his mainsails and tighten his fore-and-aft driver on the mizzenmast. That'll bring her stern around. There's the tricky part. He's got to put his helm hard alee and let go his jib and staysail sheets. Then he'll have to be ready to haul his mainsail and—"

I grew exasperated at this tedious explanation. "Who gives a damn about all that?"

"Well, you ought to."

Just about then, Fitzgerald must have spotted us plodding into the bay. It was too late for him to stay directly on our tail. He gave us a larboard broadside as he blundered by, but we were too far away to be hit. I prayed that he could not see that we had lost our topsail and with it our speed.

"If the man has any sense, he'll give up," Lovejoy said.

Usually he was the pessimist and I the optimist. This time I said, "I don't think that man will ever give up."

We fumbled our way deeper into the bay and the fog until we lost sight of the frigate. During this time Lovejoy stationed a leadsman in the bow to take soundings. It was low tide. By now Lewes lay so far behind us that it was out of the question to get a pilot. Lovejoy wanted to stop and anchor until the fog lifted. I overruled him in favor of pressing on for Philadelphia. At the time it seemed the thing to do.

Lovejoy had ordered our leadsman's soundings passed along in whispers from the bow to the quarterdeck. The water was growing more and more shallow. Cursing the low tide, he eased our heading to the north a bit more.

"Damn it, Jerry, why won't you let me drop anchor? We've lost that frigate. He'd be a fool to follow us in this fog."

"I want to get this sloop and this cargo to Philadelphia."

Hardly had I uttered these words when the *Charlotte* halted so abruptly, I was thrown off my feet.

"Goddamn it to hell, I tried to tell you!" Lovejoy roared. "We have gone aground."

"Well, don't get yourself so worked up. We'll just wait for high tide. Maybe by then the fog will lift."

We used part of the time we were stuck on that Delaware Bay mudbank to clear away the wreckage of the upper mast and sail that littered our deck. It pained me to see the *Charlotte* wounded so. But I counted it a small price to pay for the rewards of money and reputation that we would reap in Philadelphia with our cargo of sorely needed ammunition.

When the wind first freshened, my spirits began to lift along with the surrounding fog. The tide apparently had passed full ebb. I ordered a round of grog all around to reward my brave crew for their ordeal.

I blame myself for not keeping a sharper eye out astern. Sure, we were absorbed in trying to get ourselves off the mudbank and in clearing away our wreckage, but that was no excuse. I should have kept a lookout on the top of what remained of our mast. But I did not. And so the frigate was almost upon us again before we saw the infernal vessel.

She moved slowly with her mainsail half furled, feeling her away along like a giant in a darkened room. The cries of her leadsmen calling out their soundings carried clearly across the water. Even through the edge of the remaining fog, I could see her open gun ports and the faint images of her cannon muzzles.

Any doubt that they not only saw us but realized our awkward position disappeared when they dropped their anchor. The clatter of those chains struck terror in my heart worse than a broadside would have.

"Ahoy, Martin!" Fitzgerald called. "Do you surrender?"

I looked at Lovejoy. For once he had no ready answer. I was on my own. It was futile to resist. From the distance where the frigate was anchored, their cannonballs could reach us. But to surrender would mean a British prison for my crew and most likely the gallows for me.

"No!" I yelled. "You can go to hell, Fitzgerald!"

There was a long pause. I broke into a sweat, bracing myself for their broadside. But instead of cannon, there boomed Fitzgerald's voice again. "It is hopeless for you, Martin."

"Go to hell, Fitzgerald!"

I was beginning to wonder why he didn't open fire and get it over with. My men, without permission, had lain down on the deck and covered their eyes.

"Come now, Martin! Don't make me destroy that beautiful sloop."

Ephaim caught the implication of the message before I did. "Jerry, didn't you tell me he loved the *Charlotte*?"

"So he did."

"He doesn't really want to hurt the ship."

Lovejoy, who had been grinding his teeth in frustration, spoke up. "Dr. McGee has something. He don't want to damage her. Here now, you ask for time to consider. We may get out of this. I don't want to rot in prison."

"What do you say, Martin? Do you strike? Or do I open fire?"

"Wait," I yelled. "Give me time to take a vote."

"I'll give you three minutes. No tricks, now. My guns are loaded and laid."

It hurt me to see Lovejoy overseeing the frantic jettisoning of our larboard guns. One by one, our fellows lifted those beautiful bronze beauties off their carriages and dumped them over the rail into the bay.

The *Charlotte* shifted on her bed of mud and began to list to the starboard.

There was no time to consult with Lovejoy. He had turned into a sort of maniac as he whispered orders and threats to his men.

"Now the starboard guns," he said in a sort of stage whisper.

"Time's almost up!" Fitzgerald cried.

"We have a division. We must vote again."

One by one my precious French six-pounders plopped into the water on the starboard side. The deck of the *Charlotte* righted itself.

"One more minute. Don't try any tricks!"

Lovejoy put a pole over the side and probed the bottom. "The tide is rising, but we're still stuck. Stall him for another minute."

"Ahoy, Fitzgerald!" I called. "If we surrender, will you set us free?"

He was a long time responding to my question. During the pause, Lovejoy stationed a crew of our stoutest fellows on the deck, ready to haul up our mainsail to catch the breeze. The *Charlotte* remained stuck, but free of the weight of the cannon, she rocked ever so slightly in the swells.

"You will get a fair trial."

"Not good enough! We don't want to go to prison."

"No promises. Surrender, or you'll die right here."

Lovejoy took another sounding and came away from the rail, cursing our luck. "Even if the wind breaks us free, I don't see how we can get away, Jerry."

That was when I played my final card.

Quietly motioning Lovejoy to ease our boat over the larboard side, I called back to Fitzgerald, "We'll burn the ship if you don't give us amnesty."

"No amnesty!"

"No *Charlotte* then. We'll burn her!"

During the pause that followed, I debated whether to order our sail raised and take a chance on the wind pushing us free.

I put the speaking trumpet to my lips and called out, "Let my men go free, and I'll surrender."

Ephraim caught my sleeve. "No, Jerry. You can't do that!"

Lovejoy joined in. "If you stay aboard, then I do, too."

Fitzgerald's voice carried across the water again, this time free of the anxiety for the sloop that he loved as if she were a woman.

"I'll let your crew go, but you stay, Martin. Stand by. I am sending over a boarding party."

For a moment I considered the possibility of letting them send over a boat, then seizing their boarding party as hostages and trying to escape. But if that didn't work, not only would I hang but so would my crew—but we just might get away with it.

That idea faded quickly when I saw that three of the frigate's boats were being lowered into the water. As sailors climbed over the side, I ordered our fellows into our single boat.

Lovejoy would not go until I whispered my plan to him.

At his urging the men all clambered down the rope ladder into the bobbing boat. I didn't notice that Cato was not with them until they had cast off and I turned back to my chore.

"I can't leave you in a fix like this, captain."

"All right. Then make yourself useful."

Cato raised the hatch while I went down into our close-packed hold with a lantern. Using my pocket knife, I opened first one and

201

then another cannon cartridge. I spilled the pungent black grains of powder to form a trail along the narrow walkway between the stacked rows of powder casks. There was no time for careful calculations or for the emotion I might have felt at committing this atrocity against a beautifully crafted sloop that I had come to love almost as much as the obsessive Fitzgerald did, an affection akin to that I held for my good horse, Ned.

I raised the lantern to survey our work. We were both sweating like pigs from the exertion and the fear.

"Topside, quick, Cato. Get a hammer and nails. Fast."

I paused for a moment at the foot of the ladder and took one last look at the interior of the *Charlotte*. Then I ignited the corner of my handkerchief with my lantern's flame and dropped it at the end of my powder train.

The powder broke into an instant blaze. I dropped my lantern and leaped up the stairs. Cato, God bless him, was ready with his hammer to nail shut the hatch cover. Off our starboard side Fitzgerald was calling from one of his boats for me to lower a ladder. From our larboard side Lovejoy was calling for me to hurry.

"Over the side, Cato!"

"No, captain, I can't—"

I gave him a push that tumbled him into the water. I was just ready to leap myself when a voice cried from the base of our mast, "Captain, please help me."

Sweet Jesus, I had forgotten about Gwin, still bound to our mast! It would serve the bastard right to be blown up with the *Charlotte* and Fitzgerald. But damn it, the man had served me well before Halbertson had got his oily hands on him.

Maybe it was stupid of me, but I shouted for Lovejoy to pull away. I ran to Gwin and with my knife quickly sliced through his bonds.

"Over the side, or you'll be blown to bits," I said, pointing to the starboard side, where Fitzgerald was bellowing for me to put a ladder down.

I raced over to the rail and looked down into the face of my old adversary. There he was in the stern of a boat, surrounded by tough little British sailors, all carrying pistols and cutlasses.

"Wait a minute—I have to fetch a ladder," I said.

"Well, bear a hand, or I will keep you in irons the whole trip back to England. And you'll get naught but bread and water on the voyage. Your game is up, Martin! I told you I would catch you, and by God, you are caught. Now, get that ladder over the side, and be quick about it."

A sailor in the bow of Fitzgerald's boat tossed a small grappling hook over our rail.

I slipped off my shoes, turned, and was running across the deck

202

when the first explosion went off beneath my feet. The deck buckled, and I fell against the larboard rail. I felt, rather than heard, the following and far more violent explosion of our cargo. It was like one of those dreams in which one thinks he has the power of flight. Like an albatross, I soared up, up into air and out over the water. It was as though a mighty hand had plucked me off the deck of the *Charlotte* and hurled me head over heels over Delaware Bay.

PART SIX

1

WHEN I RECOVERED at least some of my senses, I was in the water, swimming as though by instinct toward the Delaware shore. I should have wondered, but did not, at the tomblike silence. The leaden weariness of my arms and legs indicated that I must have been swimming hard for a long while. Rolling onto my back, I raised my head and saw a cloud of black and white smoke hanging over the water several hundred yards behind me. I started to shout but thought better of it.

I continued to swim on my back, trying to conserve my strength and collect my addled wits. If only I had laid a longer powder trail or had not paused to nail down the hatch or to free Gwin. Free Gwin, indeed! He was the scoundrel who had got us into this fix. And what good had I done him? He had surely been destroyed along with my comrades—steadfast Lovejoy Brown, sensitive, intelligent Ephraim McGee, loyal, stalwart Cato, all gone, all blown to eternity along with that peerless sloop. Yes, and along with Fitzgerald and his three boatloads of sailors. And perhaps his frigate as well? I raised my head again. No, through the fast-lifting fog still loomed the masts and spars of the frigate. If I had to destroy the *Charlotte* and kill my comrades, why could not I have let the frigate come alongside and then set off our cargo? At least I would have struck a meaningful blow for my homeland.

Several times during the next hour, I was tempted to give up the struggle and let the bay claim me. My arms and legs ached. I was chilled to the marrow of my bones. Death seemed to offer sweet release from my turbulent life. What good had I ever done anyone? Who would mourn me? The first mate of the British frigate would enter the events in his log and send a report to London about the destruction of a pesky American privateer and the sad loss of their captain and a score of brave British sailors. In time, word of our destruction would reach Philadelphia and Statia. Jason and Kate McGee would weep over the loss of their son, and Laura Mason would mourn him as well. In Marblehead, Mother Brown would shed bitter tears over the fate of her Lovejoy and, aye, tell her neighbors it was all the fault of that worthless fellow from Virginia. Perhaps, back in Statia, Abraham D'Balboa would say a prayer for me in his synagogue. On the one hand, Halbertson would congratulate himself that his trick of subverting one of my crew had worked, but on the other, he would regret that he had failed to return the *Charlotte* to his employer.

And Sir Francis—how would he react to the news? Would his satisfaction at my demise balance his chagrin at losing a treasured sloop? I pictured the hawk-faced old man in London or Barbados, wherever the news reached him, cackling at having evened the score with me while regretting the cost of his victory.

Ephraim had quoted his father as saying I had as many lives as a cat. I lost one of mine there in the chilly waters of Delaware Bay. But I moved on to my next one when my feet touched the sand and I realized that I had nearly reached shore. Onward I struggled, too tired to think, too exhausted at first to see that a clump of people were waving their arms at me from the edge of the water.

They had to wade out and lift me from the water, for I was too weak to rise from my knees. They laid me on my back, and one of them threw his coat over my shivering frame.

At first I thought I had been rescued by a gaggle of deaf-mutes. They gestured and their mouths worked at a great rate, but no sound seemed to come from their throats. One, an old gentleman with thinning gray hair, bent down until his face was so close, I could smell his stale breath as he soundlessly worked his lips.

"Martin," I said. "I am Jeremiah Martin. My sloop just blew up."

The old man jerked away from me as if I had struck him a blow.

"I said my name is—"

And then I realized that I had been shouting, but I could not hear myself.

The old man cupped his mouth between his hands and said something else, but I pointed to my ears and shook my head.

A pair of stout fellows, fishermen by the smell of their clothes, helped me to my feet and half carried me along the sand to where a narrow trail led inland and finally to a hut, out of sight of the water. They sat me on a stool before a fire and put a blanket over my shoulders. There I sat, shaking so much that I thought I would rack the legs off the stool. Then one of the fishermen brought me a cup of rum, and soon the warmth of the brew ceased me from shivering and gave me the strength to stand.

The silence was maddening. They now understood that I was deaf and so had stopped trying to communicate with me. Instead they talked to each other, pointing out the door toward the sea. Suddenly I grew angry at them, as though they were to blame for my difficulty. I took a deep breath and exclaimed "Damn it, don't stand about doing nothing! Help save my crew!"

They jumped as though I had touched them with a goad. The old man put one hand over his ear and turned up the palm of the other in a gesture of helplessness. My brief spurt of energy gone, I sat down again.

The woman of the house, a dumpy old thing with no front teeth, dipped a bowl of fish stew from the kettle over the fire. Seeing that I lacked the strength to hold the bowl and spoon, she fed me the rude but nourishing stuff. After I wolfed it down, I looked up at the old man and gestured that I wanted writing materials. He spoke first to the woman and then to the men, and they all shrugged or shook their heads.

I did not protest when they lifted me from the stool, led me to a low bed, and laid me on it. In seconds I fell into a deep sleep.

A gentle hand on my shoulder drew me back to consciousness. There stood a chap wearing a long frock coat, knee breeches, and stockings. In one hand he held a low-crowned, broad-brimmed hat; in the other, some writing materials. The benign expression on his face as well as his dignified garb marked him as a clergyman.

They helped me from my bed and led me to a table, where I sat down and quickly wrote an explanation of who I was and how I came to be washed up on their shore. I ended my little report, "I am concerned about my men. Can you tell what happened to them?"

The clergyman read what I had written and then penned a reply, which informed me that he was Brother Silas Cochrane, a Methodist lay preacher. He was sorry to inform me that no sign of any other survivors had been sighted. He lived five miles away and had wondered what caused the explosion that rattled his windows that morning. He marveled at the fact that I had been aboard the destroyed vessel and had survived. God must have preserved me for some mysterious purpose, and I should fall on my knees and thank him for his providence.

I seized the quill from his hand and wrote, "I wish God had extended his providence to my men. Are you sure that none survived?

Has the fog lifted?"

"We must not question God's judgment in these affairs," he wrote in reply. "The fog lifted long ago. The frigate has departed the bay."

This back-and-forth correspondence went on until we had very nearly used up the preacher's little stock of paper. I learned that the explosion had sounded to the people on the near shore like "a hundred thunderclaps all at once." No one had actually seen the *Charlotte* explode; the fog had been too thick for that. Nor could they see what had happened for a time, even after they had been aroused by the mysterious and powerful explosion.

I spent the rest of the day walking along the shore, hoping against hope that I might find a sign of my old comrades, but all was in vain. The Reverend Mr. Cochrane stayed with me until darkness fell and then persuaded me to ride to his house with him. Sunk in my deaf misery, I rode behind him on his rough-gaited horse to a small but neat house on the road from Lewes to Dover. His wife, a dark, cheerful woman, fed me a good supper at the table with their two little sons, who were so awed by my presence that they stared at me through the entire meal.

The next morning the preacher hailed a horse-drawn dray bound for Philadelphia and persuaded the two wagoneers to allow me to ride with them. I slept that night under a horse blanket at Wilmington. It was nightfall the following day before the wagon lumbered into the city.

Liz Oliver was sitting in her tavern kitchen drinking a cup of tea when I arrived at her door, barefoot and crusty from my long immersion in sea water. The instant before she recognized me, her face had looked old and her plump shoulders sagged. Because I could not regulate the volume of my voice, I had given up trying to speak. I waited mutely until she recognized me.

Her face brightened in a flash. She clapped her hands and bounded into my arms. Her face fell again when I pointed to my ears and shook my head.

As every room in the tavern was full, she made a pallet for me in her little pantry. After feeding me until I was ready to burst, she covered me with a blanket. I slept the sleep of the dead until nearly noon the next day.

Dogood Mackey was amazed and delighted when I showed up at his office door the next afternoon. He was distressed at my deafness but would give me no rest until I had sat down with quill and paper and written a complete report of my adventures of the past twelve months.

He shook his head over the loss of the *Charlotte* and her crew.

"This war is a sad thing," he wrote. "Friend Jason McGee will be devastated. He loved his son so very much."

I nodded my head, and tears stung my eyes.

"I am sorry about thy sloop, too."

I shrugged.

"It was inevitable that the sloop be captured or destroyed sooner or later," he wrote. "That is no great matter. Thee has earned thy investment in it many times over. In fact, thee is a rich man. Thee would have been far richer, had thee brought that cargo to port. Washington needs every grain of powder and every pound of lead. This war is coming to a head. The issue may be settled within the next few weeks."

Using a map on his office wall, he pointed out Washington's encampments up in New Jersey, around Morristown, then indicated the position of a new British army under Burgoyne that had moved down from Canada into the upper Hudson Valley.

He wrote, "Howe and his army remain in New York with the British fleet at their disposal. It is feared that he will move up the Hudson against Washington, while Burgoyne moves down to meet him. If they succeed in that strategy, they will cut the country in two, separating New England from the other colonies."

Then with his usual efficiency, he drew out his books and gave me a full reckoning of my earnings from our cruises in the West Indies. I had never dreamed I would have so much money—well over ten thousand pounds, it came to. Yet it seemed a hollow triumph.

That behind us, he had one of his clerks lead me around to a tailor shop, where the proprietor took my measurements and promised to work through the night to turn me out a good suit. Then it was on to a cobbler's to be fitted for new boots.

Back at The White Swan, Liz gave me a good supper. Later, after she had packed Master Oliver off to bed, she joined me in the pantry, and there did help me forget my troubles.

To this day I am partially deaf in my left ear, and I have two recurring nightmares. In one I am struggling in the ocean, and in the other I am in a crowd of people who are speaking in voices I cannot hear and, at the same time, pointing their fingers at me. Often have I awakened filled with rage at the callousness of those faceless phantoms. Given a choice between losing my sight and losing my hearing, I am not sure which I would choose. Perhaps blindness on even days of the month and deafness on odd. But some hold that every handicap has its compensations; mine did eventually.

Wealth has obvious compensations. I could now afford to rent Mistress Oliver's very best second-floor room. There, while waiting for my hearing to be restored, I wrote letters to Laura Mason and Jason McGee informing them of the death of Ephraim, and to Mother Brown in Marblehead.

Steeped in my silent misery, I was as rich as Croesus and as empty of contentment as he, except for occasional furtive visits from my landlady. Except for Liz and Dogood Mackey, I shunned human contact, staying in my room and brooding over the loss of my comrades and the *Charlotte*. The New Testament contains a great truth in the question, "What doth it profit a man to gain the whole world and lose his own soul?"

At the urging of Mr. Mackey, I did go with him one evening to the office of the Marine Committee of the Continental Congress. There in the presence of the chairman, John Hancock himself, and the representatives from each of the colonies, I — still not trusting my voice — sat like a dumb creature while Mackey told them about my experiences. They attempted to question me by means of written notes, but the tedious procedure soon wearied them. I reflected bitterly that it would have been glorious to stand and hold that august body enthralled with accounts of our adventures. Instead, I sat like a village idiot while they discussed me with my mentor.

Mr. Mackey occasionally persuaded me to venture out to dine with him at The London Coffee House or The City Tavern to read the war news. We were at the latter place when we learned that Ticonderoga had fallen to Burgoyne, giving him clear sailing down Lake Champlain. Hard on the heels of this unwelcome news came reports from New York that a goodly part of the British army had gone aboard transports. Did they intend to sail up the Hudson or strike elsewhere so as to draw Washington out of Burgoyne's path? And if so, where? Boston? Charleston? Or Philadelphia?

Congress, which had taken to its collective heels the previous December at the approach of Howe, again became nervous for the safety of Philadelphia and ordered the forts below the city to be strengthened and for obstructions to be placed in the river.

Then came the news that the British fleet with some fifteen thousand men had set out to sea.

During this same period, the little mulatto maid who worked for the Mason family delivered to me a letter from Laura Mason. She had been prostrated by my report of Ephraim's death, or she would have written sooner. She had admired him more than anyone she had ever known or was likely ever to know, she wrote. She would ask me to come round and tell her more about Ephraim's experiences aboard my ship, but her father would not permit it. Besides that, she was in poor health.

I toyed with the idea of shadowing her house until her father left for his medical rounds but decided that I would only cause her and myself embarrassment. Besides, fresh war news began to take my attention away from myself and my tribulations. Worried by the departure of a British army from New York by sea, Washington had shifted his headquarters from northern to southern New Jersey and had ordered further strengthening of the forts downriver from

Philadelphia and the emplacement of additional obstructions in the water.

A curious event took place at about this time, late in July. It had to do with my hearing and our landlord, Phineas Oliver. Previously he had treated me with obsequious courtesy, but he now acted as if I did not exist. He did not even bother to nod to me during his infrequent appearances in his tavern. By then, the staff of The White Swan had grown accustomed to my deafness. One morning I was sitting at a table by myself waiting for my breakfast and recalling with pleasure the night I had just spent in Liz's arms. It was late, and I was the only patron in the place. Suddenly, very faintly and through one ear only, I just barely made out the voices of the two servingmaids.

"Wonder what the dummy wants this morning?" one was saying. "Shall I ask him?"

"You know he can't hear a word. Give him his usual eggs and scrapple."

"Better not let herself hear you talking so of him. He is her special pet, is that one."

"Aye. Do you suppose she thinks no one knows of her slipping into his room of a night when Master Oliver is away?"

"I ain't so sure he don't know what's going on."

I was at the point of shouting, "I can hear!" but wisely kept quiet.

"She was in his room again last night, the entire night. Where do you suppose her husband was?"

"Germantown again, I reckon. Suppose he keeps a woman out there? It would serve herself right if he did."

"I ain't so sure it was Germantown. Coming to work yesterday morning I seen him riding south along Front Street with two saddlebags and wearing his cloak."

Not certain whether to be amused or outraged, I made the mistake of looking up at the gossips. This caused them to withdraw to the kitchen to fetch "the dummy" his eggs and scrapple.

Throughout that day, the hearing in that one ear grew stronger, but I told no one, not even Dogood Mackey. He came around to share the news that scores of the enemy's ships had been sighted off the Delaware capes and that George Washington himself was expected to visit Philadelphia to confer with Congress.

Philadelphia braced itself for a naval assault. The cobblestones rang with the boots of militiamen. Congress met long into the night. Despite the partial return of my hearing, I observed all this activity with a sort of jaundiced detachment. None of this war seemed to have anything to do with me anymore.

That night I was awakened by the sound of my door opening, and without thinking I said, "Who's there?"

"It is only me," Liz said. She paused to disrobe and then slid in beside me. We had become almost like a well-adjusted married couple, each having learned what the other liked. And so, after a few preliminaries, we got down to business. After this had come, so to speak, to a satisfactory conclusion, I pillowed my head on her ample bosom and went happily off to sleep.

I awakened at dawn to see her up on one elbow scrutinizing my face.

"How did you know when I entered the room last night?"

I laughed and told her about the return of my hearing.

She was very quiet for a while, then asked, "You have really been deaf, though?"

"As a post. Until yesterday morning."

"What will you do now that you can hear?"

"I don't know, Liz. There is nothing I am much interested in anymore."

"Poor Jerry," she said. "You need a woman."

"I've got you," I said.

"For the time you have. But for better or worse, I have a husband. And I am not the right woman for you, not in the long run. You draw people to you as a candle draws moths. I have seen it. That is why Sir Francis Bolton took such pains to make your acquaintance."

I sat up and threw aside our cover. "What do you know of old Bolton?"

"Ah, Jerry, don't hate me." She then proceeded to reveal that her husband had long been in the employ of Sir Francis. "Not in a big way, but on a sort of retainer, you know. Don't be angry now. We couldn't have bought this tavern without his assistance."

Suddenly I recalled my first tumble with Liz. She had pressed me for my opinion of Sir Francis the night she had waited up for me in her kitchen. And she had eavesdropped on my heart-to-heart conversation with Jason McGee upon our reunion, then passed the information on to her husband.

I started to lash out and accuse her of duplicity but was deterred by the sight of her pained expression.

Thereafter, I kept my door barred at night, which was just as well since Oliver remained about the premises most of the time. Liz and I conversed, but our intimacies were discontinued. She was solicitous of my health, inquiring often about the progress of my hearing, but I stopped exchanging either confidences or embraces with her.

With the partial return of my hearing, I began taking my meals at other taverns both to avoid the Olivers and to hear the lively talk about what the British were up to. Their fleet had massed as if in preparation to sail up the Delaware and disgorge Howe's army for an assault on Philadelphia. But it inexplicably stood out to sea again. All the talk now was of an attack on Charleston, South Carolina, and of Burgoyne's continued advance south from Ticonderoga.

Later in August came a thrilling report and a chilling one. Colonel John Stark of New Hampshire, the same man whose militiamen had slaughtered the British light infantry on the sandy edge of the Mystic River in the struggle for Bunker Hill, had beaten and routed a large raiding force of Burgoyne's Hessians at Bennington. And up from Virginia came the news that the British fleet had been sighted standing in to Chesapeake Bay, apparently with the intention of landing in Maryland. This report was followed quickly by the news that Washington's army was crossing the Delaware and shortly would be passing through Philadelphia on its way to confront the British.

2

I NEVER had seen so many people on the streets of Philadelphia—or of any other city—as early as I did on that Sunday morning, August 24, 1777. Despite the rain that had fallen the night before, by six o'clock they had begun to gather along Front Street in front of Dogood Mackey's office, Mr. Mackey and I among them. Within an hour we stood shoulder to shoulder, straining our eyes and ears in the direction of Hartsville to the north. With my still-impaired hearing, I did not pick up the sound of drum and fife as early as those around me did, but being taller than most, I was one of the first to see the head of the parade.

There he rode in the lead, the great man himself. I recognized him from my visit to Philadelphia on Dr. Warren's behalf. Back then he had been wearing a Virginia militia uniform, which had seemed rather silly for a member of the Continental Congress. Now I wondered at my lack of perception. This big, strapping man, clad in the brilliant uniform of the commanding general of the American armies and riding his horse with rare grace, looked born to command. He exuded a power and dignity that at first seemed to awe even a boisterous Philadelphia crowd.

Then a fellow with a deep voice shouted, "Washington! Hoorah for General Washington!" And the crowd took up the cry.

The great man raised his hat and turned that impressive countenance from one side to the other as though bestowing a blessing on us.

I took little notice of the anemic-looking young man wearing a major general's sash who rode at his side, until Mr. Mackey explained that he was the Marquis de Lafayette, newly arrived from France to join our revolution.

No, everything was Washington, Washington, that day. And I must confess that I got caught up in the cheering with the rest. He had earned the adulation of the crowd, this man who had forged a grab bag of New England militiamen into an army able to rescue Boston from the British; this man who, after losing New York to his adversaries, had turned the tables on them boldly at Trenton and Princeton; this man who had held together an often dispirited rabble and turned it into an army of patriots. It was hard not to believe that he could save Philadelphia as well.

I know now that Washington, although as brave as a lion, is not a gifted battlefield general. But by the Almighty he is a natural-born leader. He and his retinue of generals and staff, followed by fifers and drummers, passed our vantage point there in front of Mr. Mackey's office. But the parade was only just starting.

Next came a contingent of half a hundred tall, stout fellows, marching twelve abreast in good step, carrying light arms. What a bunch of dandies they looked, with their blue coats and white facings, their white waistcoats and breeches and black half gaiters, all wearing cocked hats adorned with blue and white feathers.

"Friend Washington's Life Guards, I think they are called," said Mr. Mackey. "Every man nearly six feet tall, and hand picked. Mostly Virginians. They protect him and look after his headquarters."

This fine-looking lot had nearly passed and I had turned my gaze toward the next unit—a rakish lot of pioneers carrying axes and wearing wool caps—when Mr. Mackey grasped my arm.

"That chap in the rear rank of the Life Guards—do my eyes deceive me?"

The rank was even with us and I could not see who he meant. But then, as they marched on, I recognized the set of the shoulders and the way he walked—like an Indian, as I had taught him back in Sherman's Valley.

"Chris!" I yelled. "Chris McGee!"

Damn it, he could not hear me above the cries of the onlookers and the music of fife and drum.

I yelled again and waved my arms, but now a squadron of light dragoons clattered past, their horses prancing nervously over the unaccustomed cobblestones.

Mr. Mackey took my arm again. "Do not agitate thyself. We can ride out to their camp later. Here now, see how handsomely the dragoons sit their horses."

It took that parade two hours to pass Mr. Mackey's little office. Down Front, up Chestnut, to the Common, and then out to Middle Ferry marched regiment after regiment of infantry, each led by its own little band of musicians. Many men wore long linen or deerskin hunting frocks and, in addition to muskets or rifles, carried tomahawks or long knives. Those who owned hats wore them as suited their dispositions: some low over the eyes; others on one side of the head; and still others far back, as if to shade their necks. And in his hatband or hair, each exhibited a sprig of greenery—by order of Washington, so Mr. Mackey said. As for their marching, there was no comparison with the orderly way I had seen British soldiers drilling on the Boston common. They kept more or less in step with the music, but they turned their feet in and out in as undisciplined a manner as they wore their hats and caps. And they were clad in every conceivable type of clothing, from striped breeches to pantaloons, from smock to tailored longcoat. And not a few lacked shoes.

It was a motley army, all right, but with Washington at their head and up to twelve thousand men freshly recruited, they were a force to be reckoned with.

I said it took the parade two hours to pass. That was according to the later testimony of Mr. Mackey. It would have taken much longer had Washington not ordered his wagon trains to go around the city, had he not forbidden female camp followers from entering the city, and had Sullivan's division not been left behind in New Jersey to watch the British remaining in New York.

After General Henry Knox and his artillery rattled by, I saw that only more of the same was coming and excused myself. I could wait no longer to find Chris McGee. I cut across to the Common and raced past the marching troops. Then, near exhaustion, I overtook the head of the column beyond the city, at the Middle Ferry on the Schuylkill River.

Washington and his staff were crossing the river on a rickety bridge of boards laid on pontoons. The Life Guards stood about at ease, awaiting their turn. They had unbuttoned their coats and were wiping their faces and congratulating themselves on the smart showing they had made in Philadelphia.

At first Chris did not recognize me, but when he did he gave out a great whoop and lifted me off the ground in a bear hug.

We bombarded each other with questions until I said, "You go first. I heard you had been taken prisoner."

Indeed, he had been captured at Quebec after Arnold's failure to take that Canadian town on the first day of '76, but he had been exchanged the following fall, in time to join the army for its Christmas foray across the Delaware at Trenton.

Although his face reflected his experiences as a captive of the British, he retained his habitual enthusiasm. "We caught them with their pants down, Jerry. Took a good thousand Hessian prisoners and lost less than a dozen men ourselves. There was never such a man as General Washington."

As for his family, his father, ailing with rheumatism, had returned to Sherman's Valley after the battle of Long Island. There

215

he was busy commanding a company of militiamen and managing the thriving grist mill his wife had built. The twins were well, yes. I was casting about for a way to learn of Gerta's welfare without having to ask outright when he stopped and frowned at me.

"Wait, Pa said in his last letter that Ephraim had gone a-privateering with you."

Tears came into his eyes and his face took on a twisted expression as he listened to my explanation.

"And there was no sign of him afterward?"

"Not a trace of him or any of the others. I am sorry."

He wiped his cheeks quickly so that his comrades would not see, then swallowed hard and said simply, "He was as good a brother as anyone could ask. This will kill Ma. She doted on him."

Then he squared his shoulders and said, "Here, let me introduce you around. Jeb Fleming, meet Jerry Martin. Jerry was my old schoolmaster back in Cumberland County—"

He was interrupted by shouts for the Life Guards to fall in and march across the bridge.

"One more thing, Chris," I said. "What happened to my old horse, Ned? I left him with you that day on the Charlestown Neck, you remember?"

"I should have told you sooner. Pa took him home. I may see him and Pa soon. General Armstrong from Carlisle commands the Pennsylvania militia now. General Washington has asked him to bring all his forces to join us. Unless Ma can stop him, I expect Pa to join us in time to help whip Howe's ass."

Suddenly he was gone, and I was once more left to my own hollow devices. I sat beside the road and watched throughout the morning as regiment after regiment of Washington's army marched gingerly across the bridge.

I was a rich man. Now that I had recovered my hearing, there was nothing to stop me from reentering the privateering trade as a landbound owner, or from accepting some congressional post, or from going into commercial trade to supply the army with grain and clothing.

My mind jumped to the future. Someday I might find a good woman, marry her, and produce children. What would I say to my family when they asked what had I done in our great war against England—"Why, I got rich from privateering"?

My mind wandered beyond the Schuylkill, where, if Chris was correct, even now my old comrade Jason McGee was riding Ned to join Washington. Somewhere down in Maryland, Howe was disembarking his army with a view to taking Philadelphia.

My old horse Ned came to mind. In company with Jason McGee, I had ridden him off to the west to Bushy Run in '63. That had been a perilous but invigorating time in my life. And now a fresh, even greater adventure was beckoning, with far more at stake than the safety of a frontier fort. Of course, I had nothing to gain from joining Washington's army—nothing except the satisfaction of serving my country, nothing except the recovery of my own self-respect. The decision burst upon me like a thunderclap. By the Almighty, I would do it!

Off I loped back to the city to turn my affairs over to Dogood Mackey, buy myself a brace of pistols and a plump little mare, and say a perfunctory good-bye to that other plump little mare, Mistress Oliver.

"What do you mean to do, Jerry?" she asked sadly.

"Serve my country," I replied. I shook her hand and mounted my new mare, then left her standing with a hurt look on her face.

I spent the next several days riding over the pretty countryside between the Schuylkill and Brandywine Rivers, inquiring as to the whereabouts of Armstrong's Pennsylvania militia. I found them in the act of setting up camp south of Chester at Marcus Hook, near the Delaware border. I recognized many of the backwoodsmen who swarmed about with their rifles. Lo and behold, there stood old Ned himself, tied to a tree. It saddened me to see that one of his eyes was glazed and that patches of gray now appeared in his mane.

At my approach, he tossed his head and whickered. As I came nearer, he stretched his neck to rub his nose against my chest. I put my arms around his lowered head.

I was interrupted in this ridiculous posture by a familiar voice demanding, "What are you doing to my horse?"

Without looking up, I replied, "This horse is mine. It was stolen from me." Then I turned and seized Jason McGee's hand before he realized it was me.

The rigors of his military service around Boston and New York, and the long hard march from beyond the Susquehanna, had taken their toll on my old friend. As I soon learned, so had my letter about the loss of his son Ephraim. We sat against the tree while I told him the entire story. Throughout the ordeal, Ned kept bending down his head so that I could scratch his nose.

When I had finished, Jason put his hand on his chin and said, "Well, his mother will want to know all about this. She took to her bed for three days after your letter came. Hated to leave her so distraught, but couldn't let my men come without me."

I offered to trade my own mare for Ned. "She has an easier gait than Ned. It will be better for your rheumatism."

"My rheumatism comes and goes. Wait, how do you know of my ailments?"

I laughed and brought him up to date on the great parade through Philadelphia and my brief meeting with Chris.

"So what will you do now that you've got your horse back?"

"Jason, we have been friends for a long time. I can talk to you frankly. I got into this war by accident, as it were. I have done my fair share of service for my country, but everything I have done has been tainted by self-seeking. The war has made me rich. It also has cost me my best friends, aside from yourself. I have seen enough of British high-handedness to know that I can never accept their rule again. Besides that, I don't want Ephraim and the others to have died in vain." I paused to get control of myself and added, "I would like to join your militia company and fight alongside of you as I did at Bushy Run."

"You got no musket."

"I have these two pistols."

"And your old war horse." He mused for a moment, then said, "Come, let's go talk to General Armstrong about this."

Armstrong, a venerable old Ulsterman from Carlisle, listened as Jason told him of our long acquaintanceship and of my desire to fight.

"He was at Bushy Run? And Lexington as well?"

"Aye, John, and his horse has seen even more service," Jason said.

Armstrong laughed. "I got enough footsoldiers, but I could use a mounted aide, I reckon. You can read and write, I hope."

3

WASHINGTON, being a surveyor by trade, had a shrewd eye for terrain. He picked a good spot to place his army so as to block Howe's ponderous advance against Philadelphia, up from his Head of Elk landing in Maryland. After pushing most of his army south into Delaware and waiting to see which way the British would move, Washington finally withdrew back into Pennsylvania behind the Brandywine River and established his headquarters in a comfortable three-story stone house atop a slope overlooking a pair of shallows called Chadd's Ford.

The great man concentrated Wayne's and Greene's divisions and all of his artillery around himself at Chadd's but spread Sullivan's division out to cover Brinton's and Painter's Fords upstream. He held Stephen and Stirling in reserve well back of the river. To screen his concentration, he strewed his cavalry over the countryside to the north and sent Maxwell's 750 light infantrymen across the Brandywine toward Kennett Square five miles to the west, where the British had bivouacked. As for Armstrong's one thousand roughcut Pennsylvania militiamen, we were shunted off like unwanted stepchildren two miles downstream to a rugged, wooded area to guard Pyle's and Corner's Fords.

Since Ned and I were employed to carry messages between Washington's and Armstrong's headquarters, I was able to keep myself well apprised of what was happening. Also, Chris was on hand at Chadd's Ford, ever and officiously ready to supply me with headquarters gossip.

The evening before the battle, I supped with my young friend and some of his fellow Life Guards in the yard of the house that our general had appropriated. Oh, he was full of his own importance and knowledge, was my young protégé, as he explained the situation to me with the help of a rough map scratched in the dirt.

"See, here is that little river. It flows generally south. And here we are at these two fords."

He drew a long line and then pointed to our west.

"That is the direct route for the British to take. But you have these other fords upstream. It would be grand if the redcoats would just charge right across and let us shoot them down. But the old man thinks Howe is too clever for that. Most likely, they'll try the same maneuver they pulled on Long Island a year ago."

I tried to tell him and his dandified comrades how stupidly the British had fought on the road from Concord and at Breed's Hill, but he shrugged off my comments.

"Howe is not Gage, don't you see? You watch. He will set up a big demonstration in front of us with part of his army, while the rest goes marching the long way around. They will cross one of the other fords to fall on our flank and rear. That was what he did on Long Island."

"What's to prevent them doing it again?" I asked.

"The old man doesn't want to prevent it, you see. They have been cooped up on ships for the past four weeks. Neither them nor their horses are as fresh as they were on Long Island. You know how long it took them to reach here from Head of Elk. So what the old man plans is to sit tight and let them conduct their demonstration, trying to fix our attention here."

He jabbed his stick in the dirt.

"Then when he knows for sure that Howe has split his army, but before that detachment can complete its march, we throw our entire force across the Brandywine and kick the shit out of the fellows making all the fuss in front of us. Then we cross back and confront the other force when they come huffing and puffing against our flank."

He stood and brushed the dirt from his hands.

"That is a very nice theory," I said sarcastically. "Let us hope the British play their assigned roles properly."

"You'll see tomorrow. We'll whip their asses for a fare-thee-well, never fear."

Back at Armstrong's headquarters as we settled down for the night under our shared tent, I told Jason what his son had said.

"Chris thinks Washington is next to God," my old friend said. "He wasn't there at Long Island. I was, and we got trounced worse than he thinks. The only thing that saved us was Glover and his Yankee boatmen. They rowed us over the East River, you know. I got no use for the British, Jerry, but never underestimate their soldiers. They are tough little monkeys. And remember, too, that Howe has been a full-time soldier while Mr. Washington has been driving his black slaves on his big plantation."

I lay awake that night under our simple canvas shelter and reflected on what I had seen of the war so far: Lexington and Concord, Breed's Hill, and my several battles at sea. This was the first time I had been part of a large army in the field with an even larger and better disciplined one poised nearby to attack. At least Washington's army was better than the rag-tag collection of New England militiamen that made the British pay such a heavy price at Breed's Hill.

The sound of musket fire across the Brandywine awakened me shortly after sunrise. The woods beyond the river were shrouded by fog. By the time the sun had burned away the mists, there was a steady noise of skirmishing to the west. This continued until Maxwell's light infantrymen withdrew to the banks of the Brandywine and the British rolled up their artillery and began booming away at our men around Chadd's Ford. General Knox unlimbered his guns and replied. We were treated to a long cannonade concert. There is nothing as stirring to the blood as the thunder of cannon and the smell of burnt gunpowder.

I rode over with General Armstrong to Chadd's Ford and watched with him as Maxwell's men splashed across the Brandywine to the safety of our main army. These hand-picked men had seen some arduous duties the past few days, having been engaged in several fair-size scraps with the advance guard of the red-coated juggernaut. While Maxwell reported to General Washington, one of their captains treated General Armstrong and me to an account of their experience across the Brandywine.

"We held them up as long as we could. Then they come at us in a straight line, shoulder to shoulder, bayonets fixed. Took no more notice of our fire than if we had been a swarm of mosquitoes. Just kept coming at a dog trot. Hessians, they were, and big fellows, too—"

A British cannonball kicked up a cloud of dirt a hundred feet away, and the captain excused himself to take cover.

Armstrong and I rode back to our camp to prepare our fellows in case the British tried one of our two fords. We were there late in the morning when Washington made his great mistake of the day. As Chris told me later, our scouts sent in a report from beyond the river upstream that they had sighted a British column marching north. But it seems Mr. Washington thought it might be only a small flanking party or a ruse. So he took a middle course—he sent off a request for confirmation but also ordered the divisions of Wayne and Greene to fall in and stand ready to charge across the river when the time came.

Armstrong had sent me back with a report that all remained quiet in our neighborhood. Although Wayne's and Greene's men made a pretty sight forming up their ranks, it gave me pause to see them seemingly preparing to advance without bayonets across a small river against professional soldiers.

Chris thought I was silly to worry. "Didn't I tell you how the old man did it at Trenton?"

"I also heard that the Hessians were all drunk or asleep. Here they have their cannon in place, and they are wide awake."

"Yes, and here we don't have to cross in boats, and there is no ice in the river. The last thing they will expect us to do is attack."

Of course, the attack never occurred, but it came close. Our fellows were loading their muskets and edging toward the river when another report came in from upstream that no British had been sighted at any of the upper fords. Now it seemed that either the earlier report had been false, or else the British had made a northward feint to cause us to think they were dividing their forces.

So Washington ordered a delay in his attack. The day wore on, with our cannon and the enemy's dueling away in a half-hearted manner. I caught several glimpses of our noble commander peering across at the redcoat-infested woods on the other side of the Brandywine or conferring with the profane, blustery Wayne, the general of his best division; the cool, professional Knox, who commanded his artillery; the intense, self-important young Hamilton, his chief aide; and various others. Maybe the redcoats would come directly across at us after all.

I was not at Washington's headquarters when a local farmer galloped up and told what at first sounded like a cock-and-bull story of seeing thousands of British soldiers on our side of the river just four miles north of Chadd's Ford up beyond a Quaker meetinghouse. Chris told me later how Washington had refused to believe the chap until he heard steady musket fire from the direction of the meetinghouse.

It was just my luck to be stuck off to the south with Armstrong and to miss the main action that followed. That first report about the British column had been accurate after all. Howe had sent Cornwallis with about eight thousand men off to the north at a rapid pace. They had crossed the Brandywine much farther upstream than Washington expected, with a considerable number of cannon. Stephen's and Stirling's divisions had tried to form a battle line, but the British descended on their flanks like a horde of disciplined vandals. Sullivan tried to face his division around to support Stephen and Stirling, but he did not have time. It was a hell of a fight, and from all I heard later, our men acquitted themselves surprisingly well. But we fought at a disadvantage, having been taken by surprise.

The sound of cannon to our north made it all too plain that something far more serious than a skirmish was taking place. I rode back to Chadd's Ford to find out for Armstrong what was going on, and arrived soon after Washington himself had galloped off to the north. He had taken Greene's men with him and left only Wayne's division and Maxwell's light infantry to guard Chadd's Ford.

From across the river, the British cannon stepped up their bombardment, and then there they came. First, two regiments of British regulars waded across the Brandywine and came up the slope. Knox's guns and Wayne's muskets drove them back to the water's edge, but damn it to hell, they were followed closely by a regiment of Highlanders. Then a horde of Hessians splashed across the river, their bayonets flashing in the late afternoon sun. It was a pretty sight, let me tell you. Our fellows gave them several volleys. The Germans returned the fire and charged. With Washington off trying to stem Cornwallis and reduced forces of our own, there was no stopping the Hessians as they swarmed around what had been Washington's headquarters. They paid us back in spades for Washington's treatment of them at Trenton.

Knox tried to blast them back with his artillery, but his gunners were unequal to the task. He lost a dozen of his precious cannon. Onward the enemy surged over a hill to pause, regroup, and advance again.

I raced back to our Pennsylvanians with my report, but by the time Armstrong got everyone in column, we were swamped by a stream of Wayne's men fleeing south from Chadd's Ford. The battle was over. Howe had outfoxed Washington on a grand scale. Up around the Quaker meetinghouse, we were beaten in stubborn, open battle by Cornwallis. At Chadd's Ford we were simply overwhelmed. All we could do was to withdraw to the east to put distance between ourselves and the seemingly invincible Howe.

It was a sorry lot that retreated east toward Chester that night, leaving our wounded and most of our artillery in the hands of an enemy too exhausted to follow up his victory. Washington tried to put a brave face on what happened at the Brandywine. He claimed to have inflicted heavy casualties on the British. The truth is that he lost over a thousand men, twice as many as Howe did.

Surprisingly, no one seemed to blame Washington. Apparently those engaged in the heaviest fighting up around the Quaker meetinghouse felt that they had acquitted themselves honorably against the British.

Would that I could boast of having played a larger and more heroic role in the Battle of the Brandywine. But no, Jason McGee and I were stuck off in a backwater, guarding a ford the British did not think worth their time to attack. But Chris McGee found plenty to boast about, for he and his Life Guards were in the thick of the heaviest fighting and under the eye of his hero, Washington.

I found myself wishing that I had instructed him in humility when I had been his teacher. But I was not the right person to preach humility to anyone—not then, anyway.

We all learned lessons from the Battle of the Brandywine. Although it was a British victory, our army acquitted itself far better than it had at Long Island. We discovered that the redcoats were not invincible; Cornwallis's men were too exhausted by their long outflanking march and by our stubborn defense to follow up on their success.

As for me, I regained a large measure of my self-respect. Without thought for personal gain—indeed, at possible financial sacrifice—I had chosen a patriotic course. To be doing my duty as a true son of America made my sense of loss over the sacrifice of my crew and the destruction of my sloop a little less painful. I have never regretted the decision I made at the Middle Ferry to join Washington's army. It set me on the road to a new sort of maturity. Mind, I say maturity, not moral perfection.

4

AFTER A FEW HOURS of licking our wounds at Chester, we sullenly marched back across the Schuylkill at Middle Ferry and on to Germantown, where we spent two days sorting ourselves out and receiving reports from scouts. Oddly, we did not feel beaten. Of course, as Chris pointed out to his father and me, General Armstrong's Pennsylvania militia had exchanged hardly a shot with the British, being stuck off to the south guarding the lower river fords. But neither Chris nor his comrades would admit that they had been whipped. No, by God, they had stood their ground as well as anyone could be expected to under the awkward circumstances of having their flanks exposed. They were ready to fight the redcoats again, anytime the great commander willed it.

Ironically, our morale may have been enhanced by the fact that our seriously wounded were left behind on the battlefield. Not only were we spared the sight of our suffering comrades, but Washington was freed of the encumbrance of conveying them, while the British surgeons had to do double duty. The same could be said, I suppose, of the British and Hessian gravediggers. It is depressing to the spirit to have to clean up a battlefield, even when you are the victor. It is not work I recommend to anyone who cherishes his tranquillity of mind.

Washington barely gave us time to catch our breath before it was back in ranks again to recross the Schuylkill and take positions around The White Horse Tavern. Many of our men had lost their blankets and even their weapons. Their shoes were worn out, and so were they. Through losses at Brandywine, straggling, and simple desertions, we had scarcely half as many armed men available to confront the British as we had had at Brandywine, but damn it if Washington wasn't standing his ground, as if daring Howe to have another go at him.

I have heard it said that Howe did not have his heart in trying to crush the so-called "rebellion." He did indeed take his own sweet time in following up his victory, but eventually he maneuvered his way to within fresh striking distance of our camps west of the Schuylkill.

Part of Armstrong's militia—about three hundred men—was placed along a ridge in advance of our left flank. They did not cover themselves with glory when a regiment of British light infantry detected their presence and moved smartly forward. They gave the militia one volley and then swept up a slope with bayonets at the ready. The militiamen took to their heels, thereby uncovering Washington's flank.

Our army was saved from a possibly disastrous battle by a rainstorm so heavy, it soaked our cartridges and drenched us to our skins. Of course, the rain fell on the British as well, but they all had bayonets and the skill to use them. So Washington wisely quit the field and marched us back through ankle-deep mud to the banks of the Schuylkill, which was so rain-swollen, we had to wait two days to cross. Unwisely, he left behind the division of Anthony Wayne to be surprised and scattered by the British in a night attack on their camp at Paoli.

Meanwhile, down in Philadelphia, after sending appeals to other states to rush all available militiamen to bolster Washington's strength, our ever-nervous congressional delegates packed up and moved themselves and the capital to the town of York, eighty miles to the west, beyond the wide Susquehanna River. Likewise, great wagonloads of army supplies were hauled out of the city, to be stored far up the Schuylkill at the town of Reading. Although our forts and obstructions below Philadelphia still prevented the British fleet from sailing up the Delaware, it began to appear doubtful that Howe could be denied his prize for long.

As for Armstrong's Pennsylvanians, we were set to digging fortifications to shield the fords over the Schuylkill while Washington's regulars jockeyed about to keep between the British and Philadelphia and between the British and his supply base at Reading.

Just as Washington had made serious mistakes in losing the Battle of the Brandywine, so General Howe made his share in winning the field and thereafter. Somehow Howe never got it in his head that his best course would be to destroy Washington's army, not to occupy American towns. At Long Island, he beat Washington but let him slip across to Manhattan Island and then contented himself with the leisurely envelopment and occupation of New York. Now here he was dancing the same sort of minuet before the approaches to Philadelphia.

In the end, Howe's capture of Philadelphia was carried off with great professional skill. He pressed a strong column north to Valley Forge, causing Washington to fall back to shield our supplies up at Reading. Then the wily British general reversed his direction and crossed the Schuylkill well above the city.

Jason McGee's company of Pennsylvania militiamen had nearly worn themselves out in digging a redoubt to cover a Schuylkill ford above the city. Jason and I were chatting one day when, lo and behold, the British came upon us like a red-coated horde. Jason McGee did his damndest to get his men to hold their position behind the freshly dug breastwork, but half of them immediately threw down their tools and took to their heels, right into the river and across to the east bank. The other half fired their muskets once or twice and followed suit.

I scrambled onto Ned's back, which gave me a better view. How awesome it was to see a long line of bayonets advancing toward us at a dogtrot! I fired one pistol; seeing that that was only going to attract their attention to myself, I left my second one in its holster.

By now Jason had hauled himself onto his little mare.

The lobsterbacks halted about a hundred yards distant and leveled their muskets. A line of smoke exploded along their front. Their musket balls sang around us like a multitude of hornets.

"Let's get the hell out of here, Jerry!" Jason said.

The Schuylkill's water came up to the belly of Jason's little mare. Ned, with his longer legs, got me across first. On the opposite bank I paused and drew out my second pistol and fired it at the red mass now swarming over our redoubt.

"You might as well fart into a cyclone," Jason said as his steed mounted the bank. "Let's round up our fellows and move the hell out of their way."

Thus did the British cross the river and get between Washington's army and Philadelphia. From there it was a simple matter of leaving half of their army at Germantown to keep an eye on us and marching the rest down into the city.

Of course, I was not there for the parade of the conquerors, but I have heard that they were greeted by a smaller if no less enthusiastic crowd than the one that had cheered the American army a few weeks earlier. Anyone in any way connected with our cause had taken his valuables and fled, leaving the city to fence-sitting Quakers and Tories.

As we marched to join the rest of Armstrong's militia, there was so much grumbling about the pace of the march that Jason halted our column and reasoned with the men. "I am sick and tired of hearing your complaints. The past two days you have complained at having to stay in one place and dig. 'We come to fight, not work like slaves,' I heard some of you say. Now you are marching, not working, and still you complain. Let me tell you something. I am ashamed of how you acted back there at the river. You ran like a bunch of rabbits."

Most of the men looked at their feet in their embarrassment, but one fellow spoke up.

"Look a-here, captain. That was just about the whole damned British army coming at us. If we had of stayed and fought, they would have killed us every one."

"All I wanted you to do was give them two good volleys. Enough to hold them up for a while and to give us time to send word back to General Armstrong. Good Lord, the bastards didn't even break their step!"

"I got a family at home. What good would it do old Washington for me to leave a widow and four children with no one to support them?"

Another man joined in. "He is right. They should not have left us stuck off by ourselves with no support. I don't mind standing my ground when there's some point to it."

Jason's face was getting redder and redder, but he ended the dialogue. "All I got to say is that I will not be proud of my company when I report on its conduct to General Armstrong. Now, let's get on with this march. I don't want to hear another word out of you."

Fortunately, Jason did not hear one private mumble, "I wouldn't mind marching, either, if I had a horse to ride."

We remained at the village of Trappe through the rest of September. During most of that time, Washington kept his main army at Fagleysville three miles away, an easy distance for Jason and me to ride to visit with Chris. From him we learned that Washington was calling in support from the militia of other states, was drawing down some remaining strength from his army in New Jersey, and was taking measures to reinforce the Delaware forts below Philadelphia.

"Howe has put his head in a noose," was the way Chris explained it to his father and me. "As long as we block the river downstream, he can't get his ships up to Philadelphia. Now our quartermaster people pretty well cleaned the city out of foodstuffs, blankets, wagons, and horses. And here we are ready to strike again as soon as we've rebuilt our strength."

Jason groaned at his son's optimism. I expressed my skepticism, as well.

Chris directed his counterattack at me.

"You have been hanging around the militia too long. Why don't you enlist with a real division, such as Wayne's or Greene's?"

Jason stood and pointed his finger at his son. "Now, you look a-here. Don't you say another word against our militia. Mr. Washington is always glad enough to have our assistance, it seems to me. My fellows marched all the way here from Sherman's Valley to fight to protect Philadelphia. If your Mr. Washington had used us properly, we could have made a big difference on the Brandywine. He treats us like dirt and then expects us to fight like professional soldiers. He just don't know how to handle militia. Our fellows are as brave as any when led proper."

Was this the same Jason who had berated his company for failing to stand up to the British? To cool down the confrontation between father and son, I switched the subject, asking Chris, "What's this about our getting ready to strike again?"

"I should not have said that. Captain Gibbs has cautioned us not to talk about anything we overhear around headquarters. But you'll see what I mean soon enough."

We began to see on October 1, when Armstrong received orders to send all ailing men back to Bethlehem and to be prepared to march south the next day. By then, Washington had moved his Continentals east from Fagleysville, first to Pennypacker's Mill and after a three-day rest south to Skippack. In other words, he was edging his way closer to Philadelphia. And now he wanted every healthy, armed man he could get his hands on to join his mysterious enterprise.

So Armstrong gathered his motley lot of militia and herded us for a leisurely march south. We splashed across the Perkiomen Creek and made camp in an apple orchard.

The next day, October 2, I rode east with General Armstrong to the crossroads at Worcester, where Washington occupied a fine stone house on a height overlooking the countryside for miles around. While Armstrong went inside to confer with the staff, I sought out Chris. He was irritatingly close-mouthed about the army's plans, but he made me promise to look after his father. "I worry about him. At his age he should be at home, sleeping in a warm bed."

"I'll do my best to see he comes to no harm," I said.

On our ride back to our camps, Armstrong proved himself more forthcoming than Chris.

"General Washington means to repay the British for Brandywine," he gruffly explained. "He feels that if we move quickly, we have a chance to strike a blow that could end the war. The news from Gates and Arnold sounds very good indeed. They stopped Burgoyne cold up there two weeks ago. Now Howe has divided his army. Half his men are at Germantown in unfortified camps. Unfortified, mind you! On top of that, the general has got word that Howe has detached troops from Philadelphia to attack our downriver forts. This is a golden opportunity."

He went on to explain that Washington meant to march all his forces through the night in order to make a dawn attack on the British at Germantown. At first glance the plan seemed simple. Wayne and Sullivan would lead their divisions directly against Germantown from the north, while Greene and Stephen would come in from the east in separate columns so as to strike the British right flank and rear. The Maryland and New Jersey militia were to swing even farther to the east to block the expected British retreat.

"And what are we to do, sir?" I asked.

"We will advance directly along the Ridge Road and slip between the Hessian camps above Wissahickon Creek and the Schuylkill. It is a bold plan, but timidity will never win this war. There were those who thought me overbold back in '56, when I led the expedition against the Indians at Kittanning, but let me tell you this—the enterprise was a fruitful one. We wiped out the Indians there, we did indeed. The wicked savages were taken by surprise. We will do the same for the British tomorrow, mark my words."

It was indeed a bold plan and far more complicated than Armstrong's attack with three hundred frontiersmen against a Delaware village of women and children. It called for eleven thousand men to march along several different roads in the dark at a pace that would deliver them to widely separated points on an arc in time to make a simultaneous attack. I kept my doubts to myself as I listened to Armstrong's orders to "inform each of our company commanders to instruct every man to fasten a piece of white paper to his hat so they can see each other in the dark, you know" and to "extinguish all cook fires before sundown" and "make sure everyone has forty rounds prepared."

Jason McGee was incredulous when I repeated these orders. "It

228

will never work. Howe could bring it off, maybe. His men are veterans, trained to execute such maneuvers. This is madness!"

But good soldier that he was, he summoned his men and gave them their instructions. We fell in on the Germantown Road soon after dark and moved south; our only light came from lanterns carried by our two local guides. Our progress was slow at first, for the road ahead was jammed with Continentals. At Chestnut Hill, the divisions of Greene and Stephen veered off to the left. Then about a mile beyond, we turned off on the Manatawny Road toward the Schuylkill. A night march, particularly one conducted by amateur soldiers, is a matter far different from a parade-ground exercise. Our men cursed their comrades behind for stepping on their heels and those in front for moving too slowly. They cursed the night for its darkness. And the officers swore at the men for talking. A thousand Trappist monks, faithful to their vows of silence, could hardly have failed to make some noise. Along the way, light after light appeared in houses as the sound of our trudging feet and barking dogs aroused the occupants.

Across an upper ford of the Wissahickon we splashed and turned south on the Ridge Road bordering the Schuylkill. Our discomfort was now made worse by a chilly fog that overlay the landscape. By the time we reached Levering's Tavern, a mile or so from the British camps, the fog had become so dense, we could no longer see the lanterns of our guides. I shivered at the recollection that a similar fog had proved the nemesis of the *Charlotte* and my fine crew in Delaware Bay three months before.

At Levering's, Armstrong allowed the men to fall out along the road and eat their rations while he conferred inside the tavern with his officers.

I held a lantern as he referred to a map spread out on a taproom table.

"The road bends just ahead of us and curves downhill to the Wissahickon just where it flows into the Schuylkill. Upstream there is a gorge. The Hessians are camped above the gorge with no breastworks."

"Hessians?" one of our captains said. "I didn't know we was to attack Hessians."

"We aren't going to attack them head on. We're to take the bridge across the mouth of the creek and press right along the road until we are beyond their camps. Then we move against their rear while the regulars are attacking Germantown."

"I don't like that fog out there."

"The fog is a blessing. They won't be able to see us."

I looked at the faces of the officers as Armstrong tried to make them understand what was expected of them. These were back-

229

woodmen, mostly Ulster Scots with a sprinkling of German and English or Welsh. They were not cowards certainly, but neither were they fools, and it was plain to see that they did not like the plan to make a night attack against well-trained mercenaries. For that matter, neither did I. And neither did Jason McGee.

Jason kept quiet until the questions had died out and then simply said, "It seems to me that we are asking to be cut off if our entire force crosses that creek. Just look at the map. All the Hessians have to do is move down to the road behind us, and we are trapped against the river."

Armstrong grew red in the face from the objections. Before he lost his temper, however, a knock sounded at the door of the tap-room, and an elderly man with a white beard entered.

"Pardon my intrusion, sir, but I could not help overhearing your discussion. I live here and know this area like the palm of my hand. What you say ain't right."

"What do you mean?"

"You said their camps was not fortified."

"So I was informed by none other than General Washington himself."

"Well, he don't know what he is talking about. Them German fellows have built two little forts up there, and they got some cannon in them."

You could have heard a pin drop. Armstrong made a face and then demanded, "How do you know this?"

"I seen them with my own eyes. And they got fellows on horse-back patrolling about as well."

When we took up the march again, there was no problem with talking in the ranks. Every man was aware that we were advancing into a dangerous situation. Even Ned seemed to sense the peril, for he walked stiff-legged, as if he were stalking prey. I cursed the creaking of my saddle. I had not experienced anything quite like this on either sea or land. On the one hand I was thrilled at the prospect of fresh battle, but on the other, I was troubled by a sense of foreboding.

Armstrong had sent Jason's company forward to feel their way down to the bridge where the Ridge Road crossed the creek. Dawn was just beginning to illuminate the fog around us when the *pop, pop, pop* of muskets rang ahead of us.

"Ride fast and see what's happening," Armstrong ordered me.

My heart pounding, I lashed old Ned into a canter down the hill through the eerie fog toward the sound of the muskets, and we nearly blundered into Jason's mare.

"Damn it all to hell!" my old friend swore. "We ran into two of them blasted Hessians on horseback, this side of the creek. They fired their pistols and took off across the bridge. Better tell Armstrong that if we don't make our attack right away, it'll be too late."

Before I reached Armstrong at the head of the column, the sound of heavy musket fire echoed from the east. Obviously the main battle had begun over at Germantown.

Armstrong raged at his leading companies to advance on the double. He left me to direct the rear half of his column to leave the road and deploy along the creek bank. To one who has never been in war, it might seem a simple matter to maneuver a few hundred able-bodied men across a field, but just try it. Every other fellow had to stop to relieve himself or to ask me for fresh directions. A crucial half-hour had passed before we were in position across the Wissahickon gorge from the Hessian camps. Although the fog still shrouded the other side, we opened fire with muskets, to which they soon replied with their artillery. Then our fellows got their cannon going, too. Then their infantry joined in the fun. And from the east the sounds of the main battle grew even louder.

I galloped Ned back down the Ridge Road to find old Armstrong beside himself with frustration. His lead companies were bunched up on the road, declining his vociferous invitations to join him in crossing the bridge and getting on with the attack.

"It's their confounded cavalry. I told them they only got sabers and pistols, but they won't budge. Now we've lost our advantage."

"Well, sir," I offered, "at least you have occupied their attention. They won't be able to reinforce their center while they are shooting at us. There is a hell of a fight going on over around Germantown."

Mollified by my observation, Armstrong told me to pass the word to his men along the creek to maintain a slow, steady fire at the enemy beyond the gorge, and then for me to ride over toward Germantown to report on our situation and ask for additional instructions.

Just beyond Levering's Tavern the Ridge Road was intersected by a road leading toward Germantown. I rode Ned along it toward the ever-louder sound of muskets, now joined by the boom of cannon. The morning sun had burned the fog off the high ground away from the river by then, so that I could see a cloud of white gunsmoke rising over the pretty village of Germantown.

In the village I found half of Knox's artillery drawn up along the road. They were banging away at a large stone house that occupied a huge grounds. This of course was the famous Chew mansion, which a resourceful British colonel had turned into a fortress when Wayne and Sullivan came charging out of the fog into the village.

Instead of leaving a few marksmen behind to keep the intrepid occupants in place and getting on with the attack, Washington held back valuable manpower and cannon to try to reduce the mansion-fortress.

Knox's gunners were sweating like horses as they swabbed, loaded, primed, and fired their cannon. They created a wonderful racket, but their balls bounded off the sturdy walls like hailstones off a turtle's shell. Our infantry poured an incredible volume of musketry at the mansion, but still the British inside returned our fire.

At one point a crew of Continentals seized a log and rushed forward to try to batter down the great door, but they had to fall back, leaving the steps littered with our dead and wounded. It struck me what a contrast this was with our militia huddled on the banks of the creek a few miles away, unwilling to advance. And whereas I had left Armstrong impotently fuming at his men, there sat Washington on his horse at the edge of the Chew grounds, calmly watching the siege. He would not have been so composed had he known that the now-alerted British were rushing reinforcements out from Philadelphia.

Washington came very close to overwhelming the foe at Germantown. He achieved near total surprise, actually chasing British regulars from their camps. Stopping to reduce the Chew house was only one of our mistakes, however. Another occurred when Stephen's division got lost in the fog and fired into the backs of Wayne's men, who, thinking themselves surrounded, returned the fire and then fell back. General Stephen had overreinforced himself against the morning fog with strong drink and had bungled his part of what was to have been a coordinated movement. For this he was later courtmartialed.

I delivered my message to one of Washington's aides, who ran and conferred with the Great One, then returned to say that Armstrong should press his attack even though the Hessians had been alerted.

So I missed the sad finale of the Battle of Germantown. This came when the reinforced British swept forward in a counterattack and put our Continentals to flight, despite the best efforts of Washington and Wayne and Greene. By the time that happened, I had lashed old Ned back to Levering's and down the road to a scene of utter chaos. A column of Hessians was streaming across the bridge and fanning out along both sides of the Ridge Road, their bayonets flashing in the morning sun. Our men were falling back in disorder.

Armstrong sat astride his horse several hundred yards to the rear, waving his arms and imploring his men to turn about and form a line of battle. The Hessians leveled their muskets and sent a hail of balls whistling about our heads. Then came the menacing line of bayonets again.

Nothing either Armstrong or I did made any difference. Our men ran right past us.

"Ride back beyond that tavern and try to hold them there!" Armstrong shouted at me.

I put my spurs to Ned's flanks and galloped back down the road past Levering's Tavern. There I halted with drawn pistols. Partly from their own fatigue and partly through my threats and curses, enough of our militia halted so that by the time Armstrong galloped up, he was able to form a new line of battle. Many of his men, closely pursued by Hessian horsemen, had scattered to the north, following the bank of the Wissahickon.

The last group to reach the safety of our new line was Jason McGee's company. Remembering my promise to Chris to look after his father, I strained my eyes for the sight of my old friend. Ah good, there came his mare, the one I had traded for Ned. And then it struck me like a blow: Her saddle was empty!

5

I HELD A PISTOL on one of the militiamen to make him pause long enough to tell what had happened to Jason.

"He rode ahead of us. Last I seen of him he was fighting with one of them Germans on horseback. Then a bunch more of them come down on us, all waving their swords, and the fellows behind me turned back, so—"

"So you ran off and left your captain behind, you cowardly bastard!"

"You go to hell!"

"You'll go to hell this instant if I pull this trigger! Now, tell me exactly where Captain McGee was."

"About two hundred yards this side of the creek at a little house in the edge of an apple orchard. A brick house. He was in the yard—on his horse."

"On the right or left of the road?"

"The side next to the river."

What I then did was an exceedingly foolhardy thing, with no rational prospect for success. Without thinking for a moment, acting purely out of reflex, I dug my heels into Ned's side and rode him toward the Schuylkill, not halting until I reached the riverbank. There I dismounted and led him through a large thicket. Of course, the sun was well up by then, and the fog had dissipated. Sure enough, there lay the orchard the militiaman had described, and there stood the little brick house as well. I tied Ned to a small tree and, bending low, ran through the orchard, ducking from tree to tree until I reached the shelter of a necessary. From the road I could hear shouts in German. I put my head around the little building and scrutinized the bare rear yard of the house.

At first, I could see only the legs and feet of the figure lying face-down at the corner of the house. My heart fell, for if ever there was a dead man, surely I was looking at one now.

"Oh, Jason," I moaned, and without thinking of my own safety I walked toward the figure, bracing myself to look into the face of my departed comrade. The boots the figure wore should have warned me, but it was not until I saw the green uniform coat and the blood-stained saber in the gloved hand that I realized that this was not Jason McGee. I crept closer and turned the man over. Sky blue eyes stared sightlessly from a strangely peaceful face, adorned with a great blond moustache.

A pair of horsemen pounded down the road toward the ford. I ducked behind the house and waited until the noise of the hoof-beats had ceased. Then I took the Hessian's body by the heels and dragged it behind the house, out of sight of the road, and confiscated his sword.

I was about to go through the German's pockets when someone called from the rear door of the house, "Who are you?"

I leaped to my feet and whipped out a pistol. It was a lad of no more than twelve. He had a shock of jet-black hair and a pair of enormous front teeth.

"Who are you?" I demanded in return.

"I live here. Are you British?"

"Do I look British?"

"German. You're not German?"

Still holding my pistol at the ready, I advanced toward the lad.

"Was there a fight in this yard?"

"There was some shooting, yes."

"Who shot this man?"

"It wasn't me."

"Then who?"

I walked closer, close enough that I could see the glimmer of blood on the doorsill.

"Where did that come from?"

"Oh, sir. I couldn't help myself. He dragged himself in the door—"

I shoved the boy out of the way and burst into the house. "Jason! Jason McGee!" I shouted.

The boy did not have to tell me where to look. A trail of blood led across the kitchen to the front room. I found my old friend lying sideways across a rope bed in the corner. His eyes were closed and the front of his coat was soaked with blood.

His pulse was so weak, I nearly concluded that he was dead. His eyes opened as I shifted him onto the bed longwise, and he moaned.

"Kate, oh, Kate, they have slain me."

"No, no, Jason. It is not Kate, and they have not slain you. It's me, Jeremiah Martin."

"Jerry, oh, Jerry, I am hurt terrible. Terrible."

So he was. The German's saber had struck him just below his left collarbone and had slashed clear down diagonally across his chest and belly, exposing the rib cage and slicing through the muscles of his upper stomach. I made him as easy as I could by removing his shoes and giving him a draught of rum from my pocket flask.

The window of the little house still shook from time to time with the boom of the Hessian artillery overlooking the Wissahickon. From the window I could see red-coated dragoons galloping about. It would be only a matter of time before they rode through the backyard and saw the body of their fallen comrade.

The boy stood in the doorway, his eyes wide with fear.

"The German outside. What happened?" I asked.

"They were fighting. The German kept swinging his sword. He tried to fight him off with his gun. Then the German struck him and he fell off his horse, but he got up on one knee. The German raised his sword and finally he got his gun to fire. See, here it is."

The boy drew Jason's musket from under the bed. The stock bore several gashes.

"Where are your parents?"

"Are you Whig or Tory?"

"I am a soldier in George Washington's army."

The boy's face brightened. "Pa is too. He is with Wayne."

"Your mother—where is she?"

"She left me here to look after the cows and chickens. But the Germans took them all."

Something about the boy's story did not ring true. Perhaps it was the way he averted his eyes, but there was no time to cross-examine him. There was nothing I could do for Jason for the moment. And that dead Hessian in the yard had to be disposed of.

Posting the boy as a lookout, I sneaked back into the yard and went through the German's pockets. I confiscated several British coins, his pocket knife, and his comb from one pocket and then from the other extracted a quarter loaf of bread and a six-inch length of sausage. These I placed on the windowsill, along with his canteen.

It was a struggle to remove the German's boots and uniform, but I wanted to strip the corpse of all identification. The boy got a stricken look on his face when I called him out to help me lug the heavy body across the yard to the necessary. After we had dumped

235

our carnal burden inside, I dismissed the lad to return and look after Jason. Then, with the Hessian's sword, I pried the boards off the privy seat and held my nose against the fumes from the fetid pit.

Very likely this man had left a wife and babies across the ocean. I wished there were time to dig him a proper grave, to lay out his corpse in a civilized way and give him a decent burial with appropriate words said over the grave. He had been a handsome man. To steel myself, I reflected on what sort of burial he would have given Jason McGee. Then I closed his eyes and, taking him by his massive shoulders, dumped him into the stinking pit.

The handle of his saber made a handy tool for nailing the seat of the privy back into place.

Returning to the little house, I was puzzled and annoyed to see that although the German's canteen remained on the windowsill, his sausage and bread had disappeared. What had happened to the food? I demanded of the boy.

He denied any knowledge of what I was talking about.

"I meant to feed it to my friend. If you didn't take it, then who did?"

Again he denied taking the food, but I could see he was lying. I took him by one frail arm and shook him.

"I didn't eat the sausage, I swear I didn't."

"Then how do you know it was sausage? You little swine! The best friend I ever had is dying in there, and you stole his food."

That was when the voice sounded from the attic. It was a woman's voice, saying, "Leave him alone. He gave me the food. It's all right, Isaac. I'll come down, now."

The trap door in the ceiling opened, and down slid a ladder. Then down that ladder descended a thin, dark-haired woman with enormous black eyes and the face of a refugee from Hades.

She told me as much as I needed to know right off. Just as the boy Isaac had said, her husband had been with Wayne since early that year. He had stopped by home for one night after Brandywine, then had marched off again "and we heard nothing from him since."

I was glad she did not know of the Paoli affair, in which Wayne had lost so many men to British bayonets.

She had been hiding in the attic ever since "them Germans came." Only later did I learn why.

They were honest people and she and the boy would never have eaten stolen food in normal times, but they had been living on rotten apples for several days.

There wasn't much we could do for poor Jason. Fortunately, the flow of blood from his horrible gash had subsided. He was able to eat some of the boiled apples the woman prepared for him. As is usual with the severely wounded, he developed a burning thirst. The boy brought a bucket from the well in the yard. The woman helped me remove his coat and shirt and wash his upper body.

As we worked together, I told her a bit about our long friendship and about the battle.

"I knowed you wasn't English, but I was afeared you might be Tory," she said. "There's plenty of them about, you know. They'd turn us in if they knowed you was here. If they knowed he killed that German . . ." She paused and added, "Or if they knowed what you done with the body."

"The boy told you?"

"Didn't have to. I seen it out the attic window. Heard you hammering out there, too. That is what every one of them black-hearted swine deserves should happen to them."

We made Jason as comfortable as we could. The German's canteen contained some excellent schnapps, with which we dosed our patient during the periods when he regained consciousness. The traffic of Germans on the Ridge Road ceased, and well before noon the sounds of the battle from over Germantown way died away.

The woman's name was Deborah Owens. Her husband had been a farmer. "Had no business going off to war and leaving us on our own, but I couldn't stop him."

As I paced through the house, I considered a hundred different plans of action. All of them were impossible to implement until darkness fell, and Deborah saw flaws in each. Wait until night fell and then load my friend on my horse and dash across the Wissa-hickon? No, that would finish him off—see how shallow his breath had become. Send for the local doctor? No, the man was a Tory, and he was too rich to be bribed. Find a boat and transport Jason across the Schuylkill? There wasn't a boat for miles around—the Americans had seized them even before the British came.

I turned to the boy. "Isaac, can you ride a horse?"

"Indeed, I can sir."

"And do you know Philadelphia well?"

"Well enough, sir. I go there often with my Pa to sell our produce."

"Have you paper and a pen?" I asked his mother.

After dark I made my way across the orchard to reclaim Ned from the thicket. Back at the house, I watered him and let him graze while I rehearsed Isaac over and over again on just what to do and say in several possible situations. When I was sure he had his part well learned, I showed him how to hide my letters in his shoe and helped him onto Ned's back.

"He's older than you by several years, lad. Don't try to race him. And remember what you are to say if the British stop you."

Deborah Owens and I spent a long night without a light listening to Jason's labored breathing. It was a night I would not like to relive. Occasionally, he would recover consciousness and I would try to assure him that all would be well.

"You're lying, Jerry. I'm finished and you know it."

I cannot remember all the promises he elicited from me that long night. He was worried about Kate and the twins at home. How would they support themselves?

"They shall have the value of Ephraim's shares from our privateering and more, too, from me as they require it."

"What will happen to Chris, about his education?"

It occurred to me that Chris would have no trouble making his own way, the brash little devil, but I promised to use my money and influence to put him through college after the war.

"Gerta. I am uneasy in my mind about her."

"She has a husband."

"He is a fool. Tory besides. Wish now you had taken her back to Boston with you. Sorry, sorry . . ."

I chewed my lip and looked away into the questioning eyes of Deborah Owens.

"Stop fretting, Jason. You are going to be all right."

We poured the last of the German's schnapps down his throat and bathed his face afresh. Mercifully, he lapsed back into unconsciousness.

I stretched out on the floor beside his bed while the woman slept in a chair in the kitchen. We were awakened near dawn by Jason talking feverishly.

"Yes, yes. Good, good. I'm glad, Ephraim. You'll be a fine doctor. Need doctors out here. No, no. Oh, mama. No, no . . . the savages . . ."

I held his shoulders until he stopped writhing and fell unconscious again.

"Who is this Ephraim?"

I explained about his physician son. I told her, too, that Jason, when a lad of only ten, had witnessed the massacre of his mother and baby sister by a band of Indians.

"He was quite a man, wasn't he, sir?"

"Why do you say *was*?"

"He can't last much longer. He's lost too much blood. I've seen this before. They generally die about sunup, you know."

I lashed out at the woman. "Don't say that! He is not dead! I will not let him die! He saved my life at Bushy Run. He is the finest man I know. He can't die. We mustn't let him—" And yet, when I looked down at his now-gray face and observed the shallow rise and fall of his horribly wounded chest, I feared that what the woman had said was true. Even if he survived the deadly hour of dawn, there was no way he could last through another day without medical help.

Seeing how crushed the woman looked, I felt sorry for her. After all, I had apparently sent her son off on a fool's errand. By all odds, the British had seized him and my horse. If they searched him and found my letters or if they broke him down, it would be only a matter of time before trouble would come to this doorstep. The British were not likely to waste much time on a wounded Pennsylvania militiaman. I would be hauled off to prison. And God help me if I were to be identified as a privateer! But even if the boy got through and delivered my letters, how could I be assured that the recipients would not either ignore them or, worse, betray me?

I wondered, too, at the outcome of the battle. Whatever hope I had had for our success had faded during the previous day. Had Washington been successful, the road in front of the little house would have been swarming with our soldiers now. For all I knew, the British counterattack had bagged Washington and his army. It was a bleak dawn for me.

The sun had just risen over the orchard when the woman cupped a hand behind her ear.

"Hark! I hear horses."

I scooped up the German's sword and uniform and Jason's musket and mounted the ladder to the attic.

"If they stop here, tell them the man forced his way into your house."

I drew the ladder up after me and closed the trap door. Crouching under the low roof, I listened to the hooves of one, two, three, horses and the crunch of wheels along the road and around to the rear of the house.

There was a knock on the rear door. I heard the woman open and say with creaking voice, "Yes, sir?"

"You have a wounded man here?"

"Oh, sir, I could not help myself. He forced his way in—"

"Well, where is he?"

That voice. It was not quite British; neither was it American. It was impatient, arrogant.

I listened as the man walked into the front room.

"McGee! Can you hear me? I am Dr. Mason."

6

I REMAINED FROZEN in my crouching position, wondering what this arrogant Tory was doing here until I heard feminine voices in the yard.

I raised the trap door and practically slid down the ladder and into the arms of Liz Oliver. I picked her off her feet in a bear hug and set her down to face, just coming in the door, Laura Mason herself.

"Mr. Mackey couldn't find a patriot doctor. Rush and the others have all have gone off to treat the wounded from Brandywine," Liz explained. "So I went round and spoke to Miss Laura, and just in the nick of time."

"Yes," Laura said. "Father was preparing to come out to Germantown to help the British surgeons. There are far more wounded than they can care for, it seems. I persuaded him to stop by here first." She lowered her voice. "He is not at all happy about this, but I told him it was the least he could do for the father of dear Ephraim."

Dr. Mason wasted no time or charm on me. He made it plain that he wished only to get his ministrations to Jason McGee over with quickly so that he could lend a hand with the casualties from the Germantown battle.

Under his imperious urging, I cleared the kitchen table and set it in the shaft of morning sunlight coming through the door. With the help of the Mason's mulatto carriage driver, I carried poor Jason into the kitchen and laid him on the improvised operating table. A downy-cheeked young medical student brought in the impressive tools of Dr. Mason's trade. The man owned enough to equip a hospital: roll upon roll of linen bandages, packages of lint, forceps, probes, scapels, saws, splints, surgical needles, and an entire apothecary chest of various potions.

And the two women, God bless them, presented us with several baskets of foods and drink.

Dr. Mason removed his black broadcloth coat and rolled up his sleeves, then donned a long white linen apron. He made a face as he surveyed the extent of Jason's wound.

Using a moistened rag, he wiped away the encrusted blood and other oozing matter to expose the angry red slash. Jason moaned at the pressure on his wound.

"Laudanum," Mason said to his assistant.

Holding Jason's head up, he poured a healthy slug of the liquid into his mouth. Then he stepped away from the table as he waited for the opium to take effect.

"Another quarter-inch deeper, and he would have been disemboweled."

"Can you save him?" I asked.

"I could have if I had seen him sooner. Now I cannot say. It will depend on his own constitution."

"You must save him."

"How dare you, of all people, say *must* to me? I would not be here at all had my daughter not implored me. Here, let's waste no more time. Felton, thread my needles and stand by to assist."

Although I detested the man's haughty manner, I had to admire the skill with which he sewed up the horrible gash across Jasons' upper body.

"Fortunate that no major arteries are involved. Too bad about the stomach muscles. That means sutures under the skin. Don't like to do that, but it can't be helped. Look closely now, Felton. Might as well learn something here. The trick is to insert the needle at the same distance from the wound as the depth of the penetration, then draw the thread across but not too tight. Don't want a pucker. . . . That's it, press the edges together firmly."

Each time Dr. Mason thrust his needle into a fresh patch of skin and drew the thread across the wound, Jason groaned and made a face. I hated to think of the even greater torment he would have had to endure without the laudanum.

So skilled was Dr. Mason that the process took far less time than I had expected. He stepped back from the table and looked smugly at the long line of stitches he had made across Jason's milky white chest and abdomen.

"See, Felton, how I have left the wound unclosed at the bottom? That will permit drainage." Then to me; "By the way, I judge this was done by a saber."

"I would assume so," I said.

"I wasn't aware that the action extended this far. I had heard that most of the fighting took place over at Germantown. What a fool is Mr. Washington to think that he could attack British regulars and win! He was swept right off the field."

"I expect you will find as many British wounded as American when you get over there," I replied.

"You are a cheeky fellow," Mason replied.

I was at the point of telling him to go to hell when the clatter of hooves sounded on the road in front of the house.

"Whose carriage is that?" a decidedly English voice called out.

My first impulse was to bolt outside, mount Ned, and dash away. My second was to slip back up the ladder and hope that Dr. Mason would not give me away. But I could not trust him that far. And either action would have left Jason at the mercy of the British.

So I took a deep breath and stepped out into the yard, taking care to conceal my two pistols under my long coat. On a fine dappled gray sat a British colonel and on either side of him two red-coated dragoons.

"Oh, sir," I said, "we are most pleased that you have come."

He rode his horse up to the open door and looked in at Jason lying on the table.

"Whose carriage is this?"

241

I proceeded to tell the colonel a preposterous story of how my wife—I pointed to Deborah Owens—and our little son—Isaac—"loyal to King George as ever you would wish," had found this poor Hessian fellow—I indicated the unconscious, drugged Jason—lying in the road near sundown the day before.

Not trusting myself to look at Dr. Mason, I rattled on that we had cowered in the house all day out of fear that "the dastardly rebels would advance upon us" until we heard "the piteous cries of this poor Hessian chap outside our home."

"We made him as comfortable as we could, sir, but we dared not venture forth into the night. Isn't that right, my dear?"

Deborah Owens, slack-jawed at my improvisation, nodded.

"Then God smiled upon us this morning when this good man, a genuine physician, came along and was kind enough to come into our humble dwelling to minister to him."

"Physician?" the colonel asked.

"Oh, indeed, sir. This is Dr. Horace Mason himself, a loyal physician from Philadelphia. A professor at our medical school there. We are honored to have him in our home, sir. And this, I believe, is his daughter."

The colonel dismounted and put his foot upon the doorstep. Dr. Mason's face had turned brick red. Before he could speak, Laura took up the fabrication, curtsying and saying in her genteel manner, "I am Laura Mason, colonel, and we are on our way to assist with the wounded at Germantown, and this is my father."

The colonel stepped inside the door and looked closely at Jason's wound.

"What makes you think he is a Hessian?"

"Oh, sir, I will show you," I said.

Up the ladder I raced and brought down the rolled-up green jacket, the buff trousers, and the boots of the dead Hessian.

The colonel frowned at the uniform.

Dr. Mason's face had turned pale. If he were going to betray us, now was the time.

"Who is this?" the colonel said, pointing to Liz.

"A cousin of my wife."

The colonel looked closely at Jason's wound.

"Damned fine job of sewing you've done there, doctor. Fellow's lucky he fell into your hands rather than into those of one of the German butchers that pass as Knyphaussen's surgeons. Treat their wounded like cattle, they do. They're all a coarse lot of peasants anyway. Goes against my grain to have to employ mercenaries, but it serves these stupid Americans right. Well, we need you at Germantown without further delay."

He paused before remounting.

"That is a saber wound, isn't it?"

"I would say so," Dr. Mason replied.

"Curious. Haven't heard of the rebels employing that weapon from horseback. Must remember to mention it at headquarters. I'll also tell the Hessians to come pick up their man."

"Oh, sir," I said, "don't trouble them. I will transport him to their camp soon as he is able to be moved. No, no, no trouble at all. Only glad to be of service to good King George."

When I returned to the kitchen, Mason was removing his apron and his assistant was repacking their medical kits. He looked at me with an expression of contempt.

"You are the most arrant liar that I have ever met."

"No matter what you think of me, you have my thanks for what you have done for my friend."

"Save your smooth words—Martin, is it? You have compromised me into lending assistance to an enemy of the crown. I resent being drawn into this affair."

"Father!" Laura said. "Mr. Martin risked his life to come to Captain McGee's rescue."

"That is his concern. He had no right to risk my reptutation. Come, let us go. There are many good, loyal soldiers of the Crown who need my assistance, and I must waste no more time on the enemy. Jethro will drive you and Mistress Oliver back after I am settled in at Germantown."

As his assistant carried the medicine chest to the carriage, he picked up the Hessian's green jacket and put his finger through the bullet hole in the front. He looked at me for a long moment, seemed about to speak, but then lay the jacket back across the chair.

Laura took my hand and smiled. "I am glad we could help. I only wish we could do more."

Then she put her arms about Liz. "You did right to come to me."

Her father took her by the elbow and swept her from the room. He paused outside and asked if Liz were coming with them.

"No, Dr. Mason. My place is here. I'll find my way back when I am no longer needed."

7

NEAR NOON, the laudanum wore off and Jason became delirious. But later in the day he calmed down enough to swallow some of the beef broth Liz had brought.

Fearful that Ned might attract the attention of the British or the Hessians, I led him back into the thicket beyond the orchard and tied him to a bush.

When I returned to the house, Liz and Deborah were deep in

conversation. They broke off their talk at my appearance, and I noticed that Deborah's face was tear stained.

That evening, after we had made Jason comfortable for the night and had eaten The White Swan's excellent roast chicken and drunk its robust ale, Liz and I stood out in the chilly October dark and talked. That was when I learned why Deborah Owens had been hiding in the attic and why she had been so terrified of me at first.

"Right in front of the boy, right out in the orchard. They took turns holding her down while the others—" Liz's voice quivered. "They are swine, those Germans. Makes me sick to think of it. The poor woman will never be the same again."

"There is one German who will never be the same again, either, Liz, if that is any comfort to you."

She was quiet for a moment; then, "Deborah warned me against using the necessary. I will say no more."

As we talked long into the night, I gained new respect for Elizabeth Oliver. She was some woman. Of course, she had known that her husband was a paid informant for Sir Francis Bolton, but she had learned that he was a British spy as well only after the occupation of Philadelphia. He had carried information about our river defenses down to Lewes when the British fleet appeared in the Delaware Bay. This information had helped persuade Howe to sail on to the Chesapeake to make his landing.

"Himself now wallows in British money. You should see The White Swan. Business has never been better. Himself acts like he's one of the gentry."

"What did you tell him about coming out here?"

"Told him nothing. I just came."

That was when I made the mistake of trying to put my arms around her. She drew herself away prissily.

"No, Jerry. Not here. Not now."

"Why not? We are alone."

"Captain McGee is in there."

Her logic escaped me, but I was not about to press myself upon a woman who had risked so much to come to our rescue.

By the next morning, Jason had recovered enough to allow us to prop him up on pillows. He recognized Liz and me. I introduced him properly to Mrs. Owens and Isaac. That afternoon, after he had eaten a stew tenderly prepared by Liz herself, it became obvious that he was out of danger, at least from his wound. But with a dead Hessian in the privy pit and two of Washington's men in the house, we were all of us in peril of prison or hanging. What if the British colonel should stop by to inquire about the wounded "Hessian," or a Tory neighbor should wonder at the presence of strangers? But it would take weeks for Jason to recover his strength enough to be able to ride a horse or walk.

Credit for the bold idea we finally settled upon belongs to Liz Oliver. She was a woman who had everything to lose and nothing to gain from coming to our assistance. Her husband was enjoying new-found prosperity and influence among the British occupiers of Philadelphia; Washington had been beaten at Germantown. The American cause appeared to be doomed. Yet she was risking her life to save a backwoods militia captain.

I asked her why.

"You wouldn't understand. He needs me."

If there is a better way to a woman's heart than to make her feel that you need her, I haven't learned it. Only Jason McGee wasn't aware of Liz's love—at least, not then. Anyway, I saw no point in arguing with Mistress Oliver. She had come up with a damned good idea, which we began to execute that very night.

It was a simple matter to lead Ned out of the thicket, down to the mouth of the Wissahickon, and thence across the Schuylkill via a ford. After a long night of stumbling through the dark, I reached one of the upper fords of the river. The next afternoon, I found Washington's exhausted army in camp back around Pennypacker's Mill.

I at first thought to recruit my rescue party from among Jason's own company of militiamen. But once Chris learned of his father's predicament, nothing would do but for him and three of his fellow Life Guards to undertake the mission. Without asking permission, we borrowed a flat-bottomed boat large enough for our purpose and, soon after nightfall, set out down the Schuylkill. Down, down we drifted until we reached the mouth of the Wissahickon.

I left one of Chris's friends to watch the boat and led the others up the creek bank and through the thicket to the edge of the orchard. There I ordered them to remain while I reconnoitered. A faint light glowed through the kitchen window. Walking quietly on the balls of my feet, as I had learned in my Indian days, I approached the little house.

I listened carefully. Hearing nothing, I imitated the cry of a hoot owl, as Liz and I had agreed. There was no response. I made it again, but without success.

Thinking that the women were sleeping, I ducked behind the necessary, waited a moment, called again. Then I slunk across the backyard. As I neared the kitchen door, I heard not voices but footsteps from within the house.

I crept to the kitchen window and looked in. Not even in battle have I come so close to soiling my trousers. For in front of the kitchen fire stood the British colonel who had appeared just as Dr. Mason was completing sewing up Jason's wound.

Liz, Deborah, and Isaac sat on a bench as quietly as if they were in a Puritan church. I put my eye to the crack for a clearer view.

245

Great God Almighty—no wonder they had not responded to my signals! They were bound and gagged.

I turned in panic to flee but ran right into the arms of a British dragoon. He tried to wrestle me down, but I gave him a blow to the stomach. He released me, but before I could get away, his companion sprang upon my back. He was a little fellow but strong as a mule, and I could not shake him off. The next thing I knew the first dragoon had recovered his breath enough to tackle me around the ankles, and down I went.

In daylight, given a fair chance, I think I could have whipped the two of them. But I knew the game was up when the colonel came out of the house and put the muzzle of his pistol against my head.

"We have been waiting all night for you," he said. "What took you so long?"

They confiscated my pistols and herded me into the kitchen.

I tried to resume my role of loyal subject of King George. I expostulated with them for treating me so roughly, and I demanded to know why they had bound the members of my family.

The colonel slapped me across the face with his heavy gloves.

"Save your lies, you scoundrel! That man in there is no Hessian. We found his musket and his militia jacket under the bed. At best you and he are rebels, and at worst, spies."

There was no point in lying anymore, but on the other hand I saw no reason to tell him the truth, either.

"All I can say to you, sir, is that you are treating me and my family in a brutal manner."

He struck me with his glove again, this time hard enough to start a nosebleed.

"Our Hessians are missing one of their dragoons. His horse came into camp without him. You were kind enough to show me his uniform. If I had examined it more closely, I would have seen that it was torn by a bullet, not by a saber. Where is the German?"

"I don't know what you are talking about."

"We will let the Hessians interrogate you themselves. Henly, Prescott, bind and gag the fellow. Then one of you ride over to the Hessian camp and ask Captain Vogler to send a squad to escort all these people to Germantown. We'll soon get the truth out of them."

My string had been played out. Not only had I failed to rescue Jason, I had put him and Liz and the Owenses in jeopardy. And with a squad of Hessians on their way, Chris and his fellow Life Guards would only lose their own lives if they tried to intervene.

So there I sat on a stool with my hands bound behind me and a rag stuffed in my mouth, looking into the eyes of Liz Oliver, while the colonel strode back and forth.

"So Master Hosea Owens, is it? You will have a great deal to explain to our German allies when they get their hands on you. Loyal subject of King George, indeed."

Each time he passed my stool, he struck me across the face or on the back of my neck with those damned gloves. He still thought I was the husband of Deborah and the father of Isaac. The woman had not betrayed me. That was some small comfort, at least.

Just the two of them were in the kitchen, the colonel and the larger of the two dragoons, as we waited for the appearance of the Hessians. God help me when they learned, as learn they must, that I had been a privateer as well as a soldier for Washington. And God help the poor Owens family when the body of that Hessian was found in the necessary. The best I could hope for at that point was that Chris and his fellow Life Guards got back to the American camps safely. Good Lord, had I not caused enough grief to the McGee family?

As I sat thinking my black thoughts, Liz's eyes opened wider and a look of amazement appeared on her face. I frowned at her. Again she first widened and then narrowed her eyes and looked sideways.

I glanced toward the dragoon. He glowered at us with his hands on the butts of his pistols, then glanced back at the colonel. Here came the bastard again, slapping his gloves against his thigh.

"You'll likely all hang. Oh, you Americans make me sick. Pretending to be loyal British subjects and all the while harboring—"

He raised his gloves again; as they descended, Liz pitched forward from her bench and fell across the colonel's ankles. He staggered back, then lost his balance when one of his spurs caught in her dress. The dragoon leaped forward to help him to his feet, at which point I arose in a crouch and rammed my head into his stomach. He fell against the table, knocking the candle to the floor.

Then all hell broke loose in the kitchen, and there was a roar of voices. For a moment I thought Hessians had come raging into the room bent on our destruction. But the next thing I knew I was being helped to my feet by Chris McGee.

In minutes the gags were out of our mouths and into those of the colonel and his dragoon.

My mind worked furiously.

"There is another soldier. They sent him off to bring back a squad of Hessians," I said. "We must get moving without delay."

One of the Life Guards was for shooting the two Britishers on the spot, but I would not permit that. The others wanted to leave them gagged and bound and be on our way.

I could not permit that, either. They would reveal to the Hessians that there were only four men besides myself, and they would come after us with a vengeance.

"We'll just carry the bastards back with us."

One of the Life Guards protested that our boat could not carry two extra passengers, as well as Captain McGee.

"We will also have two horses," I replied. "I know my way back well enough to lead them."

"Aren't you forgetting something, or someone?" Liz asked. "We can't leave Deborah and Isaac here. You don't know what the Hessians would do with them."

"What do you mean, *we?*"

"I refuse to desert Captain McGee!" she cried.

"And I want to join my husband," Deborah Owens said.

One of Chris's comrades protested that they had come to save a soldier, not to haul off two women and a boy. I told him to shut up and let me think for a minute.

"First things first," I said. "You brought your litter? Good. Two of you carry Captain McGee down to the creek. For God's sake, don't drop him. Isaac here can lead you. Then you two women gather up what you must and follow me."

Chris and one of his comrades kicked and prodded the colonel and the big dragoon across the orchard, while I waited in the yard with their horses.

I cursed the two women for taking so long. What was keeping them? They still had not come out when I heard the clatter of hoofbeats.

"For sweet Jesus' sake!" I shouted. "Come as you are! We must get out of here."

I practically hurled bony little Deborah onto the colonel's horse and then turned to Liz. She would not relinquish her hold on the two large bags she carried. It took a mighty effort to lift her onto the back of the dragoon's horse.

Liz protested that she could not ride, so I gave the reins of her horse to Deborah and told her to hurry to the thicket.

They had just set out when two horsemen charged into the yard. It was stupid of them to rush up in the dark like that. I shot the first one out of his saddle. The little British dragoon fell off at my feet, and I seized the reins of his horse.

"All right men," I shouted. "Prepare to fire!"

The second horseman suddenly developed some judgment and withdrew as quickly from the yard as he had entered it. Thereupon I mounted the horse of the dragoon and rode across the orchard toward the thicket.

At the Wissahickon I put Isaac in the saddle of the colonel's horse. I offered Liz the honor of riding behind me on the horse of the big dragoon, but she refused to leave Jason's side.

Chris assured me that it would be child's play for him to see that the boat reached safety upstream. "After all, I helped wrestle far larger ones up the Kennebec to Quebec."

248

So we put Deborah on the same horse as Isaac and placed—not too tenderly, I fear—the colonel and the dragoon, stomach down and hogtied, across the back of the colonel's own horse.

"We will await you at Matland's Ford," I whispered to Chris.

When we reached the American camp, we were acclaimed as heroes by all except for an envious few. Not only had we rescued a wounded militia captain from behind British lines, we had brought back a genuine colonel as prisoner. I regret to say that General Armstrong was among those who were not overjoyed at our exploit. That redoubtable old Indian fighter had not covered himself with glory in the Battle of Germantown, but he liked to boast that his Pennsylvania militiamen had been the last Americans to quit the field. He did not like to mention that this was because they had engaged the enemy only at long distance, and because General Washington had forgotten to send them the retreat order.

I realized that he was embarrassed that one of his captains—and Jason was an old friend at that—had been wounded and abandoned and that his rescue had been carried out by myself and Chris's fellow Life Guards rather than by his own backwoodsmen. He began to treat me coolly, giving me few assignments, until . . . but I am getting ahead of my story.

As for the Owenses, Deborah found her husband, Hosea, among the ranks of the unwounded and was put to work right away as a camp laundress. I said nothing about her being raped by Hessians, and I suspect, neither did she. Isaac joined his father as a regimental drummer. As for Liz Oliver, she rented a large stone house up near Valley Forge and hired a teamster to carry Jason to it so that she could cluck over him to her heart's content. The poor fellow was too weak to defend himself.

I wondered at her ability to pay for so commodious a dwelling and at the trouble she was putting herself to for the husband of another woman. But long ago I had given up trying to understand the hearts of the females of our species.

8

I EXPECTED to find Washington's army in a dejected mood following the repulse of their attack at Germantown. But no—despite heavy losses, the general attitude in our camps was one of triumph. Less than a month after being beaten at Brandywine, they had gone on the offensive, had taken the British by surprise, had put their vaunted regulars to flight, and had come very near to winning a victory that would have forced Howe to abandon Philadelphia and seek refuge with the royal fleet.

General Wayne's men were particularly proud of themselves, for had not their initial bayonet attack in the morning fog avenged their humiliation at Paoli?

I was still puzzling over the amazing resilience of my countrymen when news came down from New York of a great rebel victory over Burgoyne's army at Freeman's Farm. We celebrated with a parade and artillery salutes. But even these celebrations were far outdone a few days later, when we received official reports that Burgoyne had surrendered his entire army at Saratoga. Oh, that was a glorious day! Washington lined up every man in two long lines facing each other. After subjecting them to sermons by sundry chaplains, he conducted a thrilling "feu de joie," in which blank cartridges were fired off in succession beginning at one end of each line and rolling on to the other. Afterward there arose from some ten thousand throats three great huzzahs; then we broke rank to receive extra rations of rum.

As the fiery potion warmed my insides, I reflected that, two months before I would not have given us a fifty-fifty chance of overcoming the awesome power of the British. Then at Germantown we had come close to winning a victory that, coinciding with our conquest of Burgoyne, surely would have ended the war on our terms. Well, rarely do human endeavors go as we would like. Hard times still lay ahead.

Meanwhile, sobered by the audacity of the Americans at Germantown, the British belatedly threw up strong fortifications all about that locality. Then they turned their full attention to clearing the Delaware of our obstructions. Washington tried hard to keep his stranglehold on the river below Philadelphia; he detached most of Armstrong's militia, under General Potter, to harass the British line of communications between Head of Elk and Philadelphia. But in the end, after suffering much damage to their ships and with heavy casualties, the British captured our Delaware River forts, cleared away our obstructions, and opened their communications to the sea.

The weather had turned increasingly raw, and with it morale fell and desertions grew. We lacked enough tents to shelter our ragged troops, whereas Howe had himself a snug refuge in Philadelphia. Before settling himself into hibernation, Howe sent strong columns out to probe our positions. There was much marching about, with heavy skirmishing; finding us ever ready to receive their assaults, the British pulled their lines back close to the city. There was nothing for Washington to do but to locate a place to winter his ragged, worn-out army.

Valley Forge lies twenty-four miles northwest of Philadelphia at the point where Valley Creek empties into the west bank of the Schuylkill River. There, along a thickly wooded ridge, in ideal defensive terrain, was where Washington chose to base his army for the winter. It was far enough from Philadelphia to keep us out of easy reach of the British, but near enough that we could keep an eye on them.

Much has been said about the arduous winter we spent at Valley Forge. At first we had no shelter except for tents and lean-to's, but Washington soon remedied that by ordering the erection of sturdy log huts, going so far as to offer prizes for the best-built structures.

Although hampered by a shortage of axes and spades, in a few weeks our men transformed the landscape into a town crowded by huts, each of which expressed the individuality of its twelve occupants. Generally, the huts were about fourteen feet long and twelve wide, with mud-chinked log walls and steep-planked roofs. A low doorway graced one end and a crude fireplace the other. Bunks lined the windowless walls. The earthen floors were soon packed hard by the feet of the soldiers.

I wouldn't want to spend the rest of my life in one of those structures, but they did keep out the worst of the cold. We might have fared better had the weather been colder, with more snow and less rain and mud. More soldiers died of disease during that winter than had died from the bullets and bayonets of the British at the Brandywine, Paoli, and Germantown battles combined. And many more soldiers left the ranks, with or without permission, rather than endure further privations.

Our greatest want was shoes and clothing. Many a poor chap stood guard in a cold rain with his feet wrapped in rags. And many slept with nothing but firecake and water in their bellies.

Chris McGee and his fellow Life Guards endured no such hardships, however. Their huts were built right next to the stone house occupied by General and Mrs. Washington, and they were warmly clothed in their natty uniforms.

Jason, although still weak from his terrible wound, passed the early days of the winter agreeably enough in his own private room in the two-story stone house that Liz Oliver had rented about a mile from our camps.

It was to her house that I repaired upon my parting company with General Armstrong. He had taken me to task for my constant hobnobbing with Chris and the Life Guards, and I had offered my resignation. He accepted it with only a perfunctory thanks for my service.

Jason had regained enough strength to spend most of his days out of bed. Quiet and grim, he sat in front of Liz's fire while I paced back and forth venting my anger at my treatment. We were soon joined by Chris, who urged me to volunteer for his elite company.

"The Life Guards need good horsemen. You would be under the eye of General Washington himself."

251

"I am tired of playing messenger boy."

"You are well enough known and liked to win a commission as a Continental officer. Besides that, you attended William and Mary. Why not ask General Wayne for command of one of his companies? This army needs solid fighting men."

"This army needs more than numbers of troops. I saw the army parade through Philadelphia. I saw it get beat at Brandywine. I saw the ranks fill up again with green men and come damn near to winning at Germantown. But our strength has melted away as fast as it grew through desertions. Oh, yes, you may frown and shake your head, but you know as well as I that hundreds of our men kept right on retreating after Germantown, clean back to their firesides. And they weren't all militiamen, either. Who can blame them? I know you worship your General Washington and I agree that he is a mighty man, but he expects too much from half-trained soldiers. He expects them to put up with no tents, no shoes, no blankets, and not enough food."

"A soldier's life is not supposed to be easy."

"Yes, but within fifty miles of here are enough blankets to keep every man snug and warm. There is enough leather for every foot to be well shod. If you think there is not, you have not seen the German inhabitants of Berks and Lancaster Counties—their larders are overflowing. Yet our men exist on water and firecake, with an occasional gill of rum to make them forget their suffering. I would desert, too, if I had a home to desert to. What do you say, Jason?"

"You are right. This is a rich country on the whole. We just have had the wrong man as quartermaster," he said. "Mifflin was another of your precious Philadelphians. He didn't know how to run his department. Should have laid in more wagons and horses long ago. Should have recruited drovers, with their teams."

Liz was bustling about, preparing our supper so busily that I was not aware she had been listening to our talk.

She stood before us with hands on hips and said, "What you say is true as far as it goes. But our real trouble is the money. Farmers don't want to give up their produce or their livestock for pieces of paper. I myself wouldn't do it."

Later that night, after Chris had returned to his camp and Jason had retired, she and I sat around her table drinking tea, more like brother and sister than former bedmates.

"Poor Jerry," she said. "You don't know what to do with yourself, do you?"

"I could go back to sea, but with Philadelphia and New York both in British hands, that would mean traveling to Boston, where my credit is no good. Besides, I have lost my stomach for the sea after what happened to my ship and crew."

She looked at me with an amused expression until I demanded the reason for her brazen staring.

"So, you will not offer your services to General Washington as a mounted Life Guard?"

I shook my head.

She smiled again. "See here, Jerry, you told me that you and that strange old sailor conducted a thriving business supplying the army up at Boston. Here you have another army in dire need. You are a good trader. Put your talents to use. Go buy from the farmers out there, and bring it in for sale to the army."

"The Committee of Safety up in Massachusetts paid Lovejoy and me in gold. But here, Mifflin has to pay with paper money or bills of credit scarcely worth the paper they're printed on."

She reached across the table and took my hand. "Do you trust me, Jerry?"

"I have to admit that I didn't when I realized that you and your husband were in the employ of old Francis Bolton."

"Yes, but you trusted me enough to send me a message when you needed help to save Captain McGee."

"I was a drowning man snatching at a straw."

"Nonetheless, you took a chance on me. Now I am going to take one on you."

She walked about the room to make sure the doors and windows were secured, then blew out the candle. By the light of the embers from the fire, she knelt and pried up a hearthstone.

"Come here," she commanded. "Hold out your hands."

She placed first one and then another leather pouch in my hands—pouches so heavy I had to strain to hold them.

"British gold and silver," she whispered. "Part of it was paid to my husband for his spying, but most came from the pockets of British officers. Now you know why I wouldn't leave my parcels behind at the Owens house."

I whistled in amazement. "What will you do with all this?"

"Entice you into going into business with me."

As it turned out, we went into two businesses. First, I became a sutler to the army at Valley Forge. Liz doled the money out to me, and I used it—but sparingly, driving hard bargains, first for a wagon and team, and later for blankets, shoes, whiskey, sides of beef, hams, dried beans, corn meal, flour, and so forth.

It wasn't easy. Before Germantown, a huge British raid had cleaned out the area around Valley Forge. They had the country between our camp and Philadelphia to themselves, like that beyond the Schuylkill, west of the city. In fact, farmers from that area—of all political persuasions—had no scruples about hauling their produce into the city to be paid for in British money.

Our second business? The ever-enterprising Liz enlisted Deborah Owens to help and turned her house into a popular tavern and laundry for officers. Independency House, she called it. 'Twas no White Swan, but I found it a pleasant refuge from the earth-floored log hut, filled with smoke and snoring, coughing, farting, lice-ridden men.

Each week, I drove our wagon deep into the countryside to the north and west. Usually the farmers would at first deny having anything more than the requirements of their families. Then, when I mentioned that payment would be in silver or gold coin, miraculously they would remember a barrel of corn meal that they might just spare, or some cured hams. It is easy to be critical of their unpatriotic attitudes, but they had no faith in promises to pay by a government that had been chased out of its capital city.

So our business went slowly, one wagonload at a time. What Liz did not need for Independency House went to the quartermaster in exchange for bills of credit. I pointed out to Liz that she was exchanging good money for bad, but she said she knew what she was doing.

"If we lose the war, I have lost money that was not mine in the first place. If we win, the bills of credit will become valuable. Either way, we are doing something to alleviate suffering in the camps, and we are bringing a bit of cheer to our officers."

As the winter wore on, Jason grew more and more like a wounded, caged old lion. He was too well to remain in bed but not nearly strong enough to take up residence in a smoky, earth-floored hut. His men had returned to Sherman's Valley anyway. So he stayed at the stone house and enjoyed the company of the officers who flocked in for drink in the evenings. He observed with jaundiced eye my goings and comings, at once scornful of what he regarded as profiteering and yet impressed by the success of my foraging expeditions. He professed impatience at the way both Liz and Deborah clucked over him, but he wouldn't have been human if he had not enjoyed their attentions. In fact, they became like a family. The boy, Isaac, hung about him like a grandson, prying from Jason stories of his early life on the frontier and among the Delaware Indians. Chris came by regularly to inquire about his health.

I was puzzled by Liz's devotion to Jason. After two indignantly rebuffed attempts to resume our old intimacy, I realized that my cause was hopeless. She was far too enamored of Jason, and yet as far as I could see nothing carnal took place between them.

I might as well be frank and confess that on my excursions into the countryside, I did not lack for female comfort. There was a red-haired farm lass near Potts Grove, a lively widow over in Bucks County, and the wife of a long-absent sailor in Reading.

No, my winter at Valley Forge was far from unpleasant or unproductive. But nothing, either ill or good, lasts forever.

9

I HAD JUST RETURNED from an expedition to the countryside south of Reading. It was bitter cold, but my heart was light with the memory of a jolly night with the sailor's wife. My wagon was heavy with sacks of corn meal and jugs of good applejack. I delivered the meal to our commissary and received the usual bills of credit. It was nearly dark as I approached Independency House. I expected Liz would be appreciative, for she had nearly run out of spirits; and after a good, warm supper, Jason and I would sit about the kitchen fire sampling the 'jack and reminiscing about our Indian-fighting days.

But as I neared the house, I wondered at the sight of a light wagon with two horses standing outside it. As I alighted from my own wagon, I was amazed to see Liz on the back porch with a blanket about her shoulders. Her face was wet with tears, and her face bore a look of anguish.

"What is the matter?"

"She has come for him."

"Who has come for whom?"

"His wife."

It took a moment for me to comprehend.

"Kate?"

Liz nodded and dissolved into tears. I took her in my arms until her sobbing subsided and then started for the door.

"You had better not go in there. Not yet."

I paused outside the kitchen door to listen. I had last heard that German-accented voice saying that I would have to wait until I could provide for Gerta before she could become my wife.

Then, it had been low and determined. Now, it was saying with a sort of controlled fury, "No wonder you didn't come home with the others! Wounded, near death—my foot! Not too wounded to be playing house with that hussy out there! Don't think I don't know what has been going on here."

"Now, Kate, she saved my life."

"I thought it was that no-account Jeremiah Martin that saved your life."

"Jerry, and Chris and Mistress Oliver."

"Mistress Oliver, is it? Where is Master Oliver, if there is one?"

"Kate, there is no call for you to behave like this. You should apologize for the way you spoke to Liz."

"Oh now, it's Liz, is it? Why should I apologize to another woman for trying to steal my husband? She is lucky I didn't break her neck."

The coward in me wanted to tiptoe off the porch and take refuge for the night with Chris. But if ever a man needed reinforcements, it was Jason McGee. So taking a deep breath, I pushed open the door and entered into the awesome presence of Kate McGee.

Her hair had gone gray and there were a few more lines in her face than I remembered, but she was still a handsome woman. And those steely blue eyes had not lost their ability to make me squirm.

"Kate!" I cried with false enthusiasm. "How good to see you." Then to Jason, "You devil. You didn't tell me Kate was coming. If I had known, I would have brought a turkey and we could have prepared a feast." Then back to her with outstretched hand: "You look wonderful, Kate. How have you been?"

Ignoring my hand, she said, "You haven't changed, I see. Still taking advantage of your opportunities, as usual."

"Kate," Jason implored, "I would be dead now if Jerry had not come to my rescue."

"Yes, and our Ephraim would be alive if he had not turned him into a pirate."

"Please don't say things like that. Jerry, she doesn't mean it. She is upset. She doesn't understand. Please explain to her what happened. How I got wounded—."

"Yes, and how that whore out there just happened to come out from Philadelphia to nurse you. That was likely his idea, too, wasn't it? He has meant nothing but trouble to our family since you brought him back from the west. Wanted for murder and bastardy and horse-thieving, and you brought him into our home. Wanted our Gerta to marry him. He has been like a curse to our family!"

I had heard Kate give Jason the rough side of her tongue when I lived under their roof, but never had she acted in this shocking manner. Rarely have I been at a loss for words, as I was that winter evening.

She might have said or done even worse if Chris had not come in when he did. She could not avoid his hug and kiss. When she started to tune up for another vituperative chorus, he nudged her in the ribs and said,"Why, Mama, all Pa does is sit about and brag about his wife back in Sherman's Valley." Then he drew Kate aside and whispered to her, glancing at me as he did.

She looked at me and tossed her head.

"But she is a married woman."

"Well, you know Jerry."

"Why didn't your Pa tell me that?"

Before she could get her second wind, I excused myself and

stepped out to the porch to explain to Liz how things stood. She agreed to remain outside until I had finished my performance.

Kate gradually grew calmer. Her hatred of me simmered down to a hearty disdain. Jason sat wilted in his chair while Chris told the story of our rescue expedition.

"So you see, you ought to give Jerry a hug. He really did save Pa's life."

"It was the least I could do," I said with becoming modesty. "Your father saved my life at Bushy Run."

"Bushy Run or no Bushy Run, I didn't expect to find my husband living in the house of another woman. And the same woman that runs that tavern you are always talking about."

At last Chris got her calmed down enough that it was safe to invite Liz back into her own kitchen. The two woman looked at each other warily. Finally Kate said, "Mistress Oliver, I am sorry if I spoke harshly to you. I meant you no offense. I had a hard journey out here. I thank you for looking after my husband."

"No need to apologize, Mistress McGee. We all say things we regret when we are tired or upset. Now then, I expect you are hungry."

"I sure as hell am," I said. "And I brought three jugs of good applejack. Just what we need to celebrate Kate's arrival."

The mood around the table could hardly be called festive. Jason was grim and embarrassed. Kate loosened up enough to tell about the progress of the twins and the state of her milling business. Liz acted sad and distant. Only Chris and I saw the humor of the situation. We both drank more applejack than we should.

He left for camp singing a bawdy song. I arose and yawned, then took Liz's hand and said, "I expect Kate and Jason are ready for bed. What about you, my dear? Shall we turn in now?"

Liz glared at me and shook her head.

The corners of Kate's mouth turned down in disapproval. Jason looked bewildered at first but then brightened and said, "Yes, Kate, my love. It is time for us to retire."

Once inside her room, Liz turned and gave me a punch to the stomach that nearly doubled me over.

"You scoundrel, I am not going to sleep with you!"

"Just long enough for them to drop off. Then I'll slip out, if you wish me to."

"Are you sure you didn't think up this entire thing?"

"It was Chris's doing. It was the only way to get it out of her head that you and Jason were cohabiting."

"She still thinks I'm a slut."

"But not her husband's slut."

"Are you calling me a slut?"

257

"No, I think you are a sweet, brave woman whose feelings have been cruelly hurt."

"Don't try to sweet-talk me, Jerry."

"Seriously, even though I did not hear what she said to you, I imagine it was pretty bad."

"She called me—" Her voice broke. "A—a common strumpet . . . accused me of running a bawdy house—said I'd corrupted her husband."

I put my arms around her, but she pushed me away.

"Now she thinks the worst of me."

There was a bit of a struggle about my remaining the night, but upon my promise not to try to take advantage, she finally permitted me to crawl under the covers with both of us fully dressed.

And truth to tell, I did not take advantage. But poor Liz did allow me to hold her while she sobbed herself to sleep.

The next morning found Kate in a far more charitable mood. She had examined the scar across Jason's torso. Then she listened raptly to my description of Dr. Mason's medical attention. She even relented enough to ask about Ephraim's life in Barbados and aboard the *Charlotte*.

Chris came over for breakfast. In reply to his questions, she told about her letters from Gerta down in North Carolina. Gerta's husband had helped form a militia company loyal to the King, but so far there had been no fighting in their section. The more ardent of the patriots had gone north as Continental soldiers. They had two children now, a girl and a boy.

It may have been my imagination, but she seemed to relish telling me how happy Gerta and her husband were and how successful was their school.

I had to bite my tongue to keep from telling her of the wealth I had accumulated at sea.

By midmorning, that formidable woman had loaded her wagon with enough supplies for the journey back to Sherman's Valley. Chris rigged up a litter on which Jason could recline if the road proved too rough for sitting up. Kate kissed Chris and made him promise to behave himself. She condescended to shake Liz's hand and thank her for "looking after my husband."

I was tempted to give her a bear hug but decided that would be pressing my luck. So I settled for a formal bow and my best wishes for a safe journey.

While Kate was admonishing Chris to look after himself, Jason called me to the wagon and took my hand.

"I am sorry for last night, Jerry. She didn't mean it."

"I think she did, Jason, but it doesn't matter."

"Anyway, I am grateful to you for everything. And I don't hold you responsible for Ephraim, you know that."

After the wagon had pulled away from the house, Liz went into her room and remained there until noon. That night I hesitantly asked if she needed a bed partner. At first she tossed her head with a prissy No but later, after everyone else had retired, changed her mind.

It wasn't the same as in the pantry of her husband's tavern, but it was good enough. Thereafter we slept together regularly, except for those nights when I was on the road.

Thus do compensations often spring from disappointments. I lost the companionship of my old friend Jason but regained the intimacy of my mistress. For several weeks thereafter, despite the winter weather and the necessity of jolting over rutted roads and haggling with greedy farmers, I enjoyed a generally prosperous, pleasant time. But alas, the tranquillity I experience in my tumultuous life rarely lasts very long.

It was late in February that Chris brought news from Washington's headquarters that "the old man has asked General Greene to take over as quartermaster general, and Greene has agreed. Ain't that wonderful?"

Actually, it turned out to be bad news for Liz and me, for Greene ultimately corrected many of the ill's of the supply department caused or uncorrected by Mifflin. This meant that our services were not as valuable as before. But at the time, lacking the power of prophecy, we rejoiced with Chris.

"That ain't all. We got word that Congress is sending out a genuine Prussian nobleman to drill our men. He served under Frederick himself. Remember what you said long ago, Jerry? The two things this army needs most are a better supply service and better-trained soldiers."

Even with the advantage of hindsight, I cannot say who did more good for Washington's army—Nathanael Greene or Baron von Steuben. Greene scoured the countryside for wagons and teams; he sent out crews to repair roads over which supplies could be carried; he found inventories of tents and blankets that had not been recorded. Although there was much sickness during the month of March, the food and clothing of our soldiers steadily improved. In all honesty, Greene's task was rendered somewhat easier by the decline in our manpower. Through death and desertion, there remained barely half as many mouths to be fed and bodies to be sheltered as there had been at the beginning of the winter.

And thanks to Steuben (who is no more a baron than was my horse Ned), those men who did not desert or fall ill became real soldiers. He recruited men from each regiment and rigorously trained them (through interpreters, for he spoke no English) to

259

march with regular cadence and to execute parade-ground maneuvers of great complexity until they became proficient enough to instruct others themselves. He simplified the manual of arms and taught them the use of the bayonet as a weapon rather than a utensil for roasting meat.

With both the efficiency of Greene's quartermasters and the dimunition of Liz's supply of gold and silver, I found it hardly worth my while to venture forth into the countryside anymore except to purchase victuals and drink for our own establishment.

Time began to hang heavy on my hands, and domesticity palled. Liz began to act more and more like a possessive wife. She complained of my being so much underfoot. In one violent quarrel she compared me to her husband, accusing me of laziness and self-indulgence.

I would have mounted Ned and ridden out of her life except that there was no place for me to go. Eventually, we kissed and made up, but her words rankled.

Then came a fateful morning near the end of April 1778, when Chris delivered a bombshell.

Preparing for another foraging expedition, I had hitched up our team and gone into the house to receive my ration of coins from Liz together with her admonishment "to leave the women alone on this trip if you expect to share my bed on your return."

"Whatever you say, *Kate*," I replied, which fetched me a well-deserved kick to my shin.

"Hallo, in there!" Chris called from the porch. "Anybody home?"

I invited him to enter.

"See who I have with me."

I did not recognize the man at first, for he wore a blindfold. Chris led him inside and removed the cloth. There he stood, the old benefactor of the McGees and myself, Dogood Mackey himself. His countenance was as rosy as when I had last seen him, after the parade of Washington's army, but he looked troubled now. The British had persuaded him, as a presumed neutral, to come out from Philadelphia with a sealed message from General Howe for General Washington. Our pickets had led him blindfolded to Washington's headquarters. He was not privy to the contents of the letter, but it is now general knowledge that Howe did attempt that winter to convey King George's belated wishes for peace without independence. Washington had refused receipt of the letter, but his aide, Hamilton, had permitted this brief visit with me, as long as his eyes were "shut against sight of the fortifications."

He chuckled at Hamilton's notion he might be a spy for the British. "I would not have accepted this mission except that it gave me the opportunity to see you again, Friend Jeremiah. There are several items of business we should discuss."

First we went over my privateering accounts. I was shocked that my net worth was eroding fast as the value of our Continental money fell. Shrewd old duck that he was, he had arranged for me to purchase gold and other properties of lasting worth. I had only to sign the necessary papers, which he had brought along.

He also brought Liz and Chris and me up to date about Philadelphia under the British. They had taken over the homes of departed patriots and were pressuring Quakers like himself to declare for the King. The young women of the city were trying to outdo each other with parties and balls for British officers. Food and fuel had flowed in from the countryside all winter, and the redcoats were kept well clothed and armed via shipping up the Delaware.

"Yet the British are strangely restive. One hears rumors that the French may come in on our side, and that disturbs them deeply, as well it should."

I could not resist twitting him. "*Our* side, Mr. Mackey?"

He smiled. "As a member of the Society of Friends, I have tried to remain neutral in this war, as thee knows. But I must say that I do not like the swaggering, bullying behavior of our British friends. Even though both my grandfathers came here from England, more and more I feel myself an American."

He paused and slapped the pocket of his broadcloth coat.

"Now I come to the real reason for this visit."

He handed me a letter addressed to himself at "Fillidelfia." I carried it to the window for a better light but still could not make out the wretched handwriting.

"Don't strain thy eyes," he said. "Thee had a man on thy sloop named Gwin?"

"Yes, a Cornishman. He was our second mate. It was he who betrayed us. Brought about our destruction."

"Thee assumed that he was killed with the others."

"I tried at the last minute to save him. He was tied to the mast."

"And thee risked thy life to free him?"

"I don't recall telling you that."

"This letter is from Herbert Gwin. It was sent to me from his village in Cornwall, Downderry, by way of London."

I stood up in astonishment. "He was saved when the others died?"

"As the letter says, he dived into the water and a boat picked him up."

It took a moment for this to sink in.

"How did he get back to Cornwall?"

"He says Captain Fitzgerald brought him to Portsmouth aboard his ship."

"Damn! I hoped that bastard Fitzgerald had perished with my men."

"Thy men? That would mean Ephraim McGee and Lovejoy Brown and a black man named Cato?"

"Of course, and several other of the best fellows anyone ever sailed with."

"Why, my dear fellow, that is why Gwin wrote to me. He thinks that you sacrificed your own life to save his. And out of gratitude he wished to inform me that your crewmen were taken from their boat and transported in chains back to England by this Captain Fitzgerald."

I suddenly felt faint. Chris started from his chair in disbelief. Liz put her hands over her mouth.

"What happened to them?"

"Gwin says he was forced to testify against them. He tried to shape his testimony to their favor, but they were found guilty of piracy."

"And?"

"When he wrote this letter, he did not know their fate for certain."

I sat down and put my head in my hands.

"Now, Friend Jeremiah, I come to the main purpose of this visit. I would ask thy friends to excuse us while I relay yet another message."

After Liz and Chris had gone outside, he sighed and said, "Thee knows full well of the vast power and influence Francis Bolton exercises."

"Only too well."

"He has sent me a message to be relayed to thee. It seems that word of thy survival and presence in Philadelphia was reported to him in Barbados, perhaps by the husband of Mistress Oliver. At any rate, he offers you a proposition that it pains me to relate."

"What kind of proposition?"

"Thy friends have been placed under sentence of death in England, or so he says. He has asked for a stay of execution until the end of this year. If thee will surrender thyself to General Howe in Philadelphia, he will persuade the authorities to release thy friends."

I gripped the arms of the chair to keep the room from reeling.

"And if I do not?"

"They will be hanged as pirates."

PART SEVEN

1

HAVING PUT my various affairs in order, I surrendered myself at the Middle Ferry, where Washington had crossed the Schuylkill to confront Howe at Brandywine. I agreed to let Chris ride behind me on Ned's back as long as he kept his promise to avoid further discussion of my decision.

When we came in sight of British pickets guarding the western side of the bridge, I slipped from the saddle and handed him the reins.

"He has been a good horse. Now he is yours. Treat him gently, and you'll get a few more years out of him."

"You don't have to do this, Jerry. No one at home need ever know if you want to change your mind."

"It is the only way for me to undo the harm I have done. Now, say no more. Be on your way, or the redcoats will come after you. No, no, damn it, don't dismount! Just go!"

I turned away from his contorted gaze and ran toward the bridge.

The British kept me in isolation at Philadelphia's giant Walnut Street prison throughout May and well into June. It was there that I heard from a friendly guard the news of Howe's recall and replacement by Sir Henry Clinton, as well as the French entry into the war on our side. By contrast with my experience in Boston, I was treated well enough—far better than the several hundred other American prisoners, with whom I was allowed no contact. I had my own tiny room. They allowed me to exercise daily, and they fed me better fare than I would have received as a soldier in either army. They even took me to the cupola to watch the fireworks for the famous "Mischianza" that the British officers and Tory leaders of the city staged in honor of the departing General Howe.

I was not permitted even to read the Tory newspapers of the city, nor was I allowed any visitors. That suited me just as well—I had nothing to say to anyone. I was as helpless as a fly caught in a spider's web. There was no use struggling. But unlike the death of the hapless fly, my expected death would mean something: the freedom of my former comrades. Dogood Mackey, without trying to influence my decision, had assured me that Bolton would keep his word on that score. So did I resign myself to my fate.

One fine morning well into June, they put chains on my arms and marched me under a small guard from the prison down to the waterfront. There I was amazed at the number and size of the ships drawn up alongside the docks and at the mass of well-dressed civilians milling about with their baggage, waiting to go aboard.

As my guards hurried me past this crowd, someone called my name, but I was not permitted to stop until we had reached the top of the gangplank of an enormous three-master. While the sergeant turned my papers over to an ensign, I looked down at the throng below. There stood Laura Mason with her parents, waving her handkerchief. I waved back and for my pains got shoved away from the rail by the sergeant.

"So he is to be kept in chains and allowed no communication with anyone until delivered to the court at Portsmouth?" the ensign said. "What is he, a spy?"

The sergeant laughed. "Worse—a pirate. From what I hear, they mean to give him a fair trial before they hang him."

I did not realize at the time that I was witnessing the exodus of Loyalists from Philadelphia. Now that the French had entered the war, Clinton feared that their fleet would bottle him up in the Delaware. He had decided to quit the city and march his army back to New York. Howe had wasted nearly a year in taking and holding Philadelphia, but to no purpose. His objective should have been to destroy our army, not to occupy a city. He had missed several opportunities to finish us off. Our winter at Valley Forge had produced a tougher, better-disciplined, and equipped army. For that they had given Howe fireworks and a grand celebration. Now, dreading retribution from their fellow Americans—and with good reason—these native Tories were giving up their comfortable homes for an uncertain life in England.

They kept me in chains in a six-by-six locker far down in the bowels of the ship. I was fed twice a day on the same salt pork and gruel as the sailors ate. Each night, after all the passengers had retired, two sailors brought me up to the main deck and allowed me to exercise.

I have read that slaves being brought over from Africa had to be guarded during their exercise periods lest they threw themselves into the sea. Although I was not treated as badly as they, I still would have done the same, except that I anticipated seeing Ephraim and Lovejoy and the others set free.

Kept in that dark hole day after day and allowed in the open only briefly at night, I lost touch with the real world. My eyes became so sensitive to light that I could hardly bear gazing at the full moon. Hour upon tedious hour, I was left alone with my regrets and my memories. My locker lay deep within the ship, next to the armory. With no one to speak to, I began to talk to myself. Then I began to hallucinate, seeing faces and hearing voices of persons long dead.

By the time the ship reached Portsmouth in mid-August, I had become like the man in Plato's Allegory of the Cave, unable to function in the real world outside that tiny locker.

My eyes unable to bear the light of day and my legs too weak to carry my weight, I was led up to the deck of the ship. Still in chains and under close guard, I was rowed ashore to the Royal Navy Yard. There, in a jail cell little larger than my locker, I remained for several days, bereft of hope and reason.

Someday, if it can be done discreetly, I would like to obtain the records of my trial on charges of "piracy on the high seas" before that admiralty court. My memories of the brief proceedings are a blur. Not only was I unable to defend myself, I was beyond understanding what was being said and read. Men in wigs and robes rose and spoke. There was some sort of deposition from Atticus Fitzgerald accusing me of stealing his sloop and turning it into a pirate's vessel. At one point I was prodded to my feet, and I heard the man beside me say, "He pleads guilty, your honor, and throws himself on the mercy of this court."

I remember nothing of being transported across Portsmouth Harbor and up an estuary near Gosport to the Royal Naval Hospital, which had recently been turned into Forton Prison; I remember only being lifted from the boat and told to "stand up, you Yankee scum."

The hospital had consisted of two large buildings facing each other across a yard. In turning the facility into a prison, they had constructed a long, open shed across one end of the yard and had enclosed everything in a stockade, which now was guarded by more than a hundred local soldiers. Within those walls were incarcerated more than two hundred American sailors and about a hundred of other nationalities, chiefly French.

265

An ensign shoved me along from the dock to the main gate. An officer there looked at me and said, "Is this the blackguard we been waiting for?"

"Are the others ready? We're supposed to take them back with us."

"Indeed they are. Hate to see the doctor chap go. Been a great help to us here."

The gate swung open. By then I had forgotten the terms under which I had surrendered, and so I assumed that my old shipboard hallucinations had returned. For there were Ephraim McGee, Lovejoy Brown, and the brothers from Pennsylvania.

Ephraim called my name. Still, I thought, this must be a dream. He started toward me, but two guards stepped between us. I remained silent and motionless until Lovejoy Brown let out a whoop and threw his arms around me. Suddenly my senses snapped back in place like a dislocated shoulder. Bolton was keeping his word. Then, one of the guards rammed the butt of his musket into Lovejoy's back, causing him to cry out and release me from his bear hug.

Weak as I was, I flung myself upon the guard. He staggered back, more out of surprise than injury from my blow to his jaw. I tried to wrench his musket from him, only to be thrown to the ground and held by two other guards.

"Get them out of here, and be quick about it."

My friends were gone and the gate closed when they raised me to my feet.

"Here one minute, and already he attacks a guard. Well, well, lads, it will be the black hole for this one from the start. We'll see if forty days of bread and water there won't tame our wild American."

"What's that?" I demanded. "Forty days—"

"That's what we do here with them that can't behave themselves."

"You mean you're not going to hang me?"

"After a few days in the hole, you'll wish we had."

I broke into laughter so uncontrollable that they poured a bucket of water on me. They weren't going to hang me after all. I laughed again as they led me away. I heard the ensign who had brought me over explain that "he lost his senses so he could not defend himself before the court, they say."

Reserved for recaptured escapees or violent prisoners, the black hole was a pit covered with a heavy grill, just deep and wide enough to stand in. I was not kept there for forty days, however—only long enough to regain my sanity completely. Bolton had lived up to his promise and released my friends, but either he or the court had not lived up to the threat of hanging me. Perhaps the old scoundrel had meant to cause me anguish or to test my loyalty to my friends. At any rate, I still had my life.

The reason my forty-day sentence was not fully carried out was simply that my place in the black hole was needed for other guests. Late in September, a large number of prisoners tunnelled under the stockade and scattered across the countryside. The local militia pursued and recaptured most of them, and they had to be made an example of.

So after stern warnings against further misconduct, they let me emerge into the greater prison life. I was greeted by my fellow prisoners as a hero. They had heard of me and my exploits from Ephraim McGee and the others.

Normal prison life was little more unpleasant than Valley Forge had been for the average American soldier. We slept in large dormitories, in hammocks which we took down each morning. The exercise yard was spacious. We could take shelter in the shed from the rain or sun. We were allowed to make and peddle artifacts, such as carved dolls, to visitors who came out on Sundays to gawk at us. Farmers' wives brought fruit and baked goods to the gate for our purchase. To my surprise, I learned that before the hated French had turned the rebellion into a war of wider scope, certain sympathetic citizens of London and Bristol had raised several thousand pounds to be distributed to American prisoners.

Information flowed freely in and out of Forton Prison. I was delighted to learn that on June 28, the very day our convoy had sailed from Delaware Bay, a considerable battle had been fought at Monmouth Court House in New Jersey. Von Steuben's training proved itself, for our soldiers had got the better of the contest.

We learned, too, that John Paul Jones had thrown the British in a turmoil with his raids along the Scottish and Irish coasts. The French had sent a large fleet into American waters, and there were fears they might even be planning an invasion of England itself. My spirits rose with each fresh report.

Many questions continued to vex me during my captivity. I wondered whether anyone had explained to Ephraim and Lovejoy that I had exchanged myself for their freedom and been willing to lay down my life to save theirs. If not, they must have regarded it as a most curious coincidence that I was brought through the prison gates just as they were leaving. And why was Cato not with them?

I wondered, too, about the Mason family. I learned from other prisoners that hundreds, if not thousands, of Philadelphia Loyalists had come over to England in Clinton's evacuation of the city. Surely that was why Laura and her family had been on the dock the morning I went aboard ship.

As more and more captured privateer crews arrived, they brought with them stories of exploits that equaled or in some cases surpassed my own. Much of our time was spent comparing notes on the best way to conduct a chase or board a prize, and when to bluff

267

and when to run away. What a book a record of those accounts would make!

I was one of the few prisoners who had even set foot in a university. The British were glad for me and a few others to recruit and teach classes in mathematics, logic, reading, and writing. I preferred that duty to cooking or cleaning the dormitories. Soon I became known as the Professor.

They allowed us to form a drama club as well. Calling ourselves The Un-Forton-ates, we produced some tolerable versions of Shakespeare and Ben Jonson.

And a well-educated French prisoner condescended to teach me his language, so that I came to parlez-vous as well as could be expected of a rude American.

From the beginning of Forton's existence as a prison, the authorities had permitted London newspapers to be brought in. These were passed from hand to hand and preserved long after the news in them had grown stale. Prejudiced and out of date as they were, they provided me with many hours of entertainment and enlightenment. It took some reading between the lines, but I could discern the growing discomfort the British Lion was suffering from the American war.

I read with particular relish reports made to the House of Lords the previous February that 733 British ships worth well over two million pounds had been lost to American privateers. I read elsewhere that the insurance rate on cargoes bound for the West Indies had risen from two to five percent if transported in armed convoys, and fifteen percent if unescorted. I read complaints that Holland was gaining great trade advantages from Britain's troubles. Questions were also raised about the difficulty of recruiting soldiers to serve in America, and about what recompense should be made to American Loyalists for the loss of their property across the Atlantic.

My eye skipped over a small article in a recent issue, about a riot at a theater in London's Southwark district to stop the performance of a French farce. Then suddenly the name LaFontaine jumped out at me. According to the article, the audience had hooted a company by that name off the stage and had threatened to destroy the theater until the manager promised to ban the group from his stage and to produce no more French plays of any sort. My fellow Un-Forton-ates thought I was lying when I showed them the article and told them about the madam and her girls.

Hoping to prove to them that I knew her, I wrote a letter to Madame LaFontaine in care of the theater named in the article and begged her to write to me. After several weeks, however, I gave up hope of a response.

Meanwhile, the prison grapevine brought news that the British were suffering from a scarcity of sailors as well as soldiers. French and American privateers operating in European waters were still taking prizes and prisoners. These rumors were confirmed when it was announced that Benjamin Franklin, the American emissary to France, had arranged for a modest prisoner exchange with the British. Much as it went against their grain, the British had agreed to establish an exchange list and, from time to time, to trade a handful of our people for an equal number of theirs. This brought better order. Anyone who tried to escape or otherwise misbehaved got his name moved to the bottom of the exchange list.

Thus did I pass the remainder of that fateful year, 1778. As the New Year approached, I thought surely that enough time had passed for my old privateering comrades to have put themselves beyond the reach of Francis Bolton. My thoughts turned more and more toward the possibility of escape.

2

I WAS CONDUCTING a class in reading when a clerk announced that I had a visitor in the prison commandant's office. When I got there, Reuben Halbertson, bigger than life, sat reading a newspaper—no, smaller than life, for he had lost so much weight he appeared to have shrunk. He had kept his great belly, but there were folds of skin about his neck and his face was haggard.

He did not rise or even offer me his hand. He only motioned me to sit on an office stool, leaving it to me to speak first.

"So, Halbertson, what are you doing here? Come to gloat over me?"

"I am here to see if you have come to your senses."

"I am in my right mind. Are you in yours?"

"Don't be impudent with me, Martin. You are fortunate to have escaped hanging."

"They haven't hanged an American privateer yet, and well you know it. Your master knew it, too, when he lured me into delivering myself into British hands."

"Not so fast, my impetuous friend. Yours was a special case. Most privateers came by their vessels through legitimate purchase. You took the *Charlotte* without the permission of the owner, before obtaining a letter of marque. There is a fine line between privateering and piracy, and you and your crew crossed it by your betrayal of a trust."

I arose in anger. "You know as well as I that I paid Bolton!"

He gestured for me to sit. "No call to raise your voice so. I am not here to remonstrate with you. I am here to offer you a proposition that will regain you your freedom."

I sat down. "I have got in some deep troubles from your propositions."

"If you refer to Boston, remember that you did enter the city as an agent for the rebels."

"That is not true, you swine. Your Bolton hired me to deliver messages, commercial messages, and you introduced me—"

"Come, let us not hash over old matters. I am here on new business."

"Well, get on with it."

Choosing his words carefully and watching my face closely, Halbertson explained that Bolton had been "deeply and inexplicably grieved" when word had reached him that the *Charlotte* was destroyed.

"He loved his sloop that much? That old goat has ill-gotten wealth enough to buy a hundred more."

"He was more grieved by your presumed death."

"Nonsense, Halbertson. He wanted me dead, and you know it."

"You were not present to witness his fury at Captain Fitzgerald for his failure to take you alive. Nor did you observe, as I did, his joy when word reached him that you had arrived safely in Philadelphia."

"So he laid a trap for me, using my comrades as bait. He is a loathsome, grasping, conniving scoundrel. He gives avarice and duplicity a bad name. I despise him even more than I despise you."

"You crossed the ocean thinking you were to be hanged to save your friends. Such loyalty is as rare as it is misplaced."

"Waste not your flattery on me. You have not stated your business. My class is waiting for me."

He threw open his greatcoat and removed his straw hat, then drew his chair close and lowered his voice.

"You remember the day in St. Eustatius when I tried to converse with you, and you so rudely threw off my hand and turned your back on me?"

"Yes, and departed soon after to avoid your disgusting presence."

"Quite so. My proposal is the same as the one I was authorized, nay commanded, to make to you then. Only your personal circumstances have changed."

"And what, for God's sake, is the proposal? Pray have done with this beating about the bush."

"Sir Francis is not enjoying the best of health. He has sent me to England in his stead on various matters of business. One of them is to tell you that he wishes you to return to his service."

Puzzled as much by the suddenly pained look on the man's face as by his incredible proposition, I remained silent.

"Strange as it may sound, he is willing to let bygones be bygones.

270

I am to depart for Barbados within the month. You may return with me and resume your position at Bolton Hall. You will be pardoned for your piracy. All you need do is renounce your allegiance to the so-called United States of America."

He paused to draw his greatcoat about his shoulders and look about the room. "It is so miserably cold here. I think you would find Barbados marvelously warm by comparison."

If not for my fear of the black hole, I might have strangled Reuben Halbertson for making me such a blatant, insulting offer. But for once in my life reason prevailed over emotion. I took a deep breath and said in a low tone, "I cannot imagine why Bolton should want me in his employ, even in his sight."

"Nor can I. Nonetheless, he has commanded that I do what I have done. You have his message."

Playing for time to seek out the full significance of this visit, I looked at the newspaper he had been reading.

"You must find the news very upsetting."

"How is that?"

"The war has taken quite a different turn from the time we first met, or even from our encounter in Statia."

"I would not say so."

"You have lost an entire army at Saratoga. Had to evacuate Philadelphia. Came close to a disaster at Monmouth. Now, with the French on our side, things are even worse. Can it be that Bolton sees the handwriting on the wall? That he wants a true-born American on his payroll so that he can more easily reestablish himself in my country after the war?"

Halbertson snorted. "Nonsense. I know things that you do not, cannot know. Clinton is a very different general from Howe, who was too soft on Americans. Clinton is prepared to carry the war to the southern colonies, where Loyalist sentiment runs strong. An expedition has been dispatched to take Savannah. Clinton will divide the country, set South against North. The rebels have sown the wind and now must reap the whirlwind."

He grew so agitated that I knew I had struck a nerve.

I pressed my point. "Yet one reads of many difficulties here in England in prosecuting the war. Complaints over taxes. A scarcity first of soldiers to fill your ranks overseas and now of seamen to man your ships. Why else are the British permitting an exchange of prisoners in this very prison?"

"So that's it?—the exchange of prisoners? You imagine that if you bide your time, you will be exchanged. Let me tell you this, my clever young friend; you will never be exchanged. Your name will remain at the bottom of the list. And let me also make this plain: it is Sir Francis who desires your return to Barbados, not I. For my part, I was as sorry to hear of your rescue from that explosion as Sir Francis was happy. I thought I was rid of you."

He arose and slapped his straw hat over his sweaty pate.

"What if I refuse to renounce my allegiance? What if I choose to remain in this prison?"

"I could carry you back in chains to work in the sugar fields beside the black man you stole from Sir Francis."

"Cato? I thought my friends were all set free."

"Dr. McGee and the others were. The black man was returned to his rightful owner."

"Where are the others now?"

"They were taken to New York and released under parole. Now, that is that. I have done my duty. I will return in one month for your answer. Meanwhile, enjoy your stay here."

As I watched him from the window clomping across the exercise yard toward the prison gate, I wondered what hold Bolton had on him to command such loyalty. Was it love or fear? Did the old man know a secret that made Halbertson such a henchman?

Turning to leave the room, I saw that he had left behind not only his newspaper but also a rolled-up heavy sheet. I was about to raise the window and shout for him to stop, but I paused long enough to unroll the large sheet of paper. It was a map entitled "Survey of the Gosport Side from Portsmouth Harbour . . . made by order of His Majesty."

Dated 1774, the map showed in detail every road, field, wood, and village from Portsmouth's Royal Docks on the east to Hill Head on the west, from Stoke's Bay on the south to the village of Newgate on the north. There, on the estuary named Forton Lake, was the site of Forton Naval Hospital.

How careless of him to leave behind an official map of the prison area, I thought. I folded the map and put it in my pocket.

3

THERE ARE TWO time-honored ways to escape from a prison such as Forton. One is to tunnel your way out under the stockade; the other is to bribe a guard.

In the best of circumstances, tunneling is hard, hazardous work. It became even more difficult after the great escape of September 1778, when fifty-seven prisoners dug their way at least to temporary freedom. Thereafter the guards were doubly vigilant; they periodically drove iron rods deep into the ground both inside and outside the stockade to probe for tunnels.

Risks were involved in offering bribes as well. The guard might turn you in; this would put you at the bottom of a black hole on bread and water and your name at the bottom of the exchange list. Or he might simply take the bribe and do nothing.

With the advent of the exchange system, there was less motive for an American to try to break out. Except in my case. If I did not find my way out within two weeks, I would have a hard choice to make: to remain in prison at least until the end of the war or to knuckle under and accept Bolton's collar.

I puzzled both over Halbertson's offer and over his manner of making it. If Bolton wanted me back in Barbados so badly, he easily could have me brought there by force. But no, that was not his way. He wanted to own me as he did Ibo, Ramsay, Captain Fitzgerald, and Halbertson. I would have to renounce my American loyalty to get out. Yet if I refused the offer, Halbertson would order me permanently ineligible for exchange. To be honest, I began to have a lurking fear that my worst angels would gain the upper hand and lead me to decide that anything was better than rotting in prison.

Assuming it had not been accidental, what sense was I to make of his leaving behind the map? I suspected that it was some sort of trap to incriminate me and slipped it into a cookfire when no one was looking.

Barely a week before Halbertson was to return, the prison commandant announced that through the generosity of certain wealthy persons wishing to remain anonymous, we were to be treated to a play by Parker's Touring Company of actors. Our drama group, The Un-Forton-ates, were charged with transforming the largest of our dormitories into a theater. We spent two days building a stage across one end of the great hall and piecing together a curtain of borrowed blankets. The commandant lent his office next door as a dressing room.

The group arrived midafternoon in bone-chilling weather. I shivered in the wind with my fellow prisoners as the company's coach rolled through the prison gate, through our ranks, and up to the building where the commandant waited to greet his guests. So bundled against the cold were the cast that we could not distinguish their sex or their identities.

As we filed in to take our places on the floor of the dormitory hall, a guard pulled me and other members of The Un-Forton-ates out of line and told us to report to the commandant in his office.

A tall, stately woman with jet-black hair was talking to the commandant as if she were a queen receiving homage from a loyal subject.

"Mistress Parker was unable to bring her entire entourage. She finds herself shorthanded."

"Yes," she said. "Which of you knows his Shakespeare?"

She looked into our faces one by one, showing not a flicker of recognition at the sight of me.

A dozen hands went up.

"We shall perform a shortened version of *A Midsummer Night's Dream*. The parts are written out. I need four stout fellows to play the parts of Snug, Flute, Starveling, and Quince. How about you, sir, and you, you, and you?"

To my disappointment, she indicated a brawny New Englander, a stocky New Yorker, and two smooth-cheeked lads.

"And for the part of Bottom, we need someone with some talent as an ass. How about you, sir?" she said, nodding at last to me.

Whereupon, I bowed and quoted, " 'I will roar you as gently as any sucking dove; I will roar you as 'twere any nightingale.' "

"Clever fellow. You'll do nicely. Here are your lines. Now, gentlemen, come into the hall and meet your co-Thespians."

It was not a difficult audience to please, hungry as they were for any form of entertainment involving females. The girls would have been booed off the stage of some theaters for their performances but not this one, although Madame LaFontaine gave a truly professional interpretation of the Fairy Queen.

In all modesty, I rendered the donkey scene as well as I have ever seen it done. At the end, there was so much applause that Madame LaFontaine brought us back onstage for a brief reprise.

Still the audience stamped their feet and applauded. So she sent three of her girls out as Puck, Oberon, and Titania to repeat the final scene, then drew me into the commandant's office.

"Listen sharp, Jerry. Not a minute to lose. Climb in here"—she indicated an enormous cowhide trunk with handles at each corner—"quick. No time for questions. No matter what happens, keep quiet."

My four fellow Un-Forton-ates complained of the weight of the trunk as they wrestled it out the door and onto the rear of the coach. I held my breath while the commandant tried to persuade Madame LaFontaine and her actresses to remain for supper and spend the night.

"You are most kind, sir, but we have booked rooms in Cosham and must proceed directly to our next engagement early tomorrow. No, no, it is quite impossible. But neither I nor my entire group will ever forget your hospitality."

It was cold and cramped in that trunk, but I did not care. Like a bird nearing his time to leave the egg, I was about to fly free—free of prison, and free of the greater imprisonment of servitude to Francis Bolton. *Freedom*—'tis a wonderful word.

In the town of Cosham, some dozen miles from Forton on the great road to London from Portsmouth, the coach stopped. Madame LaFontaine remained while the girls went inside; then she directed the driver to draw the coach into the rear yard. There she practically ordered him to go in and have a pint of porter at her expense.

She raised the trunk lid and said softly, "Jerry, it is really you!"

"What's left of me."

I cried out in pain as I unbent my legs and stood up.

"Jump down for a moment and let me look at you. I got the largest trunk I could find. Are the air holes large enough?"

"You saved my life, dear woman."

"You'll not be really safe until we reach London. We have much to talk about, but not here. Back into your trunk. I'll slip out later with a bit of food."

"You mean I must stay in that damn torture chamber through the night?"

"And through the ride back to London tomorrow."

I groaned.

"Unless you'd rather return to the prison. I myself wouldn't mind that. Such a warm audience your friends were."

The night in the trunk wasn't all bad. I crawled out now and then between naps and walked about the inn's stable to stretch my limbs and attend to my necessaries. But the ride the next day back to London seemed an endless torment, relieved only by the chatter of the girls above the clomping of the horses' hooves and the rattle of the coach's wheels.

When we reached the jolting cobblestones of the London streets, I saw through the air holes that night had fallen. Judging from their silence, the girls had run out of gossip and had fallen asleep.

"Turn off here and take the alley to the back entrance," I heard Madame LaFontaine say.

The wheels crunched on dirt now. The coach stopped. I could hear the girls getting out and unloading their baggage. Why yes, the coachman would be glad to assist the young ladies.

Up popped the lid of my trunk.

"Out quickly, Jerry. Go down to the street and delay until the coach has left. Then return. Do get a move on!"

I nearly collapsed when I tried to stand, but I managed to hobble away.

I walked up and down the street until the coach had pulled away; then I stepped into the alley to empty my near-bursting bladder and finally rapped at the rear door.

The house was smaller and shabbier than the one on Water Street in Boston, but I was hardly in a position to quibble. They directed me to a second-floor chamber, where I slept the sleep of the dead until long past daylight.

Only two of the girls, a tiny blonde and a buxom brunette, had been with Madame LaFontaine in Boston. My favorite, Mollie, had caught the fancy of a farmer and had gone to Essex with him to rear a family. But Malinda was in the kitchen.

"Thought we had seen the end of you" was her only greeting for me.

Over one of the best breakfasts I can remember, Madame LaFontaine told me of her voyage from Boston, by way of bleak, cold Halifax, aboard an overcrowded ship full of disgruntled Loyalists.

"I miss America, Jerry. How are things there?"

I told her about the war in general and my experiences in particular.

"So now you're a rich man. I always thought you would be."

"I was rich briefly. But our money is losing its value. I gave most of what I had saved to help some friends before I left."

"Women friends, I suppose."

"Only one. I wanted her to be able to purchase the tavern her husband had owned."

"She deserted him for you? What a devil you are!"

"Not really for me."

I told her the story of Liz and Jason and, seeing that her interest was genuine, gave her a much-embellished version of Kate's arrival to rescue her threatened husband.

After she had finished laughing and wiping her eyes, she said, "Now I would like to hear from your own lips how you came to be in Forton Prison."

"And I wish to know how you managed to bring me out so deftly."

"You first."

When I had finished my tale, she looked at me solemnly and said quietly, "And you really gave yourself up, expecting to be hanged?"

"My friends would have done it for me. Besides, it was my fault they were captured."

"But they did not help you."

"No, dear woman, it was left to you to set me free. Thank God you got my letter."

"Of what letter do you speak?"

"Why, the one I wrote to you. At the Royal Southwark Theater."

"I never got a letter from you. I am no longer associated with that theater or its chicken-hearted manager. Imagine closing down our show because some dolts got it in their heads that we were a French group! It has not been safe to be French since they entered the war. That is why I have changed my name to its original."

"Wait, if you did not receive my letter, how did you know I was at Forton?"

"Why, Reuben Halbertson told me. He called to collect some money still owed Sir Francis Bolton from our Boston venture, and he took particular pains—or perhaps it was pleasure—to tell me of your imprisonment. He described in loving detail your circumstances. The name of the commandant. The fact that you had helped form a drama club."

"Did he enlist you to help me escape?"

"Not in so many words. Certainly he said nothing that could be used against him later. I did not think it unusual at the time."

"I am baffled," I said. "The man is to return on the thirty-first to hear my decision about renouncing my American allegiance and accompanying him to serve Bolton, and now—"

She asked several questions to clarify the situation, then said, "I would conclude that while Sir Francis may earnestly desire you back at his side, Reuben Halbertson does not."

"This is incomprehensible. What could be his motive?"

"Jealousy, I should think. He does not want you at the side of his master."

Suddenly I knew for certain that Halbertson had not left his map by accident. I pondered this for a moment, then said, "Now that I have escaped, I am in danger of losing my life if they recapture me. Those are the terms under which my sentence was suspended."

"Dear Jerry, from the moment we enter this life, we are all under sentence of death. There is no appeal. The only questions are the time and the manner. Meanwhile, one should live as well as one can. Come now, no brooding. Have you ever been to London?"

I shook my head.

"Malinda!" she called. "Do you remember how we showed this man about Boston?"

Malinda laughed at the memory.

"I am glad you have not been to London before. Now that I am just plain Annie Parker again with time on my hands, I should enjoy introducing you to my native city."

4

STUCK AWAY in the chests and trunks were dozens of costumes from various plays. Madame and her girls, bored by their present inactivity, delighted in making me up in different guises for our outings.

For the sake of old times, I suppose, this first day, Malinda and Madame shaved off "my disgusting beard," darkened my face appropriately, fished out the kinky wig, and made me up as Othello. Carrying a parcel, I followed them out of dingy Southwark across London Bridge to gawk at the Thames, packed with barges and small ships, and thence along the Strand to Piccadilly and down St. James Street. I had thought Philadelphia a grand city, but this one was ten times as large and twice as full of spirit and bustle.

After the household fell silent that night, I slipped down the hall to my hostess's bedroom. She was sitting up, reading by candlelight, her dark hair down around her shoulders.

"There you are, you devil! I should never have forgiven you if you had not come. Now, don't be rough or too eager. Satisfy yourself the first time, but do it gently. There should be plenty left for me later."

We tried out several different disguises after the foray as Othello. One day I was a Cockney porter; on another, a foppish gentleman from the provinces. The disguise in which I felt most secure was that of a West Indian planter. Under that guise I shed my escorts and began to explore the city on my own.

From reading the newspapers I learned that American refugees favored a coffee house just off Fleet Street. Wearing a blond wig and moustache and a wide-brimmed hat, I walked past the place and looked inside each morning. One morning I was rewarded by the sight of Dr. Horace Mason, drinking coffee and reading a newspaper. His face no longer bore its old expression of self-importance.

I loitered about the street until he had finished his coffee, then followed him through the crowds to a small house near Bishopsgate. If this was where he lived, I thought, it was a far cry from his elegant mansion in Philadelphia.

Only after he had closed the door behind him did I see the little sign reading, HORACE MASON, M.D. OFFICE HOURS AT THE PUBLIC'S CONVENIENCE.

I returned to the house at different times over the next two days. I saw him enter and leave, but no one else. Finally, on the morning of the third day, out came Laura, looking very pale. She walked very slowly, almost like an invalid, to a small park in the next street.

When I spoke her name, she whirled as if terrified. I had to tell her who I was.

When I told her that Ephraim was not dead after all, first she seemed about to faint, then she cried, and finally after drying her tears, she smiled the smile of an angel and said, "Oh, there is a God in heaven, and he does answer prayers! Where is my dear Ephraim?"

She came near to crying again when I told her that he had been near to Portsmouth when she and her parents had arrived from Philadelphia.

We sat together on a bench and talked freely for the next hour. I was sorry when she said, "I must return home. I have not been well in this London winter. Mama will wonder at my long absence."

"Can we meet again tomorrow?"

"Yes. There is so much more to ask."

We talked in that park daily for most of the next week. From her I learned of the poor reception the Masons and the other American refugees were receiving from the English.

"Poor Father has tried to set up a medical practice, but his only patients are Americans. The hospitals don't want an American. Mother's cousins had us out in the country, but it became obvious that they did not wish us to stay long. And we have such depressing news from our family lawyer back home. Our house was confiscated. It was sold at public sale for the benefit of the American government. Oh, this dreadful war! What is to become of us?"

She said all this without a trace of self-pity. I understood more and more why Ephraim McGee was smitten with her. I avoided telling her the circumstances of my present life, beyond saying that I was lodging with friends, but it never occurred to me not to trust her. I came to look forward to our daily meetings more than I did my nightly rendezvous with Madame or one of her girls.

Our meetings ended abruptly one day with the sudden appearance of her father as we were talking on our park bench.

"So, Laura, this is where you have been spending your mornings. Perhaps you would introduce me to your friend."

When Horace Mason realized who it was behind the blond moustache, I thought he would have a stroke of apoplexy.

Recovering at last, he ordered Laura to "return home forthwith and say nothing to your mother."

I was in no mood for a high-handed lecture, so I seized the initiative.

"Look, Dr. Mason, I am a desperate man. I have been through a living hell these past few months, and I don't intend to return to it. If you dare to raise an alarm, I will throttle you on the spot. Now, sit down and let's talk in a reasonable way. I have something to tell you."

I would never have dared talk to him that way in Philadelphia. To my amazement, he sat down and said calmly, "I thought you would have been hanged by now. Or at least be behind prison walls."

"I was in prison. Don't ask me how I got out. I am free and intend to remain so."

"You compromised me at Germantown, Martin. Now you seek to do so again. Is there no relief from your presence?"

"We are both refugees, Dr. Mason. And we are both Americans. Now pray hear my news."

He listened without interruption to my account of Ephraim's rescue.

"I am pleased beyond measure to hear that such a promising young doctor is alive after all. Now I understand why Laura has

279

seemed so happy these past few days. When I saw her sitting with a strange man, I thought . . . Well, that's no matter. Where is Dr. McGee now?"

Without embroidering my own role unduly, I told him how Ephraim and my comrades had been set free.

"Gave yourself up for his sake? Honor among thieves, as they say."

I swallowed my anger at that remark, reminding myself that he was the father of a very fine young woman. He showed the humanity to ask about Jason's recovery.

I told him about that and about the winter at Valley Forge, thinking as I did of the contrast with his easy life in British-occupied Philadelphia.

"Yes, I am amazed at the persistence of the rebels. Afraid we underestimated this fellow Washington."

"Many people on both sides have done so. You know, this war can only end one way. It is too bad that King and Parliament don't come to their senses and let us go in peace. Then we could all return to our homes and take up our lives as before."

"Nonsense! They have confiscated our house in Philadelphia. All my property—"

"So Laura said. I am sorry."

"Neither Laura nor her mother knows that so-called Patriot mobs broke all the windows of our house after we left. They entered our home and smashed the stair rails." His voice shook. "They even defecated on the floors and urinated on the remaining furniture. My lawyer, a good if neutral Quaker, was shocked by the vandalism. Even he has been insulted on the streets because he does not support your General Washington. Go home? How can we go back there unless British rule is restored?"

It seemed only natural to express my regrets. Instantly I wished that I had not, for his face turned white with anger and he said, "I don't want your sympathy. You are the enemy of our King. At the beginning of this interview, you dared to threaten me, sir. Now hear my threat. If I set eyes on you after this day, I shall turn you in on the spot. Hereafter I shall take care to be armed. And never, never again seek to correspond either in person or by letter with my daughter."

He arose and strode from the little park where I had spent so many happy hours talking heart to heart with Laura.

I had not told Madame of my meetings with Laura Mason. But now I had to unburden myself to someone.

"You think he might carry out his threat?"

"It is a risk I do not like to run. I must find a way out of this accursed country. Sooner or later they will discover me."

"Compose yourself. Let us talk again tomorrow."

280

We did so the next morning over our breakfast coffee. "Jerry, you know that I love London, but I cannot maintain this establishment without a source of income. I don't want to be drawn back into the sort of enterprise we were forced to conduct in Boston."

"How may I help?"

"After our conversation yesterday, I swallowed my pride. I went round to the Southwark Theater and made peace with the manager. I told him that I regretted the intemperate remarks I had made to him. He said he understood the artistic temperament and quite forgave me. To make a long story short, he feels that while it would be impossible for me to return to the stage in London, even under a new name, we might enjoy success in some of the provincial towns. Here is the itinerary he suggests."

I noted the names of Salisbury, Taunton, Plymouth, Bristol, and Bath.

"Then you would abandon me," I said forlornly.

"Never! I have hired a large coach and a team of four horses. I will require a coachman who can take some of the male parts in our plays. We would have to work on your Cockney accent. Think now—who would ever suspect a coachman-cum-actor of being an escaped privateer?"

5

WHAT A CURIOUS PICTURE we must have made as our ancient coach, groaning with the weight of six women, all their baggage, and several large trunks, careened along the streets of London and onto the great road leading west to Salisbury. I was unused to driving four horses but soon got the hang of it. I had more trouble with my Cockney accent, but Madame kept working with me on that.

We played for three nights to a half-full theater in Salisbury; then on we rolled to Taunton, where the crowds were somewhat larger.

By the time we reached Plymouth, I had begun to tire of my roles both on and off the stage. I could not spend the rest of my life in hiding. I ached to return to the war. A nation was being shaped across the ocean, and I was dilly-dallying my life away.

Madame did not wish me to leave her company. I am not sure whether she needed me or feared for my safety. But in the end she acquiesced. She packed a bag for me and gave me a small purse. She thought it best not to announce my departure to the girls, who were still sleeping.

"We may never see each other again, you know."

"Don't say that. We'll win this war, and I'll become so rich, I can set you up at the best theater in London—you'll see."

"Ah, Jerry, if you were ten years older or I ten younger, I'd not let you go. Or better, I'd go with you. Here, one last embrace and then depart quickly."

I rode a ferry over the Tamar River and hitched a ride in a cart driven by a talkative young clerk. He was headed for East Loo, which would take him right through Downderry.

Not trusting my Cockney accent, I encouraged him to chatter away. He was full of opinions about the American war ("Should hang 'em all, beginning with Washington"), the rising prices caused by the conflict ("Things have become so dear, my Nellie and I must wait another year to marry"), and naturally, the weather.

By the time we reached Downderry, I was glassy-eyed. I thanked him for the ride, then asked at the only public house where I might find " 'Erbert Gwin."

They were sitting down to an early supper when I arrived at the little stone cottage overlooking a cove. His wife came to the door in answer to my knock. A plump, worried-looking woman, she carried an infant on her shoulder.

Gwin appeared, his face nut brown. I said, "Don't you know me?"

He frowned and shook his head. Then I took off my cap and asked, "You don't recognize your old captain from the *Charlotte*?"

His complexion turned gray. He staggered back as if I had struck him a blow, and he slammed the door in my face.

"What's the matter, Herbert?" I heard his wife ask. "You look like you seen a ghost."

"It's him! He's come back to haunt me!"

"Open up there, Gwin! I'm no ghost. Come, I must talk to you." The door half opened.

"Captain Martin. You are supposed to be dead."

"Do I look dead? Now, get hold of yourself and let me in."

I ended up eating supper with the Gwin family—there was plenty of food for me. My host remained too shaken to eat his portion.

Afterward we went out to his tool shed and talked.

"I hated to testify against Dr. McGee and the others, but what choice did I have? They twisted things around to make it look like you was pirates. They had me in a bad spot, they did, seeing as I had served as your second mate. Told me I was lucky to escape being hanged myself."

"And what are you doing now?"

"I does a bit of fishing. Got my own boat. Bought it with the money Mr. Halbertson—" He checked himself.

"The money they paid you to turncoat on me?"

"Well now, I was in a most difficult position, Captain. The old man got me out of prison for smuggling, you know. And I do have

282

a family to support. He could have made it bad for them if I had refused when that Halbertson asked me. I am most grateful for what you done when you took time to untie me. I thought you was killed. We all did. I'd do anything for you after that."

"Anything?"

"Within reason, certainly."

"You say you have a boat?"

My first offer was to buy his boat and sail it across to France, but he would not accept that and offered to take me across himself.

"Meaning no offense, sir, but I have seen better sailors than yourself. Not that you wasn't a good captain, but I should hate myself if aught should happen to you. Besides which, I need my boat more than I need the money."

"Wouldn't you be taking too much of a risk if you helped a privateer captain escape to an enemy country?"

"I wouldn't be alive today if it hadn't been for you."

"Perhaps you'd like to reenlist in my service."

"As a privateer? Oh, sir, I have learnt my lesson there, although I must say they was exciting times aboard the *Charlotte*—after you took her over, that is."

Well before dawn the next morning, we set out for a cove below the cottage. Gwin's boat was a twenty-foot skiff, which he assured me was capable of navigating the distance to Cherbourg.

By the time the sun was up, we had cleared the headlands and were skimming along over a moderate sea. I embarrassed myself by getting seasick and throwing up the excellent breakfast that Mrs. Gwin had prepared for us as she wept over her failure to dissuade her husband from risking his life.

In the afternoon the sky clouded over and the seas became so rough that I thanked my stars that Gwin had insisted on ferrying me over himself.

It began to rain before nightfall. Gwin and I stayed awake to try to keep the rising and plunging skiff on what I prayed was the right course.

Dawn revealed the grayish coast of France ahead. The rain had stopped and the seas had moderated by the time we encountered a fleet of fishing craft. Drawing to within hailing distance, I marshaled the French I had learned at Forton to ask where the nearest port was.

"Le Havre. Twenty miles to the northeast."

Near noon, we passed the entrance of the harbor. Two gendarmes took us into custody at the dock and carried us before a magistrate. He was all for jailing us as spies until I thought to mention the name of Benjamin Franklin.

"Docteur Franklin. You know him?"

After much waving of hands and jabbering away, the magistrate sent one of the gendarmes out of the office. He soon returned with a man dressed in nautical garb, wearing a skipper's cap.

"Now, what's this cock-and-bull story?"

Never had an American accent sounded so sweet. The man, a privateer captain, was quickly persuaded that I was the genuine article. In fact, he had heard of the exploits of the *Charlotte*. I had mentioned Franklin—did I want to see him? he asked.

The captain saw that we got a good night's rest in a local inn. The next morning I dispatched Gwin back to his wife and children in Cornwall, and I myself set out in a hired hack with driver for the village of Passy, where I was assured I would find Dr. Franklin.

After an overnight stay at a village inn, I donned a fine broadcloth suit from Madame's wardrobe and presented myself at the pleasant house that Franklin had rented there.

The hall contained several persons waiting to see the famous and influential American. A young male secretary, whom I later learned was Franklin's grandson, asked my business. I told him just enough to pique his interest, including the fact that I had met Franklin in his home in Philadelphia in '75.

To my delight and to the apparent chagrin of the other suppliants in the hall, the secretary escorted me directly into a sunlit room. There Franklin, looking older than I remembered, sat at a desk.

At first I thought he was only pretending to remember me, but then he referred to my experience at Lexington and Concord.

He seemed fascinated by my account of my privateering and my subsequent experiences at Brandywine and Germantown, as well as at my escape from Forton Prison. In fact, he kept me so long that his grandson had to remind him that others were waiting.

"Let them wait. It is not often that I receive a genuine hero. Nearly everyone who comes wants something, usually something I am either unwilling or unable to grant."

"As a matter of fact, Dr. Franklin, I want something, too."

"And what might that be?"

"I should like your advice on how I might obtain a new ship and a letter of marque. I want a schooner that can carry twenty cannon and a crew of a hundred. I am itching to get back at the British."

He laughed. "Advice is easy to give. Have you any funds?"

"I have bills of credit in my account at St. Eustatius."

Franklin pondered for a moment and called for his secretary.

"You said Monsieur Mansard is waiting."

"Not very patiently, I fear. He seems about ready to depart."

"Send him in. Tell him I wish him to meet someone."

M. Mansard was a dark, sour-looking little man who, Dr. Franklin explained, owned a shipyard in Cherbourg. He was interested in establishing trade with America.

Over lunch, we worked out an arrangement. Operating under a commission that Congress had empowered Franklin to issue, I would buy a half-interest in and sail a new vessel that was about to be launched at Mansard's shipyard.

At first, I did not like Mansard, but as I got to know him better, I realized that he was a man of integrity—albeit one who would insist on a strict accounting for every penny of our joint enterprise. This was no Dogood Mackey nor, for that matter, an Abraham d'Balboa.

So I left Passy in the company of Mansard with a bone-fide congressional commission in my pocket to operate as a privateer against the enemies of America. My head was spinning with Benjamin Franklin's words of encouragement and praise.

I never became a close friend of Pierre Mansard, but we did forge a workable business alliance. Fortunately, he had done business with Abraham d'Balboa through his agent in St. Eustatius. So after an intense cross-examination, he satisfied himself that I was who I said I was and that I could do what I said I could.

I had dreamed of commanding either a large, sharp-hulled schooner or a small frigate with which I would be able to take larger prizes. The newly launched vessel now being rigged at the Mansard shipyard was a brig, broad-beamed with a deep hold.

At my protest, Mansard replied with practical Gallic logic. "My friend, there are more than enough ships available to fight the British now that my country has entered the war. And there are more than enough privateers on both sides. But there is much to be done to keep your armies and ours in North America well supplied."

"But I have a letter of marque from Dr. Franklin."

"Quite so, and it will not be wasted. We will arm this brig well enough that she can defend herself, if need be, and that she can take smaller craft if they should cross your path. You will find that the real money is in transporting gunpowder, lead, cannon, muskets, and other items of war to your native country."

I protested again, but he cut me off with a reminder that we were in France, where crews had become increasingly hard to recruit.

"I have a thousand Charleville muskets crated and ready to be loaded. Several hundred pounds of choice gunpowder. Two tons of lead. Also some excellent wines. If you do not wish to use your letter of marque, you should return it to Dr. Franklin."

I knuckled under and agreed to set forth with his cargo for Philadelphia as soon as we could scrape up enough men to sail our brig.

PART EIGHT

1

WE NAMED HER the *Nannette,* after Mansard's wife. Like her name-
sake, she was no great beauty but she was nimble for one so sturdily
built, and she was generally easy to handle.

With a crew of twenty ill-assorted seamen, we sailed across the Atlantic in five weeks without any undue difficulties, except my own
in trying to issue commands in French.

Beyond a shocking increase in prices and an absence of loyalists,
I found Philadelphia little changed from when I had left it a year
before in chains, thinking I was on my way to be hanged.

Dogood Mackey was elated to see me but not surprised, as he had
since learned that there had never been any serious danger of my
being executed.

I was even more elated than he when he informed me that
Ephraim McGee had returned safely and was now employed as a
physician at the Pennsylvania Hospital. But my elation turned to
concern when he added that one of his patients was my old sailing
master.

"Lovejoy Brown is ill? What is wrong?"

"He signed on as mate on a schooner, but after one trip they dismissed him for drunkenness. I fear that rum has wrecked his
health."

I found Ephraim at the hospital. We jabbered away at a furious rate. Finally, exhausted by the emotion of seeing each other after so long a time, I asked about Lovejoy.

"They called me to take him off their hands when his schooner returned from the Indies. He had developed alcoholic delirium. I released him once, but he promptly started drinking again. Do you want to see him?"

I stood by Lovejoy's bed until he opened his eyes. He promptly shut his eyes and began shaking and sweating.

"No, no," he moaned.

I put my hand on his shoulder. He opened his eyes again. It took a moment for him to realize that I was not one of the creatures he had been seeing in his alcoholic fantasies. Then he gave a whoop and tried to get out of bed, but his legs would not support him. He sat helplessly as tears streamed down his leathery cheeks.

Later, when he had composed himself, his eyes shone as I told him and Ephraim about the *Nannette* and my letter of marque from Franklin.

"Say you got a bunch of Frenchies? Is there a sailing master?"

"I did my own navigation across the Atlantic."

"You're lucky you got here."

"I expect to start looking for a sailing master tomorrow."

"They are hard to find."

"Particularly good, sober ones. That's the only kind I would accept."

"Now, Jerry, after all we been through together, what do you want to tease me like that for? I'd work for half wages if money is a problem."

"And I'd pay you double if you stopped drinking, started eating proper food, and got yourself back in shape within, say, two weeks."

For the sake of old times, Ephraim and I continued our reunion at The White Swan. There we found Liz in full control, but she was not as overjoyed to see me as I had expected. The reason was that although her husband had abandoned her to flee with the other Philadelphia loyalists, a robust young shipping clerk had taken up permanent residence at The White Swan.

"He can be a bit jealous," she explained. "So I ask that you not act familiar with me. It hurts to say that, seeing as how you have done so much for me."

"And you for me. But a word to the wise, dear Liz. I will do or say nothing to upset your new domestic arrangement."

Actually, I was relieved that she did not expect to resume our old roles as lovers. So did Liz Oliver become a closed page in my life's book.

Dogood Mackey was pleased that the terms of my partnership

with Mansard called for the *Nannette* to haul cargo rather than seek prizes. This was more in accord with his Quaker principles. The problem now was in finding a profitable load to carry to Statia. Wheat and other foodstuffs were in great demand in the West Indies, but it was too early for us to collect such produce and I did not want to wait about until harvest time. From talking to other captains, I learned of the tremendous profits to be made from the sale of tobacco, to be then transshipped from Statia in neutral ships to England or France. I also heard that plenty of newly cured tobacco was now available in tidewater Virginia.

I thought that Lovejoy, who had recovered from his illness, would object to my plan. But no, he thought anything better than "hanging about with our fingers up our arses." As for Ephraim, he was unenthusiastic about returning to the sea, but, I suppose out of a sense of gratitude to me, he did agree to accompany us "at least for this one voyage."

So we cleared the Delaware Capes together and headed due south. We hugged the coastline and kept a sharp eye out for British cruisers until we came to the mouth of the Chesapeake.

Up we sailed through the mouth of the James and finally into the Appomattox River itself. We dropped anchor at Port Walthall, where I had often seen ships with my father. Ephraim went ashore with me.

A boatman rented a pair of horses to us when he learned that we paid in gold. After warning us of the idiosyncrasies of each steed, he gazed at me closely. "You look familiar. Don't I know you?"

"Can't think why you should," I lied.

We rode out to my old home. I was shocked at the disrepair into which it had fallen. The fields around the house were neglected. I did not recognize my mother at first, nor she me. Her hair had turned iron gray, and she was stooped. When at last I convinced her that the burly chap confronting her was indeed "my precious Jeremiah," she sat down and sobbed. I could not be sure whether she was happy or sad at my reappearance.

I introduced Ephraim, who proceeded to tell her of all the kindnesses I had done his family and of my seafaring deeds.

Before I could inquire of her husband, the man himself entered the kitchen. He walked with a cane and had gone completely bald. His neck had become lean and corded, while his girth had increased.

"See here, Horace, it is Jeremiah returned to his home at last."

This one-time great bully blanched. His eyes opened wide, and he held his cane as if to ward off an attack. If ever a man was in fear of his life, it was that scourge of my youth. My momentary feeling of triumph quickly faded into a feeling of pity as I saw him tremble. I held out my hand, and after a moment's pause, he extended his. That once-great paw that had so often wielded a strap across my backside had shrunk, so that I felt I might crush it to powder in my own.

"Yes, it is me. I have come home. And this is my dear friend, Ephraim McGee."

If there had been a fatted calf about the place, my mother would have killed it for me. Indeed, the cook, who had been but a child when I had left, killed a chicken and served it up with potatoes, collard greens, and cornbread.

As word of my arrival spread about the plantation, the slaves came up to the big house one by one to greet "the young master." I was saddened to hear that my favorite, Virgil, had died two years before. Ephraim, who had grown up in a land where slavery was rare, seemed fascinated by the scene.

Often while in prison or at sea, I had dreamed of returning to my childhood home to reclaim my mother and restore my father's old plantation. But by the end of our meal, I had run out of things to talk about with my mother. I saw her now for what she had always been: a weak, fearful woman entirely lacking the shrewd wit of Madame LaFontaine, the cheerful spunkiness of Liz Oliver, or the elegant charm of Laura Mason. My stepfather had become a sour old shell of a man, and his attempts to get back on a good footing with me only made him more contemptible in my eyes. But we spent the next two nights in my old home.

The next morning we went about the neighborhood and by noon had contracted for enough hogsheads of good Virginia tobacco to fill the hold of the *Nannette*. In another two days we had our cargo securely aboard.

My mother and I made one last try at reestablishing our old bonds of love and trust. But it was too late. She tearfully confessed that they had fallen into financial distress and that Gouge was thinking of selling off some of the slaves, so I presented her with a purse of gold worth enough to see them through several more crops.

She and Gouge took their decrepit carriage down to the wharf to see me off. I shook the hand of my old nemesis, accepted his expression of thanks for my generosity, and kissed my poor mother good-bye.

As we were rowed back to the *Nannette*, Ephraim said, "I should feel very melancholy if I were saying farewell to my family in such circumstances."

"You are lucky," I said. "You have a family. I lost mine when my father died."

Only after we had gone aboard the *Nannette* and raised anchor did it occur to me that not one word had been said of the circumstances under which I had fled my home sixteen years before, nor of the various warrants that had been issued against me.

Shortly after dawn one day six weeks later, Statia loomed into view on the southern horizon and by afternoon we had anchored in the waters off Oranjstad. The lower town was even more crowded than when I had last seen it. There were so many warehouses, so closely built together in the shadow of the cliffs, that some merchants had to remove their roofs to find barrels and bales to be shipped off to Europe. Even with this new construction, much of the produce awaiting transshipment was simply piled on the ground with only tarpaulins to protect it against the weather.

D'Balboa was not surprised to see me, for Pierre Mansard had written to him about my escape and our partnership. His wife was stouter and even more uncommunicative than before, but Rebecca had blossomed into a rare beauty. She hung about listening to every word of our adventures.

"This war has taken a turn for the better for your country," Abraham said. "The Spanish have declared war on the British. With them and the French no longer neutral, the Dutch have more business than they can handle—and so do my fellow Jews. Welcome back, my friend. And you, too, dear Dr. McGee."

Abraham was in full agreement with Mansard's order to carry cargo rather than seek prizes. "You would need a frigate with twenty-four guns and a hundred fighting men to be as successful now as you were with your sloop. I know you like to fight, but believe me, you'll do your country more good by supplying its armies. Despite the entry of the French and Spanish, they will need weapons and ammunition more than ever. The British still have strong land forces, and they will seek to put them to use before the French can send over troops."

He explained that the *Nannette* should be able to make three or four round trips between Statia and Philadelphia per year, "if you dawdle not in port and if you have good agents at either end standing by to receive your cargo and give you assistance in finding a new one."

In three weeks we loaded our brig with a cargo of sugar, rum, and lead and headed north again. We were making good time, until northwest of Puerto Rico we encountered a storm. The *Nannette* weathered it well enough, but it blew us off course. When the seas calmed and the weather cleared, Lovejoy found that we were near the Bahamas. He cursed our luck, but it is an ill wind that blows no good—had it not been for that storm, we would not have caught sight of a sloop laden with salt from Turk Island. Fortunately, the captain of the sloop had overloaded his craft, and we were able to catch him before he could dump his burdensome cargo overboard to gain speed.

The cargo carried by the craft was much in demand in Philadelphia, and the sloop brought a handsome price after being libeled and auctioned off.

I was going over our accounts in Dogood Mackey's office when Ephraim McGee entered and asked to speak with me in private.

"Jerry, I have had enough of this war. It is time I returned to my profession."

I tried to change his mind, pointing out how useful he had been as the *Charlotte*'s surgeon.

"True enough, but now that you are hauling cargo, I am needed far more here in Philadelphia."

Actually, I knew it was a waste of his skills to serve aboard the *Nannette*, but I was still reluctant to part company with him. The full truth about his decision was slow to come out, but finally he confessed that he wanted to establish himself as a physician so that when peace came, he could offer Laura Mason a secure place to live back in her native Philadelphia.

"How can you be sure her parents will ever accept you, no matter who wins this war?"

"You said yourself that they felt out of place in London. Laura has always loved Philadelphia, and so do I."

Then he told me that he had used his share of the proceeds from the various cruises of the *Charlotte* to purchase the great home of the Masons from the Patriot merchant who had bought it before at a knock-down price.

"I will live there and practice medicine. They cannot refuse Laura the opportunity to marry and live once more in her childhood home."

Seeing that his mind was made up, I wished him well and got on with planning my next voyage.

2

BOSTON was one of the last places I would have chosen as my next destination, but Dogood Mackey convinced me that I should go there to pick up a cargo of the salt fish so much in demand in the Indies.

"I have a consignment of flour and cornmeal for Boston. With the British in control of New York and the lower Hudson, it makes eminently greater sense to send the stuff by water."

Lovejoy agreed, adding that he would like to see his mother again.

At my protest, he said, "Well, I agreed to go to Virginia so you could see your mother. I reckon I love mine as much as you do yours."

I let the old seadog think he had persuaded me to make Boston our destination. But it was actually the price Mr. Mackey assured me our flour and meal would bring that settled the question.

We spent the last two weeks of 1779 in Boston, unloading our cargo and waiting to accumulate barrels of salt fish to carry to Statia. While Lovejoy went off to visit his mother in Marblehead, I walked through the steep, narrow streets. I retraced my steps between Madame LaFontaine's former establishment and the great jail, Province House, and Copp's Hill. The rector of the Old North Church grudgingly allowed me to climb into the church tower to look across the Charles River at the now brown, frozen earth over which Gate's valiant grenadiers and light infantry had advanced against the withering musketry of the militia.

As I huddled in my greatcoat against the frigid wind, I reflected on my experiences of the past four years and on those of my native land. From this tower, the story went, a signal lantern had been shone to warn the minutemen across the Charles that the British were sending their troops against Concord. In another four years, it would be the end of 1783. Would the war be over by then? I climbed down the ladder from the belfry, pressed a donation on the rector, and hurried to The Green Dragon for a mug of hot buttered rum.

Lovejoy returned from Marblehead to report that his mother was in good health but remained unresigned to his life at sea.

"What did you tell her?"

"Told her my country needs me more than herself."

We reached Statia with our cargo of fish at the end of February. Abraham got a high price for this staple of the slave diet. We celebrated our success with an excellent feast of turkey at his house.

Abraham was better posted on the war news than I was. A joint French-American attempt to retake Savannah from the British had ended in miserable failure with the loss of some eight hundred men, mostly French. He was strangely pessimistic about Statia, too.

"The Dutch would be well advised to curb their greed. Sooner or later, I fear, the British will stop tolerating this great supply depot for the American rebellion. In the past it made a convenient exchange point for their plantations' goods and those from Europe, but just look at our anchorage. Every other ship is American. The others are Dutch or Spanish, and they have brought powder in chests labled 'tea' and muskets in crates marked 'agricultural implements.' I tremble for our safety."

"And I for the safety of my country if aught should happen to close this vast marketplace. Come, a toast to St. Eustatius."

With a cargo of spirits, medicines, tents, and a dozen beautifully crafted brass field artillery pieces, we set out on the familiar journey to Philadelphia. We eluded a British frigate in the Mona Passage between Puerto Rico and Hispaniola and sailed on without further incident until we neared the Maryland coast.

En route, at Lovejoy's urging, I had ordered our gunports covered with canvas. I put our gun crews through extra drills, both to keep them occupied and as a precaution.

We had just changed course to head into Delaware Bay when we sighted a rakish schooner fast overtaking us off our larboard quarter.

Lovejoy studied her carefully. "Damn good sailer. Wish we had her ourselves. I count twelve guns. Half the crew are black. No doubt about it, she means business."

"How much freeboard?"

"She's riding high, but then so are we, even higher."

"How many men?"

"Looks like they got us beat there."

"Well enough. Let her draw a bit closer, and then we'll break out our French colors."

At my direction, our crew cheered and waved when the schooner responded with the American flag.

Lovejoy let us plod along like a good French housewife on her way to market until the schooner had drawn far enough ahead to put a shot across her bow. Obligingly we fired our little swivel gun to the leeward and slacked off our sail.

Once more I instructed our men on how to hoist the nets to ward off boarders and how to light the fuses on the explosive shells brought up from the hold.

Then came the delicious moment when the schooner put her helm over and glided toward what his crew must have regarded as a helpless, trusting Frenchman. Well, if she did turn out to be an American, the other captain and I could have a good laugh over drinks in my cabin.

The schooner slacked off his sail until he was near enough to satisfy me that our gun deck rode considerably higher than his. I could see that many of his crew were armed with pistols and cutlasses, while others stood by with grappling hooks.

"Ahoy there, who are you?"

In my best French accent, I yelled back, "We are the *Nannette* out of Cherbourg, bound for Philadelphia."

"And we are the *Grayhound* out of New York. Strike your colors, or we'll blow you out of the water."

Down came their American flag and up went the British.

"I do not understand," I called.

"You heard me! Strike, or we'll slay every mother's son of you."

"Please," I shouted, "no bloodshed!"

I waited until they had thrown over half a dozen grappling hooks. Then I gave the signal for the canvas cover to be lowered from our gunports and our cannon to be run out with barrels depressed. That way our adversaries would be looking right into the muzzles.

Then, as if they were carrying out a routine drill, my lot raised nets all along our rail.

The crew of the schooner stood with mouths open.

"Ahoy there, captain of the *Grayhound*! Do you strike?"

"Go to hell, you French son of a bitch!"

"I am not French, and my mother is an honest woman. Our guns are double-loaded with grapeshot, and we have a full supply of bombshells. At a word from me, you will all die."

Several of my crewmen held up their bombshells and smoking linstocks.

A man I took to be the first mate conferred with the captain. Their gunners had backed away from their cannon. I noticed several other crewmen take cover behind the ship's boat.

The mate said, "We made a mistake. We did not know you were American."

"You thought we were French."

"Why, yes."

"But you know that the French are our allies."

"We are willing to forget this entire incident," the captain said. "You go your way, and we will go ours."

"Stand by your guns, men!" I shouted. "Grenadiers, prepare to light your fuses. Sharpshooters, at the ready! Surgeons, prepare to handle the enemy wounded!"

"Don't fire!" the captain yelled.

"Do you strike?" I shouted back.

The faces of the schooner's crewmen glistened with sweat. Lovejoy's complexion had turned beet red from his effort to suppress his laughter.

"Have you a surgeon to help with your wounded? The slaughter will be great!" I yelled.

"We don't have a surgeon," one of their crewmen cried.

"You have ten seconds," I shouted.

"Wait, wait! Don't fire. We strike!" the captain cried.

The *Grayhound* was worth far more than the French cannon and other cargo we had brought up from Statia, but I considered it a good investment to forgo auctioning her. Instead, I asked for and got a congressional letter of marque to operate her as an American, rather than a Tory, privateer.

3

I SHOULD HAVE KNOWN that I was ill. Upon entering Delaware Bay and waiting for a pilot to come out from Lewes, I felt bone tired and listless rather than triumphant over our capture of the armed Tory schooner.

Lovejoy asked what the matter was, and I replied, "Perhaps it is nerves. I feel as though my strength has drained away."

Our arrival at Philadelphia seemed only to make my lassitude worse. Dogood Mackey expressed his concern at my sickly appearance and lack of spirit.

I told him of my symptoms. He put a hand on my forehead and, declaring me to be feverish, insisted on personally delivering me to the former Mason residence, one of whose front rooms had been transformed into the office of Ephraim McGee, M.D.

Ephraim wasted no time on civilities. He asked me several rather personal questions and then had me piss into a glass jar. After that he helped me removed my shirt and proceeded to tap and probe my torso.

In the end he declared that I had something he called tropical fever, for which the only cure was several weeks of bed rest on a diet of water, vegetables, and fruits.

"No wine? No rum?"

"Nor any heavy foods of any sort, and plenty of peace and quiet."

I protested that with two ships to manage, I could not spare the time for an illness.

"You have no choice. You will stay here in my care. I have far more room than I need. You will see visitors for no more than an hour a day. I have plenty of books to keep you occupied."

"To hell with that," I said. "Give me my shirt."

Alas, I lacked the strength to dress myself. Ephraim helped me up the stairs to a well-ventilated corner room with a large bed, and there I remained for five weeks.

Besides reading, I occupied my long hours in bed with catching up on the war news, much of it bad. The British had just taken Charleston after trapping and capturing an American army of five thousand under General Benjamin Lincoln. Cornwallis, the British general, had sent out a call for the loyalists of the Carolinas to rise up in support of their king. Meanwhile, Washington had put down mutinies of first the Massachusetts, then the Pennsylvania, and finally the New Jersey Line a few months before; now in his camps around Morristown, New Jersey, he had to repeat this performance to keep the Connecticut Line from marching off with their arms. Fortunately, Clinton remained ensconced in New York City with several thousand redcoats, while Cornwallis ravaged the South.

Ephraim said that Chris, who was still a mounted Life Guard for Washington, had written that the winter they spent at Morristown had been far worse than the one at Valley Forge and that the Continental soldiers had just grievances over their lack of pay and continued poor living conditions.

"But he thinks their problem is that they have fought no major battles since Monmouth, nearly two years ago. He says they have had too much time for brooding."

"And I had thought the war would be well nigh over with the entry of the French," I said.

"The worst may be yet to come."

Although there was nothing devious about Ephraim, still he could be devilishly secretive. He did not tell me that he had written to his parents about my illness.

Jason McGee tried to make it appear that his only reason for riding down to Philadelphia was to attend to a business matter, but I quickly realized that the old warhorse had really come to visit me.

God, I was glad to see him! We talked as long as Ephraim would permit on the first day. Ephraim had told him of our prison experiences. Jason thanked me for bringing about the release of his son and added, "Kate particularly asked me to tell you how grateful she is."

The next day, following Ephraim's orders, I remained silent and let Jason tell me of his experiences the previous year as part of Sullivan's expedition to punish the Iroquois for the infamous Wyoming Valley and Cherry Valley massacres of '78.

"It was a hard and bitter campaign, as hard as anything in this war, let me tell you. They assembled us in Easton, and we passed through Wyoming Valley and seen what the dirty savages done there, with the help of Tories. We seen the remains of hundreds of houses they burned down. And the graves of women and children would sicken you. After seeing all that, we marched over into New York and gave one lot of Indians a good whipping at a place called Newtown."

As Jason recounted the massacres of settlers in the upper Susquehanna Valley in Pennsylvania and the methodical destruction of Iroquois villages across the New York frontier in retaliation, I marveled at what a vicious contest this war had become, setting brother against brother, neighbor against neighbor, subject against sovereign, and race against race.

"It's the same old story, Jerry. Folks in the east pay no mind to what's happening in the west until it's too late. They call on us to protect their cities, but we have to defend ourselves."

Jason might have talked all day about Sullivan's expedition if Lovejoy Brown had not shown up to ask me some questions about recruiting men for the *Grayhound*.

297

I lay back on my pillows and listened to my two comrades relating their experiences on the frontier and on the sea. Each of them had saved my life at one time or another. It gave me deep satisfaction to realize that they liked each other. One's best friends often don't.

I had never heard of Ramsour's Mill in North Carolina until the day before Jason had to return to Sherman's Valley. Dogood Mackey arrived with a report that on June 20, just two weeks before, some four hundred Whig militiamen had surprised more than a thousand loyalists which had been recruited to assist Cornwallis, and had scattered the Tories in bitter hand-to-hand fighting.

"Where was this?" Jason asked.

"At a German settlement about twenty-five miles west of Charlotte."

Jason frowned. "It seems to me that Gerta mentioned that place in one of her letters."

This visit from my old comrade did me more good, I think, than the ministrations of his son. In another two weeks I was back on my feet. I worked with Dogood Mackey to obtain a congressional letter of marque for the *Grayhound* and with Lovejoy to scrape up enough men for a crew.

By August, we had our crew and a cargo of dear-bought barrel staves and salt-cured beef. The high prices we had to pay opened my eyes to the illusionary nature of the paper wealth I had been accumulating. In '76, I could have bought 145 pounds of flour for a hundred dollars; now the same amount of money got me only five pounds. The army soaked up food and clothing. There was a shortage of farm labor caused by the recruitment of soldiers and the demands of hauling materials to camp. Farm laborers got more money than one would have thought possible—as much as twenty continental dollars a day during the height of the harvest.

But thanks to my reputation and to our promises of sharing the proceeds of our privateering, we were able to man both our craft adequately. Finally we were ready to set out for yet another trip to Statia, with Lovejoy Brown in command of the *Grayhound* and myself of the *Nannette*.

I offered Ephraim yet another chance to come with us as ship's surgeon, but he declined. "If Washington and Clinton come to fresh blows, I might consider joining the army. As it is, I do my part by visiting the army hospitals hereabout."

We encountered heavy seas off Cape Hatteras; then, after weathering that storm, we were further delayed by contrary winds near the Bahamas. The *Grayhound*, being fore-and-aft rigged, could have stuck to our planned course, but she was delayed by the square-rigged *Nannette*'s tedious tacking back and forth. We felt that we should keep our vessels together, however, and the result was that as we neared the Anegada Passage east of the Virgin Islands, we were far behind schedule.

As we approached the passage, there appeared on the southern horizon two frigates that could only have been British. Lovejoy and I slacked off sail and shouted back and forth until we decided that he would engage their attention while I sailed the *Nannette* farther east.

"We'll rendezvous tomorrow morning off Anguilla and make our run together into Statia from the west the next day!" I yelled. "Take care."

"You take care," he replied.

The usually brisk southeasterly trade wind faltered soon after I changed to a northeasterly course. Throughout the afternoon, I kept an anxious eye on the *Grayhound*'s progress toward the cruisers. From our crow's nest, I observed him sail perilously close to the frigates and then veer to the northwest. Sure enough, one of the cruisers took off after him, while the other maintained its station.

At nightfall the wind almost disappeared, and the surface of the sea turned glassy smooth. The sun gave off an eerie red glow as it sank behind the horizon.

During the night I was awakened by a whining wind. At dawn it was raining, and the seas had turned rough. We battened down the ship, took down most of our sail, and put out our sea anchors. I yearned for the presence of Lovejoy Brown.

What followed was nothing like our experience of two years before, when the *Charlotte* had been caught in a hurricane. No storm's eye passed over us, and the skies cleared the following day enough for me to take a noon azimuth, so I concluded that we had been only brushed by the hurricane.

With Anguilla in sight to the west, I lay to for two days, keeping an anxious eye out for the *Grayhound*. My mind conjured up a dozen fearful possibilities of what had happened, each worse than the previous one. But I feared for our own safety so close to the British island, so I ordered our sails raised and set our course for Statia.

Nothing appeared amiss as we passed smartly between Statia and St. Kitt's in the shadow of the volcanic Quill. But I realized that something was very wrong when I saw that hardly any vessels were anchored off Oranjestad. I whipped out my spyglass and surveyed the lower town. The shoreline was littered with grounded vessels in various states of damage. The town itself resembled a child's sandcastle that had been stamped upon by bullies. Not a roof remained in place. The buildings nearest the water had been wrecked.

We dropped anchor, and I climbed into the crow's nest for a better look. Lumber, barrels, bales of cotton—every conceivable item of commerce that could float bobbed in the surf. Dotted among the flotsam there appeared, face down, the bodies of dozens of men.

I was already worried sick by the failure of Lovejoy to show up at our rendezvous, but I was nearly prostrated at the sight of the havoc wrought by the hurricane. When I reached the shore itself, however, I saw that merchants had marshaled their staffs and were beginning to clear the wreckage. Sea captains were driving the survivors of their crews to refloat their vessels. I was stopped a dozen times by persons eager to know what cargo I had brought to port.

I climbed the gullied walk leading to the upper town and made my way through debris-clogged streets to the home of Abraham d'Balboa.

Over coffee, he told me the story of the hurricane, "the worst ever to strike this island."

It had burst upon them three days before. "We huddled in the kitchen for a full day and night. Never have I felt nature's wrath like that. The rain fell in great sheets. The lightning flashed constantly. And such thunder! It was as if the Almighty wished to destroy this place. And he very nearly did."

Several hundred sailors and lower-town workers had been drowned. Hundreds of thousands of pounds' worth of merchandise had been lost.

I remarked upon the activity that I had observed in the lower town.

"Yes, we must rebuild. St. Eustatius has no reason for being otherwise. As you must have seen, ships continue to arrive. Our goods and services are still needed. But enough of our troubles. I have been concerned for you. We expected you a month ago."

I told him about our delays and my fears for the safety of the *Grayhound*.

He nodded in sympathy, and then it was back to business. Our cargo would command the best prices ever. And we should be able to find it cheaper than ever to buy goods to carry back, "if you don't mind some water damage."

"It is an ill wind—" he began.

"If I have lost my old friend and our schooner, it would be a very ill wind, indeed," I responded.

"I am sorry for my remark. It was unfeeling."

Abraham insisted that I spend the night at their house. The next morning we arose early and walked to the top of the cliff to watch several sails approach the anchorage.

At first I stifled my hopes; but as I watched, one of the vessels, a schooner, looked more and more like the *Grayhound*. When I saw that she was flying a large thirteen-stripe flag, I clapped Abraham on the shoulder and ran down to the path to the lower town.

I was waiting beside a ruined dock when Lovejoy drew up in his ship's boat.

He did not understand what all the fuss was about.

"Oh, the storm wasn't all that bad. Mainly I was worried about you. Didn't think you'd know what to do."

"What about the frigate? I saw it following you."

"I played cat and mouse with her until near nightfall. The wind almost let me down once, and I thought I would have to fight. I'm glad I didn't. He would have shown me no mercy."

"Why do you say that?"

"Did you not observe what ship she was?"

"I did not venture as close as you."

"Why, it was the bloodhound himself!"

"I know no ship by that name."

"Not the frigate, you landlubber. Captain Fitzgerald! I recognized him before I doubled back and shook him off."

Abraham was right about the cargoes we brought into Statia. Our salted beef and barrel staves were snapped up. And we were able to buy silks, lace, fine leather shoes, and other luxury items at a fraction of their normal prices. We rejected goods spoiled by the hurricane but still got some grand bargains. I felt it my duty to carry some staples, such as sugar and rum. I would like to have taken medicines and surgical supplies, but these were too badly needed on the island. Not only had many persons been injured by collapsing roofs and walls, but much sickness also followed. I was eager to get away from the place before I lost any of my crew to it.

The night before our departure, Abraham drew me out of his wife's hearing to talk. He looked more downcast than I had ever seen him, and he came to the point quickly.

"Jeremiah, I have a great favor to ask of you, and of our mutual friend Dogood Mackey."

"I cannot speak for Mr. Mackey, but how could I refuse you anything?"

"Good. I wish you to take two passengers on your return to Philadelphia."

"That is a small favor. Who are they?"

"My wife and daughter."

At my expression of surprise, he said. "Perhaps you have to be a Jew to understand. We have had it too good for too long here. I have a foreboding about this place."

"You survived just about the worst thing I can imagine, a killer hurricane."

"I feel in my bones that there is worse to follow. I would like my wife and child to go to your country until this war ends."

"What then?"

"I will join them there. America is the land of the future. I should like to spend my remaining days there."

"Then why not come with your wife and daughter?"

"I have too many commitments here."

"You mentioned Mr. Mackey."

"Yes. I know of no one more trustworthy than he. I have written a letter asking him to see that my wife and daughter find suitable lodgings. There will be more than enough funds to keep them secure until I can follow."

It was a heart-wrenching scene on the deck the next morning as the d'Balboas said their good-byes. Then we loaded their trunks aboard the *Nannette* and raised our anchor. They remained on the quarterdeck waving their handkerchiefs until they could no longer see the lonely figure on the dock.

4

I TURNED MY CABIN over to the d'Balboas and moved into the mate's quarters next door. They remained downhearted and seasick during the early days of the voyage north, but eventually they recovered their spirits. I enjoyed their company, particularly Rebecca's. She plied me with so many questions about life in America that her mother reproached her.

Whenever we spotted the occasional sail in the distance, I regretted having two females aboard, being fearful for their safety. But the voyage went swiftly and smoothly, and we docked both our vessels without incident at Philadelphia on a cold afternoon in the middle of December 1780.

Among the many faces on the dock, I spotted the beaming countenance of Dogood Mackey. I warded off the queries of speculators as to our cargoes and made my way over to him.

He opened and read Abraham's letter on the spot, then smiled and said, "You must introduce me to my new wards."

He insisted on taking Mistress d'Balboa and Rebecca to his own home to stay until he could find a house for them. I was kept busy through the night seeing to the unloading of our cargoes, so it was the next afternoon before I appeared at the Masons' old house to see Ephraim.

An attractive blond boy of about three was playing in the hall when Ephraim opened the door. He greeted me with unusual warmth.

"Well, I'm back," I said, "and you'd never guess who I brought with me."

He heard my tale of the d'Balboas and the hurricane, then said, "Now, you'll never guess who I have with me. Chester," he called to the little boy, "ask your mother to come into my office, please."

She entered, carrying an infant with blond hair the same as the boy's in the hall. She was smaller or anyway shorter than I remembered. A little plumper, perhaps. Her face looked tired. Those stunning eyes seemed sad, but they danced when she recognized me and said in those musical tones, "Jerry! Is it really you? You look so different."

My knees went weak. My head swam so that I had to steady myself with a hand on a chair back.

Her name would not come out at first. I swallowed hard and then croaked, "Gerta."

"It is so good to see you."

I was surprised at the callouses on the little hand she held out to me.

We stood looking at each other without speaking until Ephraim said, "Well here, sit down. Jerry has just arrived from St. Eustatius."

In all the thirty five years of my rarely dull life, few have been the times when I felt as I did when, sitting in Ephraim McGee's office, I gazed at the face of the girl—now a woman—who had dominated my imagination for so many years. I felt as I had when I returned from the sea to find her grown into a sixteen-year-old beauty—tongue-tied, that is.

I am afraid my conversation made little sense. She explained that she had arrived at Sherman's Valley the previous September and that Ephraim had brought her down to Philadelphia to look after his house.

Her language was plain. There was nothing coquettish about her. She looked amused at my discomfiture.

There were a thousand things I wanted to know, but I am glad I did not ask them just then. After I agreed to stay for supper and she had excused herself to return to the kitchen Ephraim answered many of them.

"She has been through hell down in Carolina," he said. "Her husband joined the Tory militia. They were getting ready to march into South Carolina and join Cornwallis, but they were waylaid by a gang of Whigs."

"At Ramsour's Mill?"

"Yes. Many of the loyalists gave up their zeal for the King after being beaten so badly there—but not her Chester. No, he slipped back to their house and packed her off for Pennsylvania with some of their like-minded neighbors. Said he felt it his duty to go join

Tarleton. That's the British officer Cornwallis sent to stir up Tory sentiment in the back country. I was amazed to find her at home when I went back last month to Sherman's Valley. But Pa is so turned against Tories, I brought her and the children here. She always wanted to live in Philadelphia anyway."

"What about her husband?"

"It is better not to ask her about him. Perhaps you've not heard, but back in October there was a great battle between patriots and Tories at King's Mountain in South Carolina. Well over a thousand men were involved on each side. More than three hundred Tories were killed, and nearly all the rest were captured. I have heard much about the battle that I dare not tell poor Gerta. Many prisoners were slain after they surrendered. The British leader, Ferguson, gathered his men atop a small mountain and sent word to Cornwallis for reinforcements. The patriots got there first. They swarmed in from as far away as Virginia and the Watagua settlements over the mountains. They surrounded the place and—"

He stopped at Gerta's announcement that supper was ready.

I cannot remember what she served us. I only recall watching her bustle back and forth between the dining room and kitchen, stopping now and then to make sure her baby still slept in his cradle in the corner. The little boy, Chester, sat beside her whining over his food.

Sitting across the table, I dared not look directly into her eyes, but when she turned to speak to Ephraim or her son, I drank in her matured beauty. Unlike many frontier women, she had lost no teeth. The streak of gray in her hair only accentuated the freshness of her skin and the violet depths of her eyes.

Her conversation was not profound or witty. She talked about their parents and the twins and asked Ephraim about his work at the hospital that day. She said nothing about her life in Carolina, nor did she ask me about my career as a privateer. It was as if there were no war.

After she excused herself to put her children down for the night, Ephraim and I remained at the table over glasses of port.

"She is still very beautiful," I said.

He nodded.

"And what about her husband?"

"We have no word of him. Some of Ferguson's men got away, of course, either from the battlefield itself or later, as they were being marched up to Hillsboro in North Carolina. I have sent out inquiries, but the country down there is in such turmoil that communication is very difficult. Now, tell me more about the hurricane. And what will Mistress d'Balboa and the girl, what's her name, do here?"

Gerta, looking weary, rejoined us after putting the children to bed. She listened to my story about the d'Balboas.

304

"So I am not the only war refugee in Philadelphia," she said very simply. "Ephraim, perhaps we should invite them for supper. And you must come with them, Jerry."

The d'Balboas came two nights later, and with them came Dogood Mackey and his wife, a dumpling of a woman with a disposition as genial as his. Mistress d'Balboa acted ill at ease, but Rebecca quickly came out of her shell and was soon talking to Gerta as if they were sisters.

I had planned to turn our vessels around within a week and head back to Statia with fresh cargo, but the presence of Gerta deterred me, Lovejoy Brown was chafing at the bit so that I was half tempted to send him and the *Grayhound* on without me. Even though it was exquisitely sweet torture, I lived for the moments when I could be in her company and hear her correct her little boy and coo over her baby girl.

Chester was shy with me at first, but after several visits, he came to trust me enough to "ride horsie" on my foot and let me carry him about on my shoulders.

He and his mother came down to the docks one day with Ephraim, and I showed them about the *Nannette* and the *Grayhound*.

Still there remained a barrier between Gerta and me. Did she have any inkling of the pain she had caused me by marrying another man? I wondered. Trapped in the role of backwoods schoolmaster's wife, had she ever daydreamed of marriage to me and life in Boston or Philadelphia? I ached to talk to her as easily as I had with Liz Oliver and Annie Parker "LaFontaine"—and for that matter, Laura Mason in London.

Oddly enough, it was Laura Mason who finally eased the restraint between us. We had spent more than an hour over supper and were waiting for her to put her children to bed and bring out the dessert when a woman knocked at the door with an urgent request for Ephraim to come and look after her husband, who had suffered a seizure.

When Gerta returned to the dining room, I explained Ephraim's absence and said, "Perhaps I should go, too."

"No, my dessert must not go to waste."

This was the first time we had been alone. Again, I was overtaken by that accursed reticence. Glancing up from my dessert, I looked directly into her face. She was half smiling in a way that defied me to avert my gaze.

"Ephraim told me that you got him out of prison in England."

"He would have done as much for me, I suppose."

"No, that took uncommon courage. He also told me that you had seen this Laura Mason in London. I should like to know more about her. Ephraim seems so much in love with her."

As I talked about Laura, my words came easier and easier. Whenever I stopped, she prodded me on with a fresh question. At last she said, "Do you think she is the right girl for Ephraim?"

"He certainly seems to think so, and that is what counts."

"What about her father and mother? Would they ever permit her to marry him, now that—"

"That he has been tainted by his service with me? We won't know until this war ends. I know Ephraim will be mightily hurt if she turns him down after all the trouble he has gone to."

I waved my hand to indicate the house he had purchased.

Our conversation ran out. I was at the point of excusing myself when she said, as bluntly as her mother might have, "Poor Jerry. I hurt you very much, didn't I?"

I looked up with tear-blurred eyes at her face gleaming in the candlelight.

"More than anything in my whole life."

"I was only sixteen, you know. I did not understand what love meant. I dreamed of an easy life in a comfortable house like this one, of servants and rides in carriages over paved streets. Then that dreadful constable came from Virginia, and after that Chester Peebles."

"Would you like to know more about the Virginia business?"

"Ephraim told me all about that and his visit with your mother. You have had a hard life, haven't you, Jerry?"

"I've grown used to it. I always manage to bounce back."

She laughed. "I must learn to do that. It is not so easy for a woman, especially one with children."

After another awkward pause, she asked in a low voice, "Have you forgiven me?"

"I do now."

She looked at me, again half smiling. "If there were no war, no bitterness, I would wish you to meet Chester. He is so well read, so intelligent. He helped me grow up in more ways than one. You would like him."

I started to say that I had heard a different view of him from her own brothers but wisely held my tongue.

"Pa feels bitter toward him for sending me back here, but he thought he was doing the right thing. He believes very strongly in loyalty to the King."

"That is what makes this war so bad. Both sides feel so strongly that compromise is impossible."

"I hope you have found another girl, one who really deserves you."

I forced a smile and replied, "None bad enough to deserve such punishment."

Upstairs, her baby began crying. We waited for her to stop, but she only got louder.

"Why don't you go to her?" I said. "I'll let myself out."

5

I HAD PLANNED to sail on December 20, but Ephraim prevailed on me to spend Christmas with them. I had declined until he said, "I was hoping to surprise you, but you force my hand. Chris has written that he has obtained a leave and will spend it here with us."

That Christmas of 1780 in the old Mason house in Philadelphia was one of the happiest of my life. Gerta decorated the rooms with holly and cedar branches and placed candles in the windows. Unaware that neither Quakers nor Jews celebrate Christmas, Gerta invited the Mackeys and the d'Balboas to dine with her and Ephraim, and they accepted.

I arrived early to find Chris in the stable at the rear of the house, unsaddling a bay horse. He radiated good health and animal spirits.

"Where's Ned?" I asked.

"Someone should have told you. He died two years ago, at Monmouth. Of heat exhaustion. It was a terrible hot day. I rode him hard. The poor old fellow just gave out."

Later, in the house and out of Gerta's hearing, he rhapsodized about the "genius" of George Washington.

I pointed out that the man had won only two outright victories, one at Trenton and one at Princeton, "and they occurred four years ago."

"You were not at Monmouth,' he replied hotly.

"I was not aware that he did more than stand his ground in that battle."

"Had General Lee followed his orders, we would have wiped out half of Clinton's army and taken all his baggage train. Even so, we warded off the best of their troops and held our positions at the end of the day while the British limped away."

Ephraim joined in the fun. "That was just what Clinton was trying to do when Lee attacked his rear guard—march his army back to New York from Philadelphia."

"They left three hundred dead behind on the battlefield."

"Many of whom died of heat stroke," Ephraim rejoined.

Chris looked like his father when he stood up and declared with scarlet face, "You wouldn't dare speak so of our commander in our camps. If the British had him on their side, they would have won this war long ago. He does far more than direct just our one army. Don't you understand that he is the commander-in-chief of all our armies? And let me tell you this—his strategy is working."

"That might be news to Cornwallis. He has a death grip on South Carolina. His man Gates was soundly trounced at Camden."

"What about King's Mountain?"

"I understand that no British were involved there except for Ferguson himself," I said.

Ephraim's gestured toward the kitchen, where Gerta was preparing our meal; Chris lowered his voice and continued.

"Don't call Gates 'his man.' He is a horse's ass who was foisted off on the old man by Congress."

"I thought he was the great hero who captured Burgoyne and his army at Saratoga."

Chris snorted. "He had Arnold and Morgan there, two of the best fighting generals in America."

"Speaking of Arnold, Chris," I said, "were you not shocked to learn of his treason?"

"Of course I was. Everyone was. I followed the man to Quebec, remember? He was as good a general as we had. If Congress had not put Gates over him, he would have finished off Burgoyne even faster, and he would not have been tempted . . ."

When the Mackeys arrived with their houseguests, Chris was explaining that Washington had appointed Nathanael Greene to replace the humiliated Gates as commander of the southern forces. Thinking, perhaps wrongly, that Dogood Mackey might not wish to discuss a fellow Quaker who had been turned out of meeting for his military interest, we dropped the subject of war and turned to the celebration of the birth of one who came to bring peace to the world.

I could delay our departure no longer. Our vessels were loaded with lumber and other building supplies and tools that I knew would be much in demand to replace buildings destroyed by the hurricane.

I stopped by Dogood Mackey's office, and I knew that something was wrong as soon as I saw his face.

"Yes," he said, "there is bad news. Very bad news, indeed. Thee knows of the concern the McGees have felt for the husband of Gerta?"

"And with good reason."

"Very good reason, indeed. I have sought to help them with their inquiries through fellow Friends living in North Carolina. I heard this morning that he died of wounds at King's Mountain. Seems that one of his neighbors on the Whig side recognized him lying near the spot where Ferguson fell and helped bury him."

I sat down, a mixture of emotions boiling within me.

"Poor Gerta," I said.

"Yes, my wife has gone there to break the news and to comfort her. This cruel war . . ."

In the hall of the old Mason house, little Chester ran toward me with arms outheld but Ephraim stopped him.

"Where is she?"

"Upstairs, with Mistress Mackey and Rebecca."

"May I see her?"

"Let me ask Mistress Mackey."

While I waited, I held the boy on my lap and talked to him softly. Then Ephraim returned.

"All right, Jerry. Don't stay long. And be very careful what you say."

The drapes were drawn in her bedroom. The baby slept in the corner. Mistress Mackey and Rebecca left us alone.

I stood in front of her, trying to discern her expression in the darkened room.

"Gerta, it is me. Jerry."

"I know."

"I am so very sorry."

"Thank you, Jerry."

"Is there anything I can do to help?"

"It is too late for anyone to do anything."

"We are to sail in the morning. I could not go without telling you, without saying something, to let you know . . ."

"Sit down for a moment. I am glad you came."

"If I thought it would help, I would delay our departure."

"No. Ephraim says they need your cargo badly at that place. Besides, what could you do? What can anyone do? The only thing that can help is the passage of time." She paused and sobbed, then recovered to say, "He was a good man, no matter what my family thinks. He was good to me. It is not fair what happened. He had such hopes. First we would build a school for the young people in that area. Then he planned to enlarge it and take boarding students, hire additional schoolmasters. Eventually, he thought we might have a college, like your William and Mary. He was so ambitious. But all we ever had was twenty students."

There was nothing I could do except listen, which I did for half an hour as she poured out the bitterness of her heart at life's unfairness, at fate's way of dashing one's ambitions just as they seem near realization.

The baby awoke and cried. Mistress Mackey reentered the room. I arose and held Gerta's work-worn hand.

"It will take about six weeks to sail to St. Eustatius. We will remain there for one week. Sometime around the first of April, we should return. Do you think you will still be here then?"

"Where do I have to go?"

"I will be thinking of you."

As she arose, I realized that I had not released her hand. Still holding it, I bent and kissed her on her cheek.

"Little Chester will miss you," she said, then added, "and so will I."

With the taste of her tears still on my lips, I left the room. As I descended the stairs I heard her cry of sorrow and the sound of Mistress Mackey's attempts to comfort her.

That night I visited Mistress d'Balboa and gathered all the messages she and Rebecca had for Abraham. Then, back aboard the *Nannette,* I wrote one of the longest and most heartfelt letters of my life and gave it the next morning to Dogood Mackey, to be delivered in three weeks to Gerta.

Aboard the *Grayhound,* Lovejoy Brown stamped his feet like a racehorse eager to leave his stable. We let our pilot off at Lewes late that afternoon and by nightfall were back at sea.

I have tried, God knows I really have tried, to take no joy from the report of Chester Peebles's death. After all, I never met the man. He did not consciously do me any harm. I was deeply disturbed to see how much she loved her husband. Never have I seen a woman more grief-stricken. And yet the fact that Gerta had become a widow hardly displeased me. And she needed me. So did her children.

I cannot say what my decision might have been had I possessed the miraculous power to restore him to life. The fact remains that he is dead. Although she had made me no promises, Gerta surely could be, would be mine by spring. All I had to do was haul our lumber down to Statia and return to Philadelphia.

As the heavy-laden *Nannette* plodded along behind the nimble *Grayhound,* I rehearsed my plans over and over. I would collect my bills of credit held by Abraham and convert them to gold, then exchange my interest in the *Nannette* for full ownership of the *Grayhound.* I would sail her back to Philadelphia and sell her with her cargo for what would surely be a fortune. There would be few richer men than I in all of America. I would offer my services to Congress and, as Washington was doing, would perform them at no salary. Then I would buy a house in Philadelphia and a country estate out in Germantown. I would raise Gerta's children as my own. And we would have others ourselves. Yes, Gerta and I would establish a family that would take its place with the Morrises of Philadelphia, the Schuylers of New York, and the Washingtons of Virginia as America's finest. When the war ended, Laura Mason would return to marry Ephraim, further strengthening our tribe.

Faith, hope, and charity are the three great Christian virtues. Is the greatest of these really charity? I wonder whether it might be hope. In looking back over my turbulent years, it seems to me that my happiest times have been those spent in expectation of great happiness. One of those periods was the one during which Lovejoy and I owned a part interest in a ketch, when I was trying to accumulate enough to enable me to return to Sherman's Valley and claim Gerta as my bride. This situation was quite different. Already

I possessed considerable wealth, or anyway credit, and I was at the point of vastly increasing that wealth. And as before, Gerta was the prize for which I strove.

Only this was not the same virginal, kittenish Gerta. She had changed into a practical, mature person, and so had I. So her family's attitude toward me had or would soon change as well. How could Kate object to a wealthy, influential man willing—even eager—to free her daughter from penurious widowhood?

Why could not word of Chester Peebles's fate have reached Gerta sooner? King's Mountain had occurred in early October. Had his death been reported in November, soon after her arrival in Philadelphia, I might have been able to speak my mind forthrightly before I sailed. She would never have married me that soon, but we might have made our promises then. What the hell, it was all the same. By now Dogood Mackey would have given her my letter. She now knew how I felt about her. As we plodded southward past Bermuda, I spent many hours speculating what she might think as she read my fervent words.

PART NINE

1

At Lovejoy's urging, we angled eastward as we crossed the Tropic of Cancer so as to approach Statia through the Anegada Passage between the Virgins and Anguilla.

By that time, we had enough experience that we could identify trouble no matter what the cut of its jib or the colors it displayed. Lovejoy, sailing a mile ahead, was naturally the first to see the frigate lying off his larboard bow. He signaled that she was a British cruiser and that he would lure her out of the path of the *Nannette* so that we could sail on to the safety of St. Eustatius.

He changed to a southwesterly course and broke out his American flag. After ordering our crew to slacken sail, I climbed to our crow's nest, spyglass in hand. There the frigate was, near the horizon, silhouetted against an approaching line of rain squalls. I watched with great satisfaction as she set all sail to give chase to the *Grayhound*.

After the frigate passed to our leeward, I ordered our sails raised and set our course for Statia through the squall line. The rain felt good on my face. It was necessary only to furl our mainsail to ease the strain imposed on our mast by the quickened wind.

For more than an hour, we could see only a few cable lengths across the rain-spattered water. As we emerged from the last of the squalls, I saw looming in the sunshine off our starboard bow the rocky peak of the island of Saba.

I was admiring the view and enjoying the warmth of the sun on my wet back when one of our crewmen yelled, "Sail ho! Off the larboard quarter."

I needed no spyglass to tell me that the craft bearing down on us no more than two miles away was that damned British frigate. She had only pretended to take the bait offered by Lovejoy and had reversed course to pursue us under cover of the squall.

I screamed for all sail to be laid on. The frigate was square-rigged also. I could turn and run before the wind, away from Statia, hoping to stay free of her until dark. Or I could jettison our sixteen guns to lighten the *Nannette* enough to maintain our lead while remaining on course. Once within the Statian anchorage, we would be safe. Or I could continue on course and try to fight her off long enough for the *Grayhound* to double back and help.

"Sail ho! Off the starboard quarter."

It was the *Grayhound*. My choice was clear.

I yelled down to our crew for all available hands to stand by our cannon. For the next fifteen minutes there was a grand scramble to bring up cartridges and cannonballs from the hold and to clear the deck of all obstructions. Following our drill to the letter, we spread sand about the deck and extinguished the galley fire.

Meanwhile the frigate had cut our lead to less than a mile.

I stood on our poop deck and addressed our crew. "Men, we have never had to fight on the *Nannette* before. As brave Americans and Frenchmen, you do not need to be reminded to do your duty. It will not be easy, but all we have to do is stand them off long enough for our sister ship to come to our rescue."

I climbed back to the crow's nest and saw the *Grayhound* still fighting her way against the trade winds. I peered closely at the frigate and the figure on her quarterdeck. Surely there were not that many squat captains with orange beards.

By God, he had his spyglass fixed on us.

I lowered my trousers, turned my backside toward the pursuing vessel, and thumbed my nose in the direction of Atticus Fitzgerald, only, of course it was not my nose.

My crewmen laughed and danced about with glee. Several of them ran to the sternrail and repeated my gesture.

We were reminded of the seriousness of the chase when a long gun in the frigate's bow boomed and a cannonball plopped just behind our stern.

I climbed down from the crow's nest and sent a pair of riflemen aloft.

The frigate's bow gun boomed again and again, each time throwing its missiles closer. The *Nannette*—as if running for her life, which she was—bore every scrap of sail her masts and rigging would hold. Fitzgerald must have seen the approaching schooner, but he was not to be deterred from his pursuit of the *Nannette*.

Ephraim and Lovejoy had told me that he had gloated over besting me with the destruction of the *Charlotte*. I could only guess at the intensity of his desire to capture me intact. His strategy was predictable. He would try to draw even, put a broadside or two into us, overwhelm us with a swarm of boarders, then cut free and fight it out with the schooner.

"Stand to your guns!" I shouted.

The gun ports of the frigate opened again, and out came the twelve ominous barrels. The violence of his broadside, even at two hundred yards, was awesome. A ball slammed into our side, just above the waterline.

"Fire!" I yelled.

Our nine starboard cannon boomed, and I yelled, "Slack off mainsails!"

Our forward motion slowed. Fitzgerald fired a second broadside, which did us no damage, and his frigate plowed past.

For the first time, I saw the stern and what was painted across it. *H.M.S. Revenge*.

Fitzgerald was taken by surprise by our halting in our tracks, but he recovered quickly. I marveled at the skill with which he brought his frigate through the eye of the wind and reversed course. He sailed past us on our starboard side, close enough for us each to fire two broadsides at each other. Both times one or two of his balls found their mark in our hull, but he did us worse injury when he cut behind us and raked our stern with his broadside.

My quartermaster, a sturdy French lad, had been standing at the helm at one moment; at the next, his headless body was flying across our quarterdeck. Wiping the gore from my blouse, I took the helm.

I had been so absorbed in dodging the blows of my adversary and trying to get in a few licks of my own that I had forgotten about the *Grayhound*. Suddenly she swept in like a terrier, crossed the bow of the *Revenge*, and peppered the sides of the frigate with her six-pounders. I saw Lovejoy dancing about his quarterdeck. Only later did I learn that he had dumped all his cargo overboard in his zeal to lighten his draft and come to our rescue.

Lovejoy's twelve six-pounders brought our armament up to twenty-eight guns, versus Fitzgerald's twenty-four. Although his fired heavier balls, our two vessels were able to keep him off balance. I gave up trying to orchestrate our batteries to fire broadsides and instead allowed our gunners to load and fire their individual cannon as fast as they could. And since only one side could fire at a time and we were short-handed, I ordered our gunners to run from larboard to starboard and back as our target demanded. Oh, I got double duty out of that crew that February day in the year of our Lord 1781. And Lovejoy got even greater from his lot.

For that matter, so did Atticus Fitzgerald. The battle could have gone either way until, to my amazement, Lovejoy rammed the bow of the *Grayhound* right into the stern of the *Revenge*, smashing the windows of the captain's cabin. Fortunately, the blow was a glancing one, so that the schooner did not become locked against the *Revenge*.

Soon thereafter, the frigate began to yaw. I noticed that her rudder was flopping from side to side.

Lovejoy sailed his schooner close to us and yelled through his trumpet, "I knocked his rudder out! We got him where the hair grows short now, Jerry!"

Although it seemed that Fitzgerald was unable to steer his frigate any longer, he still had more than enough guns in action to keep us at a distance. We circled him like two dogs around a wounded but still dangerous bear. Every time we tried to close in, he opened with a fresh broadside. His masts were still intact. We took turns crossing his bow and lacing him with our broadsides, but even then his bow guns kept us at a respectful distance.

This went on for more than an hour. Cannon smoke lay over the water like an acrid bank of white fog. I was running low on ammunition. Besides the quartermaster, we had three other men dead or near death and a dozen too wounded for more action. I had no idea what casualties Lovejoy had suffered, nor for that matter Fitzgerald.

We drew our vessels off and conferred. I was all for leaving well enough alone and limping on to Statia. After all, I had something to live for back in Philadelphia. But Lovejoy's blood was up. He had learned to hate Fitzgerald worse than I did because of his treatment en route to Portsmouth after the destruction of the *Charlotte*.

"We've got him down. Let's not quit now. You always said you'd like to capture a British man-of-war. When will you have a better chance?"

"Well, he's not beaten until he thinks he is. Let's offer him the chance to surrender."

I raised a white flag to signal that we wished to parley. At a similar sign from the frigate, I sailed the *Nannette* close to the *Revenge* and raised my trumpet to my lips.

"Ahoy, Fitzgerald! Is that you?"

"It is, Martin."

"Do you strike?"

"Why should I?"

"But you are beaten. Why prolong the slaughter?"

"We don't mind. Do you want to strike?"

"Don't be a fool. We have every advantage. Think of your men."

"I'll ask them." Then, turning his back toward me, he said something to his crew.

"No!" came the sound from a hundred British throats.

Down came the parley flag and before I realized what was hap-

316

pening, that son-of-a-bitch fired a broadside that I thought would blow the poor *Nannette* out of the water. The blast from the muzzles alone would have damaged a lesser vessel. And not one of those twelve cannonballs failed to find a mark in our hull. I put our helm over and ordered our mainsail raised again but was not fast enough to escape further punishment from a second and a third broadside.

Our main deck was littered with mutilated sailors and overturned cannon. We were lucky that our masts and rigging had escaped serious damage and that enough men remained in action for us to withdraw and survey our injuries. Suddenly, taking the *Revenge* was out of the question. We would do well to get the injured *Nannette* into port.

Then to my amazement, the frigate suddenly got underway once more. She turned through the eye of the wind and began heading for us yet again. There wasn't a goddamned thing wrong with her rudder. Fitzgerald had decoyed us. Once more we had become the hunted.

Lovejoy recognized what had happened as well as I did. He sailed in close and yelled for me to "throw your guns overboard and get to Statia. I'll hang back and keep him busy."

We had to work furiously to tumble our lovely cannon over the side. By so doing, we rid ourselves of several tons of dead weight. But the sorrow I felt at giving up our weapons was nothing like what I experienced at the sight of our mangled men and the sound of their anguished cries. Every hand was needed to bind up the wounded and to sail the ship. Our dead were simply stretched out on deck and covered with a tarpaulin.

Thanks to Lovejoy, Fitzgerald never got close enough to the defenseless *Nannette* to inflict further punishment. Like a small, agile boxer pitted against a stronger but clumsier opponent, the *Grayhound* crossed first in front of and then behind the *Revenge*, each time firing one or two broadsides into bow or stern.

Meanwhile, the *Nannette* drew farther and farther away. We zigzagged toward Statia and safety. When I saw how much faster we were without our cannon and balls, I kicked myself for not dumping them all overboard at the outset.

Just before the sun went down, I surveyed the scene behind us from our crow's nest. Far behind us, the *Grayhound* was still tormenting our pursuer. The sounds of cannonfire continued past nightfall.

2

I USED the last of our cannonballs as weights to sink the canvas-shrouded bodies of my ten slain crewmen. We expended the last ounces of our energy to scrape the blood-soaked sand from our decks and clear away the worst of the wreckage. Miraculously, our masts had been only grazed by the *Revenge*'s twelve-pounders, so we made moderately good time throughout the night, tacking against a stiff breeze from the southeast.

Sleep was impossible for me. Reinforced with cup after cup of strong coffee, I shuttled back and forth throughout the night between the quarterdeck and the armory, which now served as surgery for our wounded, not stopping to change from my blood-spattered, sweat-drenched clothing. Thus I was too tired to think clearly as the sun appeared over the Quill on the horizon far to the east.

By the light of the dawning sun, I surveyed the western horizon, desperately hoping to see the *Grayhound*'s sails, but there was only empty sea.

Later in the morning as we approached Statia, I found nothing amiss. Far more ships were at anchor there than I had ever seen— like a forest of masts it was. I gave up counting the ships after reaching a hundred.

It was amazing that the place had so recovered from the great hurricane in only four months. There seemed to be as many warehouses as before. And the Dutch flag flew as reassuringly as ever over the fort atop the cliffs. A small cannon up there answered my salute.

I was concerned about Lovejoy and the *Grayhound,* of course, and nagged by remorse at the loss of so many of my crewmen. Yet I also felt a curious sort of triumph at having frustrated the attempt of my old nemesis, Captain Fitzgerald, to take me captive. No, more than that—we had fought him to a standstill. He had had to resort to a cheap trick to avoid defeat. Would Lovejoy show up with a surrendered *Revenge* in tow? After the performance of my loyal old seadog the day before, I ruled out no possibility.

At last we were anchored, and I went to my wrecked cabin to sluice the dried blood and sweat from my body and to don fresh clothing. A final visit with my wounded men with a generous ration of rum for all who wished it, and down I climbed into our ship's boat.

It was unusual that the ships past which we rowed were deserted and that none of them was flying flags. I was annoyed when I saw a crowd on the dock for which we were headed. I did not feel like talking to anyone. All I wanted to do was climb to the upper town, pay my respects to Abraham, and give him his family's messages. Perhaps he would let me sleep there for a few hours before returning to offer our cargo of lumber for sale.

It took a moment for me to realize that the crowd of bearded men gathered on the dock included many familiar faces. Where had I seen those same people in a group before? Of course—I had

318

observed them entering and leaving the synagogue up on the little
street where the d'Balboas lived. Why were some weeping while
others looked merely bewildered, as if unable to believe what was
happening to them?

Two trim, smooth-cheeked fellows in tight-fitting black coats approached me as I paused on the dock to get my land legs back. One
said in an English accent, "You came off that brig. Who are you?"

I ignored the pair as I searched the faces of the Jews.

"Abraham," I called. "Abraham d'Balboa. Where is he?"

"I say, fellow, did you not hear me ask you to identify yourself?"

"Over here, Jeremiah."

Abraham stepped out of the mass of his Jewish brethren and
held out his hands in a gesture that conveyed part supplication and
part resignation.

"What is happening here?" I asked.

One of the officious pair was tugging at my sleeve. "Your name
and place of registry, you scoundrel!"

"They have banished us," Abraham said. "They ordered all our
men to report down here. They have taken all our possessions, except the clothes on our backs. They are sending us off the island."

Now the ass in black took a firm hold on my wrist and said in an
arrogant voice, "Damn it man, answer my question!"

I jerked my arm free. "Who is sending you away? Surely not the
Dutch?"

"Here, you miserable Jew, get back where you belong. Now
again, sir, identify yourself."

"Who is doing this, Abraham?"

"The British. They have captured Statia."

The other official advanced upon Abraham and shoved him so
hard that he fell at the feet of his co-religionists. His partner
stepped in front of me and seized my lapels.

"You heard the Jew. We have declared war on the Dutch. This
island is in our hands."

I have dealt more than my share of hearty blows in my time, but
none gave me more satisfaction than the one I laid against the chin
of that pipsqueak of an English ensign (as he turned out to be). I
hit him so hard, I swear his feet actually left the dock and he flew
through the air and into the clump of huddled Jews. Instead of falling upon me, his mate ran off bleating "Guards! Guards!"

I helped Abraham to his feet.

"Oh, Jeremiah, you should not have done that. There is nothing
you can do to help us. And you have put yourself in jeopardy. But
quick, before they come, how are my wife and daughter?"

"They are in good hands with Dogood Mackey. Here, I brought
letters from them. But tell me what happened here."

"Two days ago, an entire fleet of British warships—at least

319

twenty—sailed in with no warning. It was impossible to withstand them. The governor surrendered without a fight. They have put hundreds of soldiers ashore."

"I see no soldiers. Where are their warships?"

"The soldiers are off in the countryside rounding up American sailors. They sent off many of their ships to try to catch a convoy that departed for Europe just a few days ago. Their other ships are anchored close into shore, disguised as best they can. They continue to fly the Dutch flag as a lure."

There came a squad of British soldiers led by a red-faced lieutenant, who shouted, "What the hell is going on here? If you Jews are making trouble, I'll have the lot of you flogged."

They led me off to a warehouse and into the presence of a gray-haired man who was wearing the uniform of a British major general and sitting behind a table. The officer who had arrested me bent over and whispered to him.

"Well, fellow, you have assaulted a naval officer and resisted arrest. Now you can identify yourself of your own free will or have it flogged out of you."

I told him my name and that of my ship and asked, "And you, sir. Who are you?"

The lieutenant stuck his face close to mine. "Don't be impudent to General Vaughan."

As if he had not heard, the general asked, "And you have been operating under a letter of marque?"

"Issued by Benjamin Franklin, yes. I own a half interest in the brig."

"You did own a half interest. Your vessel is now the property of the British Crown. It will be auctioned off with all the other vessels we have captured and, yes, all the goods that were stored here."

It dawned on me that all the great wealth I had accumulated and left in Abraham's hands was gone, and with it the *Nannette*.

My knees suddenly felt very weak. My head swam.

"What cargo did you bring us?" General Vaughan was asking.

"Lumber, mostly."

"Good. It is much in demand on Barbados and other islands that were damaged by the hurricane last October. How many cannon do you carry?"

"None."

"Come now. You must be armed."

"We dumped them overboard to avoid capture by a British cruiser."

"Oh, this is a grand joke. I must tell Admiral Rodney your story. Dumped his guns overboard to get away, only to find—"

"That's him! That's the blackguard that struck me!"

Holding his swollen jaw, the ensign from the dock staggered across the room toward General Vaughan's table.

"He's the one. He's broken my jaw. I demand that he be flogged!"

My lack of sleep and the shock of losing all that I had schemed for and worked for caught up with me. General Vaughan was saying something that I could not understand. The naval officer in civilian clothing was gesticulating in my direction. It was very hot in that warehouse. The faces before me became blurred. The room began to spin. I felt myself slump down into a dark whirlpool.

When I recovered my senses, I was stretched out on a bench in a narrow room with a high ceiling. A gallery ran across one end of the room. The other was occupied by an altar. All about me stood men in nautical garb. They were speaking with American accents.

"Where am I?"

A nut-brown face bent over me. "Where are you? They've jammed us into this Jewish church. I'd give you a drink, but the British scum have left us nothing. Here now, don't sit up so fast. My name is Wise. I'm off the *Enterprise*, out of Boston. Who are you?"

I sat up and told him who I was, and he introduced me to several others, who in turn informed me of what had happened. But caught in port as they had been, without warning, they did not know the full story. Admiral Sir George Rodney, the British naval commander in the West Indies, had been notified that a state of war existed with the Dutch and was ordered to descend on St. Eustatius with his fleet of twenty men-of-war and an army of three thousand commanded by his crony General Vaughan. Governor de Graaff had heard nothing of the declaration of war until the sea off his island was suddenly swarming with British warships. He was given only minutes to surrender or be subjected to bombardment. The commander of a Dutch frigate in the harbor asked for permission to make a ceremonial resistance. After giving and receiving a broadside-or two as a salve to his honor, he lowered his flag and de Graaff his, which the British promptly ran up again.

All told there had been more than two thousand American sailors and merchants on the island. Many of the sailors withdrew to the countryside with arms but were quickly overawed by Vaughan's professional soldiers. Now they were being jammed into makeshift prisons such as this synagogue.

The Jews of Statia were given special treatment. Every man of their community had been ordered to report to the dock with all his money and jewels, which were promptly taken from them. Their wives and children were allowed to remain in their homes, but the men were to be transported from Statia. Only later did I discover the reason for this persecution.

I had learned my lesson about prison informers from my experience in Boston and now asked far more questions of my fellow prisoners than I answered. Throughout that day and the next, more

321

and more Americans were brought to the synagogue until there was barely room to stand. Twice a day, soldiers brought black slaves to serve us weevily bread and watery stew and to remove the tubs containing our body wastes.

There always is some measure of hope even in the worst of situations. My dream of returning to Philadelphia with enormous wealth had been shattered, but by the Almighty I still had some credit there with Dogood Mackey. And Gerta meant more to me than all the ships at Statia. The general opinion of my fellow prisoners was that we would be paroled, that there were too many of us to be packed off to prison. So, reasoned I, if I kept my mouth shut and did nothing to call attention to myself, I would be treated like everyone else.

My anonymity ended dramatically about a week after my capture. I was awakened from a doze by a great English voice bellowing, "Jeremiah Martin! Where is Captain Jeremiah Martin?"

Bewildered, with every eye on me, I arose from my spot against the altar to see who was summoning me. Standing in the door was the lieutenant who had arrested me after I struck the ensign.

"Who wants me?"

"General Vaughan has sent me to escort you to the headquarters of Admiral Rodney. Why do you hang back, man? I should think you'd be happy to get out of this stinking hole."

3

As I FOLLOWED the captain through the upper town, I wondered what was in store for me. Surely the least punishment they would mete out for striking a naval officer would be a flogging. But would they hale me before an admiral for that? They must have learned all about me, including my suspended sentence and my escape from Forton, and meant to hang me.

Admiral Rodney had taken possession of Governor de Graaf's old house overlooking the anchorage. I was led into the downstairs office, now occupied by British army officers, and then up the steps to the same large room in which I had presented de Graaf with Dogood Mackey's letter for his predecessor. General Vaughan was standing in the doorway leading to the second floor veranda.

"Ah, there you are," he said. Then he turned to address a little man who was standing on the veranda with a spyglass aimed to sea.

"Here he is, Admiral."

"Who?"

"That fellow Martin."

"Wait. I want to make sure about this bark coming into harbor. By heavens, we have caught ourselves another one! There, she re-

322

turns our salute. Dips her flag. 'Come into my parlor, said the spider to the fly.' "

He limped into the room, and I noticed that one of his feet was wrapped in linen bandages. He was a slender man of about sixty, almost effeminate in appearance, with an elfin face and a high-pitched, self-assured voice. He slid into a chair and propped his bandaged foot on a stool.

"Sir Francis said you were a stout fellow. And impetuous as well."

"You know Bolton?" I said.

"More than forty years. I have no better friend. I spent much time with him at Bolton Hall just last month. He gave me particular instructions to look out for you and your Jewish friends."

"Well, sir, you have got me now, but I can't say that I admire your methods."

"What do you mean?"

"Flying a false flag. Taking the property of private citizens. Banishing a religious group en masse."

"Pish tish. You wish to quibble. Sit ye down, sir. As you seem to be Sir Francis's friend, I shall pay you the compliment of explaining."

Since I was anxious to hear what he had to say, I bit my tongue to keep from protesting that Bolton was no friend of mine.

"All's fair in love or war, they say. My little subterfuge is nothing compared to what has been perpetrated on this supposedly neutral place for the past five years by Jews and Dutchmen and, sad to say, English planters as well. This rock of only six miles in length and three in breadth has done England more harm than all the arms of our most potent enemies. This place alone has supported the infamous rebellion of our American colonies."

"But surely there are rules to be observed in war?"

"Against a nest of vipers, a nest of villains? Nonsense! They deserve scourging, and they are being scourged."

General Vaughan broke in. "They are that. And we have brought about this conquest without losing a man."

"Indeed, so. You may not have heard of me, young man, but I have served my sovereign in war and peace since I was a lad of thirteen. I commanded a ship at our great victory over the French at Ushant in '47. Aided in the capture of Louisburg in '58. In '59 I broke up a French fleet preparing to invade England."

"Don't forget Gibraltar," Vaughan said.

"Quite so. Just a year ago, on my way out here, I lifted the Spanish seige of Gibraltar. But"—he removed his gouty foot from its stool and leaned that strangely feline face toward me— "never in the annals of warfare has there ever been a more important stroke made against any state whatever than this blow made here by General Vaughan and myself."

He drew himself up and pointed out the window.

"The riches of this place are beyond all comprehension. We caught 130 sail of ships in the road out there. All the magazines and storehouses of this place were filled. Even the beaches were covered with tobacco and sugar, worth tens of thousands of pounds sterling."

"And the convoy," said Vaughan. "Tell him about the convoy."

"Quite so. If you look closely at the anchorage, you will see that the number of ships has been increased far beyond those I found when I descended upon this place like a thunderclap. They had just sent twenty-three fully loaded merchantmen off under the protection of a Dutch man-of-war. I sent a squadron scrambling after them. We overcame the warship and brought both shepherd and sheep back here to be added to our loot. And at least a dozen American craft, vessels such as yours, have blundered into our trap." He paused as if to gauge my reaction and added, "Also, one British frigate came into the anchorage but yesterday. She is the *Revenge*, commanded by Captain Atticus Fitzgerald. Is the name familiar to you?"

"I know Captain Fitzgerald," I said numbly.

"He came in yesterday. Rather the worse for wear, I would say. He saw your ship anchored here. What's her name?"

"The *Nannette*," I said with sinking heart.

"Quite. He has been making rather a fuss about you. Wishes you to be brought forward for hanging."

"Did he say what happened to the schooner with which he was engaged?"

"He can tell you himself. I have sent word for him to come here. Wished to talk to you first myself."

"Another fellow has been asking about you, too," Vaughan said. "From Barbados. Says he is an agent of Sir Francis Bolton."

Admiral Rodney's expression made me think of a cat playing with a mouse as he asked the general to bring them both here.

After Vaughan had clumped down the stairs, the admiral stared at me as if collecting his thoughts. At last, as I began to fidget under his glittering eyes, he said, "You know, of course, that the game is up for the American rebels. Oh yes, we have crushed the head of the viper here on this island. Without supplies and with Cornwallis unleashed in the southern colonies, the rebellion is doomed. I am pleased that the Almighty has made me the instrument of victory."

The more the man talked, the more I thought him mad. His eyes shone as he raved about his plunder, about his determination to auction off the ships and European goods. He would raze all the commercial buildings and send the lumber to rebuild the British colonies still in ruins from the hurricane. He was ranting about what he called "the perfidy" of English planters and merchants who had been dealing with St. Eustatius "under the table" when General Vaughan re-entered the room, followed by Atticus Fitzgerald and, fatter than ever, Reuben Halbertson.

Halbertson bowed to Rodney, congratulated him on his "stunning victory," and without glancing at me, accepted Vaughan's offer of a chair in the corner, out of my sight.

Fitzgerald's left arm was in a sling. Admiral Rodney returned his salute and said, "Stand at ease, sir, and say what you wish about this Jeremiah Martin."

I imagine that those next few minutes brought Atticus Fitzgerald exquisite plesure. On and on he droned about my deceit in the matter of the *Charlotte* and about his pursuit, which had ended in Delaware Bay. Now and then his emotions slipped away from him and his voice quivered, but in the main he delivered his charges so tediously that Rodney began to fidget. Finally he interrupted to say, "Well now, such a lot of fuss about one privateer when we have taken 130 vessels at one swoop. The man was operating under a letter of marque."

"Begging your pardon, sir, I have devoted the last four years of my life to bringing this scoundrel to justice. I rejoined His Majesty's service to accomplish my purpose. For months I have lain in wait to intercept him."

"Well and good. He has served a worthy end in that respect. I hear that while waiting to take your vengeance on this fellow, you captured more than a few rebel craft."

"But none means as much as seeing this one hanged."

"I admire your singleness of purpose. Is there anything you wish to say, Martin?"

"What happened to the *Grayhound*?" I asked.

At last Fitzgerald was to have his revenge. His lip curled in a sneering smile.

"The fool lay alongside and tried to board me at night."

Suddenly, Rodney seemed no longer bored. "Is that how you lost your mast?" he asked.

"Yes, sir. But I had already shot away his. Instead of striking, he grappled us. Refused to give up."

"You brought no such prize into port," Rodney said.

"It was beyond salvage."

"The crew!" I cried. "What about them?"

"Not a man left alive and unwounded."

"The captain, Lovejoy Brown. What about him?"

"That lunatic! He leaped over our rail and made for me with a pistol in each hand. Shot me in the arm. One of my bosuns cut him down. We buried the fool at sea with the others."

I sat down and through my fog of grief heard Rodney try to dismiss Fitzgerald.

"Surely he will be hanged," the little bastard said.

"He may be, but it is not for you to decide. Now, I do thank you."

Fitzgerald paused in front of me and said between gritted teeth, "I only wish it had been you instead of that Brown chap."

"I do, too," I replied.

"Now you, Mr. Halbertson," Rodney said after Fitzgerald had departed. "What is your business?"

"With all respect, sir, I should prefer that we speak in private. I ask this on behalf of my employer."

"How can I deny any request of Sir Francis? Vaughan, would you remove our prisoner? No, don't return him to the synagogue. Put him in our basement cell. Allow the fellow to bathe. See that he has a comfortable bed. He seems much distressed and weary of spirit. Now then, Halbertson, what have you to say?"

Numb with grief over the death of Lovejoy Brown, I remained in my cell for two weeks. Neither Halbertson nor Fitzgerald bothered me. From my barred window I noted a stream of men walking about the upper town, and I heard a constant tramp of feet over my head in the main office of the de Graaf house.

One of my jailers, a British sergeant, told me of preparations for a great auction. "They have come from everywhere. Wish I had a thousand pounds of me own. There's grand bargains to be had."

He told me, too, with unbecoming glee, that he and his fellow soldiers had ransacked the houses and offices of St. Eustatius looking for gold and jewels.

"Even had us dig up the coffin of a Jew that died the day we came."

"Did you find anything?"

"No, but we got eight thousand pounds off the lot of them down in the weigh house. They were trying to sneak the money off the island."

"What will happen to the proceeds of the sale?"

"Some says it belongs by right to the King, and others says no, it is to be divided between the army and the navy. One thing, sure, none of it will get into the pockets of enlisted men such as myself. No, I reckon old Rodney will get his full share."

Later, the same sergeant described the pandemonium that took place in the lower town as a mass of greedy buyers followed the auctioneers from warehouse to warehouse.

"The stuff didn't bring a quarter of what it would have sold for otherwise. Just too much stock and not enough buyers."

"Who were the buyers?"

"Lots of them planters from St. Kitts and such places, or their agents. And there was more than a few Americans there, claiming to be King's men, but Americans just the same."

Each day, that same sergeant let me out of my cell to exercise in the yard beside Rodney's headquarters. By then I had been supplied with fresh clothing and, of course, was better than well rested, at least in body. Early one morning I was taking in the air as a group of American prisoners, under guard, passed along the street.

"Look there, who it is," one of them called. "It's the turncoat himself. Hey, Martin, you Tory dog! We heard all about you."

"Heard what?" I shouted.

"You claim to be an American privateer. You're nothing but a British informer."

"You there, guard!" a voice, unmistakably that of Admiral Rodney, called down from the veranda. "The next one of those prisoners who speaks so is to be taken off parole and put back in prison. I will not have Captain Martin treated with disrespect in my hearing."

I was too stunned to protest. As the Americans marched on toward the path leading to the lower town, I longed to shout out my innocence of Rodney's implication.

"Admiral, where are those men going?" I called up to him.

He leaned over the rail of his veranda. "To Philadelphia. They are being paroled."

"I should very much like to go with them."

"That is impossible."

"Am I not as eligible for parole as they?"

"Yours is a special case, my dear fellow. It calls for a special parole."

"A special parole, back to Philadelphia?"

"No, not Philadelphia. To Barbados. Sir Francis wishes you sent there under special parole to him."

"No, no!" I cried. "Not to Barbados. Philadelphia, please! I will post any bond you ask."

His response was to leave the veranda and close the door behind him.

4

THREE DAYS LATER the same army lieutenant who had led me into captivity in the synagogue arrived with two burly privates. They bound my wrists and escorted me down to a dock, where Reuben Halbertson waited under a huge parasol like a toad beneath a toadstool.

"You blackguard," I said. "Was this your idea?"

"It was the old man's. I would have sent you directly back to Portsmouth to be hanged, as you deserve. That is the last word to pass between us. Take him aboard."

The lieutenant, Rollins by name, and his two soldiers accompanied me in a rowboat out to a large, beautifully crafted sloop. The name *Charlotte* was embazoned across her stern, and a figurehead of a young woman adorned her bow. Rollins informed me that he and the guards were to accompany me to Barbados. In fact, he shared the mate's cabin with me. Halbertson slept next door in the captain's cabin.

The captain of the sloop was a weather-seasoned Bermudian. He was as proud of the new *Charlotte* as Fitzgerald had been of the old. A good sailor, he brought us within sight of the northern headlands of Barbados in three days. During most of that time, I remained locked in the mate's cabin, alone with my grief at the loss of Lovejoy and my ships, with my apprehension at being hauled back into the presence of Bolton, and with my blighted hopes of rejoining Gerta in Philadelphia.

Halbertson did not deign even to look at me. But through the partition between our cabins, I overheard him boasting to the sloop's captain of the bargains in ships and produce he had purchased on behalf of Bolton. From scraps of these conversations, I gathered that Bolton, like other British planters, had carried on a considerable clandestine trade on Statia but, just before Rodney's arrival, had dispatched Halbertson to sell everything and deliver the proceeds back to Barbados. Then Halbertson had returned for the great auction in time to repurchase much of the same stuff at a quarter of the cost. And he had netted me as well. No wonder the man looked so pleased with himself.

Lieutenant Rollins, by contrast, talked rather too much for my taste, mostly about his conquests of dusky women in the Indies. He knew nothing about me except that he and his two soldiers had orders to deliver me into the hands of Bolton and "to await further orders" and that he had been warned I might be dangerous.

We dropped anchor off Speightstown. After Halbertson had been rowed ashore, the boat returned for me and my guards. It was shocking to observe the unrepaired damage from the hurricane. Many houses still lacked roofs. Trees remained where they had been felled by the mighty winds.

Halbertson hired a carriage for himself and set out for Bolton Hall, leaving Rollins and his men to transport me in an ox cart along a rutted road past washed-out fields and ruined plantation houses.

Half the great palms that had lined the lane to Bolton Hall were missing. A crew was at work replacing the arms on the windmill. Another crew was repairing the veranda of the great house.

Ibo waited in the yard. As I alighted from the ox cart, he took my hand and welcomed me back to Bolton Hall.

"I will go and tell him you are here," he said. Then he turned back to whisper, "Do not be shocked at his appearance."

During the half hour we were kept waiting, the overseer, Ramsey, rode up from the fields and sat on his horse, looking at me scornfully.

"So, Martin, they have brought you back. I tried to warn Sir Francis about you, but he wouldna heed me. Bombarded us with your cannon, you did. Tried to kill us. Sir Francis should treat you as we did that nigger Cato and sell you off to Jamaica."

Halbertson finally came out of the house and told Rollins to take me in "and stand by in the hall in case he becomes violent." Ibo was waiting at the foot of the stairs. He led us up to the second floor to a front corner bedroom and opened the door.

There he lay in an enormous oaken bed, propped on pillows with a lap desk across his knees. Despite Ibo's warning, I was shocked by the way he had shrunk—everything except his nose and chin, which appeared to have grown since I had last seen him. His skin looked waxen, but his jet-black eyes shone with the same intellectual intensity, and his hands still moved with that impatient energy.

We regarded each other, he with a look of triumph and I with a look of cold fear, like one brought before the judgment seat itself. I waited for him to speak, but he remained silent. Even though a fine breeze blew through the open windows, I broke into a sweat. Still he said nothing.

At last he lowered his eyes, took up a small piece of paper, dipped his pen in his inkwell, and wrote a note.

Ibo darted to his side.

"He has lost his voice," he said as he handed me the message.

So, I have you back at last.

I crumpled the paper and dropped it on the floor.

He wrote again.

You were a fool ever to think you could escape me.

Again, I crumpled the note.

You have done me great injury. Why should I not send you on to Portsmouth for hanging?

That was more than I could take.

"I have injured you?" I sputtered. "You mad old man, you have caused me more pain and sorrow than you will ever know."

He bent over his writing board again.

You defrauded me. Betrayed my trust.

"You deceived me. Sent me into Boston with messages written in code. Then your swine of an agent deliberately compromised me. Tried to turn me into a British spy."

I rescued you from prison.

"You saved me from one prison only to try to make me your prisoner. You are a manipulative, grasping, thoroughly corrupt and evil old scoundrel."

He wrote with amazing speed for one otherwise so feeble.

Who offered you a secure position, wealth, and influence? Yet you betrayed me by purloining my sloop.

"You got tangled in your own web of deceit. I paid the stipulated price for that sloop in gold. Your lawyer received the money and gave me a receipt."

You violated the spirit of our agreement. You turned my sloop into a private vessel preying on British trade. You deserve to be hanged.

"I am an American. Every prize was taken under a proper letter of marque."

He regarded me for a long time before he wrote again.

I understand that you have lost everything.

"If by everything you mean ships and money, perhaps so. I still have my integrity. I have the knowledge that I have served the cause of my country on sea and land with courage and honor. And I have the hope of marriage and family. You have vast money and cunning and influence—oh yes, it is plain that you derived great profits from your friend's expedition against St. Eustatius. But of what profit is it to own so much and to be without family or friends?"

"Please, young master," Ibo said.

Bolton motioned for Ibo to hush and wrote again.

Was that not a masterful stroke against St. Eustatius?

I nodded.

For the first time he smiled, then wrote again.

Like yourself, I have served my country. And like yourself, I have derived some modest benefit for my service. The difference is that I still have my profits.

I shrugged.

Why should I not send you on to Portsmouth to be hanged?

I was completely in his power. He could turn me over to Ramsey to be flogged or have me hanged as a pirate right there on Barbados. Yet he was not overtly threatening me. Nor was he holding out promises. What did he want of me? The satisfaction of seeing me cringe and beg for mercy?

"You will have to decide for yourself," I said in a low tone. "I will not grovel before one who has caused me so much anguish."

His pen scratched again, and Ibo handed me the note.

It has been a long contest, has it not?

"It was not a contest of my seeking."

And I have won, would you not say?

"I do not know how the contest should be scored. You have my corporeal person in your power. But you have not broken my spirit. You have amassed a fortune, while I have lost one. But there is a

330

greater contest that is far from decided. You waited too late to pounce on St. Eustatius. We can obtain all we need directly from France."

My discourse was interrupted as a fit of coughing bent the old man over his writing board. Ibo rushed foward with a towel to wipe the blood from his lips and then tenderly laid him back against his pillows.

As Bolton lay gasping, he motioned for me to be taken away.

At Halbertson's direction, Rollins and his men locked me in a tiny building made of coral blocks. It contained the drip, an arrangement of porous stone basins for cooling and collecting water condensation. It was dark in the little building, and I could not see out. Rollins left one of the soldiers on guard with instructions to let no one come near. I remained there the rest of that day and throughout the long night.

The next morning I was released and led into the kitchen for a meal served me by Ibo. He cleverly offered my guards a large breakfast at a separate table, giving him the opportunity to mutter to me.

"I have missed you. And Dr. McGee—the master has been very ill. Unable to speak these past three months. I was most distressed when we heard that you had been blown up with your sloop. And most overjoyed when word came that you had escaped."

"Ibo!" Halbertson called. "You have been forbidden to speak to him."

"I was only asking whether he wanted more coffee."

"Sir Francis wishes you to come to him immediately. Let the cook serve Mr. Martin."

It was late in the morning before I was ushered once more into the bedroom of Francis Bolton. As I entered, Ibo whispered, "Please don't agitate him. He is very tired. Was awake all night writing."

The old man did look exhausted. His eyes were not as alert as they had been the day before. He wore an expression almost benign as he wrote a note and handed it to Ibo, who read it and padded from the room.

We were alone. My wrists were bound, but my hands were free enough. I walked over and stood beside his bed. He looked up at me first as though amused and then with with eyebrows raised. I held my hands out. It would be so simple to lean forward and give that wizened neck one powerful squeeze.

I waited for some show of alarm. He stared back at me. I had long minutes of time in which to do it. If a hangman's noose awaited me in Portsmouth anyway, why not?

Ibo's voice sounded from the stairs, speaking to someone on the first floor. The moment had passed. I lowered my hands.

The old man smiled and touched one of my hands with his fingertips. I stepped away from the bed as Ibo entered the room.

He was carrying a portrait of a woman in her thirties. Bolton mentioned for Ibo to hold it in the light from the window. The woman had long chestnut hair. Only a longish nose stopped her short of beauty. Her eyes, of a clear grayish blue, seemed to follow me as I walked around the foot of the bed for a closer look.

Bolton's pen scratched away. He held out the note for me.

My grandmother. Her name was Charlotte Foxley. She reared me. Look at her closely. Remember her face.

"You named your sloop for her," I said.

He nodded.

"That is why you have borne me such a grudge?"

He shook his head.

Suddenly a fresh fit of coughing racked his body. He waved for me to leave. I withdrew from his room, never to set eyes on him again.

5

ON MY FIRST VISIT to Bolton Hall, nearly six years ago, I rode up in style from Bridgetown in a carriage, accompanied by Ephraim and Ibo. The afternoon after my last interview with Sir Francis, with a soldier on either side and Rollins and Halbertson facing me, I was taken as a prisoner in the same carriage back down past lush fields of cane here to Bridgetown.

As Rollins rattled on and on to Halbertson about the British coup in seizing St. Eustatius, my mind went back and forth over my situation. Bolton, feeble as he was in body, was taking his revenge on me. He had won. I assumed that they would ship me directly back to Portsmouth for hanging.

So downcast was I that even Rollins's mention of the great American victory over the British at the Cowpens in South Carolina last January did not improve my spirits. Halbertson shushed Rollins. Only later did I learn more about how General Daniel Morgan, with a mixed force of Continentals and militia, nearly wiped out a contingent of one thousand British regulars under Tarleton.

Thus was I delivered in grand style here to the Town Hall Gaol in the center of Bridgetown. The basement of this massive two-and-a-half-story stone building today teems with Americans and Frenchmen captured aboard privateers, but I am not allowed to mix with them. Instead, they have shut me up in this private cell on the top floor these past six months.

Between me and my fellow Americans lie two floors occupied by courtrooms and various government offices. Except for the barred windows and door and the guard always on duty in the hall, it might be a room in a pleasant inn. I have a narrow but comfortable bed. There are two chairs and a small writing table. I have a good view of Carlisle Bay. The food is edible, just. Rollins and his two soldiers allow me to exercise in the courtyard each morning and afternoon. Thus have I passed half a year, not knowing what is happening to Gerta back in Philadelphia, speculating about what people back there think about the preferential treatment seemingly given me at St. Eustatius, mourning my lost shipmates, and wondering whether I shall be hanged. Thank God for the occupation afforded me by the writing of this account. Otherwise I should have gone mad by now.

As I have noted, I last saw the architect of all my difficulties, Sir Francis Bolton, in his bedroom that morning last April. I left him in a paroxysm of coughing. Feeling the deepest contempt rather than sympathy for him, I was removed from his presence and brought here.

I was in this prison but a week when I wondered at the tolling of bells from nearby St. Michael's Church. Rollins explained the reason when he came that evening to supervise my exercise.

"Didn't you hear? Sir Francis Bolton. He died this morning."

I tried to summon some sadness at this news. None came. That man went to extraordinary lengths to entrap me in his web of deceit and intrigue. He had wanted to own me as a sort of cat's paw for his greedy enterprises. Why should I shed tears at the news of his death? I only wonder whether his demise might affect my fate at the hands of British justice.

Halbertson came the next day. He was wearing a black armband and an expression of the deepest woe.

"Have you heard?"

"About Bolton. Yes."

"He was like a father to me."

"Not, I fear, to me."

"Say naught against him, Jeremiah. You never knew him as I did."

"Oh, it is Jeremiah again? As for Bolton, I knew him well enough. What do you want anyway, Halbertson?"

"Simply to tell you that although I do not know what fate may await you, I bear you no ill will."

"I cannot say the same for you."

"To know all is to forgive all. I have been forced by unusual circumstances to do many things that went against my natural inclinations."

"Your good wishes come rather late to be of much help to me."

"I am serious. Whatever the outcome of this war or the case against you, you must not regard me as your enemy."

"I would hope not to regard you at all. Have you anything else to say to me?"

"Only to ask if there is aught I can do for you."

"I would like to be set free, or failing that, to be brought to trial promptly and be given proper legal representation."

"That is in the hands of the authorities."

"Then how about a supply of paper, a pen, and ink? Is that asking too much?"

"I will see what I can do."

Through the bars of my window the next day, I watched the funeral procession of Francis Bolton as it passed along James Street in front of the prison and turned down High Street on the way to St. Michael's. A military band, playing doleful marches, led the way. The funeral coach was followed by a vast entourage, including the governor of the island, Halbertson, and Ibo. A contingent of British sailors and soldiers brought up the rear.

It struck me as ironic that this anemic little man, who I am convinced loved no one, who indeed despised his fellow human beings, that such an uncaring manipulator as he should be laid to rest with so much pomp.

It has been quite a contest between us, one that still continues, for although he is dead and I am alive, even from the grave he controls my fate, I fear.

Halbertson came back two days later with my writing materials and more news.

"A sloop just arrived from Wilmington. There has been another great battle."

"Indeed?"

"Yes. On March 15 at a place called Guilford Courthouse, in North Carolina, between Cornwallis and an American army under Nathanael Greene."

"Who won?"

"We drove the rebels from the field, but at a heavy loss to ourselves."

"That sounds like Bunker Hill."

"Yes, both armies retreated, Greene into Virginia and Cornwallis east to the coast. The talk is that we can afford no more of these Pyhrric victories. Everything now depends on our navy."

I looked hard at Halbertson, wondering what had caused him to become not only more communicative but even ingratiating.

"It has been a long war," I said.

"And, I fear, a foolish one."

Halbertson stood in silence so long outside my cell that I became impatient. Already I had begun to formulate how I should write this memoir, and I wanted to get started.

"Thank you for the paper," I said. "Is there something else?"

"Sir Francis did not die an easy death, you know."

"I did not know it, but am not surprised."

"Yes. It was cancer of the throat. He could not speak the last few months of his life, but he did much writing, right up to the time of his final hemorrhage. He left many instructions."

"Were there any concerning me?"

"As a matter of fact, yes. I am to sail tomorrow for England. Among my missions, I am to bring back the records of your trial on piracy charges."

"I had assumed that I would be shipped back to Portsmouth for trial."

"You will be tried, but here in Bridgetown."

And here in Bridgetown in this cell I have remained ever since. Rollins keeps me up to date on the news of the war. A large American militia force recaptured Augusta and took several hundred Tory prisoners in June. The British have retreated to Charleston after another battle, at Eutaw Springs. Cornwallis has moved his army up into Virginia. I am allowed neither to dispatch nor to receive letters, but I do get the local newspaper and have a few books. I have spent most of my daylight hours scribbling this account of all that has happened to me since that fateful early morning of April 19, 1775, when my drunken sleep in Buckman's barn at Lexington was interrupted by the rattle of drums and the tramp of booted British feet.

My nights are spent dreaming of Gerta. I pray that she remains with her two children at Ephraim's house, that she has not fallen ill or, God forbid, remarried. I fret, too, over something that Rollins told me when I told him I wished that the British would either hang me or send me back to Philadelphia.

"I should think it would be a hard choice either way."

Upon my demand for an explanation, he replied, "Oh, didn't you know? That lot of American privateers we shipped off Statia, they were uttering all sorts of threats against you. Halbertson told them you were a turncoat. They saw you removed from that Jew church and kept in Admiral Rodney's own headquarters. By now I shouldn't think you'd have much of a reputation to go back to."

When Halbertson returns from England, I shall demand an explanation for this poisoning of my reputation amongst my countrymen. It must have been part of Bolton's scheme to entrap me. Any day now Halbertson should return with the records of my trial. I must set aside my scribbling and use the time remaining to prepare my defense, futile though the effort may be.

Jeremiah Martin, Town Hall Gaol, Bridgetown—Oct. 30, 1781

Epilogue

I have spent the last two days reading over what I wrote in Bridgetown's Town Hall Gaol. Imperfect though it be, I will let the narrative stand as it is and use the time remaining aboard ship to bring my story up to date. Once ashore, there will be little opportunity for reminiscence.

As it turned out, back in Bridgetown I had no time to prepare my defense.

"Good luck to you, Mr. Martin," Rollins said to me one evening as I completed my walk around the courtyard.

"Good luck at what?" I asked.

"On your hearing tomorrow. Didn't you know? You're to be brought before an admiralty court in the morning. Halbertson has returned with your records."

"Someone might have told me," I said.

"I just did. My orders are to bring you down to the courtroom on the first floor at ten o'clock tomorrow morning."

My original trial at the Royal Navy Yard in Portsmouth had been a mockery. My second hearing in Bridgetown was an equally rigged proceeding, but with some surprising and important differences.

I stood while a red-faced judge, sweat running from under his wig, listened to a pompous little prosecutor recite the old charge of piracy on the high seas and a new one of escaping from prison. I was prepared to put up a spirited fight.

At the conclusion of the charges, the judge said "and how does the prisoner plead?" But before I could respond, a lean, aristocratic-looking man sitting behind me in robe and wig spoke in a voice that rang with assurance and authority, "We plead innocent on all counts."

"And who are you, sir?"

"I am Archibald Foxley, of Lincoln's Inns, London, and I have been retained to represent Mr. Martin."

This stranger was one of the tallest men I ever saw, with a thin, beaked nose and a flushed complexion. In a few minutes he took command of the courtroom. Several times I was at the point of protesting that I had hired no lawyer, that this man was unknown to me, and that I was capable of defending myself. But, fascinated by the effortless way in which this distinguished barrister—as I was to learn that he is—took charge, I wisely remained silent.

Each time the prosecutor, a fussy, fat fellow who looked as if nothing ever pleased him, tried to make a point, this Foxley countered with an air of disdain. At length I heard him say, "We move for dismissal of all charges against my client."

"On what grounds?" the judge asked.

"On the grounds that Mr. Martin was found guilty on misleading and insufficient evidence in his Portsmouth trial."

The judge groaned. The prosecutor protested that it was out of the question for me to be granted a new trial. "The fellow is here on fresh charges of escaping from prison and continuing to prey on His Majesty's shipping."

"May it please the court," my mysterious defender said, "we do not wish the case against Mr. Martin to be retried. We wish only to enter into the record a deposition and leave it to your honor to decide whether my client's several months in Forton Prison are not more than sufficient punishment for whatever errors of judgment he may have committed."

"What deposition is this?" the judge asked.

"May it please the court, it is a deposition in the handwriting of the late Sir Francis Bolton of St. James Parish, Barbados, witnessed by none other than His Excellency, Major General James Cunninghame, Royal Governor of Barbados."

I nearly fell off my chair. My amazement continued as the judge overruled the protests of the prosecutor and read silently and at an agonizingly slow pace a document of no more than two or three pages.

At last he looked up and removed his spectacles.

"This is a most unusual deposition."

Now the prosecutor was on his feet demanding to see the paper. He read it at a furious rate and then stammered in outrage, "Preposterous! There was sworn testimony that he stole the sloop."

"There it is in plain words," Foxley drawled. "My client had an option to buy the craft, and he exercised that option, paying the purchase price in gold."

"But," sputtered the prosecutor, "the man is an American! He has never denied that he was a rebel privateer. It is all in the record of his trial."

Acting as if the prosecutor no longer existed, Foxley approached the bench. "May it please the court, I wish to present yet another document in evidence. This paper, you will observe, is a parole from Admiral Sir George Brydges Rodney, the hero of St. Eustatius, releasing Mr. Martin into the custody of Sir Francis Bolton. And you will see that the admiral has added a note expressing his appreciation for the cooperation of my client."

I opened my mouth to protest, but a single piercing look from Foxley silenced me.

"May it please the court," Foxley said after the judge had finished his scrutiny of this paper and had handed it to a now throughly deflated prosecutor, "this war with our American colonies is no simple affair. Intrigue plays a vital part in our struggle. I could put my client on the witness stand to testify on his own behalf, but I think it

337

would ill serve our sovereign or our cause for him to reveal all that lies beneath the surface of this case. Suffice it to say that rather than jeopardize others and embarrass us in the presence of our national enemies, he chooses to remain silent and let the testimony of Sir Francis Bolton and Admiral Rodney speak on his behalf."

The enormity of the lies the barrister was telling stunned me. Every word that he uttered moved me closer not only to freedom from noose or prison cell but also to estrangement from my own people. Only thoughts of Gerta and her children constrained me from rising and shouting, "Lies! Lies! I was a privateer! I am no British agent. I have done all in my power to injure the British army and navy."

The proceedings ended with the judge ordering a recess until the next morning. Rollins led me back to my cell, my head swirling with the events of the hearing. I was sitting on the edge of my bed when Foxley, minus his robes and wig, appeared.

"So, Jeremiah Martin," he said.

"Who in the hell are you?" I said. "What was going on down in that courtroom?"

He laughed. "I do not wonder that you are confused. First, as you heard me identify myself, I am Archibald Foxley. Francis Bolton and I are distantly related—second cousins once removed, to be precise. I have represented him in many matters over the years, but none in so curious a case as this."

"But I did not retain you."

"No, I was retained by two different solicitors."

"I do not understand."

"Francis never left anything to chance. His agent, Halbertson, and the captain of his sloop, unbeknownst to each other, each had sealed instructions to be given to a different lawyer to be turned over to me."

"Why did no one consult with me in advance?"

"Francis left explicit instructions that you were to be brought into the hearing with no foreknowledge of your defense."

"What was his game? I despised that old man."

"I should speak more discreetly of my benefactor if I were you."

"He was not my benefactor, and you are not me. I am a privateer. I am a loyal American. You tried to make it appear that I was in the secret employ of Admiral Rodney. There are dozens of people who could come forward and testify to the contrary."

"But they are half a world away, are they not?"

"I do not want my freedom under such infamously false testimony. It will make difficulties for me at home. Already lies are being spread there concerning my loyalties. I would be compromised as a traitor worse than Benedict Arnold."

"Well then, return to that courtroom tomorrow and contradict all

338

that I said. Try to convince the judge that you really are a pirate and that you deserve hanging. If you wish to speak along that line, I will withdraw from the case and leave you either to hang or to be shut away as a lunatic. The choice is yours."

"Get out of my sight," I said.

He took from his pocket a thick sheaf of folded papers that bore impressive seals. He seemed about to hand the packet to me. But then, scrutinizing me as if trying to fathom my thoughts, he put it back in his pocket and said, "It is always a pleasure to quit the presence of a fool. Until tomorrow."

After a sleepless night, still in a state of befuddlement, I followed my guards back into the courtroom the next morning. I sat like a deaf-mute while the judge declared that the old charge of piracy would be reduced to one of privateering and that I should be paroled into the custody of Archibald Foxley until the end of the war.

Had the judge demanded that I renounce my allegiance to my native land, I would have rejected the parole. But it was not presented in such blatant terms. So I saw nothing wrong in giving assent by my silence nor in accepting Foxley's invitation to dine with him at the Bow Bells Tavern.

"You go along with Rollins, and I'll join you later."

For the first time in many months, I walked out into the open air without my arms being bound, a free man at last. No, not quite free—I had been paroled into Foxley's custody. And Rollins and his two soldiers accompanied me to the tavern and waited in the hall while I sat in a small private dining room.

I was baffled by the pains to which Francis Bolton had gone to employ a kinsman to win my freedom. But was this really freedom, being under guard? Something smelled here.

Bide your time, I told myself. At least you're not waiting to be hanged. Find out what their game is. Don't be rash.

Halbertson entered the room as I was quaffing a mug of ale.

"Congratulations, Jeremiah. We got you off. I am delighted."

I was about to lash out at him for spreading rumors about me to my fellow Americans when Archibald Foxley appeared, accompanied by a clerk carrying an armload of papers.

"You here, Halbertson? I left orders with Rollins that no one was to see Mr. Martin before I arrived."

"I thought you might require my presence."

"We do not. If we do, I will send a messenger for you."

Looking like a whipped mastiff, Halbertson withdrew his vast bulk from the room. Foxley, after dismissing his clerk and ordering us a light meal, got down to business.

"I have known Francis Bolton since I was a child," he said. "I must confess that I don't understand why my cousin has gone to such great trouble on your behalf."

"He has brought great trouble into my life."

"Be that as it may, here is a letter from Francis which I am charged with giving you to read. I was at the point of turning it over to you yesterday but decided to wait and see if you were stupid enough to refuse parole. It is a long letter with not one but three seals. I will withdraw while you read it. Then we will talk again, about yet another matter."

That letter was the most curious I ever I have read. I will let it speak for itself.

Bolton Hall,
St. James Parish,
March 15, 1781

Dear Jeremiah:

There is so very much I should like to say to you and so little time in which to say or write it. How I despise my mortality. If only this wretched ailment had waited a few more weeks, we might have talked out our differences and reached an understanding. But my voice has gone the way of all flesh, and the rest of my frame will follow all too soon.

This letter is intended to explain, not to apologise or berate. You stole my sloop, but I have never borne you a moment of ill will for your deception. Indeed, I must say I rather admired the way in which you brought it off. As you took pains to document, you did pay me in gold specie. I cherished my sloop, as I did my grandmother for whom it was named, but I am not so great a fool as to worship a mere sailing vessel.

While I admire your intrepid rescue of young McGee from under my very nose, it was boorish of you to later bombard my plantation from guns mounted on my own sloop. Still, I bear you no ill will for that, either. I was in England at the time, and the only damage was to an empty slave hut.

Fitzgerald was another matter. What a fool the man is. Halbertson thought himself mightily clever to enlist his grudge against you to carry out my wishes that you be brought back before me. I was exceedingly wroth when I learned that the idiot had caused my sloop to explode, ostensibly killing you, and then had taken your surviving crewmen off to England. I thought more kindly of him when I learned through my Philadelphia agents that you had survived. Do you not think it a clever stroke the way I enticed you into surrender? Always remember that. Find what your adversary prizes above all else, and use that as a lure.

It had been my intention to return to England back in '78 to save you at the last moment from the gallows, or anyway to make it seem so to you. But that was when I learned that what I thought was merely a frog in my throat was a crab, as it were, and, too weak to travel, I was forced to send Halbertson in my stead.

I should very much like to know how you escaped from Forton Prison and made your way to France. Halbertson claims no knowledge of how you did it. I have my own ideas on the subject, but they are beside the present point.

340

Here the color of the ink on the letter changes, and the handwriting appears shakier.

> This morning, when you stood threateningly at my bedside, my only fear was that you would cause your own destruction. For your sake, I am glad that you did not.
>
> You put it very well, I thought, when you said you did not know how the contest between us should be scored. Let me confess that I think you are right about the greater game being played out in the war between America and England. It is plain to me now that America will prevail. We ought never to have entered upon a war against so energetic and spirited a people.
>
> Had I been confident that a few more years of clear thought and good health were left to me, I would have let the game between us play itself out and approached you as one equal to another, but I am confounded by my mortality. I do not have the time to persuade you to become my ally. And I know you well enough to realize that the more I try to force you to my will, the more obdurate you will become. The only card I have left to play is to surrender to you. I shall instruct the only lawyer in whom I place any faith, one Archibald Foxley of London, as to the form my capitulation is to take. Trust him as do I, I implore you. He is our kinsman.
>
> Oh yes, I say "our kinsman."
>
> When we were introduced that Sunday afternoon at Franklin's house, I recognized only that you were a young man of mettle. It was only after your friend, Dr. McGee, told me more about you and your origins in Virginia that I began to piece together the puzzle of what force drew me to you. When we dined and you spoke of your great-grandfather and his Quaker background and his coming to Virginia from the West Indies as a physician, even then I thought it might be only a coincidence, but one that would bear investigation. Meanwhile, why not make some use of you?
>
> Are you mystified? Let me go back 117 years and tell you about my grandmother, Charlotte. She was the daughter of Sir Robert Foxley of Foxley Manor in Bedfordshire. In 1664 she was married to Sir Richard Bolton, the founder of Bolton Hall, and came here to live on his plantation. Twenty years her senior, he died while Charlotte was with child, and she subsequently wed a Dr. Higganbotham, by whom there was no issue. I am the son of her daughter, of whom the less is said the better, for she abandoned me at an early age and I was reared by my grandmother.
>
> Archibald Foxley is the great-great-grandson of Sir Robert Foxley, descended as he is from the older brother of Charlotte. Still, you must wonder why I say "our kinsman."
>
> I grew up reverencing my dear grandmother. Never was there a woman of stronger spirit or brighter intellect. Her first husband died when she was thirty and her second when she was fifty, and she not only ran Bolton Hall with a firm hand but made it into one of the most productive plantations on the island. She saw to my education herself until I was a precocious fifteen, at which time I was packed off to Cambridge and the care of my great-uncle in Bedford. An illness struck me soon after my arrival in England, an ill-

ness that stunted my physical development but that, if anything, stimulated that of my will and my mind.

Only after I had completed my education at Cambridge and returned to Barbados did I learn what I am about to relate.

Formerly so erect of posture and strong of constitution that she might have been taken for a far younger woman, my grandmother had turned into an enfeebled invalid. It appeared that she had kept herself alive only by sheer force of will until my return.

During the last week of her life, she called me to her bedside and made a confession, the memory of which still plagues me. I knew that I had been born out of wedlock and that my mother had run away with a Dutch sea captain before I was out of the cradle. But my grandmother told me there was more to the story than that— far, far more, as it turned out.

It seems that the same ship on which she and her husband, Sir Richard Bolton, came out to Barbados also carried Dr. Higganbotham, who was to become her second husband in time, and a strange sort of Quaker mystic and his young son from Bristol.

The Quaker's name was Moses Martin, and he had been exiled for preaching sedition against the Crown. The son's name was John. Mark that name well.

Moses Martin was indentured as a white servant. He died under unusual circumstances. He fell off a church roof while haranguing a group of militiamen, so my grandmother said. The lad was apprenticed to Dr. Higganbotham and, under his instruction, became a skillful doctor.

The man believed to have been my grandfather, Richard Bolton, was a forceful and respected leader who narrowly missed being appointed a governor of Barbados. Dr. Higganbotham, a fine gentleman by all accounts, worshipped my grandmother from afar. That is one reason I wished you to look closely at her portrait. I wanted you to see her as she was in those days, when three men—her husband, Dr. Higganbotham, and John Martin—each in his own way loved her deeply.

Yes, John Martin. He was several years younger than my grandmother. Dr. Higganbotham was a frequent guest at Bolton Hall, and he often brought along his young apprentice. While Richard Bolton was back in England to press his suit for the governorship, young Martin confessed to my grandmother that he was in love with her.

She said that she was flattered. He was a handsome young man, but she loved and honored her husband. So she rebuffed his advances. Later, during a period of unrest over a slave rebellion, there was a misunderstanding between herself and Richard Bolton, and it was then that John Martin, your great-grandfather, sired my mother.

Oh, it was never general knowledge. Dr. Higganbotham knew, but he was so smitten that he would have taken Charlotte to wife under any circumstances. At any rate, John Martin left Barbados for Virginia before my grandmother knew for a certainty that she bore a child, and also before she learned that her husband, due to

342

an early venereal infection, was incapable of fatherhood. Bolton died during the great hurricane of 1675. My mother was born six months later, and soon thereafter Charlotte married Dr. Higganbotham. She never heard again from John Martin.

After you and I met in Philadelphia in '75, I had inquiries made in Virginia and Bristol. In the latter place, I learned that John Martin had returned there from Virginia with a half-Indian wife in the 1680s. Quakers keep meticulous records, as you may know. Their visit is recorded in the minutes of their meeting.

Descendants of Moses Martin still live in Bristol, but they are persons of limited ambition, in no wise like you and me. I have not troubled myself to cultivate a relationship with them.

So there, you know as much of the story as I have strength to record. John Martin was my grandfather and your great-grandfather, which makes us first cousins once removed. I sensed the relationship after we had met in Philadelphia, but I could not corroborate it until after you came to Barbados and ran off with my sloop. Had Fitzgerald captured you, I would have told you the story then or when you were at Forton Prison, had my health permitted me to come to England.

Still, I have no regrets. I do not desire a maudlin sort of reconciliation. It is better this way. You know who I am now, and I you. We are more alike than you may care to admit. Damn this disability. It requires more strength than I possess to attend to all the details that require my attention, but for reasons that shall in time be made clear to you, it is imperative that your name be cleared by a British court.

In due course, Archibald will tell you why this is so. He has his instructions. He will know what is to be done. Meanwhile, it would be best for you to remain in custody.

I may at times have seemed to be your enemy. I was not. It may have seemed to you that we were engaged in a contest of wills. If it were a contest, then let you be declared the winner. It remains only for you to be informed of the prize for your victory.

Francis Bolton

I read the letter a second time, then called for Foxley and, without speaking, handed it to him.

When he had finished reading, he removed his spectacles and regarded me for a long while.

"This explains much that has puzzled me. Is there any doubt in your mind that what he has written is true?"

"I only know that I am descended from a Quaker physician named John Martin who came to Virginia over a century ago and who married the half-breed daughter of a Powhatan princess."

"It is most unlikely that there would be two such persons."

"I have heard it said that all of us are kin to one degree or another," I replied.

"It appears to be true in our case, Cousin Jeremiah."

"It is a touching story. Now that all this is cleared up, I should very much like to return to Philadelphia. There is a young woman there whom I wish to make my wife. And I have some business interests that require my attention."

"Not so fast, Jeremiah, I have yet another document from the hand of Francis Bolton. He charged me to reread it for you only after you read that amazing letter."

I felt my gorge rising.

"Another document? Another of his tricks, I suppose, to bend me to his will. All this business about our kinship is intriguing, but I am far more interested in returning to my native land. Am I never to be free of Francis Bolton? From the grave does he now offer me some bribe, or is it another threat to my life or happiness? Let me read the thing."

He drew a paper from his pocket. "May I close the door? Good. We must not be overheard, Jeremiah, I have here what purports to be Cousin Francis's last will and testament. It is one of the briefest and most unusual ever have I read. Pray listen."

In slow, deliberate tones, Foxley proceeded to read aloud. "I, Francis Bolton of Bolton Hall, St. James Parish, Barbados, being of sound body and mind, do hereby name Jeremiah Martin, native of the colony of Virginia and my closest living relative, to be the sole heir and beneficiary of my estate."

Thinking that Bolton was making me the butt of a final, cruel joke, I snatched the paper from Foxley's hand. Certainly the handwriting was that of Francis Bolton. Still, I could not believe it.

"This will was incomprehensible to me until I read that letter. Astounding. Well, there it is. Francis has made his wishes clear. Now, as his heir, you must be informed of his various holdings. This will take a while. I should like some tea. Will you join me?"

I was too dumbfounded to do more than nod. By the time Foxley finished his presentation, we had drunk three cups of tea each. My mind reeled with the details of the wealth that had been held by that strange little man. He owned various houses and other buildings in London. There was a majority interest in an insurance company, tin mines in Cornwall, one fleet of merchant vessels based in Bristol and another in London, an enormous portfolio of stock shares in various businesses, and a sheaf of promissory notes signed by many persons, including one by Admiral Rodney and another by General Gates. My mind could not take it all in. I looked up from the documents into the level gaze of Archibald Foxley.

"Is there anything, anybody he does not own?"

"These are only his holdings in the British Isles. They do not include Bolton Hall and other interests in Barbados. Nor his properties in America, which are sequestered under the names of other parties."

"I cannot believe that he wished to leave me everything. There must be a catch in all this."

"There is a condition attached, true."

"What condition?"

I nearly fell off my chair at his reply.

"You are required to remain on British soil."

It took a while for the offer to penetrate my thick skull. At first glance it seemed that to become one of the wealthiest men on either side of the Atlantic, all I had to do was—really, nothing. Merely accept my inheritance and remain in Barbados. But no, confound it, there was more involved than that. I would have to turn my back on my native land. Forget what I had witnessed at Lexington, what I had endured at British hands in that Boston prison. Put behind me the memories of Germantown and Valley Forge. Yes, and delay my reunion with Gerta at least until the end of the war.

It was entirely up to me, Foxley said. Even though I had been paroled into his custody, he would not interfere with my departure if I promised not to take up arms against the Crown again. But he could not delay probating the will much longer.

Foxley had many matters to attend to while in Barbados. He gave me three days to decide between a life as a wealthy British citizen or a life as an American with few worldly possessions.

He asked me if I required anything while I pondered my decision.

"It goes against my American grain to be kept under surveillance."

"Give me your word of honor that you will not flee, and I shall dismiss Rollins and his guards this very morning. What's more, you shall have the use of a horse. I have taken the liberty of booking you a room here at the Bow Bells."

"Thank you. As my bond, I will turn over this memoir, which I wrote to pass the time awaiting my trial. You are welcome to read it if you have time."

At the Bow Bells that night, I tossed and turned until dawn, then got up and without stopping for breakfast saddled my borrowed horse and rode up to Bolton Hall.

Ibo was overjoyed to see me.

"I wished so much to visit you in prison but was forbidden to do so."

"I understand. They did not treat me badly."

"And now you are free?"

"I am not sure."

Ibo listened with narrowed eyes while I told him of my dilemma.

"Most curious. I knew that the master held you in high esteem, but never did I dream that he would make you his sole heir. I do not understand why he would do such a thing."

Whereupon I let him read the letter from Sir Francis.

The nearer the end he read, the larger grew his eyes.

"This explains much that even I did not know," he said. "Poor, poor man."

"I am not asking for sympathy," I replied.

"Not you, the master. He was so lonely."

"He also was very crafty. He used people as if they were pawns in his strange games. Even now I can feel him trying to mold me to his will."

"Or by his will," Ibo said without smiling. Then he asked softly, "What will you do?"

"What do you think I should do?"

"It would give me enormous pleasure if you were to accept the inheritance and bring your Gerta and her children here. I should like that very much. But it is your happiness you must think of and not that of a poor African."

"You are one of the wisest men I have ever met, Ibo. I value your opinion. What would you do if you were in my shoes?"

"You flatter me. But suppose for a moment that I had a choice of returning to my homeland in Africa a free man or remaining here as heir of the master's estate. At my age, I would choose the latter without thinking twice. It is too late for me to return to my homeland. But it is not too late for you. Remember what I said to you that morning at the Bow Bells, as you were about to set out for America?"

"As I recall it you said, 'Do not let yourself be gelded by him or anyone else.' Correct?"

"Yes. It made you angry. Would you be angry if I repeated my advice?"

"You don't need to. I remember."

"Let me tell you another story. Have you noticed the spiders that inhabit this house and its grounds?"

"I can't say that I have."

"We have one called the golden spider because of the coloring of its legs and other parts of its body. If you walk about the yard, you will notice its webs in our torch thistle trees. I often have thought how like the golden spider the master was, always busy spinning webs and waiting, waiting to see what prey the blooms of the tree attracted. You seemed to be about to enmesh yourself in his web when you left aboard his sloop for Boston, but you eluded his capture. Now I see that the master was not seeking to entrap you. He wished to turn over mastery of his webs to you."

"I have never cared for spiders or their webs," I said.

"Quite. Perhaps my analogy is not a good one. It is a clearcut choice, I suppose, between love of wealth and love of your native land. On which do you place the higher value?"

I walked to the end of the veranda and gazed out over the cane fields down to the subtle greens and deep blues of the Caribbean. I thought for a long time.

At last I turned and took Ibo's hand.

"Many thanks for your wise counsel."

That very afternoon I sought out a haggard-looking Foxley and told him of my decision.

"I stayed up through the night reading your memoir," he said. "It is a remarkable story, like a novel by DeFoe. Your choice comes as no surprise. I would have been disappointed in you had it been otherwise."

There was a problem about transportation, however. Foxley solved it by having me sign a promissory note for ten thousand pounds made out to the estate of the late Francis Bolton for a copper-bottomed sloop named the *Charlotte* and, after a bit of three-way haggling, an African house servant named Ibo, as well as certain other personal effects of the late Sir Francis Bolton.

I reluctantly signed a pledge not to bear arms against the Crown but have no regrets about doing so for a week before our scheduled departure came the news that on October 19, Cornwallis had surrendered his army at Yorktown after a siege of three weeks' duration by Washington's army and a large French force.

After a long delay in Statia seeing to his loot from its seizure, Admiral Rodney sailed back to England. Had he taken his ships to Virginia, he might have prevented the French fleet from bottling up Cornwallis in the Chesapeake. At least that is the opinion of Archibald Foxley. He too feels that the war is nearly over.

Although I am under parole, I continue to serve my native land. The Barbadians were tired of the expense of feeding so many prisoners in the Town Hall of Goal. I volunteered to return the Americans—like myself under parole—to Philadelphia. Never was a vessel so well or so enthusiastically manned as is the *Charlotte*.

I have promised Ibo his freedom when we reach America. We pass the time here in my cabin under the gaze of the portrait of my great-grandmother Charlotte, by playing chess and talking.

Ibo has cleared up many points about Francis Bolton that had puzzled me, including his hatred of Jews and Dutchmen.

"Ah, you see his mother was not a chaste woman. There was the Dutch sea captain with whom she eloped. Earlier she had taken as lovers both a Christian minister whose wife was an invalid and a Jewish tailor of Bridgetown. It troubled the master that he did not know whether he was English or half Dutch or half Jewish."

Last evening, over a game of chess, he explained the mysterious ailment to which Bolton referred in his soul-baring letter to me.

"It was the mumps. He could not enjoy a woman. Perhaps that was why we got on so well. We were not distracted by females as you have been."

"I trust you will not discuss that subject in the presence of Gerta, please. Perhaps I should not have allowed you to read my memoir."

He moved his queen.

"Check," he said. Then he added, "Although, unlike you, he never desired a wife, yet he always yearned for a son, I think."

I moved my king, and he captured my rook.

"Mate," he said. "A rebellious son from a rebellious people was better than no son at all, I suppose."